A *Loving* HEART

A *Loving* HEART

Volume Three of The Dickens Inn Series

a novel

ANITA STANSFIELD

Covenant Communications, Inc.

Cover image *Summertime Lemonade* © Chris Elwell, courtesy of iStockphoto.com; *Blank Sign* © xyno, courtesy of iStockphoto.com.

Cover design copyrighted 2010 by Covenant Communications, Inc.

Published by Covenant Communications, Inc.
American Fork, Utah

Printed in Canada
First Printing: May 2010

15 14 13 12 11 10   10 9 8 7 6 5 4 3 2 1

ISBN: 978-1-60861-017-4

CHAPTER 1

Anaconda, Montana

Chas Leeds opened the hymn book to sing the opening song in sacrament meeting. On her left sat Charles, her fifteen-month-old son, who was being unusually good, looking at a picture book. To her right was her husband, Jackson. As he took one side of the hymn book with one hand to help her hold it, he lifted his other arm behind her on the bench and gave her shoulders a gentle squeeze. She turned to see him smile at her just before they began singing.

They'd been married a little more than two years, and they'd sat through church together many times. But this was only the second time he'd attended sacrament meeting as a baptized member of the Church. He'd chosen the Saturday before Valentine's Day for the big event, and Chas believed it was the most romantic thing he ever could have done for her—even though he hadn't done it for *her*. His conversion had been slow in coming, but was deep and profound. His heart had been healed from the unspeakable horrors of his past that had given him post-traumatic stress disorder (PTSD). And his countenance had changed. Chas could see it as much as she could feel it, and the result was a mutual happiness beyond description. They had set a tentative date to be sealed in the temple, and she was already crossing days off on the calendar, counting down to the most important day in her life.

It was snowing lightly when they left the church after meetings were over.

"I keep thinking about going to the temple with you," he said, pulling onto the road.

"So do I," she said and took his hand. "We need to decide which one, you know."

"They all work the same, right?"

"Yes, of course, but . . . we should make a vacation out of it when the time comes."

They playfully speculated on which temple they should go to together, since there were more than a hundred to choose from all over the world. But Chas saw Jackson's eyes light up when she suggested Washington, DC. His years serving in the Marines had given him an especially patriotic soul, and he'd gone there on business a great deal when he'd been working for the FBI in Norfolk. She knew he was fond of the city and its history.

"You like that idea," she said.

"I do. I'd love to take you to DC."

"Then it's settled."

"So, next year we'll celebrate Valentine's Day with a trip to Washington, DC."

"I'll be counting on it. And we'll have *two* children to contend with by then." She rubbed her belly that was just rounded enough to no longer be concealed.

"How delightful," Jackson said.

"We have that appointment tomorrow."

"I know. I can't wait."

They were both excited to be getting an ultrasound of the baby, now that Chas was about halfway through her pregnancy. Just as last time, they were eager to know the gender of the baby in order to start making the appropriate preparations. However, the baby would be sharing a room with them until they were able to complete the addition they were having built onto the inn, and they wouldn't even be starting that project until spring.

Jackson pulled the SUV into the parking lot of the Dickensian Inn, the restored Victorian mansion that comprised both their home and their place of business. It was a well-established and efficiently run bed-and-breakfast. The Dickensian theme of the place was quaint, but it also held deep meaning for both Chas and Jackson. The life and work of Charles Dickens had influenced them both a great deal, and they even joked that Mr. Dickens had brought them together.

Jackson opened the car door for Chas, then got the baby out of his seat. They went through the back door of the inn to find Polly in the office just off the hallway. She was a longtime friend of Chas's and also their right hand in running the business. She had red curly hair that she'd always worn short, but it had now grown to shoulder length. She was efficient and full of energy, and she was indispensable, both as an employee and as a friend. Since she had no religious convictions and no interest in getting any, she had no problem covering for them on Sundays while they attended meetings. Saturday nights were always busy at the inn, and consequently the Sunday morning breakfast routine was always brisk as well. But Chas did well at planning ahead and being on the ball so that work could be kept to an absolute minimum on the Sabbath. The cleaning of rooms always waited until Monday unless they were absolutely needed for Sunday evening, which was rare. Now that they were home from church, Polly left to go have dinner with friends. Jackson put Charles down for his nap, and Jackson and Chas worked together to prepare a simple Sunday dinner. It was a typical Sunday in most ways, yet it was entirely different. Jackson had come to understand for himself why Sunday was such an important day to his wife. What had separated them in the past had now created a bond deeper than he'd ever imagined. And they both knew it would only become stronger with time as they progressed toward the eternal goals they had set together.

The following day arrived accompanied by crisp sunshine. It was always a relief to have good weather when it was necessary to make the drive to Butte during the winter months. The morning was busy, but with Polly's help they were able to leave for their appointment on time, knowing that Charles and the inn were both in good hands. Chas was in good spirits, anticipating a pleasant day. Following their appointment, they were going out for an early lunch before they picked up Jackson's sister at the airport. Melinda had called the previous week from her home in Arkansas, declaring that it had been far too long since she'd come to visit. They were always pleased to have Melinda around, and they were looking forward to spending some quality time with her. For the sake of convenience, she had purposely scheduled her flight on a day when they knew they would be in the city.

Within minutes after they were on the road, Chas's mood turned sour. She had to stop and ask herself why, since she'd been so excited and positive in anticipating this day. When the reason suddenly occurred to her, she wondered how she could have blocked it out of her mind so completely. When she'd been at this point in her pregnancy with Charles, it had been one of her most prominent concerns. And this time it had completely slipped her mind—until now. She tried to tell herself that just as with Charles, they were going to find out that her worries had been unfounded and unnecessary. But a vague uneasiness nagged at her, and she couldn't decide if it was simply a ridiculous fear that she should push away, or if she was somehow being warned that the doctors would find a problem.

"Are you okay?" Jackson asked after way too many minutes of silence. She was usually the talkative one.

"I don't think I am," she said but kept her eyes focused toward the window, not wanting him to see the tears that came with admitting the truth.

"What's wrong?" he asked and took her hand. His concern was so genuine that her tears increased. When she didn't answer and turned farther away, he tugged on her hand. "Chas? What is it?"

When she realized there was no point in trying to hide her tears, she wiped her face with her free hand and turned to look at him. "What if something's wrong with the baby?"

Jackson's heart tightened. He couldn't tell her the thought hadn't occurred to him, because it had. And he couldn't tell her there was no reason to think there would be a problem, because they both knew it was a possibility. There was a history of genetic heart defects in Chas's family. There had been many more babies that had died than had survived. Chas's mother had lived with a weak heart that had taken her during childbirth. And soon after Chas had lost her first husband in a military training accident, she had given birth to a baby that hadn't lived very long, due to the same problem. When they'd gone to this same appointment for her last pregnancy, they had both been holding their breath, but the doctors had reassured them every step of the way that Charles had a healthy heart. It had been an unspeakable relief.

During the course of this pregnancy, neither Chas nor Jackson had mentioned this problem once. Jackson hadn't wanted to bring it up, even though he'd thought about it and worried, and he had assumed that Chas was doing the same. He felt sure they were both hoping for the same result, that everything would be okay. He wasn't sure what had suddenly brought it to the forefront for her, and he was even less sure of what he might say to ease her concerns. Instead he just asked, "Is there some reason you feel there will be something wrong . . . more so than last time?"

"I don't know. I had honestly forgotten all about it . . . at least for a few weeks. And now . . . I can't tell if I'm just afraid, or if . . ."

"If what?"

"If . . . I'm being prepared . . . or warned, or something."

Jackson didn't like the sound of that at all. He'd only recently come to understand and recognize the guidance of the Holy Spirit in his life, but he knew that Chas had many years of experience over on him in that regard. He might not be able to get answers the way she did, but he did know how to pray. He kept hold of her hand and silently asked God to guide his words and to give them both the comfort and strength they needed for whatever might lay ahead. He found it funny as he was concluding his prayer that he hadn't actually asked that everything would be all right with the baby. Did he instinctively believe that something *would* be wrong? Was *he* being prepared or warned? Or was he just afraid? He couldn't answer such questions in that moment, but he was able to say to Chas, "Whatever happens, we're in it together. If something's wrong with our baby, we won't love it any less. But regardless of anything else, we will have this baby forever."

Jackson figured he must have said the right thing by the way Chas's countenance shifted from distressed to peaceful in a heartbeat. He added gently, "That's not to say it won't be difficult, but we *will* get through it together."

"Yes, we will," she said and squeezed his hand. She leaned across the console between the seats and put her head on his shoulder. "And we *will* be together forever."

Chas felt calmer as they arrived at the office of her obstetrician, but she still couldn't shake a nagging feeling that they were going to receive difficult news. They waited a short while before they were escorted into a room where Chas laid back on the examination table and uncovered her belly. Jackson sat beside her and held her hand while the technician chatted with them and began the ultrasound. She asked some questions and made some notes, then asked if they wanted to know the gender of the baby. When they both said that they did, she laughed softly and said, "Oh, good. It's so hard to keep it a secret."

When a fairly clear image of the baby appeared on the monitor, Chas and Jackson both laughed as they tightened their hold on each other's hands.

"It's a girl," the technician said with firmness as she showed them the visual evidence.

Jackson and Chas silently shared their mutual joy over the revelation and continued to take in the evidence of their baby's growing life. The technician did measurements of the head and other parts of the body, saying that the growth appeared normal and the size was about right for the estimated due date of June 28.

She then became silent as she looked at the baby's internal organs. In a voice that was kind and calm, she said, "I want the doctor to look at something. I'll get him and be back in a few minutes."

As soon as the door closed and they were alone, Chas released the tears that had gathered in her eyes. They slithered into the hair at her temples. Jackson stood and leaned over her, wiping the tears away and kissing her brow. "It's going to be okay," he said. She nodded, and he wiped more tears.

It felt like forever before the technician returned with a doctor that was not Chas's usual physician, but she knew there were several doctors in this clinic. At least the amount of time they'd waited had allowed Chas to get her emotions under control.

"Mrs. Leeds, is it?" the doctor asked.

"Yes," Chas said.

He sat down and maneuvered the probe over her belly, studying the screen closely. He finally said in a kind voice, "It appears that something might not be quite right with the baby's heart." Neither Chas nor Jackson said anything, but they both nodded. The doctor said, "You're not surprised."

"It's a genetic issue," Jackson said. "It's come up before."

"These are difficult conversations to have," the doctor said. "At this point, it's difficult if not impossible to understand what's going on or if there's anything that can be done."

"We understand," Jackson said, and Chas was grateful that he could speak for both of them. She couldn't have found her voice for any reason without dissolving into helpless tears.

The doctor quickly covered possible options, some of which they would never even consider. The conclusion was that they needed to give the matter some time, and if the pregnancy went full term—meaning the baby was strong enough to live that long—then they could determine whether anything could be done to repair the problem. If the defect was severe enough that it could not be repaired, then the child would inevitably not live very long, if at all.

When the appointment was over, Chas walked out to the parking lot with Jackson's arm around her shoulders. Neither of them had anything to say while she walked blindly with her husband's guidance. He helped her into the car and closed the door, then got into the driver's seat. He started the car and turned on the heater, but he made no effort to put it in gear.

"Talk to me," he finally said.

"Listen to you," she said, trying to sound light, "encouraging *me* to talk."

"You need to tell me what you're thinking."

She tried to gather her thoughts and focus on the most prominent issue, then she sighed before she could voice them. "I was thinking about my first pregnancy . . . when I was married to Martin. I don't know if technology has just improved so much in the last fifteen years, or if my doctor wasn't that good, but . . . we had no clue that anything was wrong. I'd known that there had been many deaths of babies in my mother's family, and I knew my mother had a weak heart, but I'd never made the connection; I'd never even considered the possibility of a heart problem with my baby. When she was born, it didn't take long to know there *was* a problem. Two days. That was all the time we had together, and then she joined her father. I don't need to tell you how devastating that was for me."

"No, you don't need to tell me," he said, because she'd told him all about it before. They had visited the baby's grave numerous times, since it was near where Chas's grandmother was buried, as well as her first husband, Martin.

Chas turned to look at him. "I'm trying to figure out if it's better to know, or to not know. Is it better to be prepared . . . to know this baby is going to die? Or to believe everything's okay when it's not?"

"First of all, we don't *know* this baby is going to die. Maybe something *can* be done. It *has* been fifteen years. Medical advancements are happening all the time. And secondly, the father of this baby is right here, and I'm going to be with you every step of the way." Chas nodded, then hugged him tightly. With his arms around her, he added, "I think it *is* better to be prepared. During my years in the military *and* in the FBI, I always lived by the adage to be prepared for the worst but hope for the best. That's what we're going to do. We know there's a possibility that we're going to lose this baby." He pulled back and took her shoulders into his hands, looking at her squarely. "But we know it will only be a temporary loss, and we also know that God will be with us, to comfort us and help us through. We can still hope for a miracle, and maybe everything will be okay. Either way, we will get through this. Do you hear me?"

Chas nodded and put her head to his shoulder, crying without restraint for several minutes. Jackson just held her and shed a few tears of his own. His speech had sounded very convincing, but the raw reality was hard to swallow. When she had calmed down he wiped her tears again and said, "We need to get something to eat and get to the airport."

Chas groaned. "Oh, I'm not hungry."

"I don't care," he said and fastened his seat belt. "You have to eat. You are going to take very good care of yourself and give this baby every possible chance to have a life."

Chas took his hand and nodded, appreciating his attitude and support more than she could ever tell him. She fastened her own seatbelt as he put the car in gear and left the parking lot.

"You know," she said, "if you had married someone else, you wouldn't be facing this."

"Chas, I hate to have to point out the obvious, but if I had married someone else I wouldn't be married." He chuckled to realize how that sounded. "There is no other woman in the world that could have ever lured me away from being an eternal bachelor. But even if there had been, it doesn't matter. The commitment we share overrides everything else. This is *our* baby, and whichever genes it got from one or the other of us really doesn't matter in the grand scheme of things."

Chas sighed and closed her eyes, laying her head back against the headrest. "Where did you learn to be so sweet?"

"From you," he said. "I was never sweet until I met you." He kissed her hand. "You inspired me; still do."

She turned to look at him. "I love you, Jackson."

"I love you too," he said.

After eating a quick lunch that they both had trouble getting down, they drove to the airport. Jackson's cell phone rang when they were about five minutes away. It was Melinda telling him that she was collecting her luggage and she would be at a designated spot in a few minutes. When Jackson pulled into the passenger pickup zone they saw her waiting. He got out and hugged her before he loaded her luggage into the back of the SUV. Melinda opened Chas's door and hugged her before she closed it again and got into the backseat.

"Oh, it's so good to see you both," she said after Jackson had gotten back into the car.

"It's good to see you, too," Jackson said. "How was your flight?"

"Oh, you know," she said. "It was a flight." She chattered a few minutes about some challenges she'd had getting to the airport earlier, and about how she wasn't fond of airplanes, but since she loved to travel she had to endure them.

Melinda was as different from Jackson as two siblings could be. He was quiet and conservative in dress and nature. She was anything but. Her fluffy blond hair was much the same as it had looked in high school, and her flashy wardrobe was a part of her personality. In Jackson's opinion, his sister wore too much makeup and jewelry, and her professionally done fingernails were too long and too bright. She spoke in a thick Southern accent that Jackson had worked hard to lose since his youth. But Jackson loved his sister and respected her, and he deeply appreciated the comfortable relationship they had come to share, especially since the death of their mother the previous year. Melinda was not tied down with work or children; she owned her own business that ran itself, and her children were grown. She'd been doing a lot of traveling with friends the last several months, but the last time she'd come to Montana, their mother had come with her, and so it felt a bit strange.

They all chatted comfortably during the drive to Anaconda, and Jackson was glad that his sister had a lot she wanted to tell them about her kids and grandkids. Her daughter, Sasha, was married with children and lived in the same town as Melinda. Her son, Brian, was still single and in the military. He was currently serving in Iraq but doing well at last report. With all that Melinda had to say, Jackson hoped she wouldn't notice their subdued moods. He knew they had to tell Melinda sooner or later about the news they'd just gotten, but he was hoping to put it off until the shock had worn off a bit. His mind kept wandering to it while the conversation continued, and he found it difficult to swallow. And if he was having trouble accepting it, he couldn't imagine how Chas must be feeling. She was doing well at interacting with Melinda with apparent normalcy, but Jackson knew her well enough to know that she too was preoccupied with the doctor's report.

Once they were at the inn, they got Melinda settled into her usual guest room, while greetings with Charles had to be put off since he was napping. After Polly quickly caught them up regarding the day's business, she went home. While Melinda was upstairs unpacking, Chas went to the kitchen to start some supper. Jackson took care of a couple of items of business in the office, then found her there.

"You okay?" he asked, but he only had to glance at her to know she wasn't. Before she could answer she started to cry, and all he could do was wrap her in his arms and hold her tightly.

Chas held to her husband and cried, grateful for the love of a good man in her life, if for nothing else. After so many years between Martin's death and meeting Jackson, just having a man to hold her was not something she took for granted. Without speaking a word, he could wrap his strong arms around her and make her feel safe and loved and secure. This was tangible evidence that what he'd said earlier was true. Whatever happened, they were in it together.

"Maybe I'll get it out of my system eventually," she said, wiping at her tears.

"And maybe you won't," he said. "You can cry as much as you want, you know."

"Yeah, well," she turned away to get back to her task, "I'd prefer to save it for times when I'm not around other people. You're the lucky one who gets to deal with all the tears. I think that should be a part of standard marriage vows. A man should be warned about the commitment he's making to hold his wife through all the tears of a lifetime."

"In a roundabout way, I think it's part of the vows. I doubt there's anything more important I could be doing with my life than to hold you while you cry. You know I'm not the real sensitive type, but *that* I can do."

Chas started to cry again. "I think you're a lot more sensitive than you think you are." She took that place in his arms again and hugged him tightly. "I love you."

"I love you too," he said and pressed a kiss into her hair.

Noises on the baby monitor indicated that Charles was waking up. Jackson offered to take care of the baby while Chas put their dinner in the oven. It would be ready to eat in a couple of hours. Melinda was thrilled to see the baby, and Jackson enjoyed watching his sister be a ridiculously doting aunt.

Wendell Davis arrived right on time for his after-school job at the inn. He was barely thirteen, and his mother had passed away not many months ago. Chas and Jackson enjoyed having him spend a few hours a day in their home, where he could earn some extra money by helping out with odds and ends that no one else wanted to do. He was always given a snack when he came in, and Polly was good at looking after him when Chas or Jackson weren't around. He was well behaved and a fairly good worker, and he had bonded with Jackson through reading *A Tale of Two Cities.* Melinda was glad to meet Wendell, since she'd heard all about him. Wendell thought Jackson's sister was funny and didn't hesitate to tell him so. Jackson could only agree.

After Wendell's father picked him up at the usual time, the remainder of the evening went well; Melinda settled in and visited while she helped in the kitchen, and they all shared a nice supper. They were interrupted twice while guests checked in, but they took care of it quickly both times.

After Charles was put down for the night, the adults sat in the parlor to visit. At the first lull in the conversation, Melinda asked, "Is it my imagination that the two of you are awfully somber?" Jackson and Chas exchanged a glance that encouraged Melinda to add, "Something's wrong; I knew it. I hope you're not going to tell me that it's none of my business, because I'm family and you need me."

"Yes," Jackson said, "you *are* family, and we *do* need you. We're glad to know that we have each other, and we're glad you're here. It's just . . . the timing is a little . . ."

"What?" Melinda demanded.

"Well . . ." Jackson said when it became evident from Chas's silent plea that she wanted him to be the one to give the dreadful news, "we had a doctor's appointment this morning before we picked you up."

"Oh, that's right," she said, then her eyes widened. "What's wrong? Is something wrong with you, Chas?"

"No," she said quickly. "I'm fine."

"The baby, then?" Melinda asked, putting both hands to her heart as if to protect it from an inevitable blow. "Is something wrong with the baby?"

"Yes," Jackson said quickly. "Her heart is . . . well, it's not right; that's all we know for sure."

"It's a girl?" Melinda asked at the same moment that tears rose in her eyes. Jackson nodded, and she said, "Is this the same thing you were worried about with Charles? The genetic thing you told me about?"

"Yes," Jackson said again.

"Goodness gracious!" Melinda said. "Will she be okay?"

"We don't know," Jackson said.

"Well, the timing of my coming isn't bad at all," Melinda said. "You need me. We're going to talk this through, and we're going to face it together. You've both been there for me so very, very much, and I'm not going to let you face this alone."

"You're very sweet," Jackson said, "but there really isn't a lot we can do at this point except wait. I can assure you, however, that when the drama comes—and it probably will—we'll be glad to have your support."

"Yes," Chas said. "And I'm glad you're here . . . now. I think what we need most is a distraction. There *isn't* anything that can be done right now, and I feel . . . helpless. So let's try to have some fun while you're here."

"That's a great idea," Jackson said.

They steered the conversation to more trivial things until Melinda insisted that she needed to get some sleep. She'd been up very early packing. Jackson made certain everything was locked up and in order before he and Chas read from the scriptures and prayed together. Jackson prayed that their baby could be healthy, that they could be granted a miracle. Nothing was said after the amen, but after they'd both crawled into bed, Chas found his shoulder with her face and cried in his arms. He just held her and cried with her until they were both finally able to sleep.

* * * * *

Jackson was up early and left Chas and the baby sleeping while he went for his usual early-morning run. He came back and showered and found Chas still sleeping. Miraculously enough, the baby was still asleep too. He knew Chas didn't have to serve breakfast to their guests until later, and it was mostly prepared anyway, so he took the baby monitor with him so he could hear the baby and went to the dining room where he found his sister reading a newspaper.

"You're up early," he said.

"You were up earlier, I noticed." She set the paper aside.

"Did you sleep well?"

"Very well, thank you. I think you have the most comfortable beds for rent in the country. And I'm the lucky woman who gets to sleep on one for free."

"Hey, I just married the innkeeper."

"Good move."

"Yes, it was," he said and picked up a paper before he sat down at one of the little guest tables there.

Melinda crossed the room to the sideboard where the breakfast buffet would be set out later. "I started the coffee maker," she said. "I love the way Chas always has it ready to go before she goes to bed."

"She is very efficient," Jackson said and opened yesterday's copy of *USA Today*; the running joke at the inn was calling the paper *USA Yesterday* because they always got it a day late. He tipped the paper down when he heard a cup being set on the table, and he realized he'd overlooked telling his sister about the latest development in his life. He just kept reading, wondering how to open up the subject.

A few minutes later Melinda said, "Your coffee is getting cold." He tipped the paper down again to look at her, and she added, "I got you some coffee. It's getting cold."

Jackson folded the paper and set it aside. "Thank you, but I don't drink coffee anymore."

She looked astonished, then she laughed. "You're joking, right? *You* don't drink coffee?"

"No, I'm serious."

She turned to look at him from a different angle, as if that might help her understand. "I know Chas doesn't drink it. Has she rubbed off on you?"

"You might say that," he said with a smile.

"Not even decaf?"

"Not even decaf."

"Why?" she asked. "I mean . . . Chas doesn't drink it for religious reasons, right? So . . ."

She hesitated as if the thought had crossed her mind but she didn't dare say it, so Jackson said it for her. "And that is the same reason I don't drink it anymore. I was baptized a week and a half ago. I was going to call and tell you after you got back from your last jaunt, but then you called and said you were coming. So, here you are. You get to hear it face-to-face. Your brother has become a Mormon."

"Well, if that isn't about the most remarkable thing I've ever heard."

"Yeah," he chuckled, "it is pretty remarkable. And since you went to church with me in Arkansas on my last visit, and you were quite impressed, I assume you can't be too shocked."

"No, not *too* shocked. But I'm not sure I ever believed you would actually take the plunge."

"I never believed I would, either, but . . . well . . . one thing led to another, and . . . I just knew it was the right thing to do; I knew it was true. Chas said you told her you were going to visit with the missionaries."

"I had every intention to, but . . . I went out of town again and it just didn't happen." She leaned back and smiled, taking him in as if he'd changed colors. "Wow!" She laughed softly. "That is . . . really something."

"Yeah, but . . . you know what's at least as remarkable?"

"I surely don't."

"I finally kept my promise to Mama."

"What promise?"

"That thing she made me promise to do when she was dying." He paused just a moment for effect. "I have been able to forgive my father." Jackson saw tears appear immediately in his sister's eyes.

"To put it in a nutshell, while I was trying desperately to get past the PTSD and stop having nightmares, my counselor and Chas both suggested that I needed to forgive those who had hurt me in order to heal. Chas guided me to the means to search for answers in a spiritual vein, and . . . well, as I said, one thing just kind of led to another."

"Wow!" she said again and wiped at her tears. "That's got to be one of the best things you've ever told me."

"What was better than that?"

"When you told me you were smart enough to actually marry Chas."

"Yes," he chuckled, "that would definitely be the *other* best thing I've ever done in my life."

"I hope you're going to tell me more about this. I want to know everything."

He smiled. "Oh, you could probably talk me into that." He reached across the table and kissed his sister's cheek. "In fact, I'm looking forward to it."

CHAPTER 2

Chas came into the dining room wearing a bathrobe, and Jackson rose to kiss her.

"Good morning," he said. "How did you sleep?"

"Not too bad," she said. "How about you?"

"The same."

Chas bent over to hug her sister-in-law and asked, "How's your stay so far?"

"It's wonderful to be here, and everything is grand, as always."

Chas sat down and Jackson said, "I was just telling Melinda why I don't drink coffee anymore."

"Oh?" Chas's countenance brightened. "And I missed it?" To Melinda she said, "And what do you think of that?"

"I think it's wonderful. It's obviously a good thing. He's promised to tell me everything later."

"I can't wait," Chas said and glared comically at Jackson. "You'd better make sure I don't miss *that* conversation."

"I promise," he said and went to the kitchen to fix some cocoa for Chas and himself.

The baby woke up, and the day officially began. By the time the guests had been fed breakfast and Polly had arrived, Jackson had prepared an itinerary of activities for the week, taking Polly's schedule into consideration so they didn't overload her too much. Before they set out for the afternoon, Chas sought Polly out in the office to have a private word with her.

"There's something I need to tell you," Chas said, scooting a chair close beside Polly's.

"Oh, my gosh!" Polly said. "I totally forgot that you had the ultrasound yesterday. You know what the baby is. Come on, tell me. A boy or a girl?"

"It's a girl," Chas said, but Polly's countenance sobered when she realized that Chas wasn't smiling.

"Is something wrong?" Polly asked, reaching for Chas's hand.

Chas knew she wouldn't get through this without tears, but she still felt embarrassed as she reached for a tissue. "You remember what happened to my first baby?"

Polly's brow furrowed. "I wasn't actually around, but you've told me about it. Why? What has that got to do with . . ." She paused and gasped as it dawned on her.

Chas said it for her. "This baby has a heart defect."

"Oh, Chas!" Polly said and rolled her chair close enough to wrap her in a big hug, then she took Chas's shoulders and looked her in the eye. "What does this mean, exactly? Is there a chance she'll make it, or . . ."

"At this point, they can't tell us much of anything. *If* she makes it to full term, we'll see *if* anything can be done."

"But there's a chance . . . that she'll make it?"

Chas sniffled. "I think there's a chance. I have to believe there's a chance."

"Then that's what we're going to hold on to," Polly said, and Chas hugged her again. She appreciated her friend's positive attitude more than she could ever tell her. They talked for a while longer, and Chas filled her in on more details of how the appointment had gone. She was grateful, as always, for Polly's friendship and support. Even though Jackson was a wonderful husband, sometimes a woman just needed a female friend.

Through the remainder of the day, Chas felt immensely grateful for the timing of Melinda's visit. The distraction of doing some sightseeing and eating out was exactly what she needed. She had to remember that for now there was absolutely nothing to be done about the problem with her baby, and she had to try to press forward with faith and not allow it to mar the joy she had in her life over so many other things.

The following morning, Chas was busy preparing breakfast and managing to keep herself fairly distracted when her friend Charlotte came through the kitchen door with a tray full of baked goods, just as she regularly did every second day. Chas and Charlotte had been friends most of their lives. Charlotte was a little older than Chas and had worked at the same bakery with Chas's grandmother during Chas's youth. She was gifted at baking, something that Chas wasn't so good at and preferred not to do; therefore, they had a good arrangement. Charlotte and Chas had always been a good support for each other through life's challenges, and they'd had a lot of fun together. The huge chasm that existed between their values was something they usually just managed to skirt around. Chas didn't agree at all with the way that Charlotte lived her life, especially in regard to relationships. Charlotte was a single mother with two children from two different marriages, and now she had given up on marriage and instead focused on brief, meaningless relationships with almost any man who might look her way. But Chas had stopped offering advice and opinions on Charlotte's lifestyle, especially in regard to men. Still, they were good friends, and Chas knew she needed to share the most recent news with Charlotte.

Charlotte had barely said hello when she asked, "Did you find out what kind of baby you're having? I thought you'd call me."

"Sorry," Chas said and helped Charlotte set the tray of baked goods on the counter. "Jackson's sister flew in the same day and we've been pretty busy. Yes, we found out. It's a girl." She didn't bother waiting for a response before she finished the explanation. "And there's something wrong with her heart."

Charlotte's response was a little too dramatic for Chas's taste. Following a horrid gasp she asked, "Like your first baby?" Chas nodded and was proud of herself for *not* crying. "I just don't know how you can go through that again," she added, and Chas had to work harder to hold back tears. "You're not actually going to keep it, are you?"

Chas's tears became immediately swallowed by a shocked anger that consumed her entirely. "What are you saying?" Chas asked, not wanting to jump to conclusions, or perhaps finding it hard to believe that Charlotte would actually say something like that—and mean it.

"Come on, Chas," Charlotte said. "If the baby's not going to survive anyway, isn't it better to just put you both out of your misery now?"

Chas felt her breathing become labored so suddenly that she feared losing consciousness. She felt like a rabid animal ready to pounce on the predator threatening her young. "I *cannot* believe you would even *think* something like that," she snarled, "let alone have the *nerve* to say it to me."

Charlotte looked stunned and baffled. "You can't honestly tell me that it didn't cross your mind."

"No!" Chas shouted in a whisper, glad to know that their only guests weren't due in the dining room for an hour yet. "It *didn't* cross my mind! If this baby is meant to die, it will go *when* and *how* God wants it to go. That decision is not up to *me*. It's a life, Charlotte; a human life. How could I do something like that and wonder for the rest of *my* life if I'd lost the chance for a miracle? At least if I lose this baby, I will lose it with a clear conscience."

"What's wrong?" Jackson asked, coming into the room behind Chas.

While Chas was trying to calm down and come up with a suitable explanation, Charlotte said to him, "I think your wife is a little hypersensitive and hormonal." She picked up the plate of cookies she'd brought that was meant to go in the office and walked past both of them as if they'd just had a disagreement over what brand of ketchup was best.

Chas was so upset that she couldn't even speak. She pressed her face to Jackson's chest, and the tears rushed out. When he realized how upset she was, he pulled back and lifted her chin to make her face him.

"What happened?" he demanded, but Chas couldn't answer. It occurred to her that Charlotte would be coming back into the room any minute, so she rushed past Jackson and into the bedroom, knowing he would follow her. He entered behind her and closed the door before he asked in a voice that betrayed anger, "What did she say to you?"

Chas had a hard time actually allowing herself to say the words, but he had to know. She took a deep breath and forced herself to calm down. "She's astounded that I would even keep the baby." She saw anger rise immediately into Jackson's face and hurried to add, "Don't say a word to her about it. I told her how I felt."

"And she chalked it up to being hypersensitive and hormonal?" he asked.

"Apparently." Chas grabbed a couple of tissues and blew her nose.

Jackson groaned. "If she were a man . . ."

"What? You'd give her a fat lip?"

"Something like that."

"Well, even if she were, you wouldn't. It's not Christian."

Jackson blew out a slow, calming breath. "Okay, you got me there. I'm not sure this Christian attitude stuff comes very naturally to me."

"Just because you're human enough to feel angry does not make you any less Christian. I'm angry too. We just . . . need to be kind to her, anyway."

Jackson sighed and put his arms around her. "You're a good woman, Chas Florence Leeds. I think I'll keep you. And we are going to keep this baby and make the most of whatever God gives us." He hesitated about voicing his next thought, but felt like it needed to be aired. "And forgive me if this sounds insensitive, but . . . if we end up having to bury her next to her sister," his voice cracked, "we will have her with us eternally, because we *are* going to put the matter in God's hands."

Chas looked up at him with new tears in her eyes. "You're a good man, Jackson Tobias Leeds. I think I'll keep you . . . forever."

"Deal," he said and kissed her.

Charlotte left without Chas seeing her again. When Chas went into the office, Polly said, "Boy, Charlotte was sure ticked off about something."

Chas felt astonished. "I don't know why *she* should feel ticked off."

"Why? What did she say?"

Chas repeated their conversation, and Polly was appalled, especially over Charlotte's comment about being hypersensitive and hormonal. "I realize," Chas said, "that she and I have a vast difference in our values, but I would still think that she'd respect mine more than that."

Polly agreed, but as the conversation nagged at Chas through the day, she still felt that she needed to behave like a Christian and take the first step toward mending the situation. She called Charlotte's number and got her voice mail. She left a message that said, "I apologize if I overreacted this morning. I know there are some things over which we just have to agree that we disagree. I appreciate your friendship, and I hope you're having a good day." Once she'd taken that step, Chas was able to let the conversation go and know that she was okay with Charlotte's disapproval of her choices, because Chas also disapproved of some of Charlotte's choices. But they could still respect and support each other. They always had before. Therefore it came as a complete shock when Charlotte called her the following morning and said without preface, "I can't do baking for you anymore."

"What?" Chas asked. "Did you get another job, or—"

"Oh, I'm managing on the child support and alimony," she said, "but I've been thinking of doing something else. Maybe this will force me to make some changes."

"Maybe *what* will force you?"

"This rift between you and me," Charlotte said as if they'd been arguing for weeks. "I just can't deal with it anymore, Chas. We have nothing in common, and it's getting worse instead of better. I just can't bake for you anymore; you'll have to find someone else."

"Charlotte," Chas said, unable to disguise her astonishment. "I . . . don't understand. We had a little disagreement yesterday. We've disagreed lots of times. What's so different this time? What is—"

"You really don't get it, do you?"

"No, I suppose I don't."

"Then you're blind. I'm tired of you judging me, and—"

"Judging you? When have I ever said anything—"

"You know what?" she interrupted. "I can't talk about this right now, or ever. There's nothing to say." Chas felt certain there was nothing to say because she had absolutely no evidence of anything ever actually being said that was judgmental. She wanted to ask Charlotte *who* was being hypersensitive and hormonal. While she was searching for more appropriate words, Charlotte said, "I have to go. Good luck."

Chas hung up the phone and sat down, stunned and unable to decide how she felt. She didn't even have to search her conscience to see if there was any truth to what Charlotte had said. She knew she had always been kind and respectful to Charlotte; she knew because their differences made it something that required careful words. She also knew that Charlotte had a tendency to be offended easily and to jump to conclusions. She had a dramatic streak as well. Chas just never expected to end up being the recipient of Charlotte's exaggeration of events.

Once she'd reworked the conversation a couple of times in her mind, she went in search of her husband. He had Charles on his lap and was putting on the boy's shoes. He looked up and smiled when he saw her, then he noticed her expression and frowned.

"What's wrong?"

"Charlotte just quit."

"What?"

"She told me she couldn't bake for me anymore, that she was tired of this rift between us, tired of my being judgmental, and she said if I couldn't see the problem, I was blind."

"And *who* is being hypersensitive and hormonal?"

Chas actually laughed. "That's *exactly* what I wanted to ask her, but I bit my tongue." She kissed him quickly. "I love it when we think the same." She took Charles from him to give him a hug before she set him loose to play. "But be completely honest with me. You're around a lot when Charlotte and I are talking. Do you think I'm even a little bit—"

"No," he said firmly. "And I'm not saying that to side with you or spare your feelings. If anything, it's the other way around. *I* think she's gradually gotten more uncomfortable around you because her lifestyle is so different from yours, and she's probably just been waiting for an excuse to try to blame it on you. She probably just needs to hang out with people who are more like her."

"Well, I feel bad . . . but not bad enough to try to talk her into being my friend if she doesn't want to be. I wish her well, but I'd rather have friends who respect me and my beliefs. Polly isn't religious, but she respects me."

"Exactly."

"But I do have a problem."

"What?"

"I need baked goods."

"So . . . go to the bakery and buy some. Charlotte's good at it, but she isn't the only person in town who can bake things that taste good enough to serve our guests." He shrugged. "Talk to the manager. See if you can work out a deal with regular orders, and we can . . . I don't know . . . put out a little sign or something on the breakfast buffet that says where the stuff was baked."

"You're a genius," she said, liking the idea very much. She actually felt sorry for Charlotte, certain that her ex-friend would want Chas to have a hard time replacing her.

As soon as breakfast was over and cleaned up and their guests were checked out, Chas left the baby with Jackson while she went downtown to the bakery where her grandmother had worked when Chas was a child. It had changed management and been remodeled numerous times, but it still brought back memories for Chas. Since Charlotte had started doing the baking for the inn, Chas hadn't set foot in here once. Now, it felt good to step through the door.

There was a large refrigerator with glass doors where such delicacies as éclairs and cream-filled cakes were kept. A long glass counter was filled with all kinds of cookies and rolls and ready-made cakes. Behind the counter were shelves of bagged rolls and different types of breads. The smell of something baking offered a perfect atmosphere when combined with quaint décor and a couple of little tables where customers could eat pastries while enjoying a cup of cocoa or coffee. Chas was warmed by the familiarity of the mood, and as soon as the woman behind the counter turned around, Chas was doubly pleased.

"Oh, hi," Chas said, recognizing a woman who had recently moved into the ward.

"Hello," the woman said eagerly.

"I'm sorry, I don't remember your name, even though we've met."

"That's okay." The woman laughed. "I don't remember yours either, but I know your smile very well. I'm Jodi Holdaway."

"And you just moved here?"

"Actually," she sounded mildly embarrassed, "I've lived here a long time, but I haven't been going to church for years. A lot of people think I'm new, but . . ."

"Oh, that's wonderful! I mean . . . that you've come back. I'm sorry I didn't know who you are."

"No worries," Jodi said. "Everyone has been very kind. I'm still working on my husband, but . . . it's nice to be back at church."

"Well, I have empathy for that."

"You do?"

"My husband was just baptized a couple of weeks ago, actually. But it was kind of a struggle for him to get there."

"Oh, wow. That's great. And you are . . ."

"Chas," she said. "Sorry. I'm Chas Leeds. We run the Dickensian Inn."

"The bed-and-breakfast? Of course. I'd heard someone in the ward was running that. It's a beautiful place. I went to the Christmas open house a few years ago. So, what can I do for you today?"

"Well," Chas said, "I need a number of things. I've had someone doing baking for the inn for years, but she won't be able to anymore, so I need to pick up some things to get us through the next couple of days. But I'd also like to work out a regular order. Maybe if I could talk to the manager, or—"

"That's me," Jodi said proudly. "I took over running the bakery a little more than a year ago."

"That's great!" Chas said, feeling so blessed that she could almost hear angels singing. In that vein, she said, "My grandmother worked in this bakery when I was a child. Since she raised me, I spent a lot of time here." She looked around. "It's changed a lot, but . . . it's still the same place."

"That is amazing!" Jodi said with a little laugh.

Another customer came in and Chas said, "Go ahead and help her. I'm not in a hurry, and my order could be complicated."

"Okay, thanks," Jodi said and sold a dozen rolls before she sat down with Chas to talk about a regular order. Since Chas knew exactly what Charlotte brought in and how frequently they needed things, it was easy to work out a plan. They talked about how they would need extra things for holidays or certain weekends when the inn was especially busy. Chas agreed to call when she had reservations that exceeded the average to let Jodi know with plenty of advance notice when she needed to increase the quantity. They visited about a great deal more than baked goods for more than an hour. Jodi provided éclairs and hot chocolate that they enjoyed while they talked, and she only had to interrupt their conversation twice to attend to customers.

Jodi helped Chas carry her purchased baked goods to the car, and they hugged before Chas left. On the way home, Chas called Jackson from her cell phone and said she'd be arriving in just a minute and she needed help taking stuff into the house. He walked out the back door just as she pulled up.

"How's my son?" she asked as Jackson kissed her in greeting. Then she opened the back of the SUV.

"He's all for a marvelous time with his favorite aunt."

"You mean his only aunt."

"Yeah, her," Jackson said, then noticed the new collection of baked goods. "Looks like you did okay."

"Oh, I did more than okay," Chas said, and they stood there leaning against the car while she told him what had happened. "It's like it was meant to be, or something. She's amazing."

"So you made a new friend *and* made a business deal."

"I did," she said proudly, and they carried everything into the house.

On Sunday Melinda went to church with the family. She seemed to enjoy the meeting as much as she enjoyed the friendly greetings she received from many people. They were always amused at how surprised people were when they learned that Melinda and Jackson were siblings.

On their way to class following sacrament meeting, Chas saw Jodi in the hall, taking her two children to Primary. They exchanged a hug, then Jodi introduced her two young daughters. Chas introduced Jodi to Jackson and Melinda.

Jodi shook Jackson's hand as she said, "Congratulations on your baptism."

"Thank you," he said. "Next to marrying Chas, it's the smartest thing I've ever done."

"Maybe you could work on my husband," Jodi said.

"Is he not baptized?"

"Oh, he was baptized as a child, but somewhere along the way he completely lost any interest in going to church. I was just the same for many years, so I can't be too hard on him. But now that I've started coming again, I sure wish he'd come too. He simply has no idea what he's missing."

"I don't know that I can get him to come to church," Jackson said, "but it would be great if your family would come over for dinner sometime."

"Oh, that *would* be great!" Chas said.

"Call Chas and we'll set up a time," Jackson added.

"That should be fine." Jodi smiled. "I'll talk to Patrick and let you know for sure."

Throughout the remainder of the meetings, Melinda showed a keen interest in everything that went on. She mentioned more than once afterward that she'd really enjoyed going to church, just as she had when she'd gone with Jackson on his last visit to Arkansas. Over Sunday dinner she reminded him that he hadn't yet told her the story of being able to finally forgive their father and how it had led him to such a sure knowledge of gospel truths that the only possible outcome was baptism. Chas could hardly contain her joy as she listened to Jackson recount his experiences in detail. She had shared each step of his struggle and had endured a great deal of fear and concern while he'd contended with the effects of PTSD and an abusive childhood. But he had emerged a new man, still the same in most ways, but more at peace and happier than she'd ever seen him.

When he'd told his sister all there was to tell, she asked, "And what about the PTSD? Are you still having nightmares . . . or any other symptoms?"

Jackson shrugged. "I've had a dream once or twice, but it wasn't anything that caused a problem. It really feels as if I can put it behind me, and even if the memories will always be there, I don't have to let it affect my life—or my family."

"It's truly a miracle!" Melinda declared. Chas and Jackson both agreed.

Melinda returned to Arkansas on Tuesday, and it was hard for them to see her go. On the drive back from the airport, Chas admitted to her husband that having Melinda around had made it easier not to think of the impending concern about the baby. He felt the same way, but they both agreed to work together to replace their fear with faith, to be prepared for the worst but hope for the best. They promised each other that they would talk through any difficult feelings concerning the situation, instead of trying to ignore them. And since they were counting down days on the calendar to the date of their temple sealing, they found peace in knowing that the blessings of eternity would surely compensate for their sacrifices and struggles in the here and now.

The following evening Jodi and Patrick and their two daughters came over for dinner. It all technically went fine, and Chas was glad they'd done it. But Patrick was very quiet and seemed to feel awkward and anxious to leave. Jodi called the next day and thanked Chas for their hospitality, apologizing for her husband's poor social skills. Nothing more was said about it, and that was fine with Chas. She was glad to have her growing friendship with Jodi, and she hoped that with time their husbands might be able to connect at some level.

A few days after Melinda left, Jackson entered the parlor to see Chas looking contemplatively at the picture of her first husband on the mantel.

"Should I be jealous?" he asked lightly.

She turned and smiled. "No, I don't think that's a problem. I was just wondering how it might have been for me and Martin if we'd known the baby had a heart defect. We had a lot of strain in our marriage. I wonder if it would have made it better or worse. But it doesn't really matter anymore."

Jackson felt impressed to change the direction of the conversation. "Remember when you first found me in here, looking at that picture?"

"Oh, I remember," she said. "It's a moment we seem to enjoy reminiscing over. It's come up before."

"So it has. Well . . . it was a great moment in my life."

"You told me once that you had wanted to kiss me that day. And we'd only known each other a matter of hours."

"But I was more intrigued and impressed with you in those hours than any woman I'd ever met. When I realized that Martin and I had a great deal in common, I had the first glimmer of hope that maybe what I was feeling might come to something. And then when I saw the look in your eyes when you told me it had been twelve years—and I could see that it was still painful—I just wanted to . . ."

"To what?" she asked, turning more toward him.

Jackson opted to just show her. He gently took her face into his hands, then slid his fingers into her hair and lowered his lips to meet hers. His kiss was timid and meek, like a first kiss. He opened his eyes to look into hers, then he kissed her again—a long, deep, savoring kiss that made her take hold of his shoulders to keep from melting into the floor.

"Wow," she whispered close to his lips. "That certainly would have made an impression."

Jackson chuckled and kissed her again.

"It's probably good you didn't kiss me like that . . . back then."

"Yeah," he said and kissed her again. "But you should know I wanted to."

Again he looked into her eyes. "I almost felt like . . . my life might actually have some value . . . if I could help make up for the way you'd lost Martin."

"You really felt that way, the very first day you knew me?"

"I think I had trouble defining it at the time, but . . . yes, I believe I did."

"Who would have dreamed you were such a romantic?"

He chuckled dubiously. "Now that's a stretch."

"It's all a matter of opinion," she said. "Um . . . could you show me one more time that kissing thing?"

He smiled. "Just once?" he asked and kissed her again.

* * * * *

Jackson found Chas in the kitchen fixing dinner and commented, "You look tired. In fact, you look tired a lot lately. Are you okay?"

"I'm fine," she said, but her smile seemed forced. "I guess two pregnancies in fewer than two years has its downside. I probably wasn't really recovered from the last one."

"I'm sure that's true."

"So . . . I'm just tired, but it's okay."

He leaned up against the counter and folded his arms while she stirred something in a big bowl, then spooned it into a casserole dish. "And I'm sure that your other concerns are probably draining, as well."

"Yeah," she said, sounding sad at the thought of her other concerns. "I'm sure they are. But I can't do anything more about that than I'm already doing."

"Not in that respect, maybe," he said. "But I wonder if we should hire someone else to help around here. Business is good; we can afford it. I was thinking that Michelle is very good at cleaning rooms, but . . ." He was referring to one of the two maids that Chas had come in on a regular basis to clean; Michelle had been working for her more than five years. "Well . . . she helps in the kitchen when you need to be gone, and she's very good at it. Maybe you should have Michelle do more with the breakfast and hire someone else to clean, which is easier to learn."

Chas rinsed off her hands and dried them on her apron while she thought about that. "I really don't know if it's necessary," she said. He gave her a sidelong glare, and she added, "But I'll think about it."

"Okay," he said. "But while you're thinking about it, consider being able to spend about half the time working that you do now. Maybe this is a time to focus on your health, and *both* of your babies."

Chas nodded and got tears in her eyes. Jackson put his arms around her and just held her.

"Here I am," she said, "being hypersensitive and hormonal."

"Hormonal maybe," he said, "but we're dealing with some pretty sensitive stuff here, and you're the mother. You have the right to cry as much you need to."

A minute later she said, "I think you're right. I *do* need some help. I think I am just . . . tired. I was just wondering this morning how I'll manage when both babies get bigger than they are. Charles is getting so heavy, and . . ." She let the sentence fade.

"Okay," he said. "We'll see what we can figure out."

"We could start by asking the girls who already work for us if they know of anyone looking for work."

"Good idea," he said.

A few days later it became clear that no one currently working at the inn knew of anyone else suitable who was looking for work. Jackson told Chas he would see about advertising the position the following day, and that night when they prayed together, Chas asked that they could find the right person to help ease her work-load without any problems or challenges.

The very next morning Jackson was surprised to have one of his former superiors from the agency call him out of the blue. For several minutes he chatted with Tom Myers, catching up on the trivialities of life. Then Jackson said, "It's good to talk to you, but I know you better than to think that you just called me to shoot the breeze. You're not that kind of guy."

"It's that kind of thinking that made you one of the best," Myers said. Jackson didn't comment. He'd often felt that there was some kind of unspoken competition between them, which was entirely formulated by Myers, because Jackson simply didn't feel competitive with coworkers. He never had. When Myers offered

Jackson a compliment, he always imagined it coming with sarcasm, even though it was too mild to be addressed. Without missing another beat, Myers asked, "You still own a firearm, I assume?"

"Yes," Jackson drawled. "You should know a man like me wouldn't feel complete without one."

"I do know that, yes. And I see your permit to carry a concealed weapon is still valid."

"You've been checking up on me. Did you know I got a speeding ticket a couple of weeks ago?"

"Actually, I did. Going forty-two in a thirty zone. Shame on you, Leeds."

"That's what my wife said. Get to the point. But while you're making your point, bear in mind that I'm not leaving here and I'm not going back to work. I prefer to keep the gun in a drawer and live a peaceful life."

"There's no reason you should ever have to use it. I just want to make sure you have it."

"*Why?*" Jackson snarled, steeling himself to say no to whatever this man was going to ask.

"You know that my position includes being a liaison between our office and the U.S. Marshal's office."

"Yes," Jackson drawled suspiciously.

"I've been working with them on a special case that recently went to trial. I want to send someone to you for a while for witness protection. If you're there, we don't have to send another agent with them."

Jackson sighed. "Not *another* agent, Myers. I'm not an agent anymore. I'm retired."

"But you can keep this woman safe."

"Not if it means making my home a target for criminals."

"This is an easy case, Leeds. It's a twenty-three-year-old woman. She has no family connections that will tempt her to compromise the protocol. She's already been under the radar for weeks. The trial is over. They've even staged her death. Her new identity is in place. Since the trial we've had her escorted by an agent to four different cities in the country for a brief stay, so the trail is ice cold. Everything is as ideal as it could possibly be. She just needs a place to stay, and she needs some kind of work, or at least the appearance of it. I was thinking if you could give her room and board in return for the work, it will offer her a transition. Most people get sent into the program along with a family member, but she's alone. Of course, she's been given a significant financial allotment for her new life. More than anything, right now she needs a place to stay until she feels ready to move out on her own. But it's a neat package. It's not risky."

"You started this conversation by asking me if I still have a gun."

"That's just . . . an extra precaution."

"Why would I need any such thing if it's not risky?"

"Are you interested in helping this woman out or not?"

Jackson sighed again. He didn't want to admit that they were looking for another maid, or that they had the space to put someone up. When they'd been praying for someone to help out at the inn, he certainly hadn't wanted it to come with this kind of complication. But the timing made him wonder if it was the right course. He didn't want to admit that the idea of being able to make a difference in someone's life always held deep appeal for him—especially if that someone might be a victim of organized crime. He could only say, "I need to discuss it with my wife."

"Of course. Take your time."

"I know what that means. Take my time but you need an answer by tomorrow."

"Yes, actually. I do."

"And if I say no?"

"We'll figure out something else."

Jackson knew what that meant, too. He knew how difficult the transition could be for these people just because they'd been in the wrong place at the wrong time. The thought triggered his empathy, and his heart picked up an unsteady rhythm.

"Call me tomorrow," Jackson said. "But don't get your hopes up."

CHAPTER 3

That same afternoon, Jackson and Chas went out together to do some errands, which included a long grocery list and a stop at the bakery to pick up their order. In the parking lot of the grocery store, Jackson said, "There's something I need to talk to you about."

"Okay," Chas said as they entered the store.

While Jackson was safely buckling Charles into the front of the grocery cart, he said, "You know how we were talking about hiring someone."

"Yes," she said, looking at her list while they walked deeper into the store.

"How would you feel about hiring someone under some strange circumstances . . . but with the possibility of being able to help them with a difficult situation?"

Chas stopped walking and turned to look at him.

"I know you're all for helping people in need. I'm with you in that. But what if helping a person could bring potential . . . problems into our lives?"

They stood facing each other in the middle of the produce section while Chas took in what he was saying. "Why don't you just tell me what's going on?"

"Why don't you give me an answer that's simply based on principle before I tell you what's going on?"

"Okay," she said and thought for a moment. Her mind was taken to stories she'd heard from Church history of the early Saints taking others in when they were sick, hungry, and dying, at the expense of their own safety. Surely what Jackson might propose couldn't be as serious as that. "I think it's a Christian thing to care for others and help them if possible, whatever the risks."

"But what about enabling a person in their bad behavior. Shouldn't we also protect our home and family?"

"Is this person you're talking about someone who has bad behavior that you're concerned about enabling?"

"I have no idea. I'm just trying to make a point."

"Then . . . I think that such a decision . . . like any decision, should be based on prayer and personal revelation. I think I would be willing to help someone according to the guidance of the Spirit, believing that the Lord would let me know if my intervention would do more harm than good." She looked hard at her husband. "At first you sounded like you wanted to talk me into it, now I sense you're trying to talk me out of it—and I don't even know what we're talking about."

"I guess I just want you to be objective; I want to be objective too. A part of me does *not* want to do it, because it feels to me like it's going to open some unknown can of worms."

"Is that your instinct talking?"

He thought about it. "Yes."

"Then why even consider it?"

"Because if someone's in trouble, and we can help them . . ."

"Okay, Jackson. Enough hypothetical speculation. Just tell me."

"One of my former superiors—Tom Myers—called from Norfolk . . . just this morning. He asked if we would take in a young woman who is being put into witness protection."

"Good heavens," she said. "What does that mean, exactly?"

"I don't know the details, but it generally means that she's testified against someone who has some power and her life is in danger. So, her death has been staged, and—"

"You really did say that her death has been staged."

"I really did."

"It's so . . . television drama."

Jackson chuckled and shook his head. "It's only television drama if you've never lived it. Those dramas *are* usually based on reality. It really does happen, and it happens a lot. She's been given a new identity, and she needs a job and a place to stay to get her started. It would be temporary. And I guess if there were problems, we could arrange to have her go elsewhere."

"Do you think there could be problems?" Chas asked as Charles started to fuss. She reached into the diaper bag for a graham cracker and handed it to him. Jackson hesitated. "You just told me your instincts were telling you this isn't entirely good."

He shrugged. "I don't know what to think. That might just be the way Myers approached it."

"What did he say?"

"He asked me if I still own a gun."

"Why would he want to know that?"

"That's what I wanted to know," Jackson said. "He assured me that there was no risk, that he simply asked as an added precaution. She's going into the program alone, and I think they want to send her somewhere that will give her more of a family setting for the transition."

"Is she in danger, though? Could she bring danger to us?"

"This program was never part of my job. I just worked *with* these people a few times. It's actually the U.S. Marshal's office that deals with this stuff, but as I understand it, when people who are put into the program keep the established rules, they've never been found. It's when they break the rules and reach outside the safety net that there are problems. We have to assume this woman wants to stay safe, and apparently she has no outside connections, so there shouldn't be a problem."

"Okay, so . . . I think we need to think about it. I don't think I can say no *or* yes without some prayer and pondering. If you and I can't come firmly to the same answer then . . . well, we just need to think about it."

"I agree," he said and picked up a large bag of potatoes, putting them on the bottom rack of the grocery cart.

After the grocery shopping was done, they stopped at the bakery, where Jodi had their order ready. During the short drive home from there, Chas said, "That must be so horrible."

"What?"

"To be in the wrong place at the wrong time . . . and have to completely change your life just to stay safe. It's unconscionable."

"Yes, it is. Unfortunately I was exposed to a lot of unconscionable behavior because of my job."

"I'm sure you were," she said, taking his hand. "I bet that was hard, day after day."

"It was; some of it still haunts me if I think about it. So I try not to think about it. I just have to remember that I made a little bit of difference on behalf of the good guys. That's how we got through the days—just believing we could make a difference, even if most days it didn't feel like we made much progress."

Chas was silent for a long moment. "I think we should help her."

"You haven't had time to pray about it yet."

"I know, and I will . . . we will. Of course, we need to do that to know for sure, but . . . I feel like we should help her."

"As long as you're doing it for the right reasons. The idea of hiring someone was to ease your stress, not add to it. We really have no idea what kind of person she is or what we're getting into."

"That's why we need to just go with our feelings, and if we both agree, we'll do it. Then we'll just have to take it on the best we can. When do you have to give them a decision?"

"Tomorrow."

"Oh, as long as that," she said with mild sarcasm. "Well, I'm going to pray about it, and unless my feelings change before morning, I'm going with a yes. You'll have to let me know what you think."

"And what if I don't know *what* I think . . . or rather, what I feel? I'm not as practiced at this spiritual decision-making stuff as you are."

"The best way I've learned to define it for myself is based on what it says in the sixth section of the Doctrine and Covenants. I love the phrase 'peace to your mind.' And that's how I would describe it. I've rarely had an overwhelming answer. I've just figured if I felt peace in my mind, and in my heart, the course was right. The absence of peace—or confusion—meant that the decision was wrong. I think it takes faith to move forward on something as simple as peace to your mind."

"Okay, I can live with that." He glanced at her. "When have you had an overwhelming answer about something? You said it was rare, but . . ."

"When it came to asking God about having you in my life, the answer was usually pretty undeniable."

"How'd that work out for you?" he asked with a sideways smile.

"Oh, it's working out more marvelously every day."

"I'm glad to hear it," he said and pulled up near the kitchen door of the inn to unload the groceries.

The following morning they both agreed without reservation that they should take the young woman into their home. Jackson called Tom Myers and accepted the challenge. Myers was pleased until Jackson said, "But if I'm taking this on, I want to know about the case."

Myers was silent a long moment and said, "I don't know if—"

"Tell me or I'm not doing it. I get the feeling there's some kind of extenuating circumstances that motivated you to ask for my help. I don't need all the details. I just need to have some idea of what I'm dealing with."

"She testified against Reggie Dinubilo; he's getting life."

"Of the Dinubilo Textile Industry?"

"The very same."

Jackson wanted to renege already. But he couldn't dispute the answer that he and Chas had both gotten when they prayed.

The Dinubilo family was almost classic organized crime. Their front company that imported and exported textiles was a clever coverup for importing and exporting a variety of illegal goods. But they were good at what they did and very careful. It was almost impossible to pin anything criminal on any of a number of family members who had ended up close to suspicious activities, but never quite close enough. Working for the FBI in the same city as the Dinubilo family made it impossible to not know all about them.

"So, what did Reggie do to give us the good fortune of putting him behind bars?"

"He killed Bruce Nuccitelli."

Jackson almost choked. The Nuccitelli family was the *other* ring of organized crime in the same area. The families were competitors in their front business *and* in their illegal doings. The result had been a longtime feud. They were little better than street gangs when it came to the interactions between the two families. But a killing hadn't occurred in many years.

"You're kidding," Jackson said. "I mean . . . you're kidding. You're sending me the person who actually witnessed this going down?"

"I told you yesterday that she's been under the radar a long while now, and we've staged her death. She's been in a different state, far from here, for a couple of weeks now. Everything is free and clear."

Jackson didn't know if it was simply his prior knowledge of the kind of criminals involved that caused him to bristle, or if his instincts were being alerted. Either way, he *still* couldn't dispute what he knew he was supposed to do. "Okay, well . . . I'm hoping you're right. You'd *better* be right. If my family ends up in any danger over this, you will sorely regret it."

"You should know by now that your threats get nowhere with me."

"Now, that's not true," Jackson said lightly, but with an edge to his voice. "I threatened to retire, and here I am."

"Yes, there you are," Myers said. "I'm having an agent put her on a plane. I need you to meet her when she gets off."

He gave Jackson the necessary information, and they ended the call. Jackson leaned back in his chair and offered a silent prayer that they wouldn't end up regretting this. He went to fill Chas in on what to expect. No one but the two of them could ever know that this woman was in witness protection, and he wanted her to go with him to the airport.

"Okay, I guess I can," Chas said, "but if you—"

"It's more appropriate," he said. "When I was an agent, we always went in pairs. Now I'm a married man and I'm not going to pick her up at the airport by myself."

"Okay," she said. "When?"

"Tomorrow morning," Jackson said. "I think we should put her in the Little Nell." He was referring to one of their guest rooms, most of which were named after Dickens characters. "It's a nice room with a good view, but it's one of the least rented so we won't miss it too much."

"I was thinking the same," she said and noticed his expression. "You're worried about this."

"I admit that I am, but as you pointed out, since we both feel that this is right, we just have to take it on the best we can."

"Agreed," she said.

"Of course, she doesn't have to live here permanently. If she decides to stay in Anaconda, she can work toward getting a place of her own. We'll just give her some time."

"What's this woman's name?"

"Cortney Waterton."

"Is that her real name or—"

"That's the name that comes with her new Social Security number and birth certificate. It's the only name we will ever know her by. Actually, Cortney is probably her real name. When a person is so accustomed to their name, it causes problems to change the first name. The rest is all new."

"Wow," Chas said and went upstairs to see if the Little Nell needed any special preparations to actually have someone move into it on a semi-permanent basis. She couldn't imagine having to take on a completely new identity, but she wondered if such people could choose whether or not they kept their given name. If she were to change her name, she would definitely want something a little more feminine than the abbreviation for Charles. But it was her official name, and she did take some pride in being named after the great author. Still, something like Isabelle or Rose would be nice. She laughed at herself over such a silly thought, then she was struck with a sudden idea and put a hand to her rounded belly. "Isabelle Rose," she said aloud, and the sound of it came back to her with a sense of warmth. She hoped that Jackson liked the name, and she hoped and prayed that Isabelle Rose might live long enough for her parents to get to know her and find joy in her life. Then she focused on the woman they would be bringing into their household, wondering what she would be like.

The following morning when they arrived at the airport, Chas said to Jackson, "How will we know it's her?"

"Myers gave me a description," he said, transferring Charles from his car seat to his stroller. "She'll be the woman fitting the description who is waiting for someone to pick her up."

"Okay," Chas said and chuckled.

"What's funny?" he asked.

"Remember the first time I went to Virginia to see you, and you couldn't get away to pick me up? You sent Veese and Ekert."

These two men had worked closely with Jackson for many years, and they had been through some tough things together. The three of them were still good friends, although Jackson was closer to Elliott Veese. Jackson spoke to him regularly and often teased him about coming to stay with them for a vacation. Since Veese was a bachelor in his thirties, Jackson also teased him about coming to Montana to find a wife and settle down. It's what Jackson had done, but they all doubted the same thing would ever happen to Veese. It was good fodder for teasing him, however, and Jackson loved to take advantage of that.

"Yeah, I remember," Jackson said. "Is that funny?" They walked into the airport and headed toward baggage claim, where they would meet Cortney.

"I asked you how I would find these agents, and you said they would find me because they were FBI."

"And they did."

"Yes, they did. But they didn't know I was your girlfriend. I think they thought you were going to interrogate me or something."

Jackson chuckled. "Yeah, that's funny."

They only waited in the right place for about five minutes before Jackson spotted a tall, blonde woman wearing sunglasses and carrying a big purse over her shoulder. She set a large soft bag at her feet and looked around as if she didn't know what to do. "I think that's her," he said and Chas followed him, pushing the stroller.

"Cortney?" he asked, approaching her.

She turned and took off her sunglasses. Chas was a little startled by how beautiful she was. She had the face, the hair, and the figure that showed up in magazines and on television. She made bold eye contact with Jackson and said, "I need to know who you are, or I'm not going with you."

Chas expected him to assure Cortney regarding who he was, but instead he pulled out his wallet and opened it to show her his driver's license.

"Okay," Cortney said and took a deep breath of relief.

"This is my wife, Chas, and our son, Charles."

"Hi," Cortney and Chas said at the same time, then Chas added, "We're glad to have you with us, Cortney. I hope you'll like it here."

"I'm sure I will," Cortney said. "Thank you."

"Do you need to get any luggage?" Jackson asked, motioning toward the baggage claim.

"Nope. This is it," Cortney said.

"Let's go home, then," Jackson said, and they all walked to the car while Chas made small talk with Cortney about the flight and the weather. The drive home was mildly awkward since Cortney didn't say much. She played with Charles a little and asked Chas when the other baby was due. She commented on their being so close together, but so had everybody else who knew Chas was pregnant. Cortney also made multiple comments on the snow and how much of it there was. She was clearly not fond of snow.

When they arrived in Anaconda, Cortney said something about it being a small town. Her voice sounded like she was trying to be positive and complimentary, but it was obvious that she didn't really feel that way. She did perk up a little when they arrived at the inn.

"You run this place?" she asked.

"We do," Jackson said. "This is where you'll be working, although cleaning rooms isn't very exciting. But the hours aren't bad."

"Oh, I'm grateful for any work," Cortney said, getting out of the car. She looked up at the beautifully restored Victorian home and added, "It's the most beautiful house I've ever seen." She turned to Chas, who was waiting while Jackson got the baby out of his seat. "Where do you live?"

"Here," Chas said. "It's home and work all rolled into one."

"How marvelous!" Cortney said.

"You'll be staying in one of the guest rooms," Chas added. "I hope you'll like it."

"I'm sure I will!" Cortney said and followed them into the house.

Jackson was glad to take the baby with him to the office and check in with Polly while Chas gave Cortney a tour of the house, explaining meal times, house rules, and what would be expected of her. Chas told her she could start work the next day when Michelle came in at nine to train her. They would work together for a week, then Michelle would be taking over other duties in the kitchen. Cortney seemed pleased with the setup and eager to do whatever was asked of her. She was thrilled when they came through the door of the Little Nell, the room that she would be using as her own. Chas told her that this was the only place in the inn where she could leave her things lying around, and she was welcome to make herself at home. Just as with all of her guests, Chas told her that if she needed anything or had any questions, she could pick up the phone in her room and reach Chas, Jackson, or Polly, who would have a cordless handset with them. Cortney thanked Chas for everything and said that she needed to settle in and rest, so Chas left her on her own.

Chas found her husband at the desk while Polly was out doing an errand. Charles was playing with his collection of toys that were kept in an office drawer.

"So, what do you think?" Chas asked her husband.

"It's hard to say," Jackson said. "I have a hard time imagining us sharing every meal with her for some undetermined amount of time. She seems nice enough, but not really our type. I hope it doesn't continue to feel so . . . awkward."

"Yeah, that's about how I feel too. It's not like we can ask her where she came from or why she's here."

"No, that would be even more awkward."

"So . . . one day at a time, right?"

"Right," he said.

Chas noticed his expression and commented, "Something's bugging you."

He looked surprised, then said, "Yeah, something *is* bugging me, but it's probably nothing."

"Are you going to tell me?"

"She has a cell phone."

"She does?"

"It was in the right front pocket of her jeans," he said.

"Ah, this is that special agent inability you have to avoid observing every detail of a person."

"I'm afraid so."

"And . . . she has a cell phone. Is that significant?"

"Under the circumstances, I think it's *highly* significant."

"I'm not following you."

"She's in witness protection, Chas. She is supposed to have broken contact with *everyone* in her life. According to Myers, she didn't really have family or friends to begin with. She's been living in safe houses."

"So, her only company has been FBI agents?"

"No, her only company has been U.S. Marshals."

"Lucky her," Chas said with sarcasm.

"The point is . . . why does someone who is starting over with no contacts have a cell phone?"

"Maybe she just got it."

"She supposedly hasn't been anywhere without a legal escort for months. And where was she going to have the bill sent?"

"Maybe it's one of those prepaid cell phones?"

"Maybe. And again, who is she going to call? It doesn't feel right."

"Okay, well . . . I guess you can either go ask her why she has a cell phone, or we can just give the matter some time and be . . . observant."

"I'll go for plan B."

"Plan B it is," Chas said.

"Oh, you have a message." He handed her a piece of paper with a note in Polly's handwriting. "Looks like your grandfather called. You should call him back."

"I will," she said, her mood brightening. "I've been thinking we're overdue to see him. Are you okay with inviting him to dinner Sunday?"

"That would be great. Maybe he can figure Cortney out, or at the least, he could entertain her."

"Yeah," Chas chuckled. "We'll see how that goes."

Chas put on the headset that went with the cordless phone, which she put in her apron pocket. She headed back to the kitchen while she dialed Nolan Stoddard's number so she could talk as long as she wanted and have her hands free to do some work, which would put her ahead for the next few meals. Chas had discovered the fact that she had a grandfather not so many months earlier. Since her conception had actually been the result of a criminal act, and her mother had died in childbirth, she'd been raised by her grandmother, never knowing either of her parents. Now she knew that her father had died in prison while serving time for what he'd done to her mother. But it turned out that he'd been the black sheep of the family, and her grandfather had tracked her down when he'd gained a desire to get to know her following his wife's death. The results had been marvelous so far. They got along well and enjoyed getting together on a regular basis. She hadn't yet met any of his children or other grandchildren, but it was something she hoped might happen before too long.

As Chas listened to the phone ringing at the other end, her mood darkened as she recalled that she'd not yet given her grandfather the news about the baby. When he answered, they exchanged such comfortable and natural greetings that it was difficult for Chas to believe she'd only known the man for a few months. While she put on some soup for lunch and prepared a chicken dish that could go in the fridge for supper, Chas told her grandfather all about the baby, proud of herself for getting through the conversation with very few tears. Nolan was kind and compassionate, and his concern was genuine. He assured her that whatever happened, he would be there for her as much as she needed. When there was no more to say about that, she told him about Cortney, omitting anything about witness protection. She simply told him what she and Jackson had agreed on, that she was the friend of a friend and had been in need of a job and a fresh start. She said quite honestly that she really hadn't gotten to know Cortney yet, and she could only hope that it worked out well for everyone. She thought of the cell phone issue while she was talking and couldn't deny that according to Jackson's logic, it did seem rather strange. She invited her grandfather to Sunday dinner, and he eagerly accepted the invitation.

Chas ended her phone call and had some lunch with her family before Jackson went to put Charles down for his nap while Chas cleaned up. She'd told Cortney that lunch would be at twelve-thirty—but it was past one and she hadn't shown up. Thinking she might be feeling shy, Chas considered taking a tray to her room, then she wondered if Cortney might be sleeping. She'd already told Cortney where she could find sandwiches and snacks in the guest refrigerator, so she slid a note under her door that simply reminded her of that.

Chas found Jackson in the parlor talking to Veese on the phone. She listened for a minute to their typical banter, then went to the office and found Polly busy there. They went over a few things and chatted a bit about the situation with Cortney, although Polly was getting the same version that Chas had given her grandfather.

Wendell came after school to do his usual simple jobs, and Jackson made a point to see that they did a couple of chores side by side so they could talk, mostly about the books they were reading. After the boy left, Jackson found Chas in the kitchen and offered to help her.

Cortney didn't show up until supper time. She apologized for not coming down earlier, saying that she'd fallen asleep. The meal was mildly awkward, with very little conversation, but Cortney was kind and expressed her appreciation for the meal and for everything else. She talked to Charles a little bit as if he were an adult, which was actually quite endearing. She helped clear the table when they were finished eating and asked Chas if there was anything else she needed help with. When Chas told her there wasn't, she said she was going to take a little walk, even though it was cold, and then she'd just hang out in her room.

"You don't need to hide in your room," Chas said. "You're welcome to use the parlor, or—"

"Thanks," Cortney said, "but I'm kind of used to being a loner. Don't worry about me. As long as I have a safe place to stay, I'll be fine."

"Okay," Chas said. "Just find me . . . or call me, if you need anything."

Chas watched her bundle up and go outside and felt decidedly sorry for her. She couldn't even imagine how it might feel to look at life through Cortney's eyes. She wanted to know more about her. She wanted to know where she'd worked, what she liked to do, and what kind of family she'd come from. Perhaps with time they could gain enough trust to come to that conversation. For now, Chas could only do her best to make Cortney feel at home.

The next day Cortney came down for breakfast at eight. Jackson was still out for his usual early-morning run and Chas had just finished getting Charles dressed.

"Good morning," Chas said. "How did you sleep?"

"Oh, that bed is luscious!" Cortney said. "Everything is wonderful; thank you."

"You're welcome. There's some coffee on the sideboard in the dining room. Since this is a bed-and-breakfast, most mornings there will be a buffet set out and you can help yourself. On mornings when we don't have guests, there's cereal and toast and other odds and ends. Again, just go ahead and help yourself."

"Which kind of morning is it?" Cortney asked.

Chas smiled. "I'll have some breakfast out in about twenty minutes. Michelle will be here about nine and you can start working, but it shouldn't take very long today. I'm going into town later if you'd like to come along."

"That would be great," Cortney said, and poured herself a cup of coffee.

By lunchtime the rooms were all cleaned, and Michelle reported discreetly to Chas that Cortney was doing fine with the work. After eating some sandwiches, Chas and Cortney left Charles with his father and went into town for some errands. Chas tried to initiate some conversation, and they did a little better than the previous day, but it was more about preferences with food and movies and such. It was a start. When they returned to the inn, Cortney helped Chas bring things in from the car and put them away. She asked if she could do anything else, then she went up to her room and didn't come down until supper. Again she was mostly quiet but polite, and she was helpful in cleaning up after the meal. Then she disappeared again into her room.

"Well," Jackson said to Chas after Cortney had gone up the stairs, "as least she's not loud and obnoxious."

"No, she's certainly not that," Chas said. "Do you think she's just naturally shy, or has being on the run from the mob and living in safe houses made her clam up?"

"I don't know," he said. "Could be some of both. But I think she'll be fine."

"I hope so," Chas said, realizing that she'd developed an increasing care and concern for Cortney.

On Sunday Cortney politely declined their invitation to attend church, which wasn't a surprise to either of them, but they wanted her to feel welcome to join them. That afternoon, Nolan came for dinner, and Chas was always pleased to see her grandfather. Jackson had also taken to him quite well, and they all had a great time visiting. Nolan was very kind to Cortney, and he got her talking more at the dinner table than she'd ever talked before.

Because Nolan didn't know Cortney was starting a new life with a new identity, he didn't hold back in asking her about herself and her life before coming to Anaconda. Chas and Jackson kept exchanging discreet glances of amazement to hear the convincing tale she'd concocted about her past. But it was difficult to tell which parts were the truth, and which were not. Knowing that much of it was *not* true, Jackson felt mildly uneasy to realize that she was an *excellent* liar. He had to counter that with the reminder that she had been trained by her protectors these last several months on how to start a new life, and she'd probably been practicing her story. She *needed* to be a good liar to stay safe.

Everyone worked together to clean up dinner, then they all went to the parlor to visit. Cortney hung around for a short while, then excused herself to go to her room. Jackson and Chas were both surprised when Nolan said, "I suspect that story she told us about her past wasn't entirely true."

Jackson realized that maybe Cortney wasn't such a great liar, after all. He hoped that *he* was when he said, "We know very little about her, only that she's been in some trouble in the past and she might be trying to hide from it. We should probably just leave it at that." He gave Nolan a subtle nod, which was returned as a silent understanding.

Nolan knew Jackson was ex-FBI and he could probably put pieces together. Fortunately, Nolan could be trusted completely, and Jackson knew it. They just had to be careful in their explanations to other people. He hoped that Cortney fully understood that.

The following day, Chas brought in the mail while Jackson was in the office. Polly had gone to the kitchen in need of a snack and had taken Charles with her. It was sweet to see how much Polly enjoyed helping with the baby and how comfortable they were with each other.

"You have a package," she said to Jackson, setting the small padded envelope in front of him while she shuffled through the rest of the mail.

"What on earth?" he said, then glanced at the return address and laughed.

"From Elliott?" she asked.

He looked momentarily confused, then said, "Uh . . . yeah." Even though he'd known Elliott Veese for years, he'd always known and referred to him mostly as just *Veese*. It was Chas who had started referring to him by his first name.

"What is it?" she asked, looking over his shoulder.

"Mostly a practical joke, I think," he said as he tore open the package. "He threatened to send me one of these, but I told him I wasn't going to wear it."

He pulled out a folded shirt and held it up as he explained. It was a rather silly custom-designed T-shirt that had been made for the agency's softball team. Jackson explained that Veese had been teasing him about not being around to do his part to win an important game, but they were going to make him an honorary member of the team anyway.

"I think you *should* wear it," Chas said.

Jackson chuckled. "Maybe for painting or something."

"I'm going to wash it anyway," she said, taking it from him. "Then it'll be ready when you're in the mood . . . to paint or something."

With the shirt in one hand, she reached out to pick up the empty padded envelope to throw it away since she was closer to the wastebasket. She was startled when Jackson put his hand over it and said, "That's okay. I'll take care of it."

"I was just going to . . . throw it away," she said.

"I know." He smiled. "I'll take care of it. Why don't you go . . . get some rest or something."

"I'm fine."

"Okay," he said. "Good." With his hand still over the envelope, he changed the subject and asked if she wanted him to go with her to the standard pregnancy checkup the following day.

"Yes," she said, "I *would* like you to go. I've already talked to Polly about watching Charles."

"Okay. Let's get lunch out while we're in the city."

Chas tried to dismiss his mildly odd behavior and left the room, dreading tomorrow's appointment with all her soul.

CHAPTER 4

As soon as Chas had left the room, Jackson peered into the padded envelope, then carefully removed a tiny electronic device that had been taped inside. He examined it, then put it safely away where no one else could ever find it. He might never need it, but he was glad to have it—just in case.

Chas's appointment the following day went as well as could be expected under the circumstances. Other than knowing there was a heart defect, everything appeared to be going well. Beyond Chas feeling excessively tired, she was healthy and strong. They would continue to do ultrasounds throughout the pregnancy to keep a close eye on the baby's heart. The baby's current heartbeat seemed fine.

After the appointment, Chas cried in the car; being reminded of the situation made it necessary to face it emotionally once again. But Jackson quickly distracted her with a nice lunch out, and then they went shopping. They ended up buying some baby clothes for a girl, both agreeing that it was a gesture of faith, and if this baby didn't live to wear them, they would hope for another daughter someday that could.

March brought a series of snowstorms that made business slow and going out difficult. Cortney commented more than once on not being fond of snow, but she liked the feeling of safety being at the inn and not having to go out at all. She and Chas both agreed that snow had more charm when you could sit by a warm fire and look out at it through the windows.

Jackson, Chas, and Polly all felt sad when Wendell came by with his father to tell them that the family was moving out of state. A possible transfer had come up for Wendell's father to a place that would put them closer to family. Since Wendell's mother had passed away the previous year, this additional support would be a good thing for all of them. The following weekend Wendell had a sleepover at the inn. They watched a movie and had pizza and popcorn, and then he got to sleep in one of the guest rooms. A few days later the family moved, but Wendell made them promise to send him e-mails. He was a great kid, and they were all more than willing to remain connected.

Later that month, snatches of warming weather made it possible to begin a project that had been in the planning stages for months. Jackson and Chas had made the decision to use an inheritance he had received from his mother to build onto the inn. Living in the inn was wonderful, but a growing family needed room for children to play and make noise without affecting a business where customers wanted peace and quiet. Since the actual property surrounding the inn didn't amount to very much space, they'd not been able to consider their desire to build an addition. Then, the little house next door had gone up for sale. The house was small and old and had many problems, but the property was priceless to Jackson and Chas. They'd purchased it last fall, and the blueprints for the addition had been custom made according to their unique specifications. It would be attached to the inn via what was now the kitchen door that exited to the side of the inn, with a sidewalk that went around to the back. The addition would be built for practicality, with a large common room and sufficient bedrooms and bathrooms to raise a family comfortably. They could still use the parlor and formal dining room of the inn for special occasions and to entertain guests. Their new home would have a private entrance and a fenced backyard that could only be accessed by the family. The home would be wired so they could hear when someone entered the inn, and one or the other of them always carried a cordless phone continually, anyway. With the money Jackson had received from his mother's estate, and an amount they'd had in savings, the mortgage required to build the home was minimal and would be easily affordable with the average amount of business they took in.

Now, with spring finally on the horizon, the project they'd been planning and discussing could begin. They had made an agreement with the contractor in charge of the project so that no construction could take place prior to ten A.M. or after seven P.M., since they had to be considerate of their guests. Construction might proceed a little more slowly, but it was necessary to keep their business running.

During the last week of March, the house next door was leveled and the rubble removed. A hole was dug for the basement and foundation of the new house. The kitchen door of the inn was blocked off, and a construction fence ensured the safety of anyone on the premises. A streak of bad weather in April put the next step on hold, then a stretch of lovely warm days made it possible to pour the concrete.

While winter was merging into spring, Cortney seemed well settled into life at the inn. She did her work efficiently and was always helpful and polite. But she mostly kept to herself except for meals, and it was difficult to know whether she was doing all right or not. Jackson and Chas agreed that all they could do was be mindful of her and give her time. They both suspected she wouldn't end up staying in Anaconda terribly long, simply because she didn't like cold weather or small towns. Perhaps that was the reason she made no effort to get out and meet people or acclimate herself to the community.

Jackson and Chas took turns trying to discreetly check on her and make certain all was well, or at least give her fair opportunity to discuss any concerns she might have. When it was Jackson's turn, he mentioned to Chas some things that had been on his mind, and they both agreed that he needed to talk to Cortney about them.

When Jackson knew she had just wrapped up her work for the day, he asked her if she would come to the office and sit down.

"Are you doing okay so far?" he asked.

"Yeah, I'm fine," Cortney said. "Thank you."

"You know, of course, that our agreement is that you work for your room and board, meaning we will house and feed you, but the job doesn't come with any wages."

"Yes, I know," she said, seeming alarmed. "Is there some problem with the work I'm doing? Do I need to do more to earn the—"

"No, what you're doing is fine for now. Michelle and Chas both tell me that you're doing a good job. We may need to reevaluate the situation at some future time, but for now it's fine. I would think that eventually you'd want to get your own place, and not necessarily in Anaconda."

"It's a nice little town," she said, "but . . . I'm a city girl."

"And you're not too fond of the cold weather," he said and she smiled. Wanting to be certain that she truly had all she needed, he went on. "I was told you were given a financial allotment that you could use to start over."

"Yes, that's right," she said.

"Forgive me if it seems like I'm being nosy. I just want to make certain you have what you need."

"Oh, I do, thank you."

"It's just that . . . I haven't seen you actually *spend* any money."

She shrugged. "I haven't needed to buy anything. You and Chas take very good care of me."

"Okay, I'm glad, but . . . what about a car? Would you like me to help you use some of that money to get yourself a car? Then you wouldn't be so . . . stuck. You can't enjoy being cooped up all the time."

"It's okay, really," she said. "I'll have to do that eventually, but right now I'm fine. I'm used to being cooped up. Maybe I feel more . . . secure after what's happened." She shrugged again.

"I'll have to work up to getting out in the big, bad world. But for now . . . I'm fine, really. There's no need for you to worry about me."

"Okay, fair enough. Please let us know if you have any problems."

"With as many times as both you and Chas have made that offer, you can be sure that I will."

She got up and left the room while Jackson wondered what it was that made him feel mildly uneasy after such conversations. But he couldn't very well corner her and insist that she tell him why his instincts were alerting him to something about which there was absolutely no evidence of logical cause for concern. What could he do besides hope that this situation would end well, for Cortney as well as his family?

* * * * *

The construction of the house got fully underway, with work proceeding more quickly some days than others, depending on the weather. Melinda came for a short visit, and Cortney seemed to enjoy her company. She didn't open up any more than she had before, and she still didn't say much, but she did spend more time out of her room while Melinda was there. When Melinda went back to Arkansas, Cortney went back to hiding away in her room. Neither Jackson nor Chas could imagine spending that much time holed up in a room with the television on. She didn't have any books, and she rarely got any more exercise than going for a walk. But it was their job to keep her housed and fed, not to offer any judgments on how she spent her time.

In May, the new section of the house began to take shape. Chas was becoming more uncomfortable with her pregnancy, and more tired. She was so grateful for Jackson's foresight in having Michelle mostly covering the daily breakfast for the guests, while Cortney took over her cleaning duties. Chas still helped here and there, and she worked one or two mornings a week so that Michelle didn't have to come in every day. But the arrangement was much more conducive to helping Chas get through this pregnancy while she had a toddler to contend with.

Chas was surprised to get a phone call from Charlotte out of the blue with no apparent purpose but to say hello and see how she was doing. Chas was thinking that it was nice to hear from her—and she told her so. Then the conversation shifted to Chas's pregnancy, and Charlotte made more than one passive-aggressive comment about all the misery Chas could have spared herself by just having it over with a long time ago. In as polite a voice as Chas could manage, she told Charlotte she would enjoy keeping in touch with her if she could keep her opinions to herself. Then she hung up before she burst into tears. She waited to do that until the call was over. When she'd calmed down, she found Jackson and told him about the call. He listened and hugged her and assured her that she was a good woman making sacrifices to do the right thing—no matter what Charlotte or anyone else believed.

The following day they went into Butte for the usual checkup. They'd gone there the previous week for another ultrasound, but they hadn't waited around for the results. Today was six weeks from the due date, and Chas felt a sense of doom in anticipating the date. She'd adjusted to the idea that this baby might not make it, and she'd managed to keep herself distracted by other things in life if only to avoid thinking about it. Jackson was continually telling her not to give up hope, but deep inside she wondered if she already had. She couldn't even comprehend having a healthy baby at the end of this journey. After losing her first child soon after its birth, she wondered if it was just too frightening to invest any hope at all that it might turn out differently this time.

They ended up waiting a long time, since the doctor had needed to leave to deliver a baby. They were given the option of rescheduling, but Chas wanted to have it over with. Besides, the drive into Butte was no small thing.

When the doctor finally returned, he listened to the baby's heartbeat and opted not to perform any other exam. Then he asked them to come into his office. After they were seated across the desk from the doctor, Chas put her trembling hand into Jackson's, wondering what this conversation would bring.

"Now that the baby is a little bigger," the doctor explained, "we can see more detail on the ultrasound images of what exactly is going on with her heart. I took the liberty of sending the most recent images to a doctor I've learned of who has had great success with pediatric open-heart surgery."

Chas took in a sharp breath and tightened her hold on Jackson's hand. Could it be possible? Was that hope she felt?

The doctor went on. "If the baby makes it full term—or rather, *almost* full term—I think we might be able to correct the problem enough to save your daughter's life."

Chas realized she was trembling, and in the same moment she knew that Jackson was too. He was just better at covering it. "Tell us," she said. "Tell us what we need to do."

"This surgeon works through Primary Children's Medical Center in Salt Lake City. It's one of the best pediatric hospitals in the country. You would need to give birth at the University of Utah Medical Center, which is right next door. The delivery would need to be done C-section, early enough that we don't run any risk of you actually going into labor. We don't want to take any chances that might put any strain on the baby. We would need to maintain complete control over the delivery, and the surgeon would be on hand to do the surgery on the baby right away, once it's established that she is strong enough to withstand the procedure."

The doctor paused, but Chas couldn't speak. She turned to Jackson, hoping he could find his voice. She saw her own astonishment mingled with hope mirrored in his eyes. He turned back to the doctor, cleared his throat, and spoke with a mild quiver in his voice. "So . . . I assume this doctor believes there's a good chance for success, or he wouldn't be willing to do this."

"That is a true statement," the doctor said, and Chas had to clap her free hand over her mouth as the sound of her hope threatened to jump right out of her throat. She whimpered behind her fingers and put her head on Jackson's shoulder as he shifted to put his arm around her. "Of course, there are always risks with *any* kind of surgical procedure, and there are no guarantees. But there's a lot higher chance that she'll live than that she won't."

Chas's tears mingled with laughter, and she moved her hand away from her mouth when it became pointless to hide her emotion from the doctor. "That's the best news we've heard in a long time," she said.

The doctor leaned back in his chair and smiled. "It's nice to be the bearer of good tidings once in a while. If you're prepared to move forward with this, I'll make all of the arrangements."

"Yes, make all of the arrangements," Jackson said eagerly.

"You'll need to drive to Salt Lake City," he said, "because flying just brings on too many variables at this stage of pregnancy. I'll have one of the schedulers call you with appointment information, but I want you to plan on being settled there before you hit thirty-seven weeks, which is three weeks prior to your due date. There are options available for housing in association with the children's hospital so that you can have a place to stay nearby while the baby is recovering."

Recovering. Chas really liked that word. The hope that she had struggled to hold on to since the news had first come of the baby's heart defect was suddenly something that she could feel. They left the doctor's office laughing and speculating and planning their lengthy stay in Salt Lake City.

"It *is* the Mormon capital of the world," Chas said. "We can see some of the sights while we're there."

"Do you think Polly can manage running the inn for that long?" Jackson asked. "We don't know for sure how long it will be."

"She did just fine while we were on our honeymoon. I'm sure she'll manage. We'll talk to her about it. I would bet we can get some help from people in the ward if we need it."

"That's true. And what about Charles? We can't expect Polly to take care of him, too."

"I'm sure Melinda would be more than happy to come and take care of him, and she could help Polly a little as well."

"Now *that's* a good idea," Jackson said. "Let's go home and call her."

"Let's call her on the *way* home. But let's eat first. I'm famished."

Melinda was thrilled with the news and eager to come and take care of little Charles for as long as they needed. She didn't have any conflicts on the calendar, but she declared that even if she did she would change them. When they arrived at the inn and spoke to Polly, she was equally excited with the good news and fully committed to doing whatever it took to keep things running smoothly so that they could get through this with no worries about what was going on at home. Cortney came into the office while they were talking, so they shared the news with her. She seemed pleased but lacked the enthusiasm the others felt, although that was understandable since she wasn't actually emotionally involved with the situation. She asked a few questions, wished them well, and went out for a walk.

Later that day, Jackson was walking down the hall and noticed that a wall hanging was crooked. He stopped to straighten it and wondered if he'd ever stopped before to actually read what it said, even though it had been there long before he'd ever arrived. In lovely hand stitching, framed and behind glass, it read, *A loving heart was better and stronger than wisdom. Charles Dickens*

Jackson read it three times, taking in the profound depth of meaning he was finding in the words. Of course, wisdom was necessary, but nothing was more powerful than love. Chas had taught him that. She'd loved him unconditionally in spite of his many struggles and mistakes. And she loved those around her, even when they caused her grief and brought challenges into her life. Chas *was* very wise. She was sharp, and she knew how to use her head and apply her experience to life. But it was her understanding of love that made her so amazing.

Jackson turned to see the subject of his thoughts come into the hall from the dining room. When she saw him there she approached and asked with a smile, "What are you doing?"

"It was crooked," he said, pointing to the wall hanging's present straightness with great pride. "And then I read it, and then I had to think about it."

"Oh, so you're going all philosophical."

"Maybe," he said.

Chas looked at it and said, "It's from *David Copperfield.*"

"I like it," Jackson said.

"I like it too." Chas looked at him skeptically. "But . . . may I ask why you're suddenly so taken with it?"

"It reminds me of you," he said and kissed her before he walked away with no further explanation. Chas read the quote again and smiled. From her husband of few words, she would certainly take that as a compliment.

The following day Chas saw Jodi at the bakery when she went to pick up her order. She always planned a little extra time to just sit and visit, and today she told Jodi the wonderful news that had given her so much hope. When Chas was talking about the arrangements they needed to make, Jodi eagerly offered to help out at the inn if she was needed. Since business at the bakery was running smoothly and she had plenty of help, it wouldn't be a problem to get away if the need arose.

Chas thanked her, and then felt a strange sense of heavenly love when Jodi added, "And my sister and her husband live in Salt Lake. He's a very successful businessman, and they have a big, beautiful home. Most of their kids are grown and gone, and they actually have a separate living area in the basement. They've let people stay there for all kinds of reasons. If it's vacant, I know they'd love to have you stay. They're all about helping someone out. I'll give her a call."

"Oh, that would be great!" Chas said, but she hadn't expected Jodi to pick up the phone that moment and call her sister. Chas sat and listened to Jodi's side of the conversation as she explained what still felt dreamlike to Chas. Jodi hung up the phone and smiled at Chas. "It's all good. You have a place to stay for as long as you need. Their basement has three bedrooms, two bathrooms, and a kitchenette."

"That's incredible!" Chas said, realizing she could cross that off her list. She was glad to know the hospital had options available, but she didn't know what limitations there might be, and maybe there was someone else with fewer options available that could benefit more from what the hospital had to offer.

Driving home from the bakery with Jodi's sister's contact information in her purse, Chas realized that if Charlotte hadn't quit, she wouldn't have become friends with Jodi, and this blessing wouldn't have come to pass. She felt tempted to call Charlotte and thank her, but decided against it.

* * * * *

Less than four weeks prior to Chas's due date, everything was arranged for them to leave for Salt Lake the following week. Melinda would be flying into Butte the day before their departure, and everything at the inn was being taken care of. Chas had spoken to Jodi's sister, Kate, on the phone several times, and their home away from home was waiting for them. All of the appointments were scheduled so that they could meet with the doctors ahead of time, and the delivery and heart surgery were all set and good to go. Jackson and Chas sat down together at breakfast to double-check everything and make sure that nothing had been overlooked. They both admitted to being excited and nervous, and neither of them was even going to consider the possibility that the baby might not make it. They would cross that bridge *if* they came to it.

Later that day, Jackson was at the side of the inn by the driveway, pulling weeds in the flowerbed, when he looked up to see Cortney standing close by.

"Did you need something?" he asked, noting that she looked expectant, perhaps nervous.

"Um . . ." she wrung her hands, "I just . . ."

Seeing that she was *really* nervous, he stood up and brushed the dirt off his hands. "Is something wrong?"

"I guess I'm just . . . worried." Her voice broke. "What happens if they find me?"

He felt confused. "You've been here for months. Why is this an issue now?"

"I don't know. I guess I just . . . got thinking . . . about them, and . . ." She became mildly upset.

"Every possible precaution has been taken, Cortney."

"But that doesn't mean they won't find me," she said. "You're FBI. You know more than most what these people are capable of."

"I admit I know that, but I also know that an enormous amount of effort goes into keeping people like you safe. If you do everything they ask you to do, there's no reason you can't expect to be protected."

"Oh, I hope you're right," she said and threw her arms around him, crying against his shoulder. He did his best to offer comfort without returning the embrace. He recognized the symptoms of a victim becoming emotionally attached to their protector, and he knew how to offer assurance and sincere comfort without leading her on or being inappropriate.

What bothered him even more than the awkwardness of the moment was the fact that he'd never seen any hint of behavior leading up to this. He wondered if he'd missed something, but he knew he'd been watching her like a hawk. He felt the same way he had all along, that she wasn't being entirely honest with him, or rather, that she was withholding information from him that was vital.

He stepped back and took her shoulders into his hands, if only to keep her at a distance. He looked at her intensely and said, "Cortney, is there something you're not telling me?"

"Like what?" she asked with a defensiveness that bristled him.

"Anything. Anything at all that you haven't told me or the people who helped you get here."

"No, there's nothing," she said, but she looked down abruptly when she said it. She leaned toward him again as if to initiate another embrace, but he let go of her and stepped back, startled to realize in the same moment that he had the sensation he was being watched. He checked his feelings and told himself that it could just be a neighbor glancing out their window. While he was trying to analyze all the mixed messages his instincts were getting, he realized she had stepped close to him again. She looked up with coy eyes and said, "You've been so kind to me, Jackson. I don't know what I ever would have done, if . . ." Her sentence faded as she let her eyelids fall slowly closed, like a woman who was about to be kissed.

Jackson stepped farther back and hurried to say, "If you're being honest with me, Cortney, you have nothing to worry about. If there's more going on here than you're telling me, you could be in a lot of trouble." *From me,* he added silently and hurried inside. He told himself to separate the issues here and focus on the problem at hand.

Jackson went straight to the kitchen where Chas was cutting a cantaloupe into bite-sized pieces. There were washed strawberries and a watermelon waiting in line for the same process. Charles was sitting in his high chair, the tray covered with toys and Cheerios.

"How are the weeds?" Chas asked while Jackson washed his hands.

"I got interrupted," he said.

"Something wrong?" Chas asked in a tone that indicated she had picked up on his sour mood.

"Cortney came out to talk to me. Apparently she's scared."

"Does she have reason to be?"

"Not if she's being honest with us."

"Do you have reason to think she's not?"

"Maybe," he said, drying his hands.

"Your instincts?"

"Yeah. I think she's holding something back. I know that look in a person's eyes, but I can't force her to talk unless I have her in an interrogation room."

Chas gave him a dubious glare. "And then you could?"

"Most likely." He felt restless, but knew there was more he needed to tell his wife, so he started slicing strawberries and she went back to the cantaloupe. "If I tell you something, will you promise not to be angry with Cortney?"

"*Should* I be angry with her?"

"Depends on what you think her intentions are."

"What do *you* think her intentions are?"

"You don't even know what I'm going to tell you yet."

"Maybe I should know her intentions first."

"I think she's scared and feeling vulnerable and she doesn't know what she's doing."

"You think her withholding information is based in fear, then?"

"I'd like to think so. Truthfully, right now I'm having a hard time not being angry with her myself. But I'm trying to give her the benefit of the doubt. I just wish I knew exactly what she was afraid of."

"Is that what you wanted to tell me?"

"No. She was flirting with me."

Chas set the knife down and turned to lean her hip against the counter, folding her arms over the top of her pregnant belly. "Flirting how?"

"Are you angry?"

"Maybe. Flirting how?"

"We were talking outside about the situation. She started to cry and hugged me. It's far from the first time I've comforted a distressed victim."

"So . . . for you this hug was . . . purely professional?"

"Yes. But then she got a little too coy, and then she got that look in her eyes."

"What look?"

"That 'I wouldn't mind if this got romantic and I wouldn't stop you from kissing me' look." Jackson studied her expression and concluded. "You're angry."

"Yeah, I'm a little ticked off."

Jackson stopped slicing and wiped his hands on the towel before he turned and leaned against the counter to face his wife. "This is something I've dealt with dozens of times, Chas. Agents are trained in this sort of stuff. It's not uncommon for a victim to become emotionally—or romantically—drawn to the protector. I never gave in to that kind of thing when I was single, and I certainly wouldn't give in to it now. Even *if* I felt some attraction to the victim—which I do not—I'm more disciplined and appropriate than that, and I can assure you that I did nothing to encourage her."

"Were you ever attracted to the victim . . . when you were single?"

"Once or twice, mildly, but that's irrelevant."

"What *is* relevant?" she asked. "You're telling me that a young, beautiful woman who is living in my home is attracted to my husband."

"I think Cortney is scared and confused and doesn't know what she's doing. I'm old enough to be her father."

"Still attractive," Chas said, and he shrugged.

"I don't think she would ever consciously do anything to hurt you, or me. And I think if she stopped to think about what she was doing she would feel mortified. I also think that you shouldn't be angry with her. She needs compassion and guidance, not judgment. And since I'm not keeping any secrets from you, we can work this out together. If anything else happens, you'll be the first to hear about it."

Chas breathed in his logic and assurance and blew out the anger she'd been feeling. "Okay," she said. "Thank you . . . for telling me, and for having the right perspective." She pushed her arms around his waist. "You're a good man, you know."

"I try, but . . ." As his sentence faded Chas noticed something uneasy about his manner.

"What else?"

"What do you mean?"

"I get the feeling there's something else on your mind. Did anything else happen with Cortney?"

"No, but. . . ." He sighed, realizing this was hard to admit. "I felt like I was being watched . . . outside, just now. We both know I haven't had any symptoms of PTSD for a long time, but when I did, I promised that I would always tell you if something felt strange or wrong."

"Do you think this has something to do with Cortney?"

"I hope not. And I really hope it was just my imagination."

"I hope so too," she said.

He sighed, and she asked, "What else is wrong?"

"I really feel like Cortney is holding something back. I want to believe that what just happened outside has nothing to do with anything but what it appeared to be, but . . ."

Chas felt terribly uneasy about the whole thing, but she wanted to let it settle in a little before she panicked. He'd just told her that they needed to give Cortney the benefit of the doubt, and Chas agreed.

"I'm sure everything will be fine," she said and kissed him.

"I'm sure it will," he said and kissed her again. Chas was just beginning to really enjoy it when she heard a noise and turned to see Cortney, looking a little astonished. Perhaps she needed clear evidence that Jackson was very much taken.

"Sorry," Cortney said and went upstairs.

The following morning Chas took a reservation from a man asking for their best room, and he wanted to rent it for ten days. He would be arriving with his wife the following week. Later that day Polly told her a man with a thick accent had called and asked about renting a room for two weeks, possibly more, and he would be arriving the following day. Chas mentioned it to Jackson over supper, saying lightly, "Before you came along, I almost never got people who stayed more than a few days; now they're all over the place. It'll be more like a boarding house."

When Jackson's response showed no sign of humor, she asked, "Is something wrong?"

"Don't you think that's a little odd?"

"What?"

"What you just said. Two reservations on the same day for such lengthy stays?"

Chas was assaulted by an involuntary shiver. "You think it's significant?"

"I don't know," Jackson said, not wanting to alarm her by admitting to the high alert of his instincts. "Maybe it's nothing. I guess we'll see what these people are like when they get here, but since we're leaving for Utah in less than a week, they'll mostly be Polly's problem."

"Lucky for Polly," Chas said with light sarcasm, and they went on with their supper.

The next day Chas went to the office to go over some business with Polly, who immediately handed her a large manila envelope, saying, "That just came with the mail. I didn't open it because I don't know what it is."

Chas didn't recognize the return address, which only had an out-of-state location and no name. It was addressed to Mrs. Jackson Leeds, which seemed odd; it was rare these days for a woman to be referred to only by her husband's name. She opened the envelope and slid out the contents, gasping the moment she realized what she was looking at.

"What is it?" Polly asked from the other side of the desk, and Chas was grateful that Polly couldn't see the photographs she was holding.

"It's nothing important," Chas said and hurried to find Jackson, who had just finished changing the baby's diaper.

"What's wrong?" he asked, doing a double take when he saw her expression.

"My vote is that your instincts are as sharp as ever," she said and handed him the envelope.

"What's that supposed to mean?" he said, looking skeptically at what he was holding.

"*You* tell *me* what it means," she said and nodded toward it. He cautiously removed the photographs, making no effort to disguise his astonishment. The instinct that told him something wasn't right roared to life as he viewed the photographs of himself and Cortney outside the inn. They showed detail that was evidence of being taken by a telephoto lens, and the angle of their innocent embrace and the closeness of their faces when they'd been talking screamed of romantic implications. Jackson was more grateful than he could express that he had come directly to his wife with an explanation. If he hadn't, the real issues at hand might have become tangled up in hurt feelings and strained trust.

"What does it mean?" Chas asked again, sounding as afraid as Jackson felt. "Is she in danger? And if that's the case, why didn't they just kill her or kidnap her? Why pictures? And why send them to me and not you? I don't understand, Jackson."

He continued looking at the photographs, asking himself all the same questions and a few more. He said conclusively, "She knew they were being taken."

"What?" Chas practically shrieked.

"She knew. That's why she came to talk to me while I was working outside. That's why she hugged me and behaved the way she did. She knew."

"But why?"

"She's either not who and what she's pretending to be, or she's being threatened. Either way, she's in danger."

Chas felt more horrified than she could even articulate. Her only comfort was knowing that her husband was very good at protecting himself and the people around him—and his instincts were good.

"Tell me what to do," she said, scooping the baby up as if she could personally keep him from being affected by any threat against their home and family.

"Come with me," he said, pushing the photographs back into the envelope as he hurried from the room. Chas followed him into the office where he said to Polly, "Would you please take the baby and tell Cortney to come here. I need to talk to her."

"Sure," Polly said, tossing Chas a skeptical glance as she took Charles and left the room, making it evident she knew something was wrong but didn't want to ask.

"What are you going to do?" Chas asked her husband.

"I'm going to talk to her, and I need you to just observe and stay quiet."

"In other words, you're going to interrogate her, and you want me to be a witness to whatever she says."

"That's right," he said, and she felt so nervous she could hardly breathe. This was all too surreal and frightening for her to handle.

"And then what?" she asked.

"That depends on what she says, and whether or not she's telling me the truth."

"How can you tell?"

"I can tell," he said as they heard footsteps approaching in the hall.

CHAPTER 5

Cortney entered the office, looking alarmed. In fact, she looked so alarmed that Chas felt certain she knew something was wrong. If Jackson was right—that she'd been holding something back from them, and that she'd somehow known she and Jackson were being photographed—she certainly had cause to be nervous. Chas just didn't know if Cortney's concerns should make her own concerns more or less intense.

"Close the door," Jackson said. "And sit down."

Cortney looked at him, then at Chas, as if she wanted to run. She hesitated a long moment then did as Jackson had asked. He immediately tossed the envelope down on the desk in front of her and leaned against the desk, folding his arms over his chest. "You want to explain this to me?" he asked.

She hesitated to pick up the envelope, but Chas saw a lack of confusion in her expression that indicated she had some suspicion of what she might find in the envelope. She opened it and slid out the photographs, looking mildly surprised and undoubtedly upset.

"I don't understand," Cortney said.

"That makes three of us," Jackson countered, "except that I get the feeling you understand a lot more than we do."

She glanced at him to gauge his reaction, then quickly darted her gaze toward the floor. Chas then saw a transformation take place in her husband. The man she had become familiar with instantly became the FBI agent she had only gotten glimpses of previously. His entire demeanor became tough and intimidating as he leaned toward Cortney and spoke in a voice that signaled the difference between conversation and interrogation. "We have opened our home to you and trusted you. I have given you multiple opportunities to come clean with me, but I know you've been lying to me. I cannot and will not protect you another minute unless you tell me everything."

Cortney was breathing so hard that Chas could hear it from across the room, but she wouldn't look at Jackson, and she didn't speak.

"Everything!" Jackson shouted only inches from Cortney's ear, at the same time hitting a fist on the desk. She and Chas both jumped, then Jackson added, "Now!"

Cortney started to cry and shook her head, clearly terrified. But Chas realized what she felt sure Jackson already knew: she was more terrified of someone or something else than she was of Jackson.

Jackson's skill at seeing beneath the surface and getting answers became evident when his voice transformed into perfect compassion and he spoke in little more than a whisper. "Who are you afraid of, Cortney? Who is threatening you?"

Cortney's eyes shot to his so quickly that it was evident he'd hit on the truth and had surprised her. She looked down again and said, "What makes you think someone is threatening me?"

"Are you wearing a wire?" he asked, his voice even lower.

Her surprise over the suggestion was clearly genuine. "No!"

"Have you planted any video or listening devices anywhere in this house?"

"No!" she said more firmly, now keeping eye contact with Jackson.

"Then there is no reason you can't tell me the truth."

Cortney's chin quivered, and she bit her trembling lip. Her hands were shaking as she put the photographs and envelope on the desk, then took hold of the arms of the chair.

Again Jackson spoke in a voice of compassion. "I am capable of protecting you, Cortney, but not if I don't know what I'm dealing with. If you're honest with me, we can work this out without anyone ever knowing that you told me anything."

She searched his eyes as if to measure whether or not she could believe him. He tightened his gaze with a look that Chas knew well. His integrity and trustworthiness were overtly evident in his eyes.

"Tell me, Cortney," he urged.

She glanced at Chas, then back to Jackson. She sobbed through a whisper, "They said they'd hurt . . . someone I love."

Jackson leaned closer to her. "Who? *Who* threatened you? And *who* are you trying to protect?" When she hesitated, he said, "I thought you didn't have any family connections."

"I don't."

"Then who is this someone you love?"

"I can't tell you," she said, looking away. Jackson felt his ire go up, but he remained calm.

"Then tell me who threatened you." He slapped the envelope on the desk. "Who took the pictures? And why?"

"I don't know why," Cortney cried. "And I don't know how they found me. They must have followed me."

"No one followed you," Jackson said, and Chas noted that his compassionate attitude had dissipated with her reluctance to talk to him. Chas felt entirely confused with Cortney's answers and felt sure Jackson did too. A part of her felt sorry for Cortney, but not enough to want to rein Jackson in. She wanted answers as much as he did.

Still Cortney made no effort to comply, and Jackson asked, "Where did you get the cell phone?"

She shot her head up, astonished. "What cell phone?"

Jackson chuckled if only to keep from shouting. He shook his head and glared at her. "You are not nearly as good a liar as you think you are. Or maybe you're better at some lies than others. Let's try that again. Where did you get the cell phone?"

"What makes you think I have a cell phone?"

"I can have Polly go search your room right now while I frisk you right here."

Cortney sighed like a disgusted teenager. "A friend gave it to me just before the trial."

"A friend?" Jackson echoed. "I thought you had no friends, no connections, no one you were having contact with—at all—since you went into protective custody long before the trial."

She looked guilty but snapped. "I didn't."

"But a *friend* gave you a cell phone? You tell me who it was . . . now!"

"It's not that big of a deal," she insisted. "It was . . . the victim's brother."

Chas was startled to see Jackson go a little ashen, and he gripped the desk more tightly. Cortney, however, was oblivious, staring at the floor.

"The victim's brother?" Jackson countered in a voice that didn't betray what Chas had just seen. Her heart quickened while she wondered what it meant. What did Jackson know that she didn't know? "So . . . you're telling me that the person you saw murdered . . . *that* victim . . . his *brother* gave you a cell phone?"

"Yes," she said, apparently baffled over there being any problem. "He came to the trial. He was there every day. We talked at the courthouse a couple of times just for a minute. He was very kind to me. His brother had been killed. Of course it was upsetting for him. He said that his family was grateful for my courage in putting away the killer. They wanted to help me make a fresh start. He gave me some money and a cell phone and wished me well. The agents saw me talking to him, but they didn't know he gave me anything. But . . . what's wrong with that? It's just a cell phone."

Jackson felt a fury that was impossible to contain. "I cannot believe that you would be that *stupid.*"

"Jackson!" Chas said, needing to protest against him resorting to petty insults.

He glared at her, then shifted his gaze to Cortney. "You would think with as much TV as you watch, you would know that a cell phone is as good as a tracking device. It probably has a GPS locator." Cortney gasped, and the color rushed from her face. "Nobody followed you, Cortney; they didn't have to. Not only have you given your position away, you gave it away to one of the biggest crime families on the East Coast."

"What?" Chas exclaimed, feeling her blood pressure rise. Jackson gave her a look of calm reassurance that seemed completely out of place in the conversation, but she was sharp enough to catch his silent message. He knew what he was doing and everything would be okay. She'd never been more grateful to know that her husband was an experienced agent. He'd been one of the best according to his coworkers, and she knew for a fact that his instincts were still sharp.

Cortney whimpered and said, "I . . . had no idea. I'm . . . I'm so sorry. I never meant to bring something like this into your home; I never would have knowingly led them to you."

"That's the first truly honest thing you've said since you sat down," Jackson said. "And that's something, I guess. But I need to know what happened."

Cortney just continued to cry, and Jackson could visibly see her humble apology merge into her desire to cover up her own agenda. Whatever was going on, she had ulterior motives and he knew it. They were probably innocent motives; he couldn't quite imagine her actually having any real involvement with criminal activity. But whatever she thought she was going to gain had gone too far. "Tell me what happened," Jackson insisted, barely holding his anger back. "Take it from the top."

"I don't know what you want from me," she said, crying like Scarlet O'Hara in *Gone With the Wind* when she was trying to manipulate a man into feeling sorry for her.

"I would think it's pretty clear," Jackson said harshly. "Harry Nuccitelli gave you a cell phone and tracked you here."

"How did you know who it was?" she asked, that dumb-founded astonishment on her face again.

"You said it was the victim's brother. He only had one. So, Harry, who is now in line to take over his father's businesses—all of them, the legal ones and the ones that bring illegal drugs and weapons into this country—gives *you* a cell phone and money out of the goodness of his heart."

"I should have known it wasn't as nice as it seemed."

"Yeah, you should have known. You should have kept the rules and given it to the agents assigned to protect you. You should have told them what happened."

"Yes, I should have," Cortney cried, "but I didn't, and now . . ."

"Now, what?" Jackson demanded, but she said nothing. "Let's get one thing straight," he said. "If you do not tell me *everything* right now, I will take you to the airport *now*, and we will sit there until we can get you on a flight straight back to the city you were trying to escape from, and into the hands of the U.S. Marshals so that you can start over with them." She looked terrified even before he added, "Everything! Now!"

"Harry called me a few times. At first he was just being nice; said he hoped I was doing well. He thanked me for putting Reggie behind bars. Reggie Dinubilo; he's the one who shot Harry's brother."

"I know who he is," Jackson said, and Cortney looked surprised. "Keep talking."

"Then Harry told me he needed me to do something for him. I told him it was silly and made no sense. He got mean about it. He said if I didn't do it, he would hurt . . . my friend."

"Have you had contact with this friend since you came here?" Jackson asked.

"No!"

"And the photos? Did Harry give you any explanation as to why he wanted to send my wife something in the mail to upset her?"

"No," she said a little more humbly. "He just told me that he wanted me to . . ." She glanced guiltily toward Chas, ". . . to distract you." She looked back at him and added, "You're not an easy man to distract."

"That's the smartest thing I've ever heard you say," Jackson said snidely. Cortney jerked her head to look away, still retaining the countenance of a spoiled child who'd been caught stealing candy.

Jackson was silent for at least a minute while he stared at Cortney, trying to assess *her* body language, *his* instincts, and all the different pieces of information. He couldn't think of one logical reason to let her stay. He had every reason to think it would be better for everyone involved if he put her back in the hands of the U.S. Marshals—immediately. But the very thought of sending her away made him sick to his stomach. He didn't know why, but he knew beyond any doubt that he needed to keep her here— against his better judgment. He reasoned that he could never know the possible outcome of her staying or going. But God knew, and Jackson had to trust his feelings. He'd rarely felt anything stronger than what he felt in that moment.

Jackson wrestled silently with the decision for a couple of long grueling minutes while the silence was visibly torturous for both Cortney and Chas. He made firm eye contact with his wife, hoping she would perceive that he knew he was doing the right thing. They could talk more about it later. He looked firmly at Cortney and finally said, "You know what? I think you're not being entirely truthful with me." He found it interesting that she didn't protest his statement. "It's tempting to just send you packing. You've got money—and a cell phone. You should be able to find your way in the world. But lucky for you, I actually care about what happens to you, and my wife probably cares even more. She's just that kind of person. I think you've made some stupid mistakes, but that doesn't mean I think you deserve to be thrown to the mob."

"I can stay?" she asked, and Jackson wondered why her being *here* was so important to her.

"For now," he said. "On one condition."

"What?"

"Give me the cell phone." He held out his hand. She hesitated, and he snapped, "Give it to me, or you can leave *now.*"

"Fine," she snarled, reaching up behind her blouse to where it was clipped to the waistband of her jeans. She slapped it into Jackson's hand and left the room in a huff, slamming the door.

Jackson stared at the door a long moment, then turned to Chas, who looked like she'd just experienced an earthquake and was waiting to see if an aftershock would bring the house down.

"I don't think it's as bad as it seems," Jackson said, but Chas couldn't tell if he really meant it or if he was just trying to soothe her fears. "You look like you could use some fresh air."

"Okay," she said, noting a seeming hidden message in his eyes. He stuffed the cell phone in his pocket and took her hand to help her to her feet. They stepped outside while he kept his arm around her, walking casually around the yard as if they were talking about the flowers.

"What are we doing out here?" she asked.

"I don't know if she's telling the truth. I feel more comfortable talking out here."

"You think the house is bugged?" she asked in a whisper as if they might be overheard.

"I don't think it's likely, but since I have no idea what's really going on, I'd rather be safe than sorry." He took her shoulders and turned to face her. "Listen, I know what was said in there sounded dreadful, but—"

"There's no 'but,' Jackson. It was dreadful. We're in danger, aren't we? We actually brought someone into our home who—"

"Listen to me," he said. "If I really believed we were in danger I would remove us all from the premises immediately." He carefully explained what he'd been feeling during his conversation with Cortney, and he knew that she understood. But that didn't erase her concern.

"If Cortney is truly afraid that someone is going to harm her," Jackson went on, "then I'd wager she will be gone in an hour. I don't know what she's thinking or what she's hoping for, but I feel very confident that we are not in any danger."

"How can you know that?" she demanded.

"Because I've studied these families and they— "

"*These* families?"

Jackson took a deep breath and tried to become as calm as he wanted Chas to believe he was. "The murder that Cortney witnessed was a member of one crime family being killed by a member of another crime family. I was familiar with the activities of these families when I was with the agency, even though I was never actually on any case that dealt with them directly. But this is not like some . . . gangster movie, Chas. They don't just go around shooting people and blowing up things. There *is* criminal activity in the families and they *are* dangerous people, but they are also relatively reasonable—if that makes any sense. They still have their own code of ethics, even if that sounds like an oxymoron. They have no grudge against me or any member of my family. This is not about *me.*"

"Are you sure?"

"Absolutely!" he said and meant it. "My only connection to this is that my colleague sent Cortney to my home."

"Do you think he knew she was going to be so stupid?"

"If he did I'd like to give him a bloody nose, but I don't think so; not *this* stupid, anyway. The thing is, whatever these people are after, they're going to do it as quietly as possible, and they're not out to create collateral damage." Of course, he knew that collateral damage could happen anyway, and it often did. But he kept that to himself.

"Do you think Cortney is in danger?"

"I don't know; maybe. But if she won't be honest with me, there's not much I can do to protect her. Now, listen to me. I'm going to deal with this. I know what I'm doing. If I know beyond any doubt that keeping her here is the right thing—and I do—then we just have to deal with it the best way that we can. I want you to concentrate on getting ready to go to Utah, and let *me* worry about Cortney. The Lord will keep us safe, Chas. I really believe that one or both of us will be prompted if there is some kind of action we need to take. I don't think Cortney will stay much longer. Just . . . let me handle it."

"What are you going to do?"

"I think it's better if I don't tell you."

"It's dangerous?" she shrieked in a whisper.

"No, it's not dangerous. It's just . . . better that I keep it to myself. But don't worry . . . I won't be taking care of it *myself*. That's all I'm going to say. Now, let's go back in the house and go about our day."

Chas took a long moment to absorb what he'd said and give him her trust in the matter. Everything he'd said made perfect sense. And even if something could be done, she certainly wasn't the one to do it. These were things far out of her realm of understanding or control. She took a deep, sustaining breath and nodded. "Okay," she said. "I'm going to trust you on this."

"Okay," he said, "thank you." He put his arms around her. "It's going to be okay."

They returned to the inn, and Chas went to find Polly and take over with Charles.

"Is everything okay?" Polly asked.

"I think so," Chas said. "I hope so." Thinking of the possibility of her home being bugged, she avoided shuddering visibly and added, "Nothing that concerns us. Jackson will take care of it."

"Okay," Polly said skeptically and went back to the office where Jackson was putting photos through the paper shredder, but he kept the envelope and put it in a safe place. He left Polly to her work and went out to the garage.

* * * * *

Jackson came in from the garage more than an hour later, and the impression to call Veese was so strong that he couldn't think of anything but walking to the office and picking up the phone. He was glad that Polly had gone out on some work-related errands. While he was dialing, he considered what to say and how to say it. Agency training and protocol came to mind, and he wondered if it was really necessary. He tried the office number first and was connected to Special Agent Veese at his desk.

"Hey, buddy," Veese said. "What's up?"

"Oh, not much," Jackson said. "How about you?"

"Same old same old. Did you just call to shoot the breeze?"

"I called to see if you've finally come to your senses about getting that long overdue vacation. There's plenty of sunshine here, and you should get in on it."

Jackson heard the momentary silence on the other end and read volumes of Veese's thoughts into it. Veese knew that the word "sunshine" introduced into the conversation was an indicator that something was wrong. Even if Jackson had said, *There's no sunshine here,* Veese would have known there was a problem.

"So, it's not raining there, huh?" Veese asked, sounding completely natural. The reference to rain was as good as saying, *Can you talk without compromising your safety?*

"Not at the moment, but you know how the weather can change. You can't get too comfortable. Oh, before I forget, tell Myers hello for me. I heard he's been sick." Jackson *hadn't* heard that Myers was sick, but Myers was the one who could tell Veese the information he needed to know.

"Well, maybe it *is* time I took that vacation," Veese said. "Things are pretty slow here, so the timing could be good."

"Lucky for me," Jackson said. "You tell me when you're coming, and I'll have a really great room ready for you."

"I'll check my schedule and call you back," Veese said. "So, how's the family?"

"Good. We're all good. How's everybody there?"

They went on with friendly chitchat for several minutes, the kind of conversation that would completely avert any suspicion if it was overheard. Jackson told himself he was probably just being paranoid. He had no reason to *really* think that the inn or the phone was being bugged, but he didn't trust Cortney, and something just didn't feel right. His years of experience had taught him over and over that it was far better to err on the side of too much caution than to inadvertently let something slip.

Near the end of the conversation, Jackson said, "Oh, remember that stupid shirt you sent me?"

"Oh, I remember."

"Well, I think I'm finally going to break down and wear it. So, you tell the guys to imagine me wearing it, and we'll all be on the same team, even if I'm here and everybody else is there."

"I'll spread the word," Veese said. "You can count on it."

Jackson was glad to hear by his tone of voice that Veese knew *exactly* what Jackson meant. He needed help from the other end, as well as having Veese come to Montana.

Following a little more light conversation, Veese said, "You know, I'm looking at my calendar here and . . . it's just blank." Jackson could imagine that he wasn't just looking at his calendar. He was probably making hand signals to other people in the office, or writing notes to them. "I think it's time I stopped procrastinating and finally come to see this great inn you're always bragging about. I'll call you when I've got a flight."

"You want me to pick you up at the airport?"

"Nah, I'll just rent a car, then I can get around."

"Sounds great," Jackson said, already feeling better.

* * * * *

Chas was chopping vegetables for a salad when she had a sudden urge to speak to Jackson about their plans regarding their tempo-

rary move to Salt Lake City. She was surprised to come into the hall and see Cortney just outside the office door, leaning against the wall as if she was listening.

"What are you doing?" Chas asked, and Cortney jumped, looking guilty.

"Just hanging out," she said and hurried away.

Chas entered the office to find Jackson sitting behind the desk, talking on the phone. He smiled to acknowledge her and she sat down. It quickly became evident he was talking to Veese and that he was wrapping up their conversation, so she waited.

When he hung up the phone, she asked, "How is Elliott?"

"He's fine. I finally talked him into coming for a visit."

"That's wonderful!" she said, catching something discreet in his expression that let her know this was not a coincidence in regard to other happenings. "But we're leaving."

Jackson still felt hesitant to speak openly without knowing for certain why. He kept up his nonchalant attitude as he said, "That's okay. He can get lots of rest and relaxation whether we're around or not."

Chas felt the need to say, "Um . . . Cortney was just—"

"Baby still asleep?" Jackson asked and stood.

"Yes," she said, motioning toward the baby monitor in her apron pocket.

"Good," he said. "I could use some fresh air. Let's go for a little walk."

Once outside and several paces away from the inn, Jackson said, "Cortney was just what?"

"I was coming to talk to you about something, and . . . she was outside the office, like she was eavesdropping."

"Unbelievable," Jackson said.

"I asked her what she was doing. She said 'just hanging out' and ran off. But she looked guilty. What do you think she was hoping to hear? You arranging to get the carpets cleaned, or something?"

"I think she wanted to know who I might call after I figured out that she's been lying to me. Maybe she thought I was going to call headquarters and have her carted off."

"But you didn't. You were talking to Veese."

"Yeah, I called him because I want him to come here. I know I was prompted, Chas. Whatever is going on, I absolutely know that God wanted me to call Veese and tell him that he finally needed that vacation." He explained how the conversation had taken place with prearranged innuendos, and that Cortney couldn't have overheard anything suspicious. He was glad now for following his instincts on that count. He didn't know what Cortney did or didn't know, or what exactly she was hoping to accomplish. But he didn't trust her. Again he cautioned Chas to behave normally and just get through the next few days until they left for Utah.

"What were you coming to talk to me about?" he asked when he had nothing more to say.

"I don't even remember. Maybe it was nothing. Maybe I just needed to catch Cortney in the act."

"Maybe," Jackson said, wishing he knew a lot more than he knew. But he had a level of calm he wasn't accustomed to, and he was very grateful for that. The guidance of the Holy Ghost was something he sure could have used during his years working as an agent. But as Chas had once pointed out to him, it had probably been guiding him to some degree and he simply hadn't recognized it for what it was. In truth, what he'd always referred to as his gut instincts probably had a lot more to do with divine intervention than anything. Chas had told him that in his efforts to protect innocent people, God would have surely been there to assist him. Jackson felt confident that God was with him now, and that it was important to keep Cortney here for the time being, and that it was right to have Veese come. Beyond that, he could only keep praying that nothing happened to bring any harm to anyone.

"Oh, I remember," Chas said before they got to the door. "I was thinking that under the circumstances, I don't know if I'm comfortable leaving Melinda and Charles here while we're gone. What would you think about having them come with us? The apartment is apparently spacious and comfortable."

"I think that's very wise," he said. "I'm sure you're right. I hadn't thought about it, but I'm not comfortable with that, either."

"What about Polly?"

"Polly will be fine," he said. "We'll tell her what she needs to know, and Veese will watch out for her."

"Do you think he'll stay long enough to . . ."

"He'll stay as long as he's needed, which is something we will talk about another time. I think we're spending too much time outside."

Back in the office, Jackson called his sister and told her they had decided they would just miss the baby too much and asked how she would feel about coming to Utah with them. She was eager to do whatever they wanted, and she admitted to being pleased with the prospect of being close by for the big event. They both agreed that it might be good for Chas to have Charles around, and Melinda would also be able to offer some feminine support. The plan had been for Melinda to fly into Butte the day before they were leaving, but Jackson felt good about planning to leave for Utah a day early and just pick Melinda up in Butte on their way. That put them down to four days until departure. His deepest hope was that by the time they got back from Utah, the drama would be over and Cortney would have moved on. He prayed for that and then set out to get some *real* work done so that they could leave the state for an undetermined length of time.

* * * * *

Early that evening the foreign gentleman that Polly had spoken to checked in. Jackson and Chas were both in the office when he came in, carrying two small old-fashioned suitcases—the kind with no wheels. He set them down and took off his old-fashioned hat.

"Good evening," the man said with a thick accent. "I have reservation. My name is Artem Tarasov. I spoke with young lady before on phone."

"Of course," Chas said. "Your room is ready. We'll just need you to sign here." She set a paper on the desk. "And I'll need your credit card."

"Oh, yes, yes," he said and signed his name before he dug out his wallet. "This lovely place," he added while Chas was taking care of the transaction, "is . . . uh . . ." He struggled to find words in his broken English, then seemed to give up on the thought.

"Where are you from?" Chas asked.

"Russia," he said proudly. "From west."

"And what brings you to Montana, Mr. Tarasov?" Chas asked.

"Oh." He smiled as if he felt pleased to be asked. "I travel to . . . not . . ." He said a few words in Russian and seemed frustrated at wanting to express himself.

While Chas was watching him closely, waiting with patience for him to articulate his thoughts, Jackson spoke from where he was sitting nearby—in Russian. Mr. Tarasov's eyes lit up with delight, and he spoke back to Jackson with eager fluency.

At a break in the conversation, Chas said to her husband, "You speak Russian?"

Mr. Tarasov looked on, amused.

"I do," Jackson said.

"I didn't know," Chas said, not wanting to make an issue out of it in front of someone else.

"Now you do," he said as if it were nothing.

Mr. Tarasov smiled at Chas and said in his broken English, "Could be many things woman not know of husband."

"Indeed," Chas said, not wanting to admit how annoyed she felt, but she couldn't decide whether it was toward Jackson or Mr. Tarasov.

While the two men continued their conversation in Russian, Chas couldn't help thinking of the events going on in their home in light of the timing of this man's visit. She had to wonder if there was a connection.

Jackson seemed to remember that she was there and being left out of the conversation. He turned to her and said, "Mr. Tarasov retired a couple of years ago. He and his wife . . ."

"Alina," the older man provided.

"Alina," Jackson repeated, "always dreamed of coming to America together, then she got cancer and died."

"Oh, I'm so sorry," Chas said to Mr. Tarasov, her compassion distracting her from her irritation.

"He tells me," Jackson went on, "that she made him promise that he would still come to America, just the way they'd dreamed. She had wanted to visit out-of-the-way places and stay long enough to get to know the people, rather than just making brief stops and seeing tourist attractions. He found our inn on the Internet and knew it was perfect. He's very glad to be here and hopes that he won't be any trouble."

"Of course you won't be any trouble," Chas said. "But then . . . we'll be leaving in a few days, and . . ." She stopped when Mr. Tarasov seemed confused and looked at Jackson.

After he spoke in Russian for a couple of minutes and Mr. Tarasov responded, Jackson turned to Chas and said, "I explained the purpose of our leaving and that he would be in very good hands. He told me to wish you all the best, and his hope that the baby will be well."

He smiled and nodded, and Chas said, "Thank you, Mr. Tarasov. You're very kind."

"Call me Artem," he said and held out his hand. Chas extended hers, and he took it into both of his and squeezed, rather than shaking it.

"Very well . . . Artem," she said. "I hope you enjoy your stay. You can . . ." She wanted to give him the usual instructions but felt it would be more effective coming from Jackson. She turned to her husband and said, "You tell him where to find the food and how to call if he needs anything."

"I'll do that," Jackson said and picked up Artem's room key off the desk. He also picked up one of the suitcases and spoke in Russian as Artem picked up the other and they both left the office.

Later that night, Chas was sitting in bed reading when Jackson came out of the bathroom and joined her. When he noticed that she wasn't actually reading, he asked, "What's wrong?"

"I'm just wondering why I feel so uncomfortable around Mr. Tarasov."

"Suspicious, you mean?"

"Maybe," she admitted.

"Could it be because he pointed out that there are still things about me that you don't know? Maybe it's *that* more than it's *him.*"

"I have to admit it's disconcerting to learn such things about you. I mean . . . Russian? You speak Russian?"

"I worked in Russia for more than a year," he said as if it were nothing.

"So, what else don't I know about you?"

"I don't know," he said. "Nothing that matters." She didn't look convinced, and he took her hand. "Listen to me. It was a job. But it required some strange stuff. If we had been married at the time, there still would have been a *lot* that I couldn't tell you. I'm just glad that it's in the past. You know everything about me that has happened from the minute I met you. *Everything!* And that's all that matters."

"Okay," she said and pondered that a minute before her mind went back to the beginning of the conversation. Jackson shifted and put his head in her lap. "So, what do *you* think of Mr. Tarasov? You and your great instincts."

"I think he's exactly what he says he is."

"And it's just coincidence that he shows up here for such a lengthy stay when so many weird things are going on?"

"Yes, Chas. The problem with Cortney has to do with American organized crime, not international spy rings. I don't think the

Nuccitelli family *or* the Dinubilo family would send a Russian operative. And if they *did,* he would be a lot younger. He's just a nice old man, Chas. You've seen too many James Bond movies."

"I've seen very few James Bond movies."

"One too many, apparently."

CHAPTER 6

The following day Mr. Tarasov left the inn after breakfast, declaring that he wanted to drive around the area and get a good look at it. Chas took Polly out to lunch, which was something they did on occasion to spend time together just as friends. And since Chas would be gone and she was relying heavily on Polly to cover for them, she thought it would be a good idea. Jackson fed the baby his lunch and put him down for his nap, then he went to the office and found Cortney frantically searching through the drawers in the desk.

"Looking for something?" he asked and startled her. If she'd been more sneaky and quiet she might have heard him come in.

"I need that cell phone," she said like an addict asking for cocaine.

"Why?" he asked. "If you need to make a call . . ." he motioned to the phone on the desk, "go for it."

"I need the cell phone," she repeated. He'd predicted this, and he actually *wanted* her to take it back now that he'd had some time with it. But he *hadn't* predicted the way she reached up behind her blouse and pulled out a small pistol.

"Are you kidding me?" he asked, not ruffled in the slightest. He'd had so many guns pointed at him in his life that it didn't faze him much unless he believed the person holding it would actually pull the trigger. And he knew Cortney wouldn't. "Where on earth did you get that?" he asked. "I know you didn't bring it with you, because you only had a carry-on bag when you came."

"I bought it," she said. "Now, put your hands up and give me the cell phone."

"I can't put my hands up *and* give you the cell phone, Cortney. Which is it going to be?"

"Just . . . give me the cell phone." She sounded flustered and nervous.

"Why do you need it badly enough that you think you need to pull a gun on me?"

"I don't have to tell you anything," she insisted and corrected her aim. He was grateful for the undeniable verity of knowing that he needed to allow her to stay here; otherwise he'd be dragging her to the airport in the next ten minutes.

Jackson kicked the chair beside him which made just enough noise to distract Cortney. He lunged and grabbed her wrist. The gun fell into his other hand. He twisted her arm up behind her back, just far enough to make her unable to move but not enough to hurt her.

"You *do* have to tell me *everything,*" he said behind her ear, "because if anyone in this house gets hurt because of what you think you're going to accomplish here, I will make you *wish* the Nuccitelli family had found you first. Or maybe they already have. Apparently they know *exactly* where to find you, and I wonder what you'll do if I have *no* incentive to protect you." She whimpered and tried to squirm out of his grasp, but he didn't let go. "So I'll make you a deal. I'll trade you the cell phone for the gun. You go ahead and call whoever you think you need to call and compromise your safety a little more, but if you had any brains at all you would tell me *who* you're calling and *why,* and you would tell me the truth. Although, I bet I could *guess* who you're going to call and why."

He kept hold of her wrist so she couldn't leave, and he turned her to face him. "I'd bet your friend isn't a friend at all. I bet it's actually some love interest you've been stringing along, and you're thinking your boyfriend is going to find you here and rescue you.

So call him. Tell him to come and get you. The sooner the better. And if you both actually stay alive once you leave here, it will be a miracle."

"You think you have all the answers," she snapped. "Believe it or not, I know what I'm doing. I'm not stupid."

"You were stupid enough to go into witness protection carrying a GPS locator given to you by a criminal. What more do I need to know?"

She gave him a disgusted glare. "Can I have the cell phone?"

"Tell me who you're calling."

"I *am* calling my boyfriend, if you must know. But don't worry. I'll be out of your hair before you know it."

"I'll be counting the days," Jackson said and let go of her. He took keys out of his pocket and unlocked a cupboard behind the desk. He took out the phone and handed it to her. "Have a good chat," he said and watched her leave the room, hoping that he wasn't being a fool to let her stay here even another minute. But something in his gut told him that she needed to be *here,* now more than ever. He didn't understand why; he only knew it scared him—in spite of all his precautions. But he wasn't going to tell Chas that. He prayed for the millionth time since Cortney had come here that his home and family would remain safe. He looked more closely at the gun in his hand and wasn't surprised to discover that it wasn't loaded. He put it in the safe and went back to work, certain that Chas didn't need to know about this latest bit of drama.

* * * * *

After sharing a nice lunch with Polly, Chas initiated a little stroll through the park. When they were well away from anyone's earshot, Chas said, "There's something I need to talk to you about before we leave. I'm really not *supposed* to talk about it, but Jackson and I agreed that you need to know, and we both trust you completely, so I know you won't repeat any of this to anyone."

"You know I can keep a secret," Polly said, sounding concerned.

"Of course."

"Is this about the baby?"

"No, no, no. I've told you everything we know about the baby, and what our plans are. But the situation at the inn probably won't be completely normal while we're gone. First of all, we've made the decision to have Melinda come with us and bring Charles, as opposed to her staying here with him."

"Oh, that'll be better for you," Polly said.

"Melinda was going to help you some around the inn, but you know you can call on Jodi if you need to, and Michelle told me she'll take all the hours you can give her. Stacy too," she said, referring to the other girl who came in to clean rooms on a regular basis.

"And Cortney," Polly said.

"I don't know if you can count on Cortney. Actually, this has to do with her."

"It's no secret that something weird has been going on," Polly said. "I've tried to mind my own business, and I can't for the life of me figure her out, but I know there's something weird."

"Yeah, there sure is." They sat together on a park bench, and Chas just said it. "She's not really the friend of a friend. She's in the witness protection program. She came here to help give her a jump start into a new life since she was given a new identity."

"Good grief!" Polly said. "Is that like . . . I mean . . . did she . . . that means she saw somebody do something really bad? And she put them away?"

"That's right. It was a murder, and it involved two large crime families."

"Good grief!" Polly said more loudly. "Are we in danger having her there?"

"Jackson says we're *not,* but Cortney has done some stupid things. When people in this program follow the rules, they *do* remain protected. But Cortney broke the rules. I think she's a very confused and not terribly bright young woman. I can't tell you details, but you need to know that *someone* involved in this crime knows where she is." Polly gasped, and Chas went on. "However, Cortney's attitude is contradictory. You would think she'd be so afraid of being found that she'd be eager to move on. But it seems she's more concerned about something else. We think she's hoping to meet up with someone. I don't know. It's all way too confusing to me. I don't know what she's doing, but Jackson feels it's better to just bide our time and she'll soon be on her way. He tells me that he knows the way these families work, and they're not going to randomly hurt anyone just for the sake of it. As an added precaution, one of his friends from the agency is coming to stay at the inn for as long as he's needed. Jackson didn't come out and say it, but I believe the agency is working with them on this. So, the good news is, you'll have your very own FBI agent on the premises while we're gone."

"Is it Veese?" she asked, having heard Jackson talking to and about him quite a bit.

"Yes, it is."

"So, I finally get to meet him."

"Yes, but I'm not sure he'll want to be known as an FBI agent while he's here, so we should be careful about that, I guess. Jackson told me to tell you that you shouldn't be afraid, you should tell Elliott—that's Agent Veese—if you need anything or observe something suspicious or out of the ordinary, and that everything will be fine."

"And you believe that?" Polly asked, mildly concerned.

Chas took a deep breath. "I want to believe that. I think Jackson is giving me the optimistic version. I think there could be danger, and I believe he thinks so too, but he doesn't want to alarm anyone. I have to trust him on this. I believe he knows what he's doing. And, well . . . whether it's something you understand or not, we're praying very hard that everyone will remain safe. We have to trust in God."

"Oh, I get that," she said. "I may not go to church, but I've seen too much amazing stuff in your life to doubt that He's up there. You just keep praying, and I'm sure we'll manage. I'm glad you're going to be out of the picture for a while. That's got to be so stressful."

"It has been, yes. I'm just worried about you. I don't want to leave you in a difficult situation. I don't want you to be scared, or anything."

"Oh, don't worry about me," Polly said. "If Jackson thinks I can handle it, I believe him. And maybe we need something like organized criminals in town to spice things up around here. I'm sure we'll manage. If you were leaving me alone to deal with it, I might have a problem. But if you're leaving me an agent . . ." She laughed softly and they stood up and walked on, talking again about speculations over the outcome of having this baby.

When they were back at the car, Chas told Polly how much she appreciated her friendship, and Polly said the feeling was mutual.

"And you look really pretty today," Chas said, noting how her red, curly hair had grown out to where it hung around her shoulders, and that the dark green shirt she was wearing looked great on her.

"Thank you!" Polly said with enthusiasm. "I've lost fifty-eight pounds, you know."

"Really? I hadn't heard the update for a while. That is amazing! You've worked hard, and I'm proud of you. It's taken a lot of discipline; I don't know if I could do it if that were an issue for me."

"Well, when I realized that my health was at risk, I knew I couldn't put it off any longer. My goal was to lose sixty pounds, so I'm almost there. Now, I just have to keep doing what I've learned and stay healthy."

"Amen. And it's a good thing you're brimming with energy," Chas said, "because it looks like you're going to need it."

"Ah," she pushed her hand through the air, "it'll be an adventure." A minute later she asked, "Do you think Mr. Tarasov has anything to do with this?"

"Jackson says absolutely not. He believes this man is exactly what he seems to be, and he has some good logic to back it up. I trust his instincts—and his logic."

"Well, I'm glad. He seems like a very nice man. I'm glad he's staying for a while. I'd like to get to know him better."

"I'm sure the two of you will get along marvelously while I'm gone."

"He *is* a widower," Polly said lightly.

"And old enough to be your grandfather." Chas laughed. "I think you need to get out more."

"Yeah," Polly said, "I probably do. But I like my life, so we're good."

* * * * *

Jackson felt some relief when Cortney left the house, but since she wasn't carrying a suitcase, he assumed she was coming back. He peeked out the window to see her walking down the street, and he realized he was actually alone in the inn except for the baby, who was sleeping. It was a rare occurrence and somewhat strange. He'd spent most of his life living alone, but now that he'd become accustomed to living with a family and working in an inn, he far preferred *not* being alone.

The thought barely materialized in his brain when he heard the back door open and close. He looked up from the desk to see who would come through the doorway.

Since the inn was technically open in the afternoons for the public to come and look through it, he figured that was a likely possibility—even though it didn't happen very often. Or it could be a potential customer.

Despite the fact that he'd called Veese and asked him to come, he still felt surprised to see him standing there. He honestly hadn't expected him to arrive so quickly.

Jackson laughed to see him lean casually in the door frame without saying a word. He just smiled. "So, here you are . . . finally," Jackson said.

"Finally?" Veese chuckled. "You just called me yesterday."

"I've been trying to get you to come here for years."

"Yeah, but you know how guys like us are about taking vacations."

"Yeah, I know," Jackson said, knowing that if a need for his agent skills hadn't brought him here, he might have never come. Jackson walked around the desk and shook his friend's hand, then they shared a guy hug.

Veese glanced into the hallway and asked quietly, "Is she . . ."

"Out, at the moment. It's just me, except for the baby sleeping."

"You have an open house, I hear. So, I can look around?"

"Make yourself at home," Jackson said. "The only room that's locked . . ." He didn't finish the sentence; he just handed Veese a master key.

Jackson continued with his work and Veese came back a while later, declaring firmly, "No bugs. No phone taps. The place is clean." He gave the key back to Jackson.

"Good," Jackson said. "I wasn't too worried, but . . . it's nice to know."

"It's a very *nice* place," Veese said. "Which room do I get?"

"The Dombey," he said. "It has the best view of the parking lot so you can see people coming and going. Here's your key." He handed it to him, then helped Veese carry his bags up the stairs. He knew that Veese had brought a computer and a few other needed items along with the usual things a man would travel with. "I'd prefer that no one know you're with the agency. Consider yourself undercover."

"So why am I here?"

"You'll come up with something."

Jackson got Veese settled into his room, and they discussed the situation a little more before noises on the monitor he had hooked to his belt told him the baby was stirring. He left Veese to freshen up and went downstairs, passing Mr. Tarasov on the stairs. He barely had the baby's diaper changed when Chas and Polly came in. He found them in the office and told them that Veese had arrived, and they needed to be discreet about his purpose for being there. He was glad to know that Polly had been informed of the situation, and assured them both that everything was under control.

"Is it okay for us to be talking like this?" Chas asked him, since their last few serious conversations on the topic had taken place outside.

"It's fine," Jackson said. "Veese has checked it out. There are no unwanted electronic devices in the house. Well, maybe that old toaster . . ."

"I'll see what I can do," Chas said with mock disgust.

"Cortney's gone out, so for the moment we're . . ."

"Hello," Veese said from the doorway of the office.

Chas laughed and gave him a big hug. "So, we need a crisis to get you to come and see us?"

"Apparently," he said with a chuckle. He glanced around. "I really should have come sooner. It's a beautiful inn, and a nice town from what little I've seen." He smirked at Jackson. "I can see why this old boy didn't want to leave here."

"Does this mean you're staying?" Jackson asked. "You know you hate your job."

"And it's dangerous," Chas added.

"Yeah, well . . . don't get too hasty," Elliott said. "There are things about my job I hate, but it's a good job. I think I'll be keeping it for a while yet."

"He is very good at what he does," Jackson said.

"You never told me that before," Elliott said with exaggerated surprise.

"When you were actually working for me, I didn't want you to get a big head."

"Oh, thank you very much," Elliott said with light sarcasm, then he realized there was someone else in the room. "And who is this?" he asked.

"Oh, sorry," Chas said. "This is Polly. We've been friends forever, and she's our right hand around here."

"And our left sometimes," Jackson added.

"Hello," Elliott said, holding out his hand.

"Hi," Polly said, shaking Elliott's hand. "I've sure heard a lot about you. And I've answered the phone a few times when you've called."

"Of course," Elliott said. "It's nice to put a face with the voice."

"Excuse interrupt," Artem said, and they all turned to see the Russian gentleman standing in the doorway.

"What can we do for you?" Jackson asked kindly.

"I wonder if . . . recommend . . . good place . . . supper."

"We can recommend a number of good places," Jackson said. "In fact, there is a list of local restaurants in a drawer in your room."

"Oh, good. Very good," Artem said. "Thank you. I go look."

"However," Jackson said, "I think that *tonight* you should have supper with us."

Chas felt surprised but knew Jackson wouldn't be offering if he wasn't willing to help in the kitchen. For the sake of being gracious, she added, "Of course. You should." Thinking that it might be good for Polly and Elliott to get to know each other a little better if they were going to be helping each other out, she also said, "Polly's staying for supper too."

"I am?" Polly said, then quickly added. "I am."

"And, of course, Elliott will be eating with us," Chas said. "One more is no trouble."

"Thank you . . . very much," Artem said. "Such honor . . . eat with fine family."

"We'll be eating about six o'clock," Jackson said, and Artem glanced at his watch and nodded.

Elliott became distracted by little Charles and wanted to hold him. He'd not seen him since months earlier when Jackson and Chas had a made a visit to Virginia. Elliott admitted that he'd never been around babies much, but he sure liked this one.

"It's amazing how much he looks like you," Elliott said to Jackson. Artem looked on with a gleeful sparkle in his eye, as if a baby of any size was a great fascination.

They heard the back door, and Cortney rushed past the office and up the stairs, apparently oblivious to anything going on. Jackson gave Veese a subtle nod, and they all turned their attention to the baby's antics, as if nothing in the world was wrong.

* * * * *

Elliott hung out in his room, either resting or taking care of business, and Jackson insisted on doing most of the preparations for dinner while Charles played on the kitchen floor. Chas helped a little in the kitchen and then sat with her feet up, delightedly enjoying her husband's efforts to take very good care of her.

"I bet you didn't imagine a day like this when you were a bachelor FBI agent on stakeout."

"No," he chuckled, "I certainly didn't. But I should have. It would have made it easier to get through if I'd known *this* was waiting for me." He paused to kiss her, and Charles let a out a string of comical jabbering that they couldn't understand, but it made them laugh.

When six o'clock came, Polly entertained Elliott and Artem in the dining room while Chas and Jackson finished putting the meal on the table. They were barely seated when Cortney entered the room and hesitated.

"I didn't know it was going to be a party," she said. "Maybe I'll just . . . take my food to my room and—"

"No, no, no," Artem said and stood abruptly, taking hold of Cortney's arm.

"We need pretty girl. Other men have pretty girl. You sit by me."

Cortney offered him an awkward smile but sat down as Artem helped her with her chair.

Following the standard blessing on the food, Cortney said, "What's the occasion?"

"Mr. Tarasov is a guest," Chas said and briefly explained the situation while Artem smiled and nodded.

When her explanation was done, Cortney turned to look at Elliott. "Who are you?" she asked with suspicion, but Chas couldn't really blame her for that—even if she'd brought it on herself to some degree. But she felt a moment of panic, realizing they should have come up with an established explanation for Elliott's presence. She hoped that he or Jackson had something to say.

Without missing a beat, Polly said, "We're dating." Chas wished she could have covered her surprise as smoothly as Jackson and Elliott. Fortunately, neither Cortney nor Mr. Tarasov were looking at *her*. "You see," Polly went on with perfect ease, "we've been doing the online thing for a long time now." She looked at Elliott. "How long has it been, honey?"

"Oh, months," he said and reached for her hand on the table, giving it a loving squeeze.

"Yeah." Polly laughed softly. "I've lost track. Anyway, he was finally able to get the time to come and stay so we could get to know each other face-to-face."

"How quaint," Cortney said, bored and entirely *un*suspicious.

"It's too bad we're leaving town soon," Chas said to Elliott. "We'd love to get to know you better, as well."

"Yes, we surely would," Jackson said with sarcasm that was too subtle for those who didn't know him to pick up on. "I'm not entirely sure that you're good enough for Polly." He said the last with a smile and a wink at Polly, who smiled back. "And I'm absolutely sure I'm not entirely comfortable leaving the two of you here at the inn without supervision."

This made Polly blush slightly. Given the fact that their relationship was a pretense, her response added validity to those observing.

"I be here," Artem said with a jovial grin. "I keep watch young people. I be good . . . what you say? Cha . . ." He snapped his fingers trying to think of the word.

"Chaperone," Jackson provided.

"Yes!" Artem said with enthusiasm, pointing at Jackson. "I be good chaperone. Not too much . . . what you say? Smooching?" They all laughed, and Artem laughed with them. "Smooching not right word?"

"It's the right word," Jackson said.

"Ah," Artem said, "not too much smooching with young people. I keep them company."

"How delightful," Polly said with a genuine smile toward the old man.

* * * * *

Later that evening, while Cortney was out, Jackson went to Veese's room and made himself comfortable, recalling the weeks he'd stayed in this same room when he'd first come to the inn.

"So," Veese said, sitting in the other chair and stretching out his long legs, "you really think Nuccitelli is going to show up here?"

"Yes. I don't know *why;* I just think he will. He gave her the cell phone so he could track her, then he got her to distract me with that stupid picture-taking episode."

"You think that was simply a distraction tactic?"

"Yes. I think he wanted Cortney to cause an upset; maybe he was even hoping we'd kick her out."

"But who was taking the pictures?"

"Who knows? He could have hired someone local just to do that, or he might have someone hanging around the area. One thing I don't understand is why they've waited so long. Why all this time passing? If Nuccitelli has known all along where she is, what's he waiting for?"

"I can answer that question," Veese said. "We tracked that number . . . the one that called the cell phone that wasn't Nuccitelli. It's a correctional facility. And guess who's there? Bobby Dinubilo. And guess who Cortney was dating when the murder went down?"

Jackson took it in and shook his head in amazement. "Well, that all makes perfect sense, doesn't it."

"Yep, it sure does," Veese said eagerly. "I'd wager that Harry Nuccitelli wants Bobby Dinubilo, and he's using Cortney for bait. All the waiting is because—"

"Bobby's been in jail."

"Yep. And he's getting released next week. Who knows how long it will take him to get here, or how he'll travel? And we don't know if Cortney is actually going to wait here for him, or if they're going to meet somewhere else."

"I'm hoping for the latter. I hope she'll just leave."

"I can't protect her if she leaves," Veese said.

"I don't think you can protect her here," Jackson said. "She's holding back on telling me the truth, and she's convinced that she knows what she's doing. Her involvement with someone like Bobby Dinubilo makes me question her ability to reason."

"As if accepting a cell phone from the Nuccitelli family *wouldn't* make you question it."

"Yeah," Jackson said with chagrin. "I'm sure glad you're here. If something's going to go down here, I want it to go down when my family isn't here. But I need you to take good care of my home, and especially take good care of Polly."

"I'm your man, boss," Veese said with a grin.

The next morning when Veese arrived at the dining room for breakfast, Jackson was the one to serve it to him.

"*What* are you doing?" Veese asked when Jackson put a plate in front of him, complete with daintily arranged fruit and a mint leaf for garnish.

"It's Michelle's day off and Chas is tired, so I fixed breakfast," Jackson said with a mild scowl.

"Okay," Veese chuckled. "It's just that . . . when we were working together . . . I never would have imagined you serving me breakfast."

"And I never would have," Jackson said, giving Veese a cup of coffee. "What exactly did you think I was doing when I took up life as an innkeeper?"

"I don't know . . . but . . ."

Jackson's scowl deepened. "This place *is* called a bed-and-breakfast, you know. I'd suggest you eat your breakfast before I give you a fat lip."

"I'm eating," Veese said, then added with his mouth full, "This is good. Did you make it?"

"I'm a man of many talents," Jackson said and sat down across from him to eat his own breakfast.

Veese took notice of Jackson's cup of cocoa and said, "I thought you liked your coffee black. That looks to me like mostly milk."

"It's cocoa," Jackson said, amazed at how many people had noticed his coffee habits—and now the absence of them. "I don't drink coffee anymore."

"Why not?" Veese asked and took another bite of his blueberry pancakes.

"It's against my religion," Jackson said.

Veese laughed until he realized Jackson was serious. "You have a religion?"

"I do now."

"Since when?"

"Since February."

"And you didn't tell me?"

"It didn't come up."

"So, now it's come up."

"I'm a Mormon now."

"Like Chas?"

"That's right."

"Wow," Veese said. "I think I'd like to hear more about that."

He asked some questions, and Jackson told him the simple version. He'd expected Veese's reaction to such news to tend more toward teasing, but he seemed both surprised and impressed by Jackson's decision, even though he didn't say much. The topic shifted to the current situation, and later that morning, Jackson had to conclude that the best option all the way around was to convince Cortney to give up this madness. He called her into the office and had a long talk with her, frankly and kindly telling her what he knew and what he suspected. She was surprised but tried not to show it.

"I don't know what you expect me to do about it," she said in a snotty teenager voice that he hated.

"Let's start over, Cortney. I'll make all of the arrangements. You can start over in the program; new identity, new location. They'll never find you. You'll be safe. You can have a life. You don't need this guy, Cortney. You deserve better."

"You have *no* idea what you're talking about!" she snapped, coming to her feet.

Jackson felt more concerned about her well-being than her disrespect. "Cortney, please," he said gently. "You're putting yourself and a lot of other people in danger. Just let me call the—"

"I'll be fine," she insisted, apparently oblivious about anyone else who might be affected. "I just need to stay here another week or so, and then I'll be gone and you'll never see me again." She reached into her pocket and drew out her cell phone, which she put on the desk. "And you can have that."

"Why?" he asked.

"It doesn't work anymore," she said and left the office, leaving Jackson to wonder whether she had some kind of learning disorder. Or was her self-esteem so horrid that she truly believed she needed—or deserved—a guy like Bobby Dinubilo?

Later, he talked to Chas about his conversation with Cortney and his concern for her. She assured him that they had both done all they could, and the matter was out of their hands. They simply had to hope that she would slip away without causing any problems, and that all would be well while they were out of state.

* * * * *

On the morning they were scheduled to leave, Jackson found Chas in the bedroom doing a final check of her packing. In his opinion, she looked beautiful in her full bloom of pregnancy. It was a magnificent wonder to him that she had shown up in his life and changed it so completely. And that she was capable of creating life this way seemed a miracle beyond comprehension. Then he noticed the worried crease in her brow and he felt sick to think of the situation here in their home that was causing them both so much concern. But he'd done everything he knew how to do, and it was time to focus on one thing only.

"Are you the woman who runs this place?" he asked, and she looked up, showing a wan smile.

"Yes, may I help you?" she said, going along.

"Then you're the woman I need to talk to," he said, leaning one shoulder on the door frame. "I met a fortune teller who told me I must go to the Dickensian Inn, and there I would find my future wife. She said I would give up everything in my old life to be with her, and she would be the mother of my children."

Her smile widened. "No fortune teller is that good. A time traveler, perhaps."

He chuckled and walked toward her. "Thankfully, it was neither. God sent me here. There's no other explanation for such miracles." He took both her hands into his. "So . . . I have one question to ask you."

"Ask away."

"Will you have my baby?"

She laughed. "Either you've had a sudden lapse in memory, or you've completely lost your eyesight."

Jackson put one hand to her rounded belly and the other around her neck, pulling her head to his shoulder. "What I really mean to say is . . . we are going to walk out of this place in about twenty minutes and we're not going to think about anything but having this baby . . . together." Chas took hold of him and started to cry, which was as good as admitting that he'd hit the nail of her present concerns right on the head. "We're not going to talk about anything else, or speculate, or stew, or worry. It's all about the baby now. Everything is under control here at the inn. I've done everything I can do. Now we're going to put our home in God's hands, and we're going to devote ourselves to doing everything we can to bring this child safely into the world. Agreed?"

"Agreed!" she said, nodding against his shoulder. She sniffled and looked up at him. "I love you so much."

"I love you too. Now, hurry up. Let's get out of here. What can I do to help?"

"Zip up that bag and take it out to the car. The other bag will be ready in ten minutes, then you can take that, too."

"You got it," he said.

Half an hour later they were finally on their way with strong assurances from both Polly and Veese that everything would be fine. Jackson felt an indescribable relief wash over him as he drove away from the inn. He took a quick glance back at Charles, safely strapped into his car seat, then took Chas's hand and squeezed it. He silently assessed that his family was safe, and mentally went through a well-worn checklist to be certain that he had taken every possible precaution to ensure the safety of the inn and those who were there—whether guests or dear friends. Reconciled that he had done everything in his power, he consciously gave the matter to the Lord.

With a fervent prayer and a firm resolve, he pushed the matter away and focused on the road ahead. A glance at Chas reminded him that all that was most important to him was right here with him. The next several days were crucial to their little family as they focused everything on getting this baby here safely and doing everything they could to make and keep her healthy and strong.

CHAPTER 7

By the time they arrived at the airport in Butte, Melinda had been waiting at the curb with her luggage for about five minutes. They exchanged greetings, and Jackson loaded her luggage into the back of the SUV along with everything else they were taking in order to stay in Utah for an unknown number of weeks. With all the stuff they needed for Charles, the fit was tight but manageable. Melinda got into the backseat with the baby, and he let out a delighted squeal, happy to see his aunt.

The drive to Salt Lake City was approximately six hours, mostly south from Anaconda, but Chas needed frequent stops to stretch her legs and back and use a restroom. Charles was also pleased with every opportunity to get out of the car, although Melinda did well at keeping him occupied while they drove. They took it slow and stopped for a couple of meals, and the baby took a good nap during a long afternoon stretch.

As they got closer to their destination, Chas started talking about stories she'd heard and read of the Mormon pioneers coming to the Salt Lake Valley to escape persecution. Jackson felt deeply fascinated and realized that for all of his newfound conviction with the gospel, he knew practically nothing about the history of this people he'd become a part of. Melinda was also very intrigued and asked Chas many questions. He couldn't help hoping that she too would come to accept and embrace the gospel. Perhaps a lengthy stay in Salt Lake City could be good for all of them.

As they drove into the Salt Lake Valley, they all became unusually silent. The stories Chas had been telling resonated through Jackson's mind, and he felt something close to reverence to be in this flourishing valley that had risen out of a desert under the direction of a prophet of God. According to Jodi's suggestion prior to their leaving, they drove straight to the center of the city to see the temple.

"Oh, it's incredible!" Chas said as they drove past and she craned her head to see the spires.

"Yes, it is," Jackson said more quietly. He felt a strange sense of awe and comfort and reached for Chas's hand as he drove around the square and down the block in search of a parking garage. After parking and getting Charles into his stroller, they asked someone how to get to the temple. They walked briskly to their destination without saying much, as if they all had some instinctive homing device that had been activated. When they were standing next to the reflection pond on the temple grounds, looking up at the magnificent structure, the silence settled in more deeply. Even Charles was unusually silent. Jackson reached for Chas's hand and squeezed it, then put his arm around her shoulders and pulled her close to him, pressing a kiss into her hair. She looked up at him with tears in her eyes, but still neither of them spoke. There was no need. With the temple and all it represented before them, the trials of life fell into perspective, and the hope of eternity together stretched out before them. Unpredictability, opposition—and even death—lost their power with the knowledge they had of the gospel plan. Jackson felt his sister take his free hand, and he glanced over to see that she too had tears in her eyes. He put his other arm around her, wondering if this might be just what she'd needed to fan the flames of her longtime smoldering interest in the Church. He hoped so.

Charles started to fuss as if to tell them that they'd remained in one spot long enough, and their momentary reprieve became a gem they would treasure in memory. They walked around the temple and into the Square, where they ended up standing on the *other* side of the temple, looking up at it with the same kind of dazed trance—until a pair of lovely young ladies approached and one of them asked in a thick accent if they had any questions. The sister missionaries were thrilled to learn that Chas was a member and Jackson had been recently baptized. But they were perhaps more thrilled to know that Melinda was not a member and had many questions. This began a lengthy discussion that took place while they had a brief tour of Temple Square and the North Visitors' Center. The greatest moment was standing before the magnificent statue of Christ while the sisters each bore their testimony of the divinity of the Savior. And they *all* got tears in their eyes.

It was late evening before they left the Square with the intention of coming back the next day when they had more time. Chas suddenly felt very tired when they got into the car, but the experience of just being in this place and all that she had felt more than compensated for her fatigue.

Jackson set the navigation system to find Jodi's sister's home and drove around the temple once more before following its directions. Again there was silence among them, as if they all had too much to think about to ever be able to articulate it. They found the house without any trouble; it was less than ten minutes away from the temple. Jodi's sister, Kate, answered the door and greeted them with excitement. She bore only a slight resemblance to Jodi, but she was full of the same friendly energy.

Kate invited them into the house to meet her husband, Doug, and their two children who were still at home, and she wanted to know if they were hungry. They all insisted that they were fine, but she provided a snack, nevertheless. When they were finished eating, she took them back out the front door and down the driveway a short way to a set of stairs at the side of the house that led to the basement apartment. They found it to be spacious and comfortable, with everything they could possibly need, including plenty of clean linens, a washer and dryer, a crib all ready to be slept in, and some basic food supplies in the cupboards and refrigerator. When pointing this out, Kate simply said, "I knew you'd have way too much on your minds to worry about running right out to a grocery store the minute you got here."

"It's so kind and thoughtful of you," Chas said, and the others chimed in with their agreement.

"It's nothing, really," Kate said. "I had to go shopping anyway, and it's really nice to have an opportunity to help somebody. Life is all about spreading the blessings around and sharing what we have, so make yourselves at home, and let me know if you need anything at all. We'll check on you but we don't want to be too nosy."

"Don't worry about that," Jackson said.

Kate gave them two keys to the door and told them the best place to park their car so it could be off of the street and not in the way of their getting in and out of the garage. She then left them, expressing appreciation for their staying in her home, as if *they* were doing *her* a huge favor. Chas got a little teary after she left, overcome with her generosity. It wasn't just the physical evidence of a place to stay and food to eat, but it was also the evidence that God was looking out for them, and that good people could make such a difference by sharing what they had. She smiled to think that her lifetime hero, Charles Dickens, would appreciate and understand that concept very well.

* * * * *

Polly stood at the parlor window and watched Jackson and Chas drive away, hoping with all her heart that everything would turn out in the best possible way. She imagined the day they would return with a beautiful, healthy baby girl and decided she would hold on to that image, wondering how many weeks it might be before she saw her friend again. She felt only mildly worried about what might transpire here at the inn while they were away. She had her own personal FBI undercover agent looking after her, and Cortney's presence didn't seem to be anything but an annoyance. She'd become increasingly distant, which wasn't saying much since she'd *always* kept her distance. But that suited Polly just fine. When Cortney *was* around, she just seemed to bring a dark cloud into a room. She was barely polite and not very friendly. Polly far preferred other company, but with Chas, Jackson, and the baby all gone, the inn already felt too quiet. Loneliness and boredom would surely be her greatest challenge through the coming weeks.

Polly heard a noise and turned around to see Elliott Veese enter the room. He was tall and lean with dark blond hair that would have been very curly if it were any longer. Cut as close to his head as it was, it showed only a hint of curl.

"What are you up to . . . honey?" he asked with mild facetiousness. Their ruse of pretending romantic involvement was more humorous than anything. But she felt completely comfortable around him, and right now he was pleasant company. Since there were no guests scheduled to arrive until tomorrow evening, she was *really* glad for his company and hoped he might be as bored as she was.

"Just thinking how quiet it's going to be," she said. "We have a lot of guests coming in on the weekend, but no one tonight except you and Mr. Tarasov."

"Then we should . . . watch a movie or something . . . honey." He smirked playfully when he said it, and Polly smiled.

"That sounds great. Maybe we should invite Mr. Tarasov to join us, so he can chaperone."

Elliott stepped closer with his hands in his pockets and said playfully, "Or maybe we shouldn't." He waggled his eyebrows comically, and she chuckled.

"Well, he's joining us for supper, regardless."

"Good thing he's a *nice* old man. Truthfully, I've always been a little awkward with older people. I never knew any of my grandparents, so . . . I'm kind of socially inept that way."

"Just wait until you're old yourself, you'll be glad you got to hang out with Artem."

"I'm already glad," he said and stood beside her, looking the same direction out the window that she'd been looking when he'd come in. "It's nice here," he said. "Leeds told me it was nice, but I don't think I believed it was *this* nice."

"It *is* nice," Polly said. "Why don't you ever call him by his first name?"

"We worked together for years; he was my boss."

"And now . . ."

"Habit, I guess."

"Just try it. Say 'Jackson.'"

"Jackson," he enunciated so ridiculously that she laughed. "Now get him to call me Elliott."

"That's Chas's job. But I'll call you Elliott. I think it's a nice name. And it suits you."

"Thank you . . . I think."

Polly heard a door in the distance and footsteps on the stairs; she recognized the quick gait as Cortney's. "It's her," she whispered, and the next thing she knew, Elliott was kissing her. It lasted much longer than she'd ever been kissed before, and she heard the front door open and close in the midst of it. She took hold of his shoulders to keep from falling over. She couldn't decide if it was the way it had taken her off guard or the kiss itself that left her entirely unsteady.

When their kiss ended, she found Elliott looking into her eyes as if they really were romantically involved. She couldn't decide if she was more affected by his kiss or her own response to it. Either way, she felt as if she were standing on quicksand, when she'd never known anything but solid ground.

"Do you think she saw us?" Elliott asked, keeping his face close to hers.

"Let's hope so," she said, wishing it hadn't sounded so dreamy. "Since it was entirely for her benefit, we wouldn't want to waste our efforts."

He smiled but made no further comment as he stepped back. Polly cleared her throat and forced herself not to stare at him as her thoughts rushed headlong into places they'd never been before. Not once since she'd closed off her broken heart in her early college days had she even allowed herself to entertain the idea of being attracted to a man. She tried to tell herself that it was just a physical response, a reaction to a great kiss, something any woman would feel under the same circumstances. But she wasn't convinced.

Needing some space and time to think, she hurried to say, "I . . . uh . . . need to get some work done. You know where to find me."

As she made her way out of the room, Elliott said, "So . . . a movie? After supper?"

"Sure," she said, glancing over her shoulder, both terrified and thrilled over the prospect.

* * * * *

It didn't take long for Jackson to settle his family into their temporary home. Tired as they all were, it was a relief to get Charles to sleep rather quickly, and they all settled into their respective bedrooms for the night. Following a good night's sleep, they worked together to fix a nice breakfast with the food that Kate had left for them. After putting everything in order, they headed out again to Temple Square with the intention of exploring every inch of it more thoroughly, and of sitting through all the films and presentations that were available. Since they'd arrived a day ahead of their original plan, they had the entire day free.

The morning went quickly while they eagerly soaked in all they were exposed to, and Charles was relatively cooperative. Jackson and Melinda took turns handling him, since Chas just didn't have the energy. When they realized they were hungry, Jackson asked someone for a suggestion for a good place to eat that was within walking distance. They went into the Joseph Smith Memorial Building and discovered a whole new avenue for exploration. On the top floor of the building, they shared a wonderful lunch while

Melinda talked almost incessantly about what she was learning and how it made her feel.

After eating, they lingered at the windows, enjoying the view of the temple from this vantage point. They sat through a movie about Joseph Smith that touched them all deeply, then they wandered through a store that sold Church materials in the basement of the building. While the ladies were looking at books, Jackson purchased a set of scriptures for his sister and had her name engraved on them. He discreetly put them into the storage area of the stroller, then paid for a ridiculous number of books and pamphlets that indicated his mutual hunger for knowledge.

After pondering the statue of Joseph Smith in the lobby of what had once been a magnificent hotel, they went back to the Square and continued their explorations while Charles slept in his stroller. When Chas declared exhaustion, Jackson took her back to the apartment to rest while he took Melinda and the baby shopping to stock up on more groceries, diapers, and other things they would need. Back at the apartment, Melinda helped him put everything away while Chas was still resting. While they cooked supper together, Melinda asked Jackson a great many questions about the gospel and his own experience in gaining a testimony. She'd heard him tell the story before, but now it seemed as though her every sense had been awakened to it, and she listened with deeper interest, responding with more emotion.

It occurred to Jackson that if Melinda was back at the inn with the baby as they'd originally planned, her growing passion for the gospel might have been much slower in coming. Perhaps this was a part of God's plan, after all. Thinking of the reasons that they'd decided to bring Melinda along, Jackson's mind went to the issue he'd been doing his best to avoid thinking about. But he just did what he always did when he began to worry about the inn and the people there: he uttered a silent prayer, reminded himself that he'd done everything in his power, and focused on the moment, doing his best to put the matter into the Lord's hands.

That evening they shared a nice supper, and Chas felt pretty good after her long nap. The meal was winding down when Jackson excused himself and went into the other room. He came back with a bag that he handed to Melinda.

"What is this?" she asked.

"A little present," he said, taking delight in Chas's equally baffled expression. "It's evident you need one of these. I couldn't bear to think of you not having one after the way you've been behaving the last couple of days."

Chas smiled as she became enlightened the same moment Melinda pulled the box out of the bag. When Melinda opened the box and saw the beautiful quad with her name inscribed on it, she started to cry. Jackson hadn't seen her cry this much since their mother had passed away. She threw her arms around him with a tight hug and a ridiculous amount of appreciation. Then she sat at the table and thumbed reverently through the book while Jackson told her the story of how Chas had purchased the same thing for him long before he'd indicated enough interest for her to know that he was ready to receive such a priceless gift. He bore quiet testimony to his sister of the truthfulness contained in the scriptures, and his own convictions regarding the divinity of Jesus Christ. Melinda hugged him again, and Chas as well, and said she couldn't wait to start reading.

"Then go read," Jackson said. "I'll clean up the kitchen while Chas keeps track of the little boss."

"I'll take you up on that," Melinda said, but she stayed in the front room to read, where she ended up doing more talking to Chas about the scriptures. Chas gave her an extra marking pencil and pointed out some of her favorite verses, explaining their meaning. She showed her Moroni's challenge at the end of the Book of Mormon, and suggested she should start her reading with that volume. Chas also showed her how to use the footnotes, how to cross reference, and how to use the Topical Guide and Index. Melinda digested it all with eager anticipation and Chas felt certain it wouldn't be long before she took the plunge. She'd shown enough interest in the past that it wasn't terribly surprising, but it was certainly gratifying. There was little in life as joyful as sharing such wonders with loved ones.

* * * * *

Elliott realized he was counting the hours until supper, and then minutes. Throughout the day Polly had made it clear she was very busy, and he could only follow her around for so long without feeling like an absolute fool. He spent some time in his room making calls to his connections back in Virginia and researching some issues that Leeds had asked him to check into. He enjoyed feeling like he was working for Leeds again, and yet everything was different. He smiled to recall Polly's challenge to start calling his friend by his given name. Jackson. Lucky man, Jackson. What a life he'd found for himself!

Elliott was a little startled by how much he found his mind wandering to the possibility of staying in this town. In all of Jackson's teasing him about that very thing, he had *never* believed it was something he'd even consider. But it was as if he'd crossed the borders of Anaconda, Montana, and something in him came to life. He didn't know if it was like the town of his childhood imagination where he'd always *wished* he'd grown up, or if it was something else. The magical effect of the inn had only deepened the feeling, and since he was a man who never paid much attention to feelings beyond the basics of being hungry and tired, he was a little off-kilter.

And then there was Polly. He was still proud of himself for the cool way he'd concealed his utter delight when she'd blurted out that they were dating. This was by far the best undercover assignment he'd *ever* had. He just hoped that when it was over he didn't have to stop seeing Polly. Having the perfect excuse to kiss her earlier was the best way he'd ever found to overcome his usual shyness with women. It was easier for him to be an agent than it was to say the right thing to a woman. Being undercover made him feel like he could say and do the right things, whereas being himself had never worked very well.

Supper with Polly and Artem was great fun. The old man was funny and full of great stories. Polly was kind and sweet and very entertaining herself. Cortney showed up long enough to get a plate of food, thank Polly with minimal politeness, and take supper up to her room. Given Cortney's generally sour disposition, no one was too disappointed when she didn't join them for meals, but none of them voiced it.

After supper, Elliott helped Polly put leftovers away and load the dishwasher while Artem cleared the table. They made popcorn and picked out *Apollo 13* as the evening's entertainment. Elliott was thrilled to have Polly sit close to him, and he pretended that her motive wasn't in keeping up the proper guise. He held her hand and eventually put his arm around her, feeling like a teenager on his first date. But there was something in the way she looked at him that made him hopeful that it was more than pretending for her as well.

* * * * *

Later that evening after Jackson and Chas had prayed together and then climbed into bed, they snuggled close together and talked about the day. They discussed their anticipation of being sealed in the temple, their certainty that Melinda would be baptized, and their hope that all would go well with their doctor appointments the following day. Neither of them mentioned their concern for matters back at the inn, even though they both knew the other had to be thinking about it too. They'd requested protection for the inn and its occupants in their prayer, and that seemed the best that could be said.

The following morning Jackson got up with the baby and told Chas to stay in bed as long as she wanted. Their appointment wasn't until eleven-thirty. Once he had Charles dressed for the day, he found Melinda in the kitchen making omelettes. She looked a little tired and admitted that she'd stayed up late reading, but she said it with a wink and a smile, and he figured her lost sleep wasn't concerning her too much.

Melinda watched the baby while Jackson and Chas left to find Hospital Hill, as they'd learned it was called. They arrived early for the first appointment and were glad they had when parking and finding their way to the right place in the hospital proved to be a little complicated. They had a good visit with the doctor who would deliver Chas's baby, and Chas endured another round of the usual tests and exams. When the doctor reassured them that everything was as good as it could be, they went through an indoor walkway that connected the University of Utah Medical Center to the children's hospital next door where their baby would undergo open-heart surgery. They had some lunch in the cafeteria there; it had been highly recommended three times since they'd arrived.

After lunch they met with the heart surgeon who specialized in infants and young children. It was surprising to hear how many young children had serious heart problems, but comforting to realize how many successes this man had behind him. His wall was covered with pictures of children whose lives he had saved. He told them with uncompromising honesty about the risks and admitted that he couldn't always save every child, but he promised to do his absolute best and apply every bit of knowledge and ability he possessed to see their daughter through this ordeal. He told them that until he actually saw the heart, he wouldn't know for sure how long the surgery would take, or what the recovery would entail, but someone would act as a liaison between them and the operating room, and they would be kept completely updated. Since Chas would be recovering from a C-section, they would communicate in a way that would allow Jackson to stay with his wife.

Leaving Hospital Hill, Jackson reached for Chas's hand and gave her a loving smile. He could see from her eyes that she shared his hope, and he knew that together they could get through just about anything.

"Hey, Melinda told us not to hurry back. What should we do?"

"Ooh," she said. "Free time with a babysitter? So much to choose from."

"You're going to be laid up for a while, and then you'll be spending every spare minute with our daughter, I suspect. We should get some sightseeing in while we have the chance."

Chas opted for the Museum of Church History and Art, and they spent hours there, taking it all in and talking about what they saw. Chas sat down frequently but felt rather well. She felt grateful for the opportunity to be in this great city and to have this little vacation that included seeing so many wonderful things. She thought of Melinda's keen interest, and the glow in Jackson's eyes as he tuned in to aspects of the Church and its history that were new to him. On top of that, she felt tangible hope that their baby was going to be okay. Any worry about what might be going on back at the inn was pleasantly far away.

* * * * *

Polly was sitting behind the desk in the office, doing more stewing than anything else. Jackson and Chas hadn't been gone long enough for her to be wishing they'd come home, but she was. She'd talked to Chas a couple of times on the phone and knew that all was well at their end, and technically all was well here—at least as far as she was going to tell Chas. She had no intention of discussing her current predicament with Chas. She had no need to hear Chas's speculations or suggestions. Polly knew what she had to do, and she had to do it at the first possible opportunity. Under the circumstances, she couldn't go through with this ongoing charade. She just couldn't.

She looked up to see Elliott enter the room and felt entirely unprepared to face what she knew had to be faced. She hadn't thought it through nearly as much as she should have, but she was afraid if she waited she would completely lose her nerve.

"Good, you're here," she said. "I need to talk to you."

Elliott sat lazily in a chair on the other side of the desk. "Talk away, honey."

She got straight to the point. "I don't know if I'm comfortable with this whole . . . pretending we're dating thing."

Elliott glanced over his shoulder with exaggerated nervousness. "Are we alone?"

"Yes. Cortney and Artem are both out."

"Okay," he said, settling deeper into his chair, "what are you not comfortable with?"

"Can I be straight with you?"

"Of course," he said, realizing she was more serious than he'd ever seen her.

"I mean . . . really straight with you, because . . . I'm not the type to play games or skirt around the point."

"I'm good with that."

"I think we need to come up with something else; some . . . other reason you're here."

"We can't . . . change the story in the middle of the show, Polly. The people we're trying to fool already think we're dating."

Polly had to let that sink in for a moment. "Okay," she said. "You're right. I was so focused on my not feeling comfortable that I admit I didn't really think it through."

"I guess we could pretend we're fighting, but if we were, you probably wouldn't be letting me stay here."

"Fair enough," she said.

"So, why don't you tell me why you're not comfortable with this, and we'll figure out some other way to deal with it. Was it the kiss? It was the kiss, wasn't it? If you don't want me to kiss you anymore, then—"

"No, it wasn't the kiss," she insisted. "I mean . . . I guess it was the kiss, but . . . it's not what you think, and . . ."

"How do you know what I think?" he asked. Elliott felt amazed at his own ability to be so straightforward. Either he'd learned a thing or two from Jackson about saying what needed to be said, or feeling like he was undercover helped considerably. *Or* he had to consider the possibility that it was simply Polly. She inspired him, so it wasn't a stretch to think that she could provoke him to follow her example of being straight up about the situation. "And if you don't tell me what you're thinking I won't know what you think, either."

Polly stood up and looked out the window, preferring not to look at him. As straightforward as she was accustomed to being, this was proving to be harder than she'd anticipated.

"I thought you were going to be straight with me," Elliott said.

"Okay, straight out, Elliott . . . I'm not comfortable with this because I *am* attracted to you. There, I said it. How can I pretend when I don't feel like I'm pretending? And how do I know what's real and what isn't if I know that you're just pretending? If we're going to pull this off, I just need some ground rules so I know where I stand. I've hardly been out on a date since my early college days, so I'm not very good at this. And I don't really know you at all. I know that Jackson thinks you're a great guy, but since he's never had anything to do with your love life, I wouldn't expect that his opinion really has any bearing on the present situation. So if you
. . ." Her rambling was interrupted by her own startled gasp when she felt Elliott's hands on her shoulders.

"Nervous?" he asked.

"Did you get that?" she said with sarcasm, realizing how she'd been running on.

"There's no need for that, Polly. I like the way you're not afraid to say what needs to be said, and . . . truthfully, I'm glad you said it . . . because I wanted to, but I didn't know how without making you feel uncomfortable." Polly turned abruptly to look at him, and he dropped his hands. Their eyes met with what felt like an attempt to stare each other down. He smiled and added, "I'm attracted to you too." He shrugged. "Who could blame me? You're adorable."

Polly searched his eyes for a full minute while the staring continued. "You really mean that," she said with as much certainty as surprise.

"I really do," he said. "And just so you don't have to wonder, I suggest the ground rules remain uncomplicated. Beyond the fact that I work for the FBI and we had no email contact prior to my coming here, I'd say we could just call it real. If either of us needs to clarify anything, we'll do that when we're alone and can't be overheard."

Polly kept searching his eyes while she considered what he was saying, what she was feeling, and what this might mean. As if her mind grabbed onto a sudden understanding, her heart quickened, and a mild tremor rushed through her body.

"I think we need to talk," she said, unable to determine if she felt thrilled or terrified.

"Oh, we definitely need to talk," he said, then contradicted himself by kissing her. Polly was surprised at how quickly she wrapped her arms around him. His embrace secured her in a warmth that completely separated the moment from all things before or after, and the world around them. He kept his arms around her when the kiss ended, then they were doing that staring thing again.

Polly knew she had watched way too many chick flicks when the first words that came out of her mouth were, "I can't believe this is happening to me."

"Well, that makes two of us," he said.

Past experience made Polly want to question his motives and encourage distrust to overrule all else. But she'd worked hard to rise above the past, and she couldn't deny that her instincts were telling her he was a good man and he would never intentionally do anything to hurt her. Still, her sense of practicality had a strong vote in this situation. "We *really* need to talk," she said in a tone of voice that implied she wasn't thinking about talking.

"Yeah, we do," he said, and again he kissed her.

"You know," she said at the first possibility, "I really need to get some work done, and . . . then . . . we can talk . . . when we've had a chance to actually . . . think."

"Fair enough," he said, but he made no attempt to let her go.

Polly forced herself to move away, letting out a spontaneous giggle as she stepped back. "Wow," she said and sat behind the desk. "I'm not sure I can concentrate with you in the room."

"Too bad," he said and scooted another chair beside hers. "What are we doing?"

"*I* am going to reconcile the bank account. You are going to—"

"Oh, I love these things!" he said, reaching for the number puzzle book that Polly had left on the desk. It was something she did to occupy time when she only needed to be watching the office but didn't actually have any work that needed to be done.

"That's mine!" she said and comically slapped his hand.

He laughed. "But you'll let me do one lousy puzzle, right? I've been bored out of my mind. Leeds should have—"

"Jackson," she corrected.

"Jackson should have left me with a list of chores or something."

"I'm sure I could come up with a few things that need to be done, but I'm sure that Jackson didn't want you to be too distracted."

With his eyes fixed on her, he said, "Then why did he leave me here with you?"

"Just . . . do a puzzle or something and let me do my work."

"Yes, ma'am," he said as if she were one of his superiors.

Elliott focused intently on the puzzle, filling in numbers with a pencil, but Polly could hardly think straight enough to reconcile a single number on the bank statement. She kept reading the same line of figures over and over while at the same time trying to analyze how she felt and what to do about it. Elliott just kept working on his puzzle. She figured that was the difference between the male brain that focused on one thing at a time—and one thing only—and the female brain that tried to take in everything at once and figure it out. But her best multitasking skills were no match for the overload of her senses that had occurred in the last several minutes. Was this really happening? Yes. But could she ever hope for it to last? The very acknowledgment of the thought tightened her heart when she hadn't even taken a moment to wonder if her heart was involved. She'd admitted to being attracted, but . . . her heart had nothing to do with that. Did it?

Polly heard the door and wondered if it was one of the three couples scheduled to stay there that evening. As soon as the door closed, she heard quiet arguing between a man and a woman. She couldn't make out what was being said, but their tone was evident. She exchanged a look of comical alarm with Elliott, then he went back to his puzzle. Polly stood as the couple entered the office, and her first impression was negative. They were rich and they wanted people to know it. And they were unhappy. He was tall, dark, and handsome. She was blonde, slender, and striking. Something hurt and vulnerable in the woman's eyes made Polly like her, but she could see nothing but arrogance in the man.

Putting all impressions aside, she smiled at the couple and said, "Welcome. I assume you have reservations."

"Mr. and Mrs. Glass," the man said.

"Ah," Polly said, "you're planning to stay several days."

"Yeah, we'll see," Mr. Glass said. "Marriage counselor said we should get away for a couple of weeks together; some out-of-the-way place, he said. We'll see if we last that long."

Mrs. Glass let out a disgusted sigh. "You don't need to air our dirty laundry in front of strangers. Most people talk about the weather."

Polly ignored both comments and started talking about the amenities of the inn while she took the man's credit card and did the usual paperwork.

Elliott listened to the exchange with little interest while he worked on putting the right numbers in little boxes. He figured that was the best way to remain apparently nonchalant and unnoticed in every regard. A quick glance at their new guests had put his every nerve on alert. He knew those faces. They'd come up on DMV photos that had been emailed to him from the Bureau. Whoever they were pretending to be, this was Harry Nuccitelli and his wife, Bridget.

Elliott heard Polly tell them, "I'm Polly, by the way, and I can help you with whatever you might need."

"Thank you," Mrs. Glass said kindly.

"And who are you?" the man asked.

Elliott looked up, feigning mild curiosity as he realized Harry was talking to him. "I'm Polly's boyfriend," he said and stood up with perfect confidence, offering a hand. "Since she's in charge of the inn this week, I have to hang out here if I want to see her."

Mr. Glass shook Elliott's hand, apparently not caring in the slightest. "The owner isn't here?" he asked as Elliott sat back down.

"No, he's out of state," Polly said, and the imposter seemed relieved.

"It's a lovely place," Mrs. Glass commented.

"Yes, it is," Polly said. Elliott went back to his puzzle, his mind completely elsewhere.

CHAPTER 8

Jackson had just finished eating supper when his cell phone rang. He pulled it off his belt and glanced at the caller ID. Veese.

"Excuse me," he said to Chas and his sister as he stood and answered with a cheerful voice. "Do you miss me?"

"Oh, I do," Veese said. Jackson walked outside for privacy and heard him add, "I'm in beautiful downtown Anaconda . . . doing a little sightseeing."

"Does that mean you left the inn because you don't want to be overheard?"

"That's what it means," Veese said.

"What's going on?" Jackson asked, hating the way worry rushed back into him at the very mention of circumstances back at the inn.

"So, here's the thing," Veese said, "a couple checked in this afternoon; Polly said they made reservations last week. A Mr. and Mrs. Glass."

"Yeah?"

"Well, it's Harry Nuccitelli and his wife, Bridget."

Jackson swore, then silently apologized to God for letting it slip out. He was trying to do better with that. Since he'd married Chas, his life had been less subject to the unexpected dramas of his previous job, and his swearing had lessened considerably.

"Does Polly know who they are?"

"No, I didn't say anything. I figured it was better that way. Act natural and all that."

"Does Cortney know they're there?"

"Oh, yeah. She saw him and practically turned blue. He pretended not to know her, but I know she knew him. I've been putting pieces together, boss, and I have a theory on Cortney giving you back the cell phone—which is still without service, by the way."

"I'm listening."

"Her last conversation with Bobby was an agreement that he would come to the inn and get her, just like they'd talked about. He told her that she knew when he was coming since they'd already discussed it. Unfortunately, the conversation that established the time must have taken place before we were bugging the phone. But I think *Harry* heard that conversation, and *he* knows when Bobby's coming, or at least he has a pretty good idea. I think Harry had the phone service cut so that Cortney couldn't speak to Bobby and change their meeting place once she knew Harry had shown up here. He wants a face-off with Bobby as opposed to just doing him in. I don't know what's got Harry so riled up and determined, but it's obviously a big deal to Harry—whatever it is."

Jackson sighed. "It all makes sense." He resisted the urge to use more of those words he tried very hard not to use now that he'd become a Mormon. "It all makes *perfect* sense, in spite of a few missing pieces. But why does this face-off have to come down in *my* home?"

"It'll be okay, boss."

"I sure hope so."

"I'm calling someone in for backup to watch the place from the outside."

"Good. You be careful . . . and keep me in the loop."

"You got it, boss."

"And stop calling me boss. I'm not your boss."

"Sure thing, boss."

Jackson hung up and paced the driveway for a few minutes in order to sort it all out in his head and then put it away with a prayer and an effort to trust that God would protect his home.

"Everything okay?" Chas asked when he came back inside.

"Everything's fine," he said and helped Melinda wash the dishes while Chas played with Charles. Chas would be having a baby tomorrow, and he didn't want her thinking about anything but that.

Later that evening, Kate and Doug came by to see how they were doing and if they needed anything. Chas took the opportunity to ask if Doug might be willing to come to the hospital after the baby was born and bring someone else with him so that they could give the baby a blessing before she went into surgery. He was eager to help and told her that he was glad she'd asked. He wondered if she would like a blessing herself before going to the hospital. Chas wasn't about to turn down any opportunity for a priesthood blessing, and Doug called his home teaching partner. Ten minutes later the other gentleman arrived and they gave Chas a beautiful blessing. She was promised that she would come through her ordeal without any physical difficulties, and that the Lord was watching out for her and her family. Chas felt peace and comfort from the blessing, even though there was no specific mention of whether the baby would be all right.

After their company was gone and Charles was down for the night, Jackson put his arms around Chas and whispered, "I'll be glad when I can do that kind of thing."

"Yes, I will too. But you're a lot closer to being able to do it than you used to be." She looked up at him and smiled. "It's one of a thousand reasons I love you."

"I love you too," he said and kissed her. "You okay?"

She nodded. "Yeah, I'm okay. You?"

"I'm okay if you're okay," he said.

"Then we're both okay." She laughed softly and Jackson hugged her, not bothering to tell her about the guests that were staying at the inn. When this was all over, he'd like to tell her about it all in past tense—and hopefully with a positive outcome.

* * * * *

Polly was relieved when Elliott said he was going into town to pick up a few things and take in the sights a bit. It wasn't that she didn't enjoy his company. She was still trying to deal with the sensory overload of what had occurred between them—and what it implied. After playing it through in her head several times while she worked in the kitchen, she came to the firm conclusion that they really *did* need a long talk. She asked herself if she trusted Elliott Veese enough to be opening up to him about her issues, her past, her feelings. She concluded that she did. She wasn't sure *why* she did, but she did. And perhaps this was a *test* of trust. If he could listen to and accept her with all that she felt compelled to share with him, then maybe there could be something to this blossoming relationship.

She also had to realistically consider the possibility that despite the evidence that this was becoming a relationship, it could very well be only temporary. Just because he was attracted to her didn't mean he wouldn't go back to Virginia when this assignment was completed, and she might never see him again. She backpedaled a little and determined that she should probably get some idea of where *his* head was before she started spilling her every thought and feeling to him. Oh! It was all so overwhelming and confusing. She wasn't good at this! But maybe she just needed to admit it to him. She wasn't a person to want anything but straightforward honesty. She just had to be careful not to be *too* honest. In conclusion, she had no idea what to say to him or how to say it and figured she wouldn't say anything until they just had time to talk and see where the conversation went. So she focused on fixing supper and getting some preparations for tomorrow's breakfast taken care of.

"Hey there, honey," he said from the kitchen doorway and startled her. But she was so glad to see him she had to restrain herself from assaulting him with a hug.

"Are you going to keep calling me that?"

"I will call you that when those red curls have turned gray and we're wondering why the kids don't come to visit."

Polly felt a little stunned by the implication of his words, but even more so when she realized he was serious. He was *serious!*

Needing to acknowledge what seemed so utterly outlandish, she shook a finger at him and said, "You told me there was no pretending. So don't start staying things that—"

"I'm not pretending," he said, stepping closer.

Polly opened her mouth to say something, but no words came out. She closed her mouth and tried to think of some kind of protest or argument, but nothing she could think of to say seemed to have any substance. Elliott put a finger to her chin and kissed her. He looked into her eyes and smiled.

"We really need to . . . stop kissing," she said, "and start talking."

"So you keep telling me," he said and kissed her. "You want me to stop kissing you?"

"Not altogether. But . . . balancing it out with some conversation about *why* we're kissing would be wise, don't you think?"

"Yes, yes I do. So, let's talk."

"I'm . . . cooking right now, and I have to—"

"When do you want to talk? Tell me when, and I'll be there."

"Okay." She thought about it. "Eight o'clock in the parlor."

"It's a date," he said.

"Our first real date is talking in the parlor?"

"Since we're babysitting the inn, it will have to do for now."

"Yes, I suppose so." She smiled. "I'll see you at eight. I mean . . . I'll see you at supper, and then . . . I'll see you at eight."

"I'm looking forward to it . . . both . . . yeah." He chuckled and left the room, waving comically. Polly let out a ridiculously dreamy sigh and forced herself back to work. Every few minutes she found herself completely unproductive, just staring into space, her mind wandering. Then she'd snap out of it and try to accomplish her tasks, glancing frequently at the clock, counting minutes until their *date.*

Artem joined them for supper as usual, and Cortney showed up long enough to load a plate and offer patronizing appreciation for the meal. The three different couples staying at the inn all went out at different times, and before eight o'clock they had all come back in. Polly got the kitchen cleaned up, breakfast preparations completed, and the inn ready for night before she cleaned up a little and went to the parlor at two minutes past eight. Elliott was already there, seated comfortably at one end of the couch, looking at a magazine of Victorian decor that had been on the coffee table.

"You can't really have any interest in that," she said and sat at the other end of the couch, figuring some distance would be more conducive to conversation.

"Not a whole lot," he said, setting it aside. "But more than I did before I came here."

"I'm sure I have enough fascination with Victorian decor for both of us. Actually, I've decorated my own house in that mode. I'm afraid my job has rubbed off on me way too much."

"You have a house?"

"I do," she said.

"Well . . . I didn't figure you actually *lived* here, but . . ."

"I've stayed here off and on through the years, when they need me to watch the inn, or . . . during times when Chas didn't want to be alone."

"Alone?"

"Before she married Jackson. When he was missing, especially, and . . . other times." Polly didn't know if Elliott knew about Jackson being hospitalized the previous fall for PTSD. She figured it wasn't her place to tell him, so she just moved on. "Anyway, I like staying here, but it's nice to have my own place. I bought it about four or five years ago. It's not very big; a couple of bedrooms. But it's adequate, and at least I'm not paying rent."

"That's great," Elliott said, increasingly impressed with her. She was levelheaded and smart and kind. She was also funny and beautiful. And he was head over heels. He'd debated throughout the day about how much he should say about what he was feeling, and how exactly he should say it. He didn't have any firm answers to those questions, but he didn't feel any need to hold back. If this wasn't going to work out, he'd prefer to know up front. As it was, he hoped that it would, and he wasn't going to blow his chances with her by being vague or playing games.

Silence settled while it seemed there was way too much to say, and they were both hoping the other would begin. They both started to speak at the same time. They both laughed. They both said, "You go first." Then they laughed again.

"Okay," Polly said, "let's just start at the beginning. Somewhere in the middle of pretending that we had a romance going on, we both realized we were attracted to each other."

"Not in the middle," he said. "The minute I saw you I felt like we were Westley and Princess Buttercup in *The Princess Bride*." Her eyes widened, and he shrugged. "I like that movie."

"But Westley becomes the Dread Pirate Roberts."

"He never stopped loving Princess Buttercup."

Polly heard reference to the word *love* and had to get to the point. "Why don't you just say what you need to say so I don't have to wonder where you stand."

"Okay, I will. First of all I want to say that I'm not a womanizer or a player. Some of the guys I work with are, but I've never been comfortable around that kind of behavior. I know you don't know me well enough to know if I'm telling you the truth, but I suppose you could ask Jackson if I'm the kind of guy who tells the truth."

"I don't need to ask him," she said and nodded her encouragement for him to go on.

"You said that you haven't dated much. Well, neither have I. This is a whole new experience for me, Polly. I've wondered if my lack of experience is making me believe that this is more than it is. I've wondered if it's just like some . . . high school crush and I'll grow out of it." He shook his head. "But I'm not a kid, and neither are you. What I feel has got me completely out of my comfort zone here, Polly, but that doesn't mean it isn't real. I'm certain the wise course would be to give the matter some time and see if we have what it takes to make it work. Or . . . we could just decide we're going to make it work."

Polly couldn't say a word while several strained minutes of silence passed. Elliott just took her hand and held it, seeming to understand that she needed time to digest everything he'd just said. She was pleasantly surprised to analyze her instincts and realize that she felt nothing negative at all. Still, she needed to hold to the "wise course," at least to some degree. Given that, she felt the need to tell him certain things about herself before this went any further.

Noting a growing vulnerability in Elliott's eyes, she hurried to say, "Frankly, I'm blown away. I never expected this. I think a part of me had given up on ever having a man in my life."

"Why?" he asked as if the very idea were ludicrous to him.

"As a kid—and a teenager—I was labeled as 'the weird one.' I had red hair and freckles and wore glasses. We were poor and my clothes were always . . . well, embarrassing. I was very timid about any physical activity because I was very bad at it. I was the one nobody wanted on their team, and the only friends I had were kids who were considered to be weirder than I was. I have one sister who is several years older than I am, so we were practically strangers even when she still lived at home. She was married and had kids before I even got to high school. My dad was my best friend. He could always see the real me, and every day he made me feel like he genuinely cared about me. My mom was a pretty good mother, but she was busy and we just didn't connect as well. I was seventeen when my dad was killed in an accident. And that's when I started gaining weight. What little dating I had done prior to that time came to a halt. My sister lived out of state, and we barely spoke to each other. My mother became lost in her grief and had nothing to give me. My friends were introverts who were more dysfunctional than I was. In college I . . . ."

When she hesitated Elliott said, "What? You can tell me."

"It was a horrid and embarrassing experience. I've been through counseling and I've dealt with it. A couple of years ago I realized that my weight was threatening my health and I needed to do something about it. I knew instinctively that my gaining weight was tied into losing my father, and this incident in college had made it worse. So, I found a good counselor and I worked through all that stuff. I've lost a lot of weight recently, but I didn't lose it until I could accept that I was still me whether I was overweight or not. I can't guarantee that I won't gain weight again, even though my main objective is being healthy. And I'm not going to invest in any kind of serious relationship with someone who would be bothered by that. I need to be loved and respected for who I am, not how I look."

"Okay," Elliott said. "I realize you don't know me well enough to know whether or not I would be that shallow, but I wouldn't; I'm not. One of these days I'll show you my high school prom pictures."

"You still have them?"

"I do," he said proudly. "I went with the kindest, smartest girl in the school—but no one asked her to prom because she was a little overweight. We had a great time. We were friends for a long time. She's married now and lives in Oregon. We still keep in touch some. I don't know what you're worried about."

"Well, I'm not done yet," Polly said. "I really have dealt with my trust issues, and I really do feel like I can trust you, but . . . I have to tell you that in college I dated a guy. I thought he really cared about me. I was head over heels because he was great looking, popular, funny. And I couldn't believe he was interested in *me*. He took advantage of me, and then I found out that it had been a dare. *I* had been a dare."

"That's *horrible!*"

"Yes, it is. And for years I let it keep me from dating at all, and I know it was the reason why I gained more weight. Now I've dealt with that, but I still haven't dated." She shrugged. "So, back to the present. I never expected something like this to happen. A part of me wants to believe it will last longer than however many days you'll be staying in Anaconda. A part of me thinks I just need to enjoy the moment and not have any grand expectations. Then you make comments about . . . getting old together . . . and kids . . . and . . . what exactly are you implying when you say that Westley never stopped loving Buttercup? And you feel like Westley, and . . . I don't know what to make of it, Elliott. You said you would be straight with me. I want to believe that you are, but how does this make sense? We hardly know each other, and you have a life in Virginia." She chuckled at the irony. "I sound like Chas. When Chas and Jackson were . . . working it all out. Same thing. He had a life in Virginia. She knew she could never leave here."

"They made it work."

"He gave up everything to be here with her. He uprooted his life. It's very romantic and noble and it's wonderful for them. But isn't it a little idealistic to think that it would work for us, too?" She chuckled again, more in astonishment than in humor. "Listen to me. What am I saying? What are *you* saying?"

"I'm saying that when two lonely people find each other and feel this way, they ought to have the good sense to sit up and pay attention. They ought to be smart enough to do something about it, and find a way to make it work."

Polly took in his words as well his conviction and intensity. "And what might your definition be of *it?*"

Elliott sighed and eased a little closer. "From the time I was a kid, I always wanted to be an FBI agent. To me, it looked even more amazing than being an astronaut or a rock star. It's all I ever wanted, and I focused on the goal so completely that it got me through all the tough things in my life. But it also made me miss a lot that I should have probably been more involved in. I grew up in Pittsburgh. Typical inner-city kid. My dad was absent. My mom worked every minute for our survival. She died the same year

I graduated high school. All I could see was FBI; that's all I've ever been. But a few years ago, I started to wonder if maybe it wasn't really what I wanted after all. Or maybe it's more accurate to say that it was good while it lasted, but it's time for me to move on. I've been . . . restless." He shrugged. "I was already feeling that way when we thought we'd lost Leeds . . . Jackson. That whole search and rescue thing was a nightmare, but not nearly the nightmare that he endured. He doesn't know this, but *I* had to go through counseling because of what *he* suffered. I felt guilty; I thought it should have been me. No one would have missed me if I'd died; no one would have been affected if I had PTSD. And I couldn't help wondering if eventually it *would* be me. If I stay in this business long enough, will I end up dead? Or worse? All this time that Jackson has been trying to get me to come here, a part of me was scared to do it because I've looked at his life and envied it. I was afraid I *would* come here and not want to go back. But . . ." He shook his head and chuckled. "I *never* expected this. I drove into town and felt like I'd come home. I arrived at the inn and felt like I was in a dream world. Then I saw you and it was like . . . heaven." He leaned a little closer. "I don't feel like I'm being impulsive or naive here, Polly. I feel like what I've been longing for and searching for has finally shown up in my life. I would marry you tomorrow and find a way to make it work . . . if you'd have me." He drew back to a more comfortable distance. "But I'm trying to be reasonable and cautious and handle this with some maturity. So . . . there you have it." He shrugged. "That's me. That's how I feel. There's nothing more or less than this."

Polly took it all in and found it difficult not to cry. She'd never heard anything so sweet, so sensitive, so utterly honest and genuine in her whole life. "I . . . don't know what to say," she admitted.

"Just . . . tell me if there's any hope at all, or if I'm just barking up the wrong tree."

"Oh, you're definitely barking up the right tree . . . although that is a ridiculous metaphor."

"Yes. Yes, it is," he said and smiled.

"Are you saying that . . . what? You're going to retire and move here?"

"Yes, I am. Whether things work out for us or not, Polly, I knew as soon as I arrived that I needed to stay. I have nothing or no one anywhere else that really matters."

"Wow," she said and couldn't come up with another word. Her mind was spinning too fast to keep up with all she was feeling.

"So, you're speechless once again," he said. "I propose that we let all that settle in, take it one day at a time, be completely honest with each other, and . . . see what happens."

Polly smiled. "Okay, I can live with that." She scooted closer and threw her arms around his neck.

Elliott laughed and hugged her tightly before he looked into her eyes. "Now that we've talked, can I kiss you?"

"Absolutely," she said and wondered what stars had lined up to make her every dream come true—dreams that she had stopped dreaming a long time ago. It all just seemed too good to be true. But it *was* true. And she was going to make the most of every minute . . . until they were old and gray and wondering why the kids didn't come to visit.

* * * * *

Chas woke up just past five in the morning and needed to use the bathroom. Climbing back into bed, she knew she'd never be able to get back to sleep. And there wasn't much point when they had to leave for the hospital in a couple of hours and the alarm was set to go off at six so she would have time to shower. She left Jackson sleeping and decided to soak in the tub instead while she pondered what this day might bring. She'd been warned of every possible scenario, and she knew the risks. While the doctors believed that there was a good chance the baby would be strong enough to withstand the surgery, and that she would come through it safely, there were no guarantees and many unexpected things could go wrong. Chas had done her best each hour of every day to put the matter in the Lord's hands and have faith that the outcome would be according to His will. She knew and understood all of that, and she'd done her best to accept it. But the human, maternal part of her felt terrified.

The memories of losing her first baby many years ago taunted her with the belief that she could never go through that again. Of course, she *could* go through it again if she had to. And she would. But it wouldn't be easy. In fact, it would be horrible! She couldn't imagine even being able to go on, even though she knew she had so much to live for. And that was where faith came in. She had to put trust in the Lord; she had to have faith that whatever the outcome, He would carry her through. But until she might have to face the worst-case scenario, she preferred to believe that the outcome would instead be favorable in every respect.

Chas closed her eyes and focused on deep, heartfelt prayer as she prepared for what would no doubt be one of the most important days of her life. She cried a few stray tears and wiped them away, determined to put on a bright countenance and carry a positive attitude. She would give birth to a daughter today, and she imagined what it would be like when they took their little girl home.

After being awakened by the alarm, Jackson found Chas soaking in an array of bubbles, with her huge belly poking out. "The baby will get cold," he said, sitting on the edge of the tub.

"No," Chas said, rubbing her belly, "I'm keeping her very warm. Once we get to the delivery room, however, she might get cold."

"Then we can use a blanket," Jackson said and bent over to kiss her. "How are you?"

"I'm okay," she said and meant it. "And you?"

"I'm okay if you're okay," he said and kissed her again.

* * * * *

Charles was barely awake when Jackson and Chas both kissed him good-bye and left him with Melinda. The drive to the hospital was brief, and everything moved very quickly once they arrived. It seemed no time at all before Chas was being prepared for the C-section. Jackson sat next to her, holding her hand, and neither of them could see anything beyond the little curtained barrier that had been put just above Chas's belly. She was numb from the waist down, but her heart was beating fast with concern and anticipation. There was an excessive amount of medical personnel in the room, just in case the baby didn't start breathing on her own or exhibited any other immediate problems. Chas prayed silently that her daughter would come into the world strong enough to receive the life-saving surgery.

The doctor reported that everything was going smoothly, and a minute later a dark-haired baby girl emerged from the womb. Chas cried when a nurse showed the baby to her. She was beautiful and appeared normal in every way, and she had a healthy cry. Chas realized that Jackson too had tears in his eyes, and the intensity of the moment deepened her hope that all would be well. He left to go with the baby so that he could watch while the medical personnel cleaned her up and examined her. Chas closed her eyes and held the images of her daughter close while she was being stitched up and cared for.

A couple of hours later, Chas was resting in a private hospital room while Jackson sat nearby, holding the baby in the crook of his arm. Kate and her husband, Doug, arrived right on time, along with two other men from the ward. After admiring the baby and visiting quietly for a few minutes, Doug asked Jackson if he would offer a prayer, and Chas appreciated his insight in allowing her husband to have some participation in this sacred ordinance, even though he didn't yet hold the Melchizedek Priesthood. After Jackson offered a beautiful prayer, Doug and the other men gently took the baby and gave her a name and a blessing. Chas held Jackson's hand tightly and cried silent tears as Isabelle Rose Leeds was promised that she would live a good life on this earth and bring joy to all who knew her. Chas had to consider that it didn't say a *long* life, but a *good* one. Still, she felt hope and comfort and was determined to expect the best.

Less than an hour after the blessing, the doctors took Isabelle to the children's hospital next door to begin her surgery. Chas was able to sleep due to the pain medication she'd been given, but Jackson could only try to occupy his time while he waited and prayed. He called Melinda to give her a full report, then he called Chas's grandfather, who had made them promise to keep him up to date. He was excited to have another great-grandchild and expressed perfect optimism that all would be well. Jackson then called Polly to give her the news of the baby's birth and to tell her that everything was okay so far. She was thrilled and told him to give Chas her love when she woke up. He was glad to hear her report that all was calm and quiet at the inn, and she promised to pass the update along to Veese.

"Elliott," she corrected. "His name is Elliott. You two really should be on a first-name basis, don't you think?"

"I'll work on it," he promised.

* * * * *

Chas came awake feeling an unnatural grogginess, and it took her a moment to orient herself to being in a hospital room. The pain quickly reminded her that she had given birth. Jackson's hand in hers reminded her that she was not alone.

"Hey," he said gently, and she heard him scoot a chair closer to the bed. She felt his hand on her face, gently pushing back her hair. "How are you feeling?"

"Sore," she said, her mouth dry. "Drugged." The complete realization of the situation finally settled into her clouded brain and she opened her eyes fully to look at her husband. "Have you heard anything? Is she—"

"She's fine so far," Jackson said. "A nurse came just a while ago with an update. She said the surgeon had now been able to get a good look at the heart, and he believes it's repairable."

Chas let out a soft moan. The idea of the heart being repairable gave her great hope; the thought of her infant daughter on an operating table with her heart exposed brought anguish.

"But it is going to be tricky, she said, and it's going to take some time. She told us she'd be back as often as possible to keep us up-to-date."

Chas let that sink in. "Okay," she said and gripped her husband's hand more tightly. But she couldn't hold tears back as she added, "I guess all we can do is wait." In her mind she saw a flashback to the day she'd given birth to a little girl soon after Martin's death, and how alone she had felt when she'd been given the news that the baby wasn't going to survive more than a day or two. Chas's grandmother had been the only person in her life at the time. She'd had no friends; no one else. Granny had been there through the birth, and she stayed with Chas as much as she could, but Martin's absence had been indescribably painful. Chas looked deeper at her husband and brought his hand to her lips. "I love you, Jackson."

"I love you too," he said, kissing her brow. "We're in this together," he added, as if he'd read her mind.

Chas tried to distract herself from images of her baby undergoing major surgery and realized she was thirsty and a little nauseous. Jackson got her something to drink, and he called for a nurse who checked all of Chas's vital signs, gave her some medication for the nausea, and got her a little something to eat that was appropriate following her recent surgery. When the nurse offered another pain pill, Chas insisted that she didn't want to sleep until her daughter's surgery was over. The nurse assured her this was a more mild medication, and even if she drifted off a little, she could easily come awake for any news when the surgery liaison returned. Weighing the pain against her concerns for her baby, Chas took the pill and tried to relax. She lay there for a long while, keenly aware of Jackson flipping through magazines that held no interest for him, then flipping through TV channels that held even less fascination. He finally settled on a history program about the American Revolution.

Chas watched Jackson while he was watching TV. She loved the deep patriotism in his spirit, and she felt warm inside to think of going with him to Washington, DC—most specifically to visit the temple—where their lives would be changed forever. She prayed that they would be taking Isabelle with them, and not need to have her sealed by proxy.

Chas drifted off to sleep while Jackson was distracted by the TV. She woke up when he nudged her. The TV went off, and she opened her eyes to see a kind-faced nurse in the room, holding a large clipboard.

"Hi, I'm Mandy," she said, looking directly at Chas. "I spoke to your husband earlier. Little Isabelle is coming along fine." Chas was glad just to hear her name and to think of her as a real person. "As I said before, the surgery is complicated and requires some time, but it's going along as well as it possibly could."

"Oh, that's good news!" Chas said.

"Yes, it is," Mandy replied. She then sat on the edge of Chas's bed and told them in a straightforward, comfortable way exactly what the problem was with the baby's heart, and what the surgeon was doing to repair it.

While some of the medical details went over Chas's head, it was nice to know what was happening and why. Again she thought of her first baby, who had died from this problem, and she wondered if it was the very same thing that had given her mother a weak heart.

Mandy asked if they had any questions and promised to return with an update at the earliest possibility.

"She's so kind," Chas said after Mandy had left.

"Yes, everyone has been very kind," Jackson said. He kissed Chas's hand. "We're very blessed."

"Yes, we are," she agreed heartily.

"Chas," he said gently, "there's something I have to say. I'm just going to say it and get it over with so we can move on."

"Okay," she said, turning her head on the pillow to look at him more directly.

"It's nothing new. I just have to say it. We have every reason to believe that Isabelle is going to come through fine, and everything will be all right. But we were informed of the risks, and nothing is certain. I know we have to be positive, but . . . I guess there's just something in me that needs to . . . well, it's like when I told you that I need to hope for the best but be prepared for the worst. I guess I just have to prepare myself for the worst so I can set those thoughts aside and focus on the hope. Does that make sense?"

"Yes," she said.

Jackson glanced down and took a deep breath before he looked her in the eye. "If she doesn't make it . . ." His voice cracked. "If . . . something goes wrong . . . it's going to be hard. It's going to be really hard . . . for both of us." Tears trickled down Chas's face, and moisture glistened in Jackson's eyes. "But we're going to face it together, and with faith, and we're going to move on and have a good life. We'll try again. We'll keep trying until you're just not able to have babies anymore. We'll have a beautiful family no matter what."

Chas nodded, and Jackson went on.

"I just need to say that . . . I learned through all that PTSD counseling that . . . we need to grieve; we need to cry and scream if we have to. We need to talk about it and not let it come between us. I'm saying that more for me than you. I'm the one who has trouble talking about things. That's why I have to say this now. I have to clear the air. No matter what happens, we're going to make it, Chas. You hear me?"

Chas nodded again, then lifted her arms. He stood and leaned over her and they shared a long, tight embrace. "I love you," she said again.

"I love you too," he murmured and kissed her. Then he sat beside her and prayed aloud with her—again—that all would be well.

An hour later Mandy returned to report that the surgeon had been faced with a small setback with some kind of bleeding that he'd had trouble stopping. An hour after that she returned to say that Isabelle's blood pressure had dropped dangerously low but they'd gotten it under control. After that it was much longer than an hour before Mandy appeared. Jackson was pacing the room. Chas could only stare toward the window and pray that hoping for the best would not be in vain.

When Mandy finally appeared, Jackson hurried to Chas's side to take her hand, but he remained on his feet. They squeezed each other's hands tightly and both held their breath. Then Mandy smiled and said, "She's out of surgery. Everything's fine."

Jackson and Chas both laughed with relief and shared a tight hug before Mandy added, "Of course, this recovery period can be crucial and she's not out of the woods yet, but the worst is behind us."

"Thank you," Jackson said.

"The surgeon will come to talk to you a little later, and a nurse from the newborn intensive care unit will be coming to talk to you."

When Mandy left, Jackson and Chas prayed together, thanking their Father in Heaven for the success of this surgery, and asking that Isabelle would continue to improve and be able to go home with them when the time came.

The surgeon came in just a few minutes later and explained in more detail what Mandy had already told them. He felt very good about the results, but cautioned them that with newborns, the unpredictability factor in recovery was still high. A few hours later, Jackson helped Chas into a wheelchair and pushed her to the connecting children's hospital where they were able to sit in the same room with Isabelle. Chas cried when she saw her infant daughter hooked up to so many apparatuses, but her tears were more of joy and relief rather than sorrow. They had come this far, and she had good reason to believe that all would be well with time.

Throughout the next few days, Chas did her best to follow the advice of the nurses caring for her and focus on recovering from her own surgery. She couldn't hold the baby yet, but she was stable and doing as well as could be expected. When Chas's milk came in, she was able to pump it, and the nurses made certain it was properly labeled and stored so that it could be given to Isabelle until the time when Chas could nurse her.

When the doctors determined that Chas was healthy enough to leave the hospital, it was a difficult transition. During her hospital stay, she had been grateful to have Jackson push her in a wheelchair through the long walkway between the two hospitals so that she could sit with her daughter. Now she had to achieve a balance between getting the rest she needed back at the apartment, and being at the hospital as much as she could manage. She and Jackson started taking turns staying with the baby, and Melinda helped by dropping them off at the hospital so that they wouldn't have to park and walk long distances. Chas found that she was feeling quite well and able to get around, albeit slowly. Jackson and Melinda took very good care of her, and she was grateful to have little Charles there with them. Not only would she have missed him terribly, but she would have been continually worried, knowing that the inn had become a possible target for the mob. She prayed hourly that her home and all who were there would be protected. Then she put her focus on taking care of herself and watching over her daughter.

It was a sweet moment when Chas could finally hold Isabelle and nurse her. Melinda was then able to come and meet her new little niece, and Chas couldn't recall ever seeing her so happy. Now that the baby could be held, they took turns spending time with her so that she could get the positive bonding that was so important for infants. Chas spent every possible minute in the NICU nursery, allowing Jackson and Melinda to give her breaks when she needed them, and she always went back to the apartment to get a good night's sleep.

When Isabelle was ten days old, she developed some symptoms that caused alarm for her doctors, and even more so for her parents. It was a long, grueling day filled with many prayers and a great deal of pacing. But the very next day the baby was doing better again, and the doctors declared that she had definitely gotten past the worst of it and she would likely be fine. Their prayers had been answered! Chas began to think more about what it would be like to take her little daughter home and put her in the crib that they'd set up in the master bedroom prior to their departure. It was an image she clung to every hour, simultaneously praying that her home would remain safe, and that all would be well.

CHAPTER 9

Jackson came awake abruptly, heart pounding. The sensation reminded him of coming out of a nightmare, but he didn't recall dreaming. His next inclination was to think that a strange sound had alerted his sense of danger. He listened and tried to gauge his instincts. Nothing. Then he heard a voice, but not with his ears. He heard it inside his mind, but it wasn't a voice so much as an impression that clearly stated with gentle force, *Go home now.*

He didn't question the impression or stop to ponder the reality that *he* had been given such obvious divine guidance. He just got out of bed, grabbed his bathrobe, and hurried into the front room where he could use the phone and the Internet without disturbing Chas. In less than half an hour he had made arrangements for a flight, a taxi to the airport, and a rental car waiting at the other end. He paid extra for a rush on the car so that he wouldn't have to wait for it once he got there. He quietly got dressed, realizing he didn't need to pack anything, since he was going home. With a few minutes to kill, he opened the scriptures to read, but his mind starting working now that he'd done all he could do for the moment.

Why did he need to go home? Were people there in danger? It seemed a reasonable assumption. And apparently Veese wasn't going to be able to take care of it on his own. He started to feel afraid, imagining all of the things that could possibly go wrong, then he reminded himself that he'd been awakened and prompted by the Holy Spirit. God would surely not be guiding him so specifically, only to have him arrive too late to prevent something horrible from happening in spite of his efforts to heed the prompting quickly and without question. He thought of calling Veese now, but felt that it was better to wait. He just needed to hurry home.

Five minutes before his taxi was due to arrive, he sat on the edge of the bed and woke Chas with a kiss and gentle nudging. He thought of little Isabelle and felt grateful that she was doing so well; he would have found it especially difficult to leave otherwise.

"Is something wrong?" she asked, opening her eyes enough to realize that he was dressed.

"I'm flying home," he said. "A taxi will be here in a minute to take me to the airport."

"What's happened?" she asked, sitting up.

"Nothing . . . yet, that I know of. The Spirit woke me up, Chas. All I know is that I need to go home, so I made the arrangements and I'm going. I know it sounds ridiculous, but you mustn't worry."

"Yes, that sounds ridiculous."

He told her his own thoughts of reassurance. "God wouldn't wake me up and send me there just to arrive too late, nor would He let something terrible happen that I can't help or prevent."

"Okay." Chas took a deep breath. "That makes sense."

"So, we both need to trust in Him and do our best not to be afraid. I will call you as soon as I have something to tell you. I promise. You get your rest and take care of our family." She nodded, and tears rose in her eyes before she wrapped her arms around him. "It's going to be okay," he said. She nodded against his shoulder.

"I love you," she said, looking into his eyes. "You be careful."

"I love you too," he said and kissed her. "It's going to be okay."

Chas took a hard look at her husband. She knew he had good and trustworthy instincts, and when she combined that knowledge with the evidence that he was acting boldly on a spiritual prompting, she had no reason not to believe him. But she still clung to him tightly until he had to go. He kissed her once more, and she followed him to the door, locking it behind him. She watched from the window as he got into a taxi and rode away. Then she sat down and cried, praying that he would be safe, that their home and loved ones in Montana would be safe, and that all would be well here with the women and children during Jackson's absence. She prayed especially for little Isabelle, just as she did every hour of every day. She wanted more than anything to take her baby home . . . to a home that was safe and secure.

Now that she was wide awake, Chas knew she'd never be able to go back to sleep. Instead she studied the scriptures and prayed for her husband, her home, and all who were there.

* * * * *

Elliott didn't sleep at all while he contended with the feeling that something wasn't right; he was convinced that if anything was going to go down, it would be soon. Cortney had seemed especially on edge throughout the evening, and he'd spoken with the man currently acting as his backup, staking out the inn from a discreet distance across the street.

A few minutes after five, Elliott knew he heard something downstairs. Glass breaking. He radioed the other agent for a report and got no response. That was *not* a good sign. Gun poised, he went carefully and quietly down the stairs, his senses alert and his instincts screaming. A series of subtle night lights in the electrical outlets offered enough light for him to see, hopefully without being seen. He peered with caution around every corner before he proceeded, wondering if Bobby Dinubilo might have actually broken into the inn. Was he smart enough to have figured out there was an agent watching the place? Had he done something to him? Elliott's pounding heart raced faster. He found the source of the broken glass. The bathroom just off the hall on the main floor had a broken window. It had been broken, then opened, and the opening was certainly large enough for a man to squeeze through.

Hearing a sound, Elliott pressed his back against the wall in the hallway, looking cautiously one direction, then the other. He saw nothing, and only had a split-second awareness of being hit over the back of the head before everything went black. And in that split second, he thought of Polly.

* * * * *

Polly woke up with thoughts of Elliott, and she found herself humming while she showered and got ready for the day. She mentally tallied the things she had to do this morning, and antici-pated having breakfast with Elliott and Mr. Tarasov. She'd grown so attached to both of them that she didn't want either of them to ever leave. Her mind drifted for a moment to Cortney, and Polly just wished she would leave and take her problems with her. She thought of the horrid Mr. and Mrs. Glass, who were always arguing when they were around—and they managed to be around far too much. She could only hope that they would keep to them-selves and soon be on their way.

Before Polly got to the bottom of the stairs, she knew some-thing wasn't right. She paused and took in her surroundings, wondering what felt wrong. All of the draperies in the parlor were closed. The sheers were always left closed, but the draperies were *always* open. Enough daylight crept through for her to see, but it just didn't feel right. She wondered if a guest had been in the parlor late and had closed them.

Crossing the parlor with the intention of opening the drapes, Polly saw something on the floor behind the couch. It only took her a moment to realize it was a man. She gasped and took a step closer. *Elliott.* In a split second she took in the fact that his hands and feet were tied. There was duct tape over his mouth, and blood on his head. He looked dead! In that same second she understood what this meant. Her protector was no longer in a position to protect anyone or anything, and whoever had done this could still be in the house. For the tiniest moment her concern for Elliott, coupled with her growing feelings for him, cracked her heart in two. But her every nerve snapped with perfect fear when she heard a noise and turned abruptly. She gasped again to see Bridget Glass on a chair in the corner. Her hands and feet were tied, and her mouth was taped shut. But she was very much awake and alive, and her eyes were wide with terror. Polly had barely grasped what seemed to be a silent warning in the woman's expression when she heard a male voice say, "We've been waiting for you . . . Ms. Innkeeper."

Polly turned to see a man come out of the corner—holding a gun. He was tall and broad-shouldered and unusually handsome, in an evil kind of way. His entire countenance reeked of evil. He held the gun casually, as if it were just a trinket, but the threat of his ability and willingness to use it showed in his eyes.

Polly instinctively believed that this would go better for her if she displayed more confidence than fear. She swallowed her fear and forced a casual voice that sounded surprisingly convincing. "You must be Cortney's boyfriend."

He smiled. "Then you've been expecting me."

"Something like that," she said. "So get her and go. There's no reason for this kind of drama."

"The drama wasn't my idea. Your distinguished guest, Mr. Nuccitelli, has got her locked in one of your rooms upstairs. But now that I've got some leverage, he and I just need to have a little chat . . . and make an exchange."

"We have no one here by that name," Polly insisted.

"Whoever he's pretending to be, he's got Cortney, and I'm not leaving without her. So, you are going to help me."

"What do you want me to do?" Polly asked, sounding more angry than scared. Anger was easier to manage at the moment. And she was willing to do just about anything to get him to leave. She wondered if Elliott was dead or just unconscious. She wondered if anybody else was going to get hurt or die before this was over. Even with her knowledge that something strange was brewing here at the inn, she never would have imagined herself being part of a hostage situation.

"*We* are going to find the keys that you have apparently hidden very well, because they are *not* in the office, and then we are going to go unlock that door. And I'll be on my way with Cortney in no time."

"Then let's do it," she said, knowing those keys were in a drawer in her room upstairs. She started toward the stairs with the gun-toting boyfriend right behind her. She stopped and looked up to see Mr. Glass, a.k.a Mr. Nuccitelli, standing on the stairs, holding a gun to Cortney's head.

Again Polly tried not to show her fear, but her pounding heart had convinced her that this was not going to end well. The boyfriend grabbed her arm and pushed her toward the parlor, without taking his eyes off his opponent on the stairs. He pointed the gun at Polly, saying, "Don't move." He shifted his aim toward Mrs. Glass-slash-Nuccitelli and said snidely to his opponent, "I've got something you want, and you've got something I want. We trade. We go our separate ways. Life is good."

Mr. Nuccitelli let out a caustic chuckle. "That would entirely defeat the purpose, now wouldn't it, Bobby?" He moved down the stairs with Cortney tightly in his grasp. Polly could hear Cortney's harsh breathing and see her terror—a sentiment she shared perfectly.

"You see," Mr. Nuccitelli said, pressing the gun more tightly to Cortney's head, which resulted in a harsh whimper, "I know the truth about what happened that night." Polly saw fright flicker briefly in Bobby's eyes, while Cortney's widened with terrible fear. "I was there. I saw it all for myself. I'm the only person who knows beyond any doubt that your sweet Cortney here is guilty of perjury in the biggest way. She lied under oath and put your brother away instead of you. I know you don't like your brother, Bobby, but sending him to prison on your behalf was pretty low, even in our line of work." His voice lowered and took on a gravelly, sinister quality. "I know for a fact that it was *you* who pulled the trigger, *you* who killed my brother. And don't think for a moment that I'm going to let that go."

Polly sucked in her breath as the picture became very clear. She only wished she knew who was going to pull the trigger first. In an unexpected move, Mr. Nuccitelli pointed his gun at Bobby, and Cortney rushed toward her boyfriend, as if she could save him. While Polly was trying to absorb that Cortney was stupid enough to put herself in the possible line of fire, she concluded that the woman surely had some kind of brain damage. And she had a very poor sense of judgment when it came to men. But worst of all, Cortney's stupidity had created a situation that was *not* going to end well for any of them.

* * * * *

During every minute of the flight and the drive from the airport, Jackson had to remind himself that if he'd needed to get there sooner, God would have awakened him earlier. He tried to tell himself that he would return home to find everything completely under control. But that wouldn't explain the strong admonition he'd received in the middle of the night. Once he was in Montana, he tried more than once to call Veese, but it went straight to voice mail. He also tried to call the inn, but it just rang and rang without even going to the answering machine. That was the part that really made him nervous. It was rare when someone didn't answer the phone, because their policy was to have the person in charge carry a cordless phone everywhere. If Polly had been indisposed at the moment, she would have checked the caller ID and called right back. But she didn't.

When he finally arrived at the inn, he drove past it at a normal speed to get a glance without arousing suspicions. He prayed for guidance, and in that moment he knew undoubtedly that he'd been getting such guidance all through his career. What he had always referred to as his gut instinct was surely God aiding him in his efforts to protect good people and bring a little justice to the world. Now, his home and people he cared for were at stake.

His heart rate increased when he saw that all of the drapes and curtains were pulled shut, and the Closed sign was on the front door. It was put out only for a very few holidays when they closed down completely. Jackson cursed benignly under his breath and discreetly made a U-turn while he pressed a speed-dial number on his phone. He gave a thirty-second report and hung up as he pulled the car into the parking lot of the inn and hoped the closed drapes would work to his advantage.

Jackson parked near the garage and made certain not to make any noise as he got out and left the car door unlatched. He thought back to the feeling he'd had before leaving here that he should hide his gun in the garage. He'd been thinking that he hadn't wanted it in the house if anything weird went down. Now he was glad to have access to it so he could go inside already armed. He quickly found the gun and the clip and crept carefully out the back side of the garage and to the back door of the inn. He gently tried the knob, not surprised to find it locked—even though it *never* should have been locked at this time of day. Since he had the key, it was easy enough to get the door unlocked, but nevertheless he felt nervous as he pushed it open as slowly as he could manage.

He had no idea whether anyone was positioned so they could see the door coming open. It was one of those moments when he knew that if just one little thing went wrong, it could cost him his life. He didn't feel as afraid as he might have, simply because he didn't believe God would have brought him here now only to have him unable to make a difference. But he also felt a deep gratitude that this kind of thing was no longer a part of his daily life. Now that he had a family, he didn't know if he could have done it.

Safely inside the door, Jackson heard a male voice speaking in threatening tones, but he couldn't make out the words. He'd only taken two quiet steps when he heard two shots fired, muffled by a silencer. *Too late?* his mind screamed. *How could I be too late?* He moved a few more steps until he had a perfect view of Harry Nuccitelli holding the gun. Bobby Dinubilo and Cortney were both on the floor, apparently dead. It was far from the first time that Jackson had seen such a sight, but it never got any easier. His shattered hopes for Cortney tightened his heart, but he shoved emotion away. He could deal with such things later. His instincts told him the danger wasn't over and his next move was crucial. He hesitated and saw Harry move his aim toward the parlor, but Jackson couldn't see who was there. He wondered where Veese was. And Polly. Were there guests here? Mr. Tarasov? And where was Harry Nuccitelli's wife? Focusing on what he *did* know, Jackson aimed his gun at Harry's head, glad to know his presence hadn't been detected.

"You know I can't let you live," Harry said.

Jackson didn't know who had just witnessed what had happened, but he knew he had less time than it would take for Harry to pull the trigger to stop something worse from happening. He took two steps and pressed the gun to the back of Harry's head. "That's exactly what I was going to say to you," Jackson said, and Harry let out a startled gasp. "Drop the gun . . . or I'll blow you to kingdom come." Harry responded immediately by dropping the gun and raising both hands in the air.

Polly nearly fainted when she saw Jackson come out of nowhere to save her life without a second to spare. Her knees went weak, and she wilted onto the floor, sitting there as if it might swallow her.

Jackson took a quick glance toward the parlor and realized he'd just saved Polly's life. Heat burned into his throat and eyes. *Not too late, after all.* He would be grateful to save *any* person's life. But Polly was like family. He'd prayed hundreds of times that his home and loved ones would stay safe through all of this. The results were not as ideal as he might have hoped. But Polly was okay, and it was over. He wondered where Veese was, but stayed focused on this moment.

"Get on your knees, very slowly," Jackson said to Harry. "You move too fast or try anything and you'll be dead before you can take another breath." Jackson took a step forward and slid the gun across the floor with his foot. "Okay, down on the floor," Jackson said. Harry hesitated, and Jackson shouted, "Now! Face down! Do it! Hands behind your head!"

Harry did as he was told and Jackson put a foot on his back, both to let Harry know he was there and to be able to take his eyes off the man, yet be instantly aware if he tried to move. He glanced around and made a quick assessment. His years of experience in handling such things professionally served him well by enabling him to keep calm.

Bobby and Cortney were both clearly dead. No emergency there. Polly looked okay. He realized then that a woman was tied to a chair on the far side of the parlor. He guessed that it was likely Bridget Nuccitelli. But she was apparently alive and well.

Jackson looked hard at Polly and asked, "Where's Veese?"

Polly gasped and jumped to her feet. "I think he's dead," she said hoarsely and rushed to the other side of the couch.

Jackson's eyes followed, seeing only Veese's feet, but he definitely saw movement. He felt some relief as he said, "If he was dead, why would they have tied him up?" He knew Veese would have remained still even if he'd been conscious in order to keep any attention away from himself—attention that might tempt someone to shoot him.

At the sound of Jackson's voice, Veese rolled over and groaned. Polly knelt beside him and sobbed with relief as she pulled the tape from over his mouth and kissed him, glad that Jackson couldn't see them. This was not how she'd imagined letting her friends know that she'd fallen in love.

Jackson kept his gun pointed at Harry's head while he pulled his cell phone off his belt with the other hand and pushed the same number on speed dial. "It's under control," he said into the phone, "but I could still use some help. Please don't break the doors down. The back one is open." He put the phone back, and five seconds later the back door came open and local police officers filed in, poised for possible action. Jackson reported systematically what he knew of the situation. With Harry in handcuffs and officers helping Bridget Nuccitelli, Jackson joined Veese and Polly behind the couch. Suddenly feeling a little weak, he sat on the floor facing Veese, who was rubbing his sore wrists while Polly pressed a towel to the back of his head, wincing at the sight of his blood.

Veese took the towel from Polly and said to Jackson, *"What* are you doing here?"

Jackson chuckled and shook his head. "You wouldn't believe me if I told you."

"Try me," Veese said.

Jackson glanced over his shoulder at the commotion still taking place and the bodies on the floor. "Later," he said.

Polly moved on her knees to face Jackson and threw her arms around his neck. "You saved my life," she muttered, then cried like a child. He put his arms around her and got a little teary himself. He was looking forward to telling her that he couldn't take the credit for that. He'd done nothing but follow orders to the best of his ability. He'd learned the principle in the Marines, he'd lived it in the FBI, and he'd come to fully understand it through his newfound relationship with God.

"I can tell you why now, boss," Veese said.

"Why what?"

"Why Nuccitelli was so determined to face off with Bobby Dinubilo."

"Why?" Jackson asked.

It was Polly who answered. "It was *Bobby* who killed Harry's brother, not Reggie. Cortney lied to protect her boyfriend. She put away his brother instead because they didn't like him. Harry saw it all. He knew the truth."

"Unbelievable," Jackson muttered. He'd known Cortney was stupid. But perjury? He couldn't believe it!

Jackson heard a door close somewhere upstairs and looked to Polly in panic. "We have guests?" He felt sick at the thought of any innocent bystanders on vacation having been involved in this to any degree.

"Just Mr. Tarasov," Polly said, wiping at her tears. "Michelle has the day off."

Jackson jumped to his feet and hurried toward the stairs, coming face-to-face with Artem the moment his eyes took in the police officers in the room and the bodies on the floor. *"God be merciful,"* he muttered in Russian. Jackson stepped closer to him to block his view, and the old man's eyes connected with Jackson's. "What happen here?" he asked.

"It's a long story," Jackson said and took his arm, guiding him to the kitchen, away from the ugly scene and the chaos surrounding it. "Are you all right?" he asked, urging him to a chair.

"Yes, yes," Artem said, but he looked a little pallid. "I slept over," he said, and Jackson knew he meant that he'd overslept.

"That's probably good," Jackson said. "As you can see we had a horrible incident here this morning, but everything's all right now."

Artem's eyes looked distant and confused, then he focused intensely on Jackson. "Cortney?"

Jackson nodded. "I'm afraid she had some unfavorable involvement with some very bad people. We tried very hard to help her, but she made some bad choices, and . . ." Jackson couldn't finish, but Artem nodded as if he understood.

"She angry girl; very angry."

"Yes, I believe she was," Jackson said.

Artem asked if everyone else was okay, and he put his hand over Jackson's on the table as he inquired over Chas and both of their babies. He'd been asking Polly every day for the latest reports, but he was glad to hear from Jackson that all was going well, even though the baby wasn't completely out of the woods yet.

"Let's get you something to eat," Jackson said, welcoming the distraction of needing to take care of a guest. Artem insisted that he didn't need to make any fuss, but within a few minutes Jackson had gotten him a cup of coffee, some toast and jam, and one of the lovely bowls of fresh fruit that Polly had left in the refrigerator. He left Artem with instructions to avoid the scene in the hall. Artem thanked him and wished him well.

Jackson returned to the scene of the crime and was relieved to see that the coroner had arrived and the bodies had at least been covered. While Veese looked after Polly and Bridget, Jackson communicated with all of the right people, both there at the inn and over the phone, to see that everything was taken care of. He discovered that the phone line coming into the inn had been cut, and he wondered which of the idiots involved in this mess had done that. He made calls from his cell phone, one of them being to get a repairman there as quickly as possible. Going into the bathroom just off the dining room, Jackson found a broken window and knew this was how Bobby Dinubilo had probably gotten into the house. He called someone to come and fix that as well. And he swept up the glass.

The FBI would be taking over the case and working in cooperation with the local police, who were now interviewing the hostage victims, who were also witnesses. Polly and Bridget both looked a little shell-shocked, but otherwise fine. Veese just looked like he had a headache. Paramedics came to check on the injured and found that Bridget had only some minor abrasions from being tied up, and the bump on Veese's head was also a relatively minor injury. The backup agent that had been in a car across the street had also been knocked unconscious; the paramedics also brought him into the inn and examined him while he was being questioned.

Once Jackson had done everything he could, including giving his own official statement to the police, he just hovered on the perimeter of everything going on, trying to take in the surreal evidence that his home was a crime scene. He was *so* grateful that Chas wasn't here, for more reasons than he could count.

Watching as the bodies were removed, Jackson couldn't feel any regret for Bobby Dinubilo being dead. He had surely been responsible for multiple deaths during his career in violent crime. And catching Harry Nuccitelli with the gun in his hand would guarantee he would be put away—something the FBI had been trying to do for years. But Jackson felt a good deal of regret over losing Cortney. This was not how he'd expected this to end. He'd imagined her learning a harsh lesson and finding a fresh start elsewhere. This just didn't seem right. In spite of her horrible choices and her stubborn obsession with her stupid delusions, she didn't deserve this. And how was he ever going to tell Chas about the horror that had taken place in her home? The very thought of that conversation made him sick to his stomach. But the people they loved were alive and well. He had to maintain perspective and be grateful for that.

Recalling the moment he'd realized that a few seconds delay could have cost Polly her life, he found it difficult to hold back hot tears. He *had* been guided; they *had* been greatly blessed. Given his absolute knowledge that the matter had been in God's hands, he had to conclude that Cortney's death had been a part of the plan. Considering the position she'd put herself in, right in the middle of the families Nuccitelli and Dinubilo—and her blatant refusal to protect herself—he couldn't help wondering if she would have met a violent end regardless of whether it had happened here, today. If she'd gotten away from here with Bobby, would the Nuccitelli family have tracked them? Yes. He knew they would have. It was all very ugly and sorrowful, but he'd seen a lot of that kind of thing in his life. It had simply never hit quite so close to home.

Jackson kept a close eye on Bridget, waiting for the right moment to talk to her. When the officer had finished getting her statement, she was left sitting on the couch, looking disoriented and weary. Jackson approached and asked, "May I sit down?"

"Of course," she said, and he took the place where the officer had been sitting. "I don't know who you are, but you saved our lives."

"My wife and I own this place," he said, and her eyes showed enlightenment.

"I thought . . . you were in Utah; your baby is in the hospital . . . or something."

"That's right. But I felt like I should come back."

"I'm so glad you did." She looked confused. "How did you know how to . . ." She didn't finish.

"I'm retired FBI," he said, and she nodded. "You don't really think your husband would have killed you, do you?" She looked confused, and he added, "You said 'saved *our* lives.' You don't really think that—"

"Yes, actually, I believe he would have. I've been wanting to divorce him for years, but it's not an easy family to get out of." She fought for composure. "He manipulated me into coming here and going along with this madness; perhaps *threatened* is a more appropriate word." She looked alarmed. "Am I going to have to testify against him?"

"No, of course not. You're his wife, for one thing, but it won't even go to trial. He was caught with the gun in his hand. If anyone has to testify, it will be me and Agent Veese."

"Who?"

Jackson pointed at Elliott and added, "He's FBI."

"So, you knew something was going on."

"Yeah, we knew."

"He had no idea the feds were on to him."

"Well, now he's going away."

"Will it be for life?" she asked with hope.

"I wish I could say it would. With the way deals get cut in the legal system, I honestly don't know. If we could pin more on him besides what he just did . . ."

"Maybe I could help you with that," she said eagerly, then she checked herself. "But I can't put myself at risk . . . for my children's sake. I would have left a long time ago if not for them. I need to be safe and keep them safe."

"I understand," he said. "You think about it, and if there's anything you might feel comfortable telling us, you can talk to Agent Veese. I can assure you that no one but he and I will ever know the source, and we can come up with a viable story of where we got the information that will take suspicion away from you."

She nodded, and he had to hope that she could give them something that would guarantee putting Harry Nuccitelli behind bars for life.

"Are you leaving?" she asked.

"I need to go back before the end of the day, as soon as I can get a flight."

"Is it all right if I stay here for . . . I don't know . . . a few days, maybe? I think I need some time before I go back and face the family."

"You're welcome to stay as long as you like. Polly will take good care of you." She nodded again and Jackson asked, "Are you going to be okay?" She replied in the affirmative, but he felt the need to be more specific. "What I need to know is . . . whether you have any reason at all to believe that you are in danger; any reason at all."

"No," she said firmly. "Harry's father is actually very fond of me; he looks out for me. Since this is not just a matter of my word against Harry's, I'll be fine. They'll take care of us."

"Okay," he said. "You stay here as long as you need to, and let Veese or Polly know if you need anything at all, or have any concerns. Veese will give you his contact information in case you ever need to get in touch with him."

"Thank you," she said, fighting tears. "Thank you for every-thing."

"I'm glad it turned out okay," he said and stood, urging her to do the same. "Why don't you go upstairs and get some rest. I'll bring up something for you to eat in a little while."

"Oh, you don't have to do that. I know where to find food if I'm hungry . . . which I'm not at the moment. Thank you again," she said and went up the stairs. He hoped she would be all right.

Jackson turned around and saw Veese standing close by, waiting to talk to him. Judging from his expression, Jackson knew what he was going to say even before he said, "I'm sorry, boss. I let you down."

"No, you did not let me down."

"You don't even know what happened yet, because I know you weren't around when I was giving my statement."

"I've got a pretty good idea," he said. "But you're going to tell me anyway."

"I heard a window break and came to investigate. It was dark and I was quiet, but he still got behind me and knocked me out. When I came to, I could hear Bobby talking to Polly. I was sure he was gonna . . ." He paused to gather his composure in a way that Jackson had only seen once before in him, and that was when they'd lost a fellow agent in a shooting that had gone bad. He cleared his throat and shook his head. "I think we'd all be dead if you hadn't come."

"Then it's a good thing I came."

"But if you hadn't . . ."

"I did. It's done. Let's just . . . deal with the fallout, okay?"

Veese nodded, and they both defaulted to their training in dealing with problems and not letting emotions get in the way. But it was easier said than done when the problems were at your own door.

Jackson noticed that Polly was now sitting alone on the couch. Veese noticed at the same time and said, "I think she needs to talk to you. She's a lot more upset than she's letting on."

"Yeah, I can see that." He patted Veese on the shoulder. "Thank you."

Jackson sat down next to Polly and put his arm around her. "You okay?" he asked.

"No, I'm not okay," she said and started to cry. She cried so hard that he was afraid she'd hyperventilate. They were both oblivious to the officers still working nearby in the hall, but Jackson noticed Veese hovering at a safe distance, biting his lip with concern. Jackson took hold of Polly's shoulders and coached her into breathing deeply so that she could calm down enough to speak. "I'm sorry," she said. "I just . . ."

"There's nothing to apologize for," he said. "I'm sorry that I put you in this position."

"This is not your fault. *You* saved my life."

"I likely could have made some better choices somewhere along the way that could have prevented this."

"Not necessarily," she said, but he wanted to get the conversation back to *her* issues over this. "You have every right to be upset, Polly."

She nodded, and her chin quivered. "I saw them die, Jackson. One second . . . they were standing there, and the next . . ." She couldn't finish.

"I know," he said. "It's a horrible feeling."

"And I thought he was going to kill me. I really thought he would. He would have if you hadn't come. He would have, wouldn't he?"

"Yes, I believe he would have."

She groaned and pressed her face to his shoulder. Jackson felt helpless and increasingly nauseous. He was relieved beyond words when Veese approached and said to Polly, "Hey, girl. Let's get some fresh air for a few minutes."

"Okay," Polly said eagerly and took his hand. They went out the back door, in the opposite direction from the blood on the floor.

CHAPTER 10

Jackson impulsively made another phone call and was amazed to get straight through to someone who was usually too busy to answer his phone.

"Callahan," he said. "It's Jackson Leeds."

"Jackson?" he answered with pleasant surprise. "How are you? Having a relapse?"

"Not yet," he said, glad to feel completely comfortable with this man who had guided him through his PTSD. Ross Callahan was a great psychotherapist and had become somewhat of a friend through the traumatic experiences they'd shared as he'd coached Jackson to a place of healing not so many months ago. "But I do need your help. Do you do emergency house calls?"

"I might," he said gravely. "What's up?"

"There was a shooting at my inn this morning. Two people died."

"No kidding?" Callahan said. Jackson gave him a three-minute explanation, concluding with, "I've got two women here who were held hostage and nearly died. I've got to get back to Salt Lake City to be with my wife and—"

"What's she doing there?" he asked.

Jackson gave him a one-minute explanation about the baby. Callahan offered his congratulations on the birth and his best wishes on Isabelle's recovery. Then he said, "I can be there in a couple of hours."

"That's great," Jackson said, feeling a whole lot better about leaving. He knew that Callahan would be able to help Polly handle this better, and he could also see how Bridget was doing. He suspected that Bridget was tougher than Polly in some respects. She'd married into a crime family many years ago, and she also hadn't had the gun pointed directly at her. For Polly, this was way beyond anything she ever would have been exposed to, and Jackson was worried about her. He hoped that Veese would be able to stay for a while yet. He and Polly seemed to have developed a rapport, and he felt sure she'd feel better with him around. They walked back in, still holding hands, just as Jackson finished his call. He told them both about Dr. Callahan, and Polly seemed hugely relieved at the possibility of having a professional to talk to.

Jackson said to Veese, "How long will you be staying?"

"How long do you want me to stay?"

"Ideally, I'd like you to be here for as long as I'm in Utah, but I don't know how long that will be, and—"

"Do you have any idea how much vacation I have saved up?" Elliott asked lightly. "Now that I'm here, I'm not really wanting to go back very badly." Jackson smirked and noticed that he was still holding Polly's hand. "I'll stay as long as you need me to."

"Good," Jackson said. "Do we need to talk Artem into staying to chaperone you two?"

"Wouldn't hurt," Veese said, and Jackson caught the first hint of a smile from Polly.

"Something you want to tell me?" Jackson asked.

"Nope," they both said together while Veese protectively put his arm around Polly's shoulders.

The professional cleaning company that Jackson had called arrived and were there waiting for the police to finish their work. When everyone was gone except for the cleaning crew, Jackson insisted that Polly and Veese sit down and eat something. He didn't feel much like eating himself, but he knew that he needed to, and hoped it would ease the churning in his stomach. More importantly, he wanted Polly and Bridget to eat. He knew Veese could take care of himself. He found Artem still in the kitchen, nursing a second cup of coffee and looking a little dazed. He'd cleaned up his own meal and had left his dishes rinsed and neatly stacked by the sink. When Polly entered the room, Artem stood to greet her, expressing concern to the point where the old gentleman actually got a glistening of tears in his eyes. Polly hugged him and assured him that she was fine, while Jackson started fixing a tray of food for Bridget.

"What are you doing?" Polly asked when she noticed.

"I sent Mrs. Nuccitelli to her room and said I'd bring her some breakfast . . . even though it's lunchtime now. I've seen Chas do this enough that I think I can manage."

"Let me do it," she insisted.

"Why don't you sit down and let me—"

"Why don't you let me do something to keep myself busy?" she asked with a crack in her voice, and he lifted his hands and stepped back. Their eyes met for a long moment. She offered a wan smile and set to work. While she was taking the tray up to Bridget's room, Jackson started scrambling some eggs and told Veese to make some toast.

"Are you still hungry, Artem?" Jackson asked. "Would you like to join us?"

"I no hungry," he said. "But I join you. Good coffee. Good company. My new friends."

Polly returned and got out the fruit she'd prepared, some juice, coffee, and cocoa. They set the table and all sat down together in the kitchen, which had a bigger table and was less formal than the guest dining room. They chatted about the morning's events, answering Artem's questions and filling in details by comparing stories. As Jackson repeated his reasons for coming and how he had felt, every one of the men got a little choked up, and Polly cried a few stray tears.

"God work mysterious way," Artem said.

"I think I owe God my life," Polly added.

"Me too," Veese said, and there was a full minute of silence while they all contemplated the miracle that greatly offset the horror of the day.

The cleanup crew completed their tasks, and Jackson settled with them. Then he talked with Polly and Veese about what needed to be done to keep the business running smoothly with the least amount of strain for Polly. It seemed another great blessing that no guests were coming in that evening, and the following day there would be only one room rented. Veese had nothing to do but help Polly in any way that he could, and they all felt certain that between them they could take good care of Artem and Bridget and just work on coping with the recent trauma. It occurred to Jackson that because Veese had survived many violent episodes throughout the course of his work, he could likely be a good listening ear for Polly.

Polly offered to check on Bridget, and to tell her that Dr. Callahan was coming if she wanted to talk with him. Veese went to his room to check in with the home office and give them an update from his perspective. Jackson went to the office and made a few calls, using his cell phone when he was reminded by picking up the land line that it didn't work. He then went to his bedroom and closed the door, wanting privacy and quiet. He dialed Chas's phone and knew by how quickly she answered that she'd been waiting to hear from him.

"Is everything okay?" she asked in lieu of a greeting.

Jackson gave her the explanation he'd thoughtfully settled on. "We had an incident that I'll tell you about when I get back. But I just had lunch with Veese and Polly and Artem."

"So, everything's okay?" she asked, mildly frantic.

"It is now," he said.

"Then your prompting was . . . important?"

"Yeah, I'd say it was pretty important. I want to tell you about it when I see you. I've already got a flight booked. I'll be home before bedtime."

"Today? Really?"

"Really," he said. "Is everything okay there?"

"The same," she said.

"Okay, I'll see you later, and . . . I love you, Chas."

"I love you too," she said, and he could hear tears in her voice. He felt sure that her instincts were telling her something horrible had happened. He was glad to have some travel time to ponder how to tell her that Cortney was dead.

A man came to replace the bathroom window just a few minutes before a man came to repair the cut phone line. When Jackson walked outside with him to find the problem, the repairman said with alarm, "That's been deliberately cut!"

"Yeah, that would be the case."

"Who would do such a thing?" he asked in disgust.

Jackson knew it would be all over the news before dinner time, so he simply said, "It was either the man who was holding hostages, or the one who killed him."

The repairman laughed, then realized Jackson was serious. "No way."

"I'm afraid so. I appreciate you coming so quickly. I'll be inside if you need me."

He'd only been in the office a few minutes before Callahan arrived. He gave Jackson a brotherly hug in greeting, then they sat across the desk from each other and the doctor asked, "So, first off, how are you doing with this?"

"I'm okay now that I know the threat is over. I feel angry . . . with the people who did this, with myself . . . wondering if I could have done something to prevent it. I feel violated; my home was violated. It feels . . . desecrated."

"That's understandable."

"I'm sure I'll need to deal with all of this eventually, but right now . . . I've got to leave soon for the airport. My concern is mostly for Polly." He explained the situation in more detail, then they went into the parlor where Veese, Polly, and Bridget were all sitting. Apparently Artem had gone out on one of his excursions, which was good. Callahan introduced himself to all of them, and indicated that he'd like to talk to them all together for a few minutes, and then he'd like to talk to them separately. Jackson sat in on the first part, or most of it anyway. Before they were done, he needed to excuse himself to go to the airport. Bridget thanked him, Veese shook his hand and assured him that he'd take good care of Polly and the inn, and Polly hugged him tightly, getting tearful once again. He assured her that he would call every day, and that she should call him if she needed to talk. He also said, "I'm sure Chas will want to talk it all through with you, once I've had a chance to tell her. You can help each other deal with this."

"Of course," Polly said. "Give her my love. Travel safe."

Jackson drove the rented car back to the airport in Butte, surprised by a sudden rush of tears that overtook him once he knew he was completely alone. He felt sick, and he almost feared a relapse of his PTSD. But he reminded himself that he'd learned coping skills through all of his intense counseling, and he'd survived witnessing—and even experiencing—violence before. He turned his thoughts to counting blessings, and reminded himself of the miracles that had taken place. By the time he got to the airport, he was managing to keep it together. During the flight he pondered the drama going on in Utah. Chas wasn't feeling well and was preoccupied with continual concern for the baby. He prayed that little Isabelle wouldn't have any more setbacks. He just couldn't imagine facing any more heartache right now—or ever.

Jackson's inner unrest began to increase when the plane landed and he knew he was only a short taxi ride away from Chas. He desperately wanted to be with her, to hold her, and to share his grief. But he dreaded telling her what had happened. He prayed that he could find the right words and articulate them well. Once in a taxi on his way to the house, he called her, glancing at his watch as he did. Not yet nine o'clock. He hoped she was home and not at the hospital. She usually gave in and went home by now, and he hoped that was the case tonight.

"Hello, Mrs. Leeds," he said when he heard her voice.

"Are you . . ."

"In Utah," he said and heard her let out a deep sigh. "I'm on my way home from the airport. Are you there, or—"

"Yes, I'm here. Charles just went down for the night. He didn't get a nap so he was pretty cranky. You'll have to see him tomorrow."

"That's okay," he said. "We have a lot to talk about."

Following a long pause, she said, "You don't sound good, Jackson. What happened? Is Cortney—"

"I'll be home soon and we'll talk," he said. "I need to go."

"Okay," she said and reluctantly ended the call.

Jackson was barely out of the taxi when Chas walked up the driveway to greet him. The summer evening was still not completely dark. As the car drove away, she wrapped him tightly in her arms, and he returned her embrace.

"This has been one of the longest days of my life," she said.

"Mine too," he admitted and just held her, not wanting any words to mar the moment of just knowing they were both safe and together.

The moment was shattered for him when Chas pulled back and said, "Just give me the bad news, and then you can fill in the details."

"What makes you think there's bad news?" he asked. She gave him a harsh glare. He sighed and looked down for a moment before he forced himself to make eye contact. "Cortney is dead."

Chas took a step back as if she'd been struck. "Really?" she asked, and he nodded. "How?" she asked, her chin quivering.

Jackson put an arm around her shoulders and started walking. "We'd better sit down."

"Is everyone else all right?" she asked, a tremor in her voice.

"Everyone is safe; no one else was hurt except for Cortney's jerk of a boyfriend. But *all right* is relative. Everyone is kind of shaken up . . . especially Polly."

"Why?" She stopped walking.

Jackson took her arm and urged her along. "We need to sit down and I'll start at the beginning."

"Okay," she said reluctantly.

Once they were inside the apartment, she added, "Melinda's gone to a movie."

"Alone? Why?"

"She said we should have some time to talk, and that you could bring her up to speed tomorrow."

"Okay, well . . . I must admit she's probably right." He took her hand and headed toward the hall. "First I just need to see our son. I'm so grateful you and the babies were here when this all went down." They entered the baby's room, and Jackson heaved an audible sigh of relief and love as he observed the sweet, sleep-flushed face of his little boy.

Once satisfied that all was well, Jackson and Chas returned to the living room, where they sat on the couch and turned to face each other. Jackson took both her hands in his, rubbing his thumbs over her palms while he figured he should just tell her the worst and get it over with. As she had suggested, he could fill in details after that.

"I got there as quickly as I could," Jackson said. "I've gone over it in my head, wondering if I could have done anything to arrive even a minute sooner, but I couldn't have. I just couldn't."

Chas felt concerned at his evident regret. "Do you really think if you'd gotten there a minute sooner, you could have saved Cortney?"

"I know I could have," he said. "I heard the shots right after I came through the back door."

"*Our* back door?"

"Yeah," he said, unable to look at her.

"Tell me what happened, Jackson. I can't bear not knowing any longer."

He blew out a long, slow breath and began. "When I got there, the drapes were all shut and the Closed sign was on the door. Before we came here I left my gun in the garage, thinking that I didn't want anyone finding it in the house. I believe now I was prompted to leave it there. I got it and went in the back. I had to unlock the door. I went in very quietly, because the whole thing just felt wrong; felt like . . ."

"What?"

"It had the earmarks of a hostage situation."

"And was it?"

"Yes. Apparently Bobby Dinubilo—Cortney's boyfriend— showed up during the night to get her. As close as we can figure, when she didn't meet him, or leave the door unlocked for him, or whatever they had prearranged, he must have known something was wrong. He must have also realized there was an agent staking out the place in the car across the street, because the guy was knocked out and tied up. Then it appears that Bobby cut the phone line and broke the bathroom window to get into the house."

"Good heavens," Chas said, her stomach tightening. She was grateful for her present distance from her home and this horrific situation, but she could hardly believe what she was hearing.

"Veese heard the glass breaking and went to investigate. Bobby hit *him* over the back of the head to knock him out, and he tied him up as well."

"Oh!" was all Chas could say.

"We figure that Bobby knew which room Cortney was supposed to be in, but the door was locked and she didn't answer. He found Harry Nuccitelli's wife in a different room and tied her to a chair in the parlor, intending to use her as leverage to get Cortney, because Harry was holding *her* hostage, waiting for Bobby to show up."

"I can*not* believe this!" Chas said.

"Yeah, well . . . it gets better . . . or rather . . . worse. When Polly came downstairs to start the day, Bobby was there with Veese's gun." Chas put a hand over her mouth to keep from whimpering while the story unfolded. "He told Polly they were going to get the keys, which he hadn't been able to find, and they were going to get Cortney away from Nuccitelli. About that time, Nuccitelli came down the stairs with a gun to Cortney's head. It seems that the crime Cortney witnessed—the murder of Bruce Nuccitelli—was actually committed by Bobby, but she lied and said that his brother Reggie did it, because neither of them liked Reggie, so they sent him to prison. But Harry Nuccitelli saw the crime too, and he'd known all along that Bobby had done it and Cortney was lying. Bobby was arrested for a minor assault charge before the trial, and Harry's just been waiting for him to get out of jail and find Cortney. After Harry stated his business, he let Cortney go. She ran to Bobby, and . . . Harry shot them both."

Chas gasped. "Where . . . exactly?"

"In the front hall."

Chas wiped tears. "And they both died?" she asked, if only to reassure herself this was real.

"Instantly," Jackson said. "I heard the shots right after I came through the door. Then I saw Harry turn and point the gun at someone else. He said, 'You know I can't let you live.' And I had about a second to put the gun to his head before he was going to pull the trigger. After he put his hands up, I realized it was . . ." His voice cracked. "It was Polly he was going to . . ."

Chas groaned, then sobbed, and Jackson cried with her. He wiped his face and muttered, "When I heard those shots, I thought I was too late. When I saw Polly there, I . . . Oh, Chas! All through this whole thing . . . I've done my best to just . . . put my trust in the Lord to keep everyone safe. He proved that trust to me today far beyond my expectations. If I had been a few seconds slower . . . but . . . I wonder why I couldn't have gotten there a minute earlier and . . ." A thought occurred to Jackson with subtle force. It had come to him more quietly a couple of times through the day, but he'd dismissed it, wanting to believe that there could have been another way. "No, I know why," he added more calmly. "If I'd come a minute earlier, I would have done nothing but prolong the inevitability of Cortney's death. They would have killed her; I know they would. She lied to protect the man who had killed Harry's brother. But if they hadn't been killed then and there, it would have happened in some obscure way that could never be proven. As it was, Harry Nuccitelli was caught with the gun in his hand and multiple witnesses. He'll go to prison, which is where the FBI has wanted him for years. If Bobby and Cortney had gotten away, they would have ended up dying in some horrible incident that would have been made to look like an accident. But Harry manipulated this whole thing because he *wanted* to face Bobby. He wanted what he considered justice for his brother's death."

"And if you hadn't shown up, he would have gotten away with it, and he would have taken innocent lives along with the guilty ones."

"That's right. I don't think he planned to have any witnesses. It was Bobby Dinubilo that got the innocents in the middle. And when it went down the way it did . . ." He groaned and squeezed his eyes shut, shaking his head as if he could shake off the memory of bodies in the hall of the inn, and Polly coming so close to a violent death.

Chas felt horrified and shaken to realize what had occurred this morning in her home, but at the moment she was more overcome with gratitude at the outcome. She eased closer to Jackson and wrapped him in her arms, silently thanking God for bringing him home safely to her, and for preserving their home and their friends' lives.

"I'm so sorry," Jackson said.

"Sorry?" she asked, checking his expression. "Jackson, you saved lives today; lives of people who are dear to us."

"But . . . I feel like . . . the inn has been . . . desecrated. Polly has been utterly traumatized, and . . ."

"Apparently Polly isn't the only one."

"You bet I'm traumatized!" he said, sounding angry now. "I could name at least a dozen incidents during my career that were similar to what happened today. But it was never in *my* home, with people threatened that *I* care about! And it was never *my* fault that it happened."

"*Your* fault?"

"We should have never brought her into our home, Chas. And when we realized how stupid she was being, we should have kicked her out."

"And then what?"

"Our home wouldn't have become a crime scene."

"Jackson, we prayed about bringing her into our home. We both felt good about it."

"And then *I* made the decision to let her stay when I *knew* that she was tangled up in something with people who solve their problems with violence. And then I—"

"Jackson," Chas interrupted, "you're upset. You have a right to be upset. I'm upset too, but I didn't see it; I wasn't there. So . . . be upset if you have to, but try to keep some perspective."

More calmly he said, "I don't understand. We felt good about bringing her into our home. We did everything we could to give her a fair chance and help her, and what good did it do anybody?"

"I'm sure it will take time for all of this to settle and for us to make sense of it, but nobody got hurt except the people who were guilty of committing major crimes and making bad choices. I think it turned out like that because *you* are *still* a great investigator with sharp instincts. If Cortney had gone somewhere else, among people who didn't know what they were doing, maybe innocent people *would* have been hurt. We will never know, but I think it's a strong possibility."

"Maybe you're right," Jackson said. There was enough logic to the idea that he couldn't deny it made him feel a little better. At least he could find some reason to believe that his efforts had not been completely in vain. As soon as the thought settled into his mind, a warmth took hold of his heart. He remembered clearly the moment after he'd confronted Cortney about her lies and he'd been threatening to send her back to the U.S. Marshals. He had known beyond any doubt at that time that he needed to let her stay. If she'd gone elsewhere perhaps innocent lives *would* have been lost. In spite of the horror of this day, was it possible that he had really made a difference by following the feelings that had guided him so clearly? He'd like to think so.

"And," Chas added, as if to add a second witness to his own thoughts, "you cannot dispute the evidence that God was with us in this today. I believe He was with us all along. You've followed your instincts every step of the way. If He'd wanted it to turn out some other way—as far as something that you or I had control over—He surely would have prompted and guided us to do it differently. Whether or not that's true, what's done is done. The inn is *not* desecrated, and we will all work together to cope with the emotional impact." She was thoughtful a minute then said, "Maybe we should have Polly see Dr. Callahan and—"

"She already has."

"What? Already?"

"I called him before the mess was even cleaned up, and—"

"Ooh," she said at the image that came into her head. "*Who* had to clean up . . . the mess?"

"I called a professional cleaning company. There was no sign of anything when I left."

Chas sighed. "Oh, that's nice."

"And Callahan was there when I left."

"Then Polly's in good hands. Is Elliott going to—"

"Veese is staying for as long as we need him to be there."

Chas sighed more deeply. "Oh, that's nice, too. But when are you going to start calling him by his first name? He's not an agent on your team anymore."

"Today he was," Jackson said with firm sincerity.

"Okay, fair enough. But one of these days you should really conform to *Elliott.* It's a nice name."

"As long as we both know who I'm talking about, a name is a name. Speaking of Veese and Polly . . . I think there's something going on there."

"Something?"

"They were *very* concerned about each other . . . and they were holding hands."

"Really?" Chas said with a mild delight that helped push away the horrors of the day. "Well . . . maybe good things will come out of this, when all is said and done."

"Wait a minute," he said. "You don't really think that . . . Veese . . . and Polly . . ."

Chas just shrugged, but she also smiled, and Jackson felt some of that viewpoint settling over him. They were together and safe. The inn was safe and so were their friends. And they had every reason to hope that their little Isabelle was going to be all right.

* * * * *

Saturated with exhaustion, Jackson was glad to feel the bed beneath him. His outlook fell more securely into place when he had no worry about his home and loved ones beyond his ongoing concern for the baby. He imagined the inn safe and secure and drifted off to sleep with that image.

Jackson woke in the night with no recollection of dreaming, but his head was full of images of the desecration of the inn and the trauma endured by those who had been there. He turned his mind to prayer and the counting of blessings. He went back to sleep holding tightly to the memory of Polly and Veese alive and well . . . and maybe falling in love. He smiled to think of the possibility. He'd been teasing Veese for years about coming to Montana, retiring, and settling down. But he hadn't honestly believed it was a possibility. And maybe it wasn't. But for the moment, he knew they were together and taking care of each other.

Jackson pondered the realization that the episode with Cortney was behind them. It was over and done, and he was eager to put away his worry and fears. He took in a deep breath of relief, but before he had let that breath go, an uneasy feeling came over him. At first he attributed it to habit. He had become accustomed to feeling worried about the mob coming to his inn and creating havoc. Now that they had, it was done, and he needed to change his way of thinking. But after considering his feelings for another hour, intermixing his considerations with fervent prayer, he had to readily acknowledge that he felt uneasy and there was a reason for it. It wasn't over, and he knew it. He had officially reported to the FBI and the local police that he had seen a member of a notorious crime family commit a crime that would send him to prison. Was he in danger? Was his family in danger? His home? His friends? He felt sick at the thought. He felt scared and angry with himself for ever allowing Cortney to come to their home in the first place. As the fear became unmanageable, he prayed harder, knowing that God had gotten them this far. There was no better place he could put his trust, no other way to be able to face whatever might yet happen and be able to cope.

After another hour or so, he felt decidedly calm. Perhaps it *wasn't* over, but he was not going to ruin the present by fearing the unknown. He was going to do what he'd been doing all along. He was putting the matter in God's hands while he sought to remain receptive to the promptings of the Spirit. Surely everything would be okay.

* * * * *

When morning came, Chas called the hospital to check on the baby's progress. When she was told that everything was fine and Isabelle was stable, they decided to wait until later to begin the usual hospital vigil. A slow morning to catch up emotionally seemed a wise choice. Chas hadn't slept very well, and she suspected that Jackson hadn't either. He still had that subtle worried crease in his face, but she felt certain it would soften with time as he came to terms with what had happened.

Over breakfast they brought Melinda up to speed on the previous day's events. She was understandably astonished and upset. But talking it through with her helped Chas come a little closer to making peace with it. She hoped that Jackson was feeling the same way.

While Melinda insisted on cleaning up the kitchen, Jackson spent some time just playing with Charles, and Chas had a long phone conversation with Polly. Chas heard the whole story again from Polly's point of view, and they both cried a great deal. She told Chas that her lengthy visit with Dr. Callahan the previous day had helped her immensely already. She knew that feeling traumatized was normal, and that it would take time to mend. He'd told her that she would probably feel the need to talk about it for quite some time, and it was good for her to talk to other women, because women were better at wanting to repetitively talk through details. Since Chas felt traumatized by the event as well, even with her distance from it, they agreed that they would be there for each other as much as necessary.

When their conversation about the event wound down, Chas felt eager to change the subject. "So, Jackson tells me you and Elliott are getting kind of cuddly."

"Cuddly?" Polly echoed. "Jackson did not use that word."

"No, he didn't. He said you were holding hands . . . looking out for each other. Is that part of *pretending* that you're dating?"

"Actually," Polly drew out the word, "we stopped pretending a long time ago."

"And you didn't tell me?" Chas laughed. "Are you serious?"

"To be honest, I've been afraid it wouldn't last. I didn't want to make a big deal out of it, if it wasn't a big deal. But . . . I really like him . . . a lot. And he likes me. I know he does. But I don't have to tell *you* about the roadblocks here. I have no desire to ever leave Montana, and he's got a career in Virginia. Is this sounding like déjà vu to you?"

"Freakishly déjà vu," Chas said. "Wow. I didn't see this coming."

"Well . . . it may end up coming to nothing. Right now I'm just . . . trying to enjoy the moment and keep an open mind."

"That's déjà vu, too," Chas said, recalling vividly that same stage in her relationship with Jackson. She was certainly grateful it had worked out, and she couldn't help hoping for the same for Polly.

* * * * *

Jackson phoned Veese to see how the process of his paperwork was going. No longer being an official agent, Jackson was spared having to do such things following an incident. Veese told him that Myers had been stunned by the outcome and felt terrible for putting Jackson into the situation. Jackson didn't blame Myers; he blamed himself. Or at least he wished he had handled the situation differently, even if he couldn't imagine exactly what he might have done. He could intellectually add up the facts that he and Chas had discussed, and he believed that the whole thing had probably worked out the way it was supposed to. He'd certainly done what he'd felt was best each step of the way. But he still felt regret, and he still felt uneasy. He could reason out that he'd followed his feelings and instincts to the best of his ability, and a part of him believed he couldn't have done any better. But another part of him felt sick at the thought of what had happened—and what might yet happen—and he just wished he could go back and change it.

As his phone call was winding down, Veese asked, "So, how are you doing, boss?"

"I'm not your boss. And I'm fine."

"Are you fine enough for me to give you some bad news?"

"What bad news?" he demanded, knowing he *sounded* like Veese's boss with his sharp tone.

"I just have this . . . feeling that it's not over. Take it for what it's worth. But I don't know that the Nuccitelli family is going to let this go quite so easily. I don't understand their whole mindset about getting revenge for getting what they deserved, but we both know that's how it works."

"I know what you mean. But I have the same feeling, so you're not actually giving me any news. You're just telling me what I already feel . . . and believe. And we're just going to keep doing what we've been doing."

"Maybe it *is* over," Veese said. "Maybe we're just paranoid. And maybe whatever is left undone isn't all that serious."

"Maybe," Jackson said, hoping he was right. He would just be glad when he could believe that it really was *over.*

* * * * *

As much as Jackson had appreciated these few hours to relax and unwind a bit, he suddenly felt an urgent desire to see his baby daughter. Once at the hospital, he was overcome with unspeakable joy and gratitude as he held her tiny body close to his own heart. God had been merciful and kind in so many ways, and surely this sweet baby girl was evidence of His love.

CHAPTER 11

Polly managed to take care of running the inn as if nothing in the world had happened. She could chat and smile and go through the usual motions without letting on even a little that she had come within a split second of losing her life, looking down the barrel of a gun that had been pointed directly at her at close range. The moment kept playing over and over in her mind, sometimes provoking deep gratitude—an appreciation for life she'd never comprehended before. And yet at other times, it plunged her into such intense fear that she would have to find a place to be alone in order to hyperventilate for a few minutes before she could catch her breath and go back to work. She was glad that their current guests had all come from out of town and took no interest in picking up a local newspaper. They were oblivious to the horror that had taken place here, which made it easier for Polly to pretend it hadn't happened whenever she was interacting with them. The guests were able to enjoy the serenity and sanctity of the inn, with no awareness of how it had been debased by violence.

Elliott had actually been absent a great deal; he was either away from the inn, or up in his room talking to his associates on the phone, or working on his computer. She knew he was completing what he called masses of paperwork that followed the conclusion of any case. A part of her wanted him nearby every minute to lean on. But at times she was glad to have him absent, certain her growing feelings for him would only complicate her attempting to come to

terms with all that had happened. Or perhaps it was the other way
around. Each day she felt more hopeful that it was going to work
out. It seemed he was really determined to remain here in Montana
regardless of whether things between them worked out. She hadn't
mentioned this to Chas, still not daring to believe that Elliott
would really quit his job in Virginia and make such drastic changes
with his life. Still, she felt hopeful, and tried each day to find the
balance between being optimistic and realistic.

With minimal training, Elliott was both willing and able to
cover for her at the inn long enough for her to drive into Butte
for an appointment with Dr. Callahan. It was easy to see why
Jackson liked this guy so much, and when she thought of what
Chas had told her this doctor had done for Jackson, she was
doubly impressed. In facing such a traumatic event, it was nice to
know that she could trust this man and to have hope that he could
help her. The very idea of living for the rest of her life with such
images in her mind—and the fear they provoked—was practically
debilitating. As it was, Dr. Callahan assured her that with time she
would be able to get past the incident and be healthy and normal.
But he cautioned her to give it time and be patient with herself. In
the meantime, he gave her some tools and coping skills that might
help her get through the mild panic attacks and the occasional
nightmares.

Driving back to Anaconda, Polly thought of the intense PTSD
that Jackson had dealt with. She knew that the incident she'd
survived had been minuscule in contrast to all that he'd endured.
And she knew that his nightmares had been horrible. She couldn't
even imagine! Her respect for Jackson deepened as she gained just
a little bit of empathy.

It was nice to return to the inn and find Elliott there, and especially to see in his eyes how eager he was to see her. He greeted her
with a kiss, and she wanted her whole life to be this way. With the
inn still quiet, he urged her to sit down and share her feelings with
him about the incident and her appointment with Dr. Callahan.

She loved the way he didn't prod or push her in any way that felt awkward, allowing her instead to feel completely comfortable with sharing whatever she needed to talk about. She found that talking about it did help, and she appreciated Elliott's patience in allowing her to rehash it over and over. In turn, he shared with her some of his past encounters with violent situations, and she felt great relief just to know he'd remained safe long enough to be here for her now.

That evening they had supper as usual with Artem, then the three of them had a rousing game of Uno after all of their guests were settled into their rooms. Artem had never played the game before, and he laughed boisterously every time the cards were kind to him. In contrast, he groaned and stomped his foot when he did badly. Elliott told him more than once that he would be a terrible poker player, and he should never take it up. Artem promised.

The following morning after breakfast, all of the guests except Artem checked out, and no new guests were due to arrive for several hours. Polly locked up the inn, knowing that Artem had a guest key to the outside door if he came back from his sightseeing before she returned. She took advantage of a beautiful day and went into town to get groceries and do a few errands, delighted to have Elliott come along. They laughed and talked in between her various stops and while he pushed the cart up and down the aisles at the grocery store. It was all so pleasant that Polly hoped he would never leave her.

Back at the inn, Elliott unloaded the groceries and helped put them away, then followed Polly around while she made certain everything was ready for this evening's guests. When she went to the office to do some paperwork, Elliott plopped himself into the chair on the other side of the desk and made himself comfortable.

"I really enjoy your company," Polly said, "but I'm not sure what it says about you that you have nothing better to do than follow me around."

Elliott chuckled. "I'm on vacation, and there's nothing I'd rather do than follow you around. It's been so long since I've had *any* time off that it's nice to just . . . do nothing."

"I'm not complaining. Just . . . don't get too comfortable."

"Are you trying to get rid of me?"

"Never! But . . ."

"Yeah, I know. Eventually I'll have to go back to work and . . ."

"I don't even want to talk about it," Polly said.

Elliott leaned forward, mildly alarmed. "No, what I mean, Polly, is that . . . I obviously need a job, so I need to go back to work. But I'm not going *back* to the old job. I'm looking for a new one. It's official. I've already submitted my resignation."

"Oh?" she said, and her fear that this was too good to last decreased, if only a little. He then told her about some jobs he'd applied for in Butte, since there weren't presently any openings in his field of expertise right there in Anaconda. He'd already started apartment hunting, and he had plans to go back to Virginia in a few weeks, just to wrap up some things and clean out his apartment. Ironically, the lease would be up at that time, so he had no further obligations with his residence there. Polly took it all in and asked herself if she was ready to have this man in her life permanently. Of course, his moving here and getting a job wasn't a marriage proposal. He'd made it clear that he would have made that decision independent of his feelings for her. She was glad for that, but she was also glad that he *would* be staying. There was no rush. She could enjoy his company, give the matter some time, and safely indulge in some measure of hope for their sharing a future together.

Polly heard the door and Elliott said, "Ooh, guests perhaps?"

"Perhaps," she said and looked up to see Charlotte enter the office. At one time, she had enjoyed and appreciated Charlotte's friendship, and so had Chas. But ever since Charlotte had been so unkind concerning her beliefs in regard to Chas's baby, Polly hadn't seen or spoken to Charlotte, and she hadn't had any desire to do so.

Polly wondered what Charlotte would think if she knew that Chas had given birth to a beautiful baby girl who would soon be coming home. But Polly made up her mind to stay quiet about that. When the time was right, Chas could be the one to tell Charlotte that she'd been wrong.

"Oh, hello," Polly said with a polite smile. It wasn't in her nature to be unkind, even given her less than favorable feelings toward Charlotte.

"Hi!" Charlotte said with exaggerated enthusiasm, as if nothing in the world was wrong. The very number of months that had passed since they'd last seen each other was evidence that their relationship had changed dramatically. "You look busy."

"Just . . . doing the usual," Polly said, hating the awkwardness. "So . . . what brings you here?"

"I was . . . in the neighborhood and thought I'd see how you're doing . . . and Chas, too. Is she around?"

"Actually, she's not. She's . . ." Polly tried to think of a truthful explanation that would avoid the reason for her absence. "She's in Utah with Jackson and his sister."

"Vacation?"

"Something like that."

"Do you know when she'll be back?"

"I'm not sure. I can give her a message."

"Just tell her I came by," Charlotte said, and then looked Polly up and down. "You've lost weight."

"Yes, I have."

"You look so pretty," she said, as if being overweight had automatically made her ugly. Polly didn't comment and Charlotte added, "How are you?"

"I'm doing well, thank you. How are you?"

"Oh, I'm great," she said with a phony edge. "Are you sure?"

"Sure about what?" Polly asked.

"Are you okay? I mean . . . I read in the paper about what happened here. It must have been horrible!"

"Yes, it was," Polly said, wondering if the purpose for Charlotte's visit was to get the juicy details of the drama. Charlotte was all about drama, but Polly wasn't interested in telling her anything that hadn't been in the papers. "But it's over now and we're all fine."

"Chas was gone when it happened?"

"Yes, actually," Polly said. Wondering how to change the subject, she was relieved when Elliott shifted in his chair and brought Charlotte's attention to the fact that there was someone else in the room.

"Oh, hello," Charlotte said to Elliott, assuming a demeanor that Polly knew well. Charlotte was a flirt, a single mother with two children from two different fathers, and her morals were deplorable! When faced with an attractive man, Charlotte always went straight to flirting and waited until later to find out if the man was actually available.

"Hello," Elliott said and stood.

"And who is this?" Charlotte asked Polly while she eyed Elliott so overtly that Polly felt embarrassed.

Not wanting to complicate the conversation by calling him her boyfriend, or the guy she might marry someday, she simply said, "This is Elliott; he's a friend of Jackson's. Elliott, this is Charlotte." Polly left it at that, not particularly wanting to declare Charlotte as a friend.

"You're a friend of Jackson's?" she asked, turning more toward Elliott.

"Yes. Yes, I am. Well . . . actually, we worked together . . . and sort of became friends."

"You're FBI?" Charlotte asked as if he'd said he was the leader of the free world.

"Not anymore," he said proudly. "I just retired."

They continued to share apparently innocent small talk while Polly began to fume. She'd observed Charlotte's shameless flirting countless times, but never before had she been personally invested in Charlotte's target. Polly realized now that Charlotte's behavior had *always* been appalling. Polly and Chas had put up with it because the boundaries of their friendship had not been affected by her going in and out of relationships with men. But now that Polly had some distance from her prior friendship with Charlotte, she was stunned to see just how indiscreet Charlotte could be. Polly resisted the urge to get angry and call Charlotte a tramp. Instead she turned her attention to Elliott, and she was struck with a pleasant surprise. Elliott wasn't the slightest bit interested in Charlotte. He looked bored, politely impatient, and perhaps appalled. Charlotte rambled senselessly, completely oblivious to the fact that this man was not responding to her flirtations.

Polly tried to figure out a way to rescue Elliott from Charlotte's ongoing trivialities about her life, intermixed with ridiculous questions about the FBI. She couldn't think of anything that wouldn't involve some amount of rudeness. But she was spared when Elliott piped up and rescued himself—*and* her.

"Excuse me . . . it was nice meeting you, Charlotte . . . but . . . I've got some things to do and . . ." He stepped toward Polly, took her hand, and gave her a quick kiss. Polly didn't even have to look at Charlotte to know that her eyes had gone wide and that she was stunned speechless. Her silence was a good indicator of that. "I'll be upstairs if you need me, honey," he said and smiled at her as if there was no other woman in the world.

"Okay, I'll be done here in a minute," she said to him and watched him leave the room without giving Charlotte another glance.

"Unbelievable!" Charlotte said as if Polly had done something wrong.

"That's exactly what I was thinking," Polly said with an edge of sarcasm.

"You're *sleeping* with him?"

Polly made a scoffing noise. "What planet are you from?" she asked, glad if nothing else for a reason to say what she *wanted* to say. "Don't judge me by your standards. Just because you go to bed with a guy before you know anything about him doesn't mean the rest of womankind does the same thing. You're just jealous because he wasn't interested in you, and you're even more jealous because I've *never* been competition before. He's taken. So, take a hike, Charlotte. If you want gossip, go to the beauty parlor or something."

"I don't know what's gotten into you. You've become downright rude."

"How horrible of me."

"I think I liked you better when you were fat."

"And I liked you better when you weren't so self-righteous. I'll tell Chas you came by."

Charlotte huffed out as if she'd been deeply and utterly betrayed. Polly actually felt sorry for her. She wasn't the same person she used to be. It seemed her lifestyle was catching up to her, increasingly distorting her perspective of reality. But Polly knew there was nothing she could do, so she went to find Elliott and tell him how he'd made her day.

* * * * *

In spite of a nagging sensation that his dealings with the Nuccitelli family were not over, Jackson couldn't deny feeling some relief in knowing that his most prominent concerns could be put to rest. He forced any worry over the future to the back of his mind and settled back into the routine of being with his family in their home away from home. Though he struggled to come to terms with what had happened and how, he felt incomprehensibly grateful to know that his home and friends were no longer in danger. And he could only pray that whatever might yet be left undone would resolve itself without any more violence. Combined with his ongoing concern were the residual memories of the horror. He kept thinking of how precious the Dickensian Inn was to him, to his life, to his family. The house itself was beautiful. What it represented to him was beyond any tangible beauty. It had been his refuge from a damaged life, and it had become his home. It had been in Chas's family for generations, honored and revered and painstakingly cared for and preserved. And he had brought someone into this precious little oasis and created a situation that had ended with bloodshed.

Jackson spoke to Elliott each day on the phone and was reassured that all was well. He did his best to take Elliott's advice and just enjoy the new baby. Isabelle was thriving, and each day her progress was evident. His own joy in having his daughter here and doing well felt almost overwhelming, but seeing Chas's joy doubled his own. She was so happy that being with her made it easy to forget that anything had ever gone wrong in his life, before he'd met her or since.

Isabelle suddenly reached a point where her progress soared. While she still needed to be in the hospital, the nurses strongly encouraged Chas and Jackson to spend some time elsewhere in order to get some rest and relaxation before they had to go home and take care of a toddler and an infant full time. They were assured that the hospital had their cell phone numbers, and they would call if anything changed at all. It was difficult to be away from the baby, and they still spent many hours a day at the hospital, but they also spent some hours away every day, taking in some sights and getting a nice meal away from the cafeteria.

With all of the sights and activities available in the Salt Lake Valley, they were still drawn most strongly to Temple Square. Melinda couldn't get enough, and Jackson felt much the same. Chas loved every minute she spent there, but for different reasons. For her, what she learned and felt there only strengthened what she'd known in her heart for many years. For Jackson, it was all helping to build the testimony that was still new and fresh for him. Melinda was simply taking in something she'd never experienced before.

Doug and Kate had them all up to the house for dinner a couple of times, and Chas enjoyed sharing time with a real Mormon family. For all of her years of being a member of the Church, she had been the only member in her family until Jackson's recent baptism. She'd never actually seen firsthand how the principles taught about the family could be applied.

Doug and Kate didn't have a perfect family, and Chas actually liked seeing evidence that the kids didn't always get along and things didn't always go smoothly. But she also felt the Spirit when they were there late one evening and Doug invited them to join the family for prayer. And nearing the end of their stay in Salt Lake City, Kate invited them to join them for family home evening. Even though one of Doug and Kate's teenagers was in a bad mood and Charles was somewhat fussy, they shared a simple lesson on testimony, played a silly game, sang a hymn off-key, and enjoyed homemade cookies. More than once Chas felt so near tears she could hardly speak. She was imagining herself some years in the future, raising her family with Jackson at her side, living life to its fullest. Catching a tender glance from him more than once, she knew he was thinking the same.

Melinda just took it all in with an expression of serenity and awe that had become familiar since their arrival in Salt Lake City. She never said anything about her intentions in regard to the gospel, and Chas didn't ask. But she believed in her heart that it was only a matter of time before Melinda accepted the gospel fully into her heart. It would be a joyous day for all of them!

When the doctors finally declared that Isabelle was ready to go home, Chas felt ecstatic at the thought of returning to the inn with her family and its new addition. She also felt a little nervous about being in charge of Isabelle and her fragile heart. But they had been repeatedly assured that everything was fine, and regular checkups would keep her healthy and strong. It was possible that as she grew there would need to be some further surgeries. But for the time being, she was perfect.

They all went to bed for the last time in the basement apartment with everything cleaned and packed up as much as it could be without actually leaving. Lying next to Jackson in the dark, Chas let out a deep sigh and said, "It will be so good to go home."

Jackson hesitated a moment. "Yes, it will," he said, but Chas heard something in his tone that contradicted his words.

She leaned up on her elbow and asked, "Is something wrong?"

"I'll be very glad to be home," he said.

"But . . ." she urged.

"But . . ." Jackson hesitated again, knowing from vast experience that trying to keep his feelings from her never had good results. "I have a hard time not thinking about what happened there. I feel like the inn has been desecrated. I feel like it's my fault."

"We've talked about this, Jackson."

"Yes, we've talked about it, but I still feel that way. I appreciate your reassurance, and intellectually I know that I did the best I could, that I was guided by the Lord, that we were all immensely blessed. I know all of that. But I still feel . . . horrible."

"Perhaps being at home will help you get beyond it. Perhaps you need new memories to replace the old ones."

"I hope so," he said and kissed her. "In fact, I'm counting on it." He kissed her again. "Yes, it will be good to go home. It's been nice here, however. In a way I'm going to miss it."

"I know what you mean. We *have* been very blessed."

"*Very* blessed," he said. "Now get some sleep. It's going to be a long day."

Jackson avoided telling her about his uneasy feelings and his doubt that it was over. He didn't want to worry her. He was doing enough of that for both of them.

The following morning they all rose early. Melinda fed Charles and dressed him while Chas stripped the sheets from the beds and put them in the washer. Kate had asked that they do so and she would take care of the rest in getting the apartment in order for future potential visitors. And she assured them that they would be welcome to come back and stay any time they needed a little vacation. Jackson made certain all the dishes were washed up and the kitchen was in order after they'd eaten their breakfast of toast and cereal. Then the luggage was loaded and they were off to the hospital to pick up Isabelle and take her home.

Chas felt a little nervous just taking her tiny precious bundle past the hospital doors and into the outside world. But once Charles and Isabelle were safely buckled into their car seats and they were headed north to Montana, she relaxed and concentrated on going home.

* * * * *

Polly could hardly sleep due to the excitement of knowing that Jackson and Chas would soon be on their way home. She'd missed them so much! But she feared what their return might mean in regard to the comfortable place she'd come to with Elliott. He'd been wonderful in guiding her through her stress related to the incident that had threatened both their lives. He had a great deal of strength and insight due to his experience with trauma. It was impossible to be an FBI agent for years and not see a great deal of it, and he'd more than once faced death and survived it. He'd been hospitalized twice from injuries that had occurred when he'd narrowly escaped losing his life. As Polly listened to his experiences and wisdom, she gained greater understanding and a deeper appreciation for him. She felt validated and understood, not only in regard to the traumatic experience they'd shared, but in every aspect of life. He was just such a good man!

Polly finally slept but was awakened by a nightmare. They didn't happen often, but when they did she always found it difficult to go back to sleep. She finally got up and read, wishing Elliott was awake so that he could keep her company. At such moments, she longed to be married to him, and she wondered if it was really all going to work out the way that she hoped. At dawn she put the book aside and got ready for the day, counting down the hours until her dearest friends would be back. She just hoped that their return wouldn't alter the solace she'd come to feel with Elliott in their absence.

When Elliott came awake, he felt mixed emotions over knowing that Jackson and Chas would be coming home today. He couldn't wait to see them, but he'd enjoyed this little version of playing house with Polly, and a part of him didn't want it to end. Of course, what he wanted was his own permanent version of playing house. He wanted to make Polly his wife and settle down. He felt more sure about it every day. He just hoped that his own anxiousness didn't scare her off. While he kept expecting to find out things about her that would make him question his original instincts, he only found that he loved and admired her more every day. She had a tender heart and a deep sensitivity that softened him in ways he hadn't even known he'd needed, but now that he felt that softening taking place, he wondered how he'd ever lived without her. Polly had taught him a great deal about life and love in the weeks he'd known her, and he wanted to spend his whole life learning more from her every day.

Elliott went down to the dining room and found Artem drinking a cup of coffee and reading a newspaper. He'd come to enjoy the old man's company and dreaded the day that Artem would move on to his next adventure. But he'd kept his promise to be a good chaperone, and he'd been good company, too. He signaled to Artem to keep quiet, and they exchanged a smile before Elliott sneaked into the kitchen and grabbed Polly from behind, making her squeal, then giggle, then playfully hit him before he kissed her and said, "Good morning, honey."

"Good morning," she said and kissed him again.

"How did you sleep?" he asked. Polly made a disgruntled noise and went back to tending the waffle iron. "Nightmare?"

"Yeah, but I'm okay."

"It'll get better," he said.

"Yes, I think it will," she replied, meeting his eyes, certain that everything would keep getting better as long as he stuck around.

* * * * *

Jackson was surprised at how relieved he felt when the inn came into view. There it stood, like a beacon of light, beckoning him home, just as it had the first time he'd come here. Chas let out a delighted laugh when he turned into the driveway, as if she shared his sentiment. But she hadn't personally witnessed the nightmarish scene that had taken place within its walls, nor the images that had preceded the coroner removing the bodies and the cleanup that followed.

Chas chattered excitedly about being home while they got out of the car. Melinda offered to take Charles in and change his diaper while they got the baby. Chas and Jackson stepped inside and paused in the hall to breathe in the inn's familiarity. Jackson set down the baby seat that held a sleeping Isabelle and tried to push away the memories and only see the way it looked now. He was managing rather well until Chas said, "The rug is different."

Jackson looked at the rug in the center of the polished wood floor. It was a pretty good duplicate of the one that had been there before, and he made a mental note to thank Polly for taking care of the problem so well. He remembered how Cortney had fallen on the old rug when she'd been shot. The stains would have never come out. He tried without success to hurry and say something light and brief to explain. When no words would come, he swallowed hard and met Chas's eyes, offering a silent apology along with his wordless explanation.

"Oh, of course," she said, then she stepped forward and wrapped her arms around him. He wasn't certain whether she was offering comfort or was in need of it until she said, "It's okay, Jackson." Still, he couldn't speak. She drew back and put a hand to his face. "You mustn't let yourself be so troubled by this."

He chuckled tensely and looked away. "It's that obvious?"

"Yes, I'm afraid it is."

"I'm working on it," he said.

"Oh, it's you!" Polly squealed, hurrying down the stairs. She hurtled herself at Chas, and they both laughed as they hugged tightly. Jackson smiled as he watched them, then Polly turned to give him an equivalent hug.

"It's good to see you too, Polly," he said and laughed again.

"Oh, the baby!" she said as if she'd just recalled they'd come home with an extra family member. She turned to look around and caught sight of the little seat on the floor. Polly giggled and went slowly to her knees as if she were trying to pet a wild animal that might bolt and run. She eased back the lightweight blanket that was covering part of Isabelle's face. She sighed and let out a lengthy, "Aaaw! She's so . . . beautiful. Just look at her."

"We do," Jackson said. "All the time. And yes, she is. She looks like her mother."

"And a little like you, too," Polly said with firm resolve. "The pictures you've emailed have been great, but she's much prettier in person."

"I would agree with that," Chas said.

"What is all the ruckus?" Elliott said, coming down the stairs.

Chas made a delighted noise and hugged him much the way Polly had hugged her a minute ago. They both laughed and expressed how good it was to see each other, then Elliott turned and shook Jackson's hand. The handshake evolved into a hug that silently expressed a great deal of respect and appreciation.

"How is everything here at the old homestead?" Jackson asked him, not wanting Chas to pick up on the subtle overtone of the question.

"It's great!" Elliott said with a subtle lift of his brows that Jackson interpreted as assuring him that there was nothing suspicious to report. "And how are you? Long drive?"

"Not too bad," Jackson said. "Well, for everyone but Charles. He's not fond of the drive at all, and his nap wasn't nearly long enough. But Melinda's got him under control."

As if on cue, Melinda appeared with Charles and handed him to his father. "Okay, his diaper's clean, Daddy," she said. "Now you can wrestle with him until bedtime."

Jackson chuckled and smiled at his son. "Maybe that's what we need. Eh, little buddy? A good wrestle?"

"That would be great," Chas said, taking Charles from him. "But first you have to unload the car so I can start unpacking. I need Isabelle's stuff before she wakes up."

"I'm all over it," Jackson said, and Elliott followed him out to the car to help.

Once outside, Jackson said, "Is everything *really* okay?"

"Yes, Leeds," he said firmly, "everything is *really* okay. You worry too much."

"People were killed in my house, and people I love nearly died. I know you agree that it's not over."

"Yes. Yes, I agree. But there's nothing to be done about it. I'm doing what you taught me to do—to keep my instincts sharp, be careful, and not let it control my life. You also taught me that sometimes you have to let go and move on. Even *if* something else happens, what's done is done. We need to move on."

"That's easier said than done when it happens in your own home."

"We're safe. It's done. And you *need* to move on."

Jackson sighed and tried to swallow his own advice. While he was handing luggage to Elliott from the back of the SUV, he asked, "How is Polly . . . really?"

"She's doing a lot better. It's been rough, but Callahan has helped her a lot, and I've given her my shoulder to cry on at every possible opportunity."

"I bet you have," Jackson said with light sarcasm as he led the way back into the house. After two more trips, the SUV was emptied and cleaned out. Jackson took charge of Charles and wrestled with his son on the parlor floor while he visited with Elliott. Melinda helped Chas unpack while Polly sat close to the baby seat, which she'd moved into Chas's bedroom, just watching the baby sleep.

Chas was overcome with a deep delight that evolved into a bout of tears while she was putting Isabelle's things away in the corner of the master bedroom that would comprise the nursery until the addition to the house was completed. She sat down on the edge of the bed, and Melinda and Polly immediately flanked her with care and concern and empathy. The joy was simply too much to hold, but her dearest friend and her sister-in-law understood perfectly.

Charles wandered into the room, and Jackson followed twenty seconds later, but Melinda insisted that she'd watch out for Charles, so Jackson went back to the parlor. Polly enjoyed seeing Charles again too, declaring that he had changed in the weeks they'd been gone. Isabelle woke up and Polly insisted on being allowed to change her diaper. She cooed at the baby and made silly noises while Melinda looked on as proud as any proverbial aunt. Before Polly could snap the baby's clothes back in place, Chas lifted Isabelle's little undershirt to show Polly the healing scars from open-heart surgery. "Good grief!" Polly said. "That certainly looks out of place on such a tiny little person."

"Yes, it certainly does," Chas said. "But she's doing great!"

Chas held Charles and showed him his baby sister, guiding him to touch her little arms with gentle hands. It was difficult to know what Charles was thinking at his young age, but his eyes were wide with wonder for the minute that he tolerated sitting still before Chas set him free to play again. When he wandered out of the room, Melinda went after him, allowing Chas some time alone with Polly.

"So, how are things going?" Chas asked once she had the baby in position to nurse.

Polly unintentionally let out a dreamy sigh. "Oh, Chas," she said in a way she hadn't wanted to fully get into over the phone, "I am so in love."

"Truly?" Chas asked with a little laugh.

"Oh, yes!" she said.

"But . . ." Chas hesitated to say it, not wanting to throw a rock in Polly's glassy pond, but she knew it had to have come up, "won't he be going back soon?"

"He's not going *back,*" Polly said, and Chas gasped. "He told me he'd been having trouble with the job ever since Jackson went missing. When he came here, even before we met, he knew he wanted to stay. He's already submitted his resignation. I think if he had any doubts, they went away that day we both nearly got killed."

"Oh, Polly," Chas said gently, unable to avoid changing the subject. "Are you doing okay . . . with all of that?"

Polly shrugged. "Some days are better than others, but over all, I think I'm doing all right. Elliott has helped a lot. He's been through enough trauma that he's gained some good insights. And I'm still seeing Dr. Callahan. I'm sure I'll be fine."

They talked for a while about the incident, and they both cried a little, most of all expressing gratitude that the outcome hadn't been worse. When the baby had finished nursing, Polly insisted on burping her, grateful for experience she'd gained with babies by helping with Charles.

Chas eagerly took the subject back to Polly's growing relationship with Elliott.

"So . . . where do you think this is headed?" Chas asked. "You said he'd decided to stay before he met you, so I assume that decision is independent of his feelings for you. Do you really think he's the one?"

"I do!" she said, then giggled. "No pun intended." They laughed together and Polly added, "I wouldn't be surprised if he proposed soon, and I'm ready to accept. He's implied marriage a great deal, but when it comes right down to the big decision, well . . . I guess we'll see."

"I think it's wonderful!"

"So do I," Polly said. She went into the parlor, still holding the baby against her shoulder, and Chas followed. They found the men there, along with Melinda and Charles. Polly sat down on the couch beside Elliott and said, "Look what I found."

"Wow!" Elliott said, getting a good look at Isabelle. "She's for real."

"Yeah," Jackson chuckled, "she's for real. She's a very real miracle."

"We've had lots of those lately," Polly said, smiling at Elliott.

Jackson and Chas both noticed the tender look passing between them and exchanged a discreet knowing smile. Chas couldn't help thinking that maybe the drama that had brought Elliott to their home had been worth it, if only for the way it had brought Polly and Elliott together. They truly had miracles in abundance.

CHAPTER 12

For Jackson, the evening was soothingly normal and at the same time startlingly surreal. Guests for two rooms checked in. Polly and Chas worked together to prepare supper while Jackson held his sleeping daughter, and Elliott thoroughly enjoyed playing with Charles. Artem came in at supper time, thrilled to see Chas and Jackson back safely. He fussed over the baby as if she would be a future monarch. Conversation at the supper table was full of laughter and the exchange of trivialities, until Artem filled a silent moment by commenting on how grateful he was that everyone here at the table had come through the ordeal safely. Following more silence, Chas took the old man's hand across the corner of the table and agreed. Thankfully they had finished eating as the conversation steered into the events of that day, and each person expressed how it had all played out for them. Some of them shed tears; others expressed anger. But they all admitted that it was good to talk about it.

When it seemed there was nothing more to say, Jackson lightened the mood by asking Artem, "So, my friend, how much longer will you be honoring us with your company?"

"I like here very much," Artem said with a grin. "More places to see now, but . . . would like to come back someday."

"We'll miss you," Polly said.

"Yes, we will," Elliott added.

"Where will you go next?" Chas asked.

"You speak well of Salt Lake City. I think I go there."

"Excellent idea," Chas said with a wink toward her husband.

"I wholeheartedly agree," Jackson said. "We can tell you all of the best sights to see."

After supper, Artem went up to his room and Melinda took charge of Charles. Polly helped Chas clean up the kitchen, then she packed her bags, and Elliott followed her home to make certain all was well there before he returned to the inn. He then said good night to Jackson and Chas and went up to his room. Melinda also said good night and went to bed a few minutes later. With Charles down for the night, Chas and Jackson sat together in the parlor, the baby sleeping in the crook of Jackson's arm.

"It's so good to be home," Chas said to her husband.

"Yes, it is," Jackson said, hating the associated feelings. But he'd meant it when he said it was good to be home. He just wished that he could look at the parlor and the hall and not be afflicted by the horrible memories of what had taken place there. He forced his mind to the present, taking in the fact that little Isabelle was alive and healthy and finally home. And he tried hard not to think about the future, doing his best to put that matter in God's hands with the faith that everything would be all right. His wife and children were a great distraction. Adjusting to Isabelle's presence in the home was truly precious.

"She's not going to let us get much sleep, is she," he said with a little chuckle.

"Probably not."

"So . . . we're ready to go to sleep and she's been sleeping all evening."

"We'll just have to take turns taking naps tomorrow," Chas said and touched the baby's wispy dark hair. "I think it'll be worth it."

"Yeah, I think so," Jackson said and kissed his wife. It *was* good to be home.

* * * * *

Isabelle actually slept better than expected. She woke up a few times to be fed, but she went back to sleep quickly, and was proving to be a calm and contented baby. Since Charles was still practically a baby himself, Chas and Jackson were both very grateful and hoped that this temperament of hers lasted.

Michelle had the day off, so Jackson watched the kids while Chas put breakfast on for their guests, and then they ate with Elliott and Artem—who were technically guests, but felt more like family. Chas and Jackson hadn't spent nearly the time with the older gentleman that Elliott and Polly had, but perhaps the fact that he'd been here during the traumatic event gave them a certain bond.

Once the kitchen had been put in order and the inn was under control, Chas took over with the kids so that Jackson could do some necessary errands, including the need for grocery shopping. Polly was taking the day off to catch up on some personal things, and Tricia—a new maid that Polly had hired with Jackson's permission—arrived to clean the rooms that had been used. Elliott volunteered to go with Jackson, declaring that he needed some guy time.

Before they headed out, Jackson wanted to touch base with the contractor who was overseeing the addition being built onto the side of the inn. He'd talked to him on the phone every few days and he'd done well at keeping Jackson informed about the status of the project. It was nice to see firsthand how it was coming along. The framing had progressed a great deal since Jackson had last seen it. Now it was starting to look like a house, and he couldn't help anticipating its completion. At this point, the contractor felt confident that the exterior could easily be completed before the early Montana winter brought bad weather, and he was determined to have the interior finished in time for the family to move in before Thanksgiving. Jackson was all for that. While they still intended to have their formal holiday celebrations in the beautiful dining room and parlor of the inn, it would be nice to have his family settled into more spacious and private accommodations.

Elliott followed Jackson around while he perused the construction and visited with the contractor, then they left the inn and drove to the bank, dropped some papers off to the accountant, and went to the grocery store.

The moment Jackson turned off the engine, Elliott said, "Can we talk for a few minutes?"

"Sure," Jackson said and unbuckled his seat belt, but remained in his seat, turning more toward Elliott.

Elliott jumped right in with, "I'm going to ask Polly to marry me."

"What?" Jackson asked, wholly astonished.

"I thought I should talk to you first. You're the closest thing she has to a father."

"I am *not* old enough to be Polly's father."

"Brother, then."

"Polly's a friend, and she's a big girl. You don't need my permission."

"No, but . . . your advice, perhaps. You're the closest thing I've got to a friend. I mean . . . I've got friends back home, but . . . they're not the kind of guys you go to when you need to talk about the important stuff. I've always looked up to you."

Jackson's eyes widened.

"You didn't know that?" Elliott asked.

"No. Was I supposed to?"

"You know now. You're a great guy, Jackson, and you've got your life together." He looked around himself and sighed. "I like it here. I want to stay."

"You're serious," Jackson said, then chuckled. "You're not just . . . pulling my leg because I've teased you about settling down here?"

"Is that what you thought?" Elliott asked.

"You're serious."

"I'm serious."

"Isn't this kind of impulsive?"

"Fast, yes; impulsive, no. I've felt better about myself and my life since I came here than I have for years. It's time for me to settle down. And if I had any doubt at all about retiring from the Bureau, it all went away when Nuccitelli shot those people and I knew that Polly and I would be next. I'm done. I've served my time. Although, I will probably stick with law enforcement, so I guess I'm not *really* done. I just need a new direction with my career, and I want to have a family." He looked directly at Jackson. "I want to have what you have. A real home, a wife, a couple of kids."

"Wow," Jackson said, then chuckled again. "I don't know what to say."

"Tell me if you think I'm completely out of my mind."

"Polly is amazing," Jackson said. "If you love her, then you certainly couldn't do any better. And this *is* a great place to settle down. I'm just . . . surprised. For all my teasing, I never really believed you would . . . wow." Again he chuckled. "And what about a job? What will you do?"

"I've already applied for three jobs. I would eventually like to be an officer here in town, but they don't have any openings at the moment. There's an opening on the force in Butte, and I applied for a couple of different security positions there as well. I've already submitted my resignation."

"You're not wasting any time."

"Do you think I'm moving too fast? I mean . . . I don't feel like I am, but if you in your profound wisdom think I'm doing something wrong, then—"

"I only have one real regret with Chas," Jackson interrupted. "Of course, now that all is said and done, it's hard to regret the things that make us who we are, and I really couldn't have done it any other way, but . . . I knew almost immediately she was the one for me, and I used to wish I had done exactly what you're doing."

"You *used* to wish?"

"Yeah."

"Does that have anything to do with nearly getting yourself killed by those drug lords? Or is that subject taboo?"

"No, it's not taboo; not anymore." Jackson thought a moment about the experience that had been at the root of his PTSD and was surprised to acknowledge that he hadn't thought about it for a long time. Callahan would be pleased. "I've dealt with it . . . remarkably well, if you must know. But one of the things that helped me come to terms with it was realizing that if I hadn't still been with the Bureau, someone else would have gone in my place. And it probably would have been you . . . or Ekert."

"Yeah, I've thought about that. I've wished it had been me. I had nothing to lose."

"Well, I'm glad it wasn't you. Now that I'm where I am, I wonder if I needed that experience. Before I figured all that out, I was filled with regret over going back and putting myself in that position. I wished I would have just retired and married Chas right away. So, if you're going to learn anything from me, you need to just . . . do what feels right."

"I think that's the best thing you ever taught me."

"What?"

"To trust your instincts and follow them. That's what you always said, that's what you lived by. I've thought about that a hundred times since I came here. Not once have I wondered if my staying here and being with Polly was wrong. I've wondered if I should take more time, but then when I realized how strongly I felt about it, I knew I just needed to go with it."

"But you're still asking my advice?"

"Doesn't hurt to get a second opinion."

"What if she says no?"

"Oh, she won't say no." Elliott smiled and raised his brows.

"Then I guess congratulations are in order."

"Yes, I would say they are. But it looks like you're never going to get rid of me."

"I think I can live with that," Jackson said. They walked up and down the aisles of the grocery store with a couple of carts, joking about how they made great house husbands.

Back in the car, Elliott asked, "Speaking of instincts . . . are you still feeling uneasy about this Nuccitelli thing?"

Jackson wanted to feel angry with him for bringing it up. Then it occurred to him that it was nice to have someone acknowledge what he was feeling, someone to talk to about it. "I try not to think about it, but . . . yes, I just . . . feel like it's not over; like there's something undone."

"Yeah. Yeah, so do I. Do you think we're in any danger?"

Jackson thought about that. "Truthfully, for all of my uneasiness, over time I've come to feel rather . . . calm. Look at it this way . . . we came out all right last time. I really think everything will be okay this time. I hope that's not just wishful thinking."

"Nah, I think that's faith."

"I didn't think you were a religious man."

"I'm not," Elliott said, "but I know faith when I see it."

Jackson hoped that what he felt *was* faith, because he couldn't think of any other reason to believe that everything would be okay. If he'd not come to believe in God and His ability to protect Jackson and those he loved, he didn't know how he could live with the present situation. As it was, he uttered a silent prayer just as he did at each occurrence of a fearful thought, then he put his mind to finishing their errands.

After a stop at the bakery on the way home, they returned to the inn and unloaded all the groceries. Chas and Charles were both taking a nap while Melinda was watching the baby, who had eaten just before Chas laid down.

"I don't know what we'll do without you, Auntie," Jackson said to his sister. "I dread having you leave."

"I'm not in any hurry," she said. "My grandkids in Arkansas are old enough that they're not going to change too much during the time I'm gone, but this one is going to change so fast. If you can stand having me around, I think I like being the favorite aunt."

"Only aunt."

"Which makes it so easy to be the favorite."

* * * * *

That evening after supper was over and cleaned up, Elliott went to visit Polly, and Melinda watched the children while Jackson and Chas walked through what would soon be their new home. With the workers all absent, and a pleasant summer breeze blowing through, it was quiet and serene. They held hands and wandered from room to room, even though some of the walls in between them hadn't yet been erected. They were able to go upstairs and see the layout of the bedrooms and bathrooms, and also the view from the square holes that had been left for windows. They speculated on where they would put furnishings and decor, and laughed to imagine their children growing and playing in these rooms.

"We've got a good life, Jackson Leeds," Chas said, taking both his hands.

"Yes, we do," he said and kissed her.

Chas looked around. "It's good to be home." When he didn't comment she looked up at him again. "Isn't it?"

"Of course!"

"Then what's wrong?"

He thought about it, then he shrugged. "It's nothing, Chas."

"I don't believe you."

"It's nothing that anyone can do anything about. I just need to . . . deal with it."

"Okay," she said cautiously. "I can understand why it would be difficult. I have a hard time thinking about it too, but I didn't see it. Sometimes I've wondered if my imagination would be worse, but . . . I don't think so. From what Polly said, it was pretty awful. But . . . it's in the past, Jackson. Our home is safe and as beautiful as ever."

It is beautiful, Jackson thought and debated whether to close the subject or keep going. He wasn't about to let on to his uneasy feelings about the future, but his struggle over what had happened at the inn was another matter. Noting their time alone, he figured it was as good a chance as any to share his thoughts. "I don't know how to explain it, Chas. This place is . . . sacred to me. It has been since the first time I stepped through the door. It feels different now. It feels . . . damaged, scarred. And I feel responsible."

"First of all, you are *not* responsible. We were both a part of the decision to bring Cortney into our home. We've talked all of this through. You are *not* responsible."

"Okay," he said. "I know that, but I have trouble feeling like it's true. And as for the other, no matter whose fault it is or isn't, it still happened and it was ugly."

"I'm certain time will make it better," she said and hugged him tightly. "We're all together and we're safe. We just need to give it some time."

"Okay," he said more calmly. "Perhaps moving into the new part of the house will help. I don't know why, but I think it will."

Chas smiled up at him. "I'm sure it will."

After they went back into the inn, Chas left Jackson to help Melinda with the children while she made a phone call. She'd talked to her grandfather a number of times while they'd been in Utah, and kept him informed of the progress with little Isabelle; she'd also told him all that had happened with Cortney. He'd been compassionate and kind through many lengthy phone calls. Now Chas needed to let him know they were home. He was thrilled to hear from her and anxious to see his new great-granddaughter. Chas invited him to dinner on Sunday, which was only a couple of days away.

The following morning, Artem informed them at breakfast that he would be leaving within the hour.

"You should have given us more warning," Chas said. "We could have had a little party or something."

"That is why I not tell you before," he said with a warm smile. "But we have many little parties while I here. Good memories."

Melinda told Artem good-bye before she took Charles out for a walk in the stroller, knowing the day would soon be too warm with the summer sun. Isabelle went down for a nap a few minutes later since she'd been awake at the crack of dawn. Polly arrived before Artem left. She hugged him tightly, and then tearfully expressed her appreciation for his friendship during a difficult time. They all exchanged tender farewells and promised to keep in touch. Then Artem drove away, waving as he passed by the front of the inn where they were all standing on the porch.

They had barely gone back inside when Elliott announced, "Oh, by the way, Polly and I are getting married."

"Are you *serious?*" Chas demanded.

"No," Elliott said, "I just thought I'd throw it out for a little humor. Of course I'm serious." He took Polly's hand. "A guy like me would be a fool not to marry such a woman. It's the best chance I could ever get to have a great life."

Chas and Polly hugged. Jackson shook Elliott's hand then put his other arm around him and they shared a manly hug. "Welcome to the family," Jackson said lightly, but there was no humor in the way their eyes met with sincerity. Jackson had found a good life here with Chas, and he couldn't be anything but pleased to think of his friend finding that same happiness here. Polly was an amazing young woman, and he knew that she and Elliott had the potential to make each other very happy.

"Congratulations," Jackson added.

"Thanks," Elliott said. "So . . . if we're as good as family . . . we were wondering if we could get your help with a few things, just so we can . . ."

"Of course," Chas said. "Anything!"

"You know you can count on us," Jackson said.

"Let's talk," Chas said and urged everyone into the parlor, where they sat down.

"We want to get married a week from tomorrow," Polly said.

"Really?" Chas said and laughed.

"There's hardly anybody we want to invite," Polly continued. "Truthfully, my relationships with what's left of my family don't make me want to invite them; they wouldn't come if I did. And Elliott doesn't have any family to speak of. So, we're making a fresh start."

"We just want something real simple," Elliott said.

"Like when the two of you got married," Polly said. "It was so lovely."

"It *was* lovely," Chas said, taking Jackson's hand.

"Can we get married here . . . at the inn?" Polly asked.

"Of course!" Chas and Jackson said at the same time. "Yes!"

They talked out the details of their wedding plans, after which they would drive to Yellowstone for a honeymoon. They both had some money put away, and their hope was that one of the jobs Elliott had applied for would come through. In the meantime, he had some savings to draw from, and Polly had a home for which she was comfortably paying the expenses.

Melinda called from her cell phone to say that Charles was being so good she'd decided to make their walk a little longer. When the baby monitor indicated that Isabelle had begun to cry, Polly followed Chas into the other room to talk privately with her while she changed and fed the baby.

"Elliott and I have talked about it, and we don't want to wait to have children. We're both in our thirties, and we want to have two or three kids, so we need to get started."

"I think it's so wonderful!" Chas said. "Of course we'll see each other a great deal, whether you're working here or not."

"Oh, I intend to keep working here," she said. "Other than maternity leave and stuff, of course, I could never stay away. This is my second home. And you need me."

"Yes, that's true," Chas said, "but you'll likely want to cut back on hours once Elliott has work."

"Maybe. We'll see."

"You look so happy," Chas said.

"I never imagined being this happy," Polly said. "When things worked out for you and Jackson, I remember thinking that it was like a storybook ending."

"Or the beginning, really. Obviously we've been through a lot since then, and life keeps coming at you."

"Of course, but you're in it together, and I see the way you love each other . . . the commitment and respect you share . . . and I didn't believe I would ever get that." Polly started to cry. "But he's such a good man . . . and he loves me. It's a miracle for me, Chas. And I'm so grateful."

"So am I," Chas said. "You're both wonderful people. You deserve to be happy."

"Then it's all good," Polly said and laughed.

* * * * *

"There's something else I need your help with," Elliott said after the women had left the room.

"I'm not giving you a bachelor party."

"I *hate* those things!" Elliott said. "I wouldn't want you to; I wouldn't want one."

"I know. I was joking. I hate them too. Well . . . the one for Ekert wasn't too bad. It was clean, at least."

"Yeah, but I just want to get married."

"So, what can I help you with?"

"I need to go to Virginia and get my stuff. Since I helped take care of *your* stuff after you moved out here, I was hoping you'd return the favor and go out with me. I thought we could fly out and rent a moving truck; I don't need a very big one. If you're okay with that, I'll make some calls and arrange everything. What do you say?"

"I'd be happy to. I guess we should go right away in order to get back in time. As long as Polly and my sister can help Chas with the inn and the kids, I'm your man. I think I owe you *lots* of favors."

"Yeah, like what? Other than the apartment?"

"Well, you rescued me from drug lords, and you put your life on the line to protect my home."

"Yeah," Elliott said with self-recrimination, "and I ended up bound and gagged on the floor. A lot of good I was."

"No one could have done better. I just want you to know that I'm grateful you were here. And I'm glad it's working out for you and Polly. I was dreading your having to leave. Truthfully, you're one of the few people I've really missed from Virginia. It'll be nice to have you around."

"Well, the feeling is mutual, buddy," Elliott said and laughed. "I'm getting married. I'm actually getting married."

"Yes, you are," Jackson said.

Melinda came in with Charles. She set him down and he toddled straight to Jackson, giggling as his father picked him up.

"Did you have a good time?" Jackson asked, kissing his sister on the cheek.

"A marvelous time," Melinda said. "But it's getting hot out there now. Although, I'm thinking I much prefer the summer weather here rather than in Arkansas."

"You'll take the Arkansas winter over this, however," Jackson said.

"Yes, that's certainly true." She looked at Elliott. "You look awfully happy."

"He's getting married," Jackson explained. Elliott just nodded eagerly.

"That's wonderful!" Melinda said, and Elliott stood to receive her hug. "When?"

"A week from tomorrow," Elliott said. "I hope you'll be here that long."

"I've got nowhere to go," Melinda said. "I'm enjoying these

babies way too much. My daughter and her kids are busy and I don't see them much. And my son's in Iraq so I don't see him at all."

"You're welcome to stay as long as you want," Jackson said, giving her another kiss on his way out of the room. "I think the little man needs a diaper change."

Jackson heard his sister's cell phone ring on his way out of the room. She regularly got calls from her daughter and a few friends, and he thought nothing of it. He barely had the diaper changed when Melinda rushed into the nursery, so upset she could hardly speak.

"What is it?" he demanded, setting Charles down to play.

Melinda rambled and stammered in near hysteria, and Jackson only caught the words, *mortar fire, shrapnel, Iraq,* and *Brian.* His heart began to pound. He felt cold and sweaty at the same time. Chas and Polly rushed into the room, drawn there by the commotion. Chas was holding the baby against her shoulder. Both women looked terror-stricken. Jackson knew he needed answers before anyone could know how to help Melinda. The worst but most obvious possibility demanded to be confronted. He took hold of Melinda's shoulders and said firmly, "Melinda, is he dead?"

The word *dead* seemed to shock her into silence. Huge tears rose in her eyes and Jackson held his breath. Then she shook her head and muttered, "No. He's . . . He's . . ."

"Just take a deep breath and tell me what they told you," Jackson said calmly. *"Then* you can cry." He knew his sister was easily prone to tears, and he felt certain that this would bring on a great deal of them.

Melinda managed to stammer out that Brian had been hit by mortar fire and had received a great deal of shrapnel, especially in his right leg. At this point they were hoping to save his leg, but they were more concerned about seeing that he stayed alive. He was being transported to a hospital in Germany, and they would notify Melinda of any significant changes. Once she'd spilled the pertinent information, she *did* dissolve into tears, and Jackson guided her to the parlor, where he sat close beside her and let her cry. Chas gave the baby to Polly and sat on the other side of Melinda, holding her hand, offering reassurances.

"They'll take good care of him," she said. "Surely it's more likely that he'll be okay than not. We must have faith."

Melinda nodded but continued to cry. Then an idea seemed to occur to her and she sat up straight, looking panicked. "I've got to go to Germany. I've got to be with him!"

"Melinda, listen to me," Jackson said, glad for his experience in the FBI and the Marines, even though the latter had been many years ago. "You can't just . . . hop on a plane and go sit by his bedside every minute of the day. I'm certain it's complicated, at best. You'd have to go through the right channels and—"

"Then find me the right channels!" she insisted. "I need to be with—"

"Melinda, listen to me," he said again, more firmly this time. "The military is not necessarily known for great communication with family. How do you know that they won't be shipping him home at the same time you're on your way there? How do you know what the situation is over there? You need to just sit tight and wait for more information. When he's back in the States, that's another matter."

Melinda looked like she wanted to slap him, but her silence indicated she had no argument to his logic.

"In the meantime," Chas said, "you need to stay with us . . . just like you planned. You need to be with family, and Sasha is so busy with work and the kids. If you're here, someone can be around all the time so you won't be alone while you're waiting to hear."

"She's right," Jackson said. "We have no idea how long it will be before he'll be strong enough to come home. There's nothing you can do for him right now. But when he does come home, he's going to need you to be strong. This is going to be an emotional adjustment as well as a physical one."

Melinda took a moment to digest the idea, then turned more fully toward Jackson. "You would know about that."

"Yes, I suppose I would," Jackson said, pleased to realize once again that he was okay with talking about his PTSD. He hoped that was a good sign, as opposed to the times when he had wanted to avoid and ignore it.

"Then you can help him when he comes home."

"I'll do everything I possibly can, Melinda. But let's cross one bridge at a time. He could be in that hospital for weeks, even months. There's just no way of knowing right now. We need to be patient, and like Chas said, we need to have faith."

"How do we do that, exactly?" Melinda asked, turning more toward Chas. "I . . . learned a lot while we were in Salt Lake, but I don't know how to apply it to something like this. I just don't know if . . ." She started to cry again, and Chas took her hand.

"I think faith is trusting in God, Melinda. If it's Brian's time to go, we need to trust that the matter is in God's hands. And if it's not, he'll be okay. Either way, *you* will be okay too, Melinda, because I know that God is mindful of you. You're a good woman. And we're going to get through this together."

Melinda nodded and put her head on Chas's shoulder. A minute later she asked, "Can we say a prayer? Like we prayed together for Isabelle?"

"Of course we can," Jackson said and got up to close the wide parlor doors before they all knelt together. Jackson offered the prayer, expressing gratitude for all they'd been blessed with and the many miracles in their lives. He uttered a heartfelt plea that Brian would be preserved and comforted through this difficult time. He also prayed that Melinda would find comfort and peace, and that she might be filled with hope for the safe return of her son. While he was praying, Jackson felt the impression that he not only needed to keep Melinda under his roof during this time, but that when Brian came home, he should come and stay here as well. The impression took him off guard and he was silent for several seconds in the midst of his prayer, trying to take it in. What he felt had come as strongly as the urgency he'd felt to get out of his bed in Salt Lake City and get back to the inn quickly. He wondered what the implications might be in regard to this situation, but at the moment he felt only peace and joy. Brian *would* be coming back to them. He knew it! And he also knew that God was with them in this, and in all things. And that couldn't help but comfort him. Now he hoped that he could comfort and strengthen his loved ones.

Jackson continued with the prayer, and afterward he hugged his sister tightly and told her that it was going to be okay, that Brian would surely come back. She actually smiled and seemed much more calm. Now that she could actually talk without crying, she called her daughter and a few close friends back in Arkansas to give them the news and ask for their prayers.

The remainder of the day was difficult for Melinda, and that night she took an over-the-counter sleeping pill so that she could get some rest, but the next morning she admitted at breakfast that in spite of her worry for the possible severity of what Brian might be facing, she actually felt some relief to know that he was alive, and that he was in a hospital in Germany. In that regard, she could stop fearing the unknown she'd dealt with each day that he'd been living in a war zone.

After a quick breakfast, the family left the inn in Polly's care while they went to church. And Melinda was eager to go along. Chas noticed her dabbing at her nose a great deal through the meetings, but she seemed to be holding up bravely. Looking at little Charles, Chas tried to imagine how it would feel to have him all grown up and going off to war. She couldn't even imagine! She knew it was something women had faced all through history, sending their sons, husbands, and fathers off to war. And it was certainly an issue in the present. Of course, it wasn't just women who were sending off loved ones and worrying for them. In fact, there were many women serving in the military who had left loved ones behind. But Chas could only gauge the situation according to her own maternal and feminine perceptions. She thought of when Jackson had been missing in South America. Knowing the danger he'd been in had been torturous for her. But she and Melinda were far from alone in having to face such feelings. Chas prayed every day for those serving in the military, and their families, but today her prayer was deeper and more heartfelt. And she prayed that Brian would recover quickly and come home to his mother and everyone else who loved him.

CHAPTER 13

That afternoon, Nolan came to dinner. He fussed over the baby with such delight that it was a pleasure to simply observe him getting so much joy from this new addition to the family. When dinner was over, Nolan sat on the parlor floor and played with Charles for a long while, then sat on the couch and held little Isabelle while she slept, hardly taking his eyes off of her.

"You've sure made me a happy old man," he said.

"Glad we could help," Jackson said, "but we didn't do it for you."

"No, but I'm a lucky man to reap the fringe benefits. I'm so glad to know that we're family."

"Yes, so are we," Chas said.

"Speaking of family," Nolan said, turning his attention to her, "my kids are putting together kind of an impromptu family gathering. It's been a while since we've all been together; in fact, I believe the last time was at my wife's funeral. Her birthday is later this month, and the kids decided it would be good to get together and have some fun. I would like you to be there; all of you. You're family too."

"Uh . . ." Chas said and couldn't find words to finish the sentence.

"Is there a problem?" Nolan asked, concerned.

"I truly appreciate the relationship we have," she said. "We both do." Jackson nodded in agreement. "I just wonder if the rest of the family will feel the same way. You've told me that there were some hard feelings between my father and the others—for good reason. I find it hard to believe that they would be pleased with my existence, let alone your bringing me so fully into the family this way. You told me as much at one time. Are you sure it's a good idea? I don't want to cause any problems. It's the last thing I would want to do."

"I understand, sweetheart; I do. I'm not suggesting it would be wise to have you involved in every event. But I do think you should at least come to the barbecue we'll be having at the house. You at least need to meet everyone—and they need to meet you. It might take some of them longer than others to realize how wonderful you are, but that won't happen if they don't get to know you."

Chas sighed. "When is this barbecue?" She almost hoped he would say it was the day Polly would be getting married, which would give them the perfect excuse to decline.

"It's a week from Saturday; two weeks from yesterday."

Drat. No other plans to give them a legitimate reason not to attend.

"We'd love to come," Jackson said. "I'm sure everything will be fine."

"I'm sure it will." Nolan smiled at Chas. "Are you okay with that, sweetheart?"

"I'm sure it will be fine," she said. "Of course we'll be there."

Chas couldn't argue, nor could she deny that she was dreading it. But it was still two weeks away, and there were other more pressing matters that needed to be dealt with in the meantime.

Jackson and Elliott decided to postpone their trip to Virginia until after Polly and Elliott returned from their honeymoon. Given the situation with Melinda, they all felt it was best for her brother to be around for her until the situation was more settled. Also, with all that had to be done for the wedding, the help and support of the men in the house was very much needed.

Over the next few days, Chas felt suddenly overcome with more stress than she knew what to do with. Polly, who was her right hand in running the inn, was preparing for a wedding and wanting some guidance from Chas. Melinda, who had been her right hand in caring for the children, was consumed with concern for her son. She'd gotten another call that had reported Brian was stable, but he needed multiple surgeries to remove all the shrapnel and repair the injuries. The report was no more specific than that. Melinda was still helpful with the children, but she wasn't her usual cheerful and perky self, and she was often teary and emotional, reminding Chas very much of how Melinda had reacted to her mother's death.

While Chas was adjusting to caring for an infant and another child who wasn't even two yet, she wasn't getting enough sleep, and she that felt many of the "extras" around the inn were slipping. They were managing to keep things running smoothly enough that the continual flow of guests was going fine. But Chas knew she couldn't go on this way for long without feeling the brunt of it. She asked Michelle if she would be willing to put in more hours, much the way she'd done while Chas had been gone. Michelle was glad to do so, which was a huge relief for Chas. But she still felt overwhelmed, caught between Polly's absolute joy and Melinda's maternal sorrow.

Chas hardly had time to think about the upcoming barbecue with the family she had become a dubious part of. But she thought about it anyway. In fact, she thought about it a lot, and she realized that she was *really* nervous. She felt confident that Brian would be okay and come home safely. She wasn't concerned about helping pull off Polly's wedding successfully. But this barbecue with strangers who were relatives had her undeniably concerned. She talked to Jackson about it more than once, but he could do nothing but assure her that they just had to go and make the most of it. And if it didn't go well, she wasn't required to ever see them again. They all lived out of state, and she could continue her relationship with

Nolan, regardless of anything his children or grandchildren felt or believed.

"Maybe that's what concerns me," Chas said to him.

"What? I don't understand."

Chas shrugged and tried to explain. "Maybe I'm worried that if Nolan's children express their disdain loudly enough, he'll change the way he feels about me."

Jackson looked at her sideways. "You don't *really* believe Nolan is that shallow, do you?"

"No, I guess not. I mean . . . I know he isn't."

"You're worrying about something that will play out the same whether you worry about it or not. You need to go there, confident of your relationship with Nolan, and the absolute fact that whatever your father was or did, it had nothing to do with you. It was out of your control. *You* are a good person. You have a right to be treated with respect, and since you're willing to give these people respect as well, there's no reason it shouldn't be all right. If any of them truly choose to be snobby or difficult over this, we'll deal with it. Besides," he took her hand, "I will be right beside you the entire day. If nothing else, our babies will charm them all."

"That's true. They're great little ambassadors."

"They certainly are," he said and kissed her. "It's going to be fine."

The remainder of the week went smoothly. The wedding plans were easy to carry out when it was so uncomplicated, and the inn needed very little extra attention to be worthy of such an event when it was kept worthy of guests every day. It was wonderful to see Polly and Elliott so happy, and Chas was delighted to know that her friend would always remain close by. Even though Polly had taken the attitude for many years that she would probably remain single and always be there, Chas had held the possibility in the back of her mind that Polly might find someone to marry, and then move away. To know that Polly *had* found someone and that she would still remain close couldn't be more perfect for Chas. And she'd always liked Elliott Veese. To see the two of them together almost seemed magical. She wondered how often such things happened, that a married couple would each have their best friends come together this way. It was easy to imagine the four of them being greatly involved in each other's lives for the rest of their lives. And such a possibility seemed a rare and precious gift.

Chas was especially pleased with the prospect of Jackson actually having a good friend nearby. He'd never connected with any of the men in the ward or neighborhood enough to socialize outside of Church functions or an occasional neighborhood barbecue. They'd had couples over for dinner a few times, but it had never progressed beyond that. Jackson had always kept in touch with Veese; they were alike and they understood each other in many ways. While Chas knew that women tended to rely on friends emotionally more than men did, she could tell that the relationship between Jackson and Elliott was a good thing for both of them. It couldn't have worked out better if Chas herself had been in charge. As it was, she frequently expressed to her Heavenly Father how grateful she was for this chain of events.

The joy of Polly's forthcoming marriage helped keep other things in perspective. Even Melinda seemed in better spirits when she was kept busy with specific tasks relating to the wedding or the babies. Chas didn't know what she would do without her!

The evening before the wedding, Chas and Jackson sat down at the kitchen table with Polly and Elliott to go over their plans and make certain everything was in order. Seeing the obvious love between prospective bride and groom, Chas's mind was drawn to her own wedding. It too had been pulled together quickly, but it had been anything but impulsive. She reached for Jackson's hand across the table and squeezed it, warmed by his tender smile. They'd been through so much together since their marriage, but most of it had been good; at least the results had been. They had two beautiful children, and they had the promise of going to the temple in not so many months to be sealed for time and all eternity. Chas would hope to see Polly and Elliott eventually come to a place where they might have the same blessings. But she knew it would have to be up to them, and it would have to come about in their own time and way. Chas had always been very open with Polly about her beliefs, and had made it clear that if Polly wanted to know more, she could feel free to ask without any pressure. And that was where it stood. Chas's patience had paid off with Jackson. She hoped it would also pay off eventually with Polly. Being a true and genuine friend was the best missionary work that she could do.

That night, Jackson woke up in the dark, startled out of a nightmare. It was dramatically different from the dreams that had constituted the crux of his PTSD. This was a strange montage of images that meshed the bodies in the hall of the inn with the gun in Harry Nuccitelli's hand being pointed at Polly, with a sense of urgency in trying to get to the inn and save her. In the end, the bodies on the floor became Brian and Melinda, and Jackson felt like it was his fault. He woke up with a gasp, grateful within seconds to realize that it had only been a dream, and that he hadn't awakened Chas. Recalling the images, he knew it was nothing but nonsense, but he was left with an even stronger sense that something wasn't right, that maybe the Dickensian Inn had not seen the last of the Nuccitelli family. He felt sick at the thought, and tried once again to talk himself into believing that it was just an odd sense of paranoia that had no basis to it. He prayed for peace and found it, but he wasn't able to go back to sleep before Isabelle woke up for her feeding. Since he was already awake, he got her up and changed her diaper before he brought her to Chas to be nursed. His wife kissed him as the baby exchanged hands, then he snuggled close to them and went back to sleep.

* * * * *

The wedding turned out perfect in every way, except that Isabelle was a bit fussy as guests were arriving and gathering. But the baby calmed down in Melinda's arms as the ceremony was about to begin, and she had fallen asleep by the time Polly and Elliott were declared husband and wife. It had been Jackson's idea to ask their bishop to perform the ceremony, and since Polly and Elliott had been fine with that, they were pleased when the bishop said that he'd be happy to do so. Chas knew that Polly and Elliott both believed in God, even though religion had never been a part of their lives. The bishop spoke prior to the ceremony about making God a partner in the marriage, and about the importance of remaining committed through the tough times. Chas could see in the faces of the bride and groom that they were pleased with the bishop's comments and receptive to what he was saying. In the end, the ceremony was beautiful; it was perfect! Polly had never looked more beautiful, and Elliott had a smile that couldn't be wiped off his face.

Once the ceremony was over, Jodi and a couple of other ladies from the ward helped put out a lovely buffet luncheon in the formal dining room, and the small number of guests had an enjoyable time. Pictures were taken, the cake was cut and served, and the bride and groom were given a ceremonious send-off to begin their honeymoon. Chas knew they would be staying in a nice hotel in Butte tonight, and then heading to Yellowstone, a place that Elliott had always wanted to visit.

"You know," Jackson said to Chas once they'd driven away, "we spent our wedding night at the Dickensian Inn."

"Maybe Polly and Elliott are sick of the Dickensian Inn."

"Maybe," Jackson said. "I'm not."

"Good thing," Chas said and gave him a quick kiss.

"The wedding turned out very nice; you did a good job."

"It *was* nice, wasn't it," Chas said.

Nolan appeared at her side and put his arm around her shoulders, giving a little squeeze. Chas was glad that Polly had wanted to invite him. The two had hit it off during his occasional visits, and Chas enjoyed having him around. "It was a beautiful wedding, sweetheart. I wish I could have been there for yours."

"Since we got married in the same place and by the same man," Jackson said, "it shouldn't be too hard to imagine."

"No, I suppose not," Nolan said with a chuckle. "And I *do* have pictures."

Nolan stayed and helped clean up, and after everyone had gone, he stayed and watched a movie with Jackson, Chas, and Melinda. They all enjoyed it, in spite of frequently having to pause it to deal with one child or both. They finally finished it after Charles had gone down for the night, and by the end of the movie, Isabelle had fallen asleep. Chas was feeling tired but very gratified with the day and in a relatively good mood until Nolan was getting ready to leave and reminded her about the barbecue the following Saturday. She smiled and told him she was looking forward to it, then a minute after he left she said to Jackson, "I feel like I'm lying to him."

"No, you're looking forward to the opportunity to give this wonderful man what he wants most, to have his family all together. Just because you're not looking forward to the possibility of a negative encounter doesn't mean you were lying."

"Wow. That's very good. Is this the kind of strategy you used in the FBI?"

"All the time," he said and laughed. More seriously he added, "You mustn't worry. It will be fine. So stop thinking about it. Think about . . . the food we're going to take. He did say it was pot luck. I'm sure you'll come up with something remarkable."

Chas realized his suggestion to shift her worry had worked. Instantly she was concerned about taking the right dish to impress everyone with her cooking; maybe it would make up for her being the relative whose existence was an embarrassment.

The following morning Melinda was especially down and concerned about Brian. She hated the thought of him being in a hospital, surely miserable and in pain, and not having someone at his side who loved him. The wedding had been a good distraction, but now that it was over, she felt anxious and impatient.

At Chas's suggestion, they all prayed together before going to church, and Melinda felt a little more calm. She was teary through church, and just a few minutes after they got home, she got a call. She kept the phone charged and with her constantly, keeping it set on vibrate at times when having the ringer on would be inappropriate.

As soon as Melinda said hello, it was evident that the call had something to do with Brian. She hurried upstairs to her room, obviously wanting privacy and a lack of noise or distractions from the children.

"Oh, I hope it's good news," Jackson said to Chas. "This waiting is going to kill us all. Sometimes I think I *should* have sent her to Germany."

"No, I think you did the right thing to encourage her to stay here. Most family members can't *afford* to go there under such circumstances. And even though I'm sure she could have come up with the money, it would have been challenging." She sighed. "Do you really think he's going to be okay?"

"I really do," he said. "I told you about the impression I got."

"Yes, I just need you to keep reminding me."

"I should clarify that I believe he will be *physically* all right; I think he's going to need his family to help him recover."

"I can't even imagine what facing battle of any kind must do to a person."

"I'm afraid I *can* imagine," Jackson said grimly.

"Yes," she said with compassion, "you've been there . . . in more ways than one."

"Yeah, and maybe that's why we should insist that Brian come here and stay . . . at least for a while."

"I agree," Chas said. "I just hope it's not too much longer."

"Yes, and I hope that . . ." He stopped when they heard Melinda's door open at the top of the stairs. Then she hurried down, wearing a smile like they hadn't seen since they'd first gotten word of Brian's injuries.

"That was him," she said with the excitement of a child. "A nurse dialed the number and once she knew she had me, she put him on. Oh, it was him!"

"That's wonderful!" Chas said. "What did he say?"

"He told me not to worry. He said the worst is over. They've actually kept him sedated quite a bit so he hasn't been in too much pain. He's all done with his surgeries, and he said everything's going to be fine, relatively speaking." More grimly she added, "He may have a permanent limp and some loss of mobility in his leg. But the good news is that he won't be going back to active duty . . . ever. For that I am truly grateful!"

"We all are," Jackson said.

"He doesn't know for sure when he'll be coming home, but he agreed with you that it was best I didn't come."

"Did he say anything else?"

"He just . . ." Melinda got emotional. "He just . . . said that he was so glad to be alive, and he couldn't wait to see me."

Jackson wrapped his sister in his arms and let her cry, but it was nice to know that these were tears of joy and relief.

* * * * *

Melinda's mood improved considerably after actually talking to her son. With the wedding behind them, Chas couldn't help stewing over the upcoming barbecue, but had to keep reminding herself that not so long ago they had been concerned with simply remaining safe from the mob. Surely a little family gathering was not such a big deal.

Chas was sitting in the office looking over some schedules when she heard the outside door open and close. Jackson had gone into town on some errands, taking Melinda and Charles with him. The baby was asleep, and the inn was empty otherwise. It was too early for guests to be checking in. Occasionally some passerby took advantage of the standard open house that was advertised with a sign outside, coming in to simply walk around and look at the inn, which was great advertising. But it happened rarely. For all her speculation, Chas wasn't at all prepared to see Charlotte come around the corner. Her memories of their last few conversations flooded over her. The irony of knowing she had a healthy baby was gratifying but a little unsettling in light of Charlotte's suggestion to terminate the pregnancy and spare herself the pain of losing the baby. Chas wanted to just stand up and shout at her and tell her she had been wrong. Instead she put on a civil countenance and simply said, "Well, this is a surprise."

"You're here!" Charlotte said, as if nothing had ever been wrong between them.

"I'm here."

"Did Polly tell you I stopped by while you were in . . . Where were you, exactly?"

"We were staying in Utah for a while. Actually . . . Polly didn't mention it. But she's had a lot on her mind."

"Does it have to do with that guy that was here? The one she was dating?" She said it as if Polly's interest in a man was something to be looked down upon. Considering Charlotte's lifestyle, Chas found her attitude disturbing. She feared that Charlotte had lost her ability to view life realistically.

"Yes, actually," Chas said. "Polly is on her honeymoon."

"Honeymoon?" she echoed as if it were a dirty word.

"She got married on Saturday." As if to explain why Charlotte was not informed or invited, she added, "It was just a family thing; only a few people."

"You're not family."

"Close enough," Chas said and changed the topic. "So, what are you up to these days?"

"Same old stuff," was all she said, plopping down into a chair.

Chas opted for something more specific. "So, what brings you here? I haven't seen you for a long time. I can't help wondering why you're here now."

"Can't I just check up on an old friend?"

"Sure, but . . ." She wanted to say that she didn't think they were friends anymore.

"I just wanted to see how you're doing; that's all. I assume it's all over with now, and I thought that maybe you could use a friend."

"You assume that *what's* all over with?"

"Well . . . you know . . . the baby." She said the last in a tentative whisper, as if that might not make the implication sound so harsh.

"You know, Charlotte," Chas said, surprisingly calm, "I think you should be a little more careful about assuming. Like the way you assumed that I would prefer an abortion over giving my baby a chance at life. And since you haven't talked to me for months, you're just assuming that it all turned out the way that you predicted it would, which *I* am assuming is based on what happened last time."

"You don't have to get so testy," Charlotte said. "I know it must be difficult for you, but—"

"Charlotte," she interrupted, unable to tolerate the conversation any longer, "I'd like to say that I hate to say I told you so, but actually, I'm very glad to be able to say I told you so." Chas turned the framed picture on the desk around so that Charlotte could see it. It was a snapshot that Melinda had taken; it had turned out so cute she'd had it framed right away. The picture showed Jackson and Chas sitting close together on the couch, with Charles on Jackson's lap; Chas was holding Isabelle, who had a funny expression on her face that typically preceded a loud cry. Charlotte glanced at it, did a double-take and gasped before Chas said, "Isabelle is asleep in the other room. We went to Salt Lake City where she was delivered C-section and then had open-heart surgery. She's doing fine, and so are we."

The room became silent, and the silence became awkward until Charlotte said, "That's wonderful. Congratulations."

"Thank you," Chas said with genuine sincerity, then Charlotte made excuses about the time, said her good-byes, and hurried away. Chas had trouble focusing on her work for a long while after Charlotte left. She felt concerned for her but completely helpless to do anything about it. Noises on the baby monitor that indicated Isabelle was waking up came as a welcome distraction. Chas hurried to the bedroom and lifted the baby into her hands, grateful beyond words that Charlotte's prediction hadn't been right. But she knew in her heart that even if Isabelle hadn't survived, she wouldn't have regretted giving her every possible chance. As a mother, she couldn't imagine feeling any other way.

* * * * *

When the day of the barbecue arrived, Chas was unreasonably nervous. Melinda and Jackson took care of the babies while she prepared a spinach salad and a decadent chocolate cake, both of which were some of her special dishes that she felt confident in making. In spite of some unexpected diaper changes and Isabelle not cooperating with her usual eating time, Jackson and Chas were on the road with their little ones in the backseat right on time.

After driving several minutes in tense silence, Jackson said, "What's the worst that can happen?"

"What?"

"If you imagine the worst possible scenario and deal with it, then you have nothing to fear."

Chas groaned. "The worst possible scenario would be humiliating and . . . too horrid to imagine."

"I'm sure you can imagine it; if you hadn't imagined it, you wouldn't be so nervous."

"Okay, so . . . I can imagine it. It's too horrid to imagine having to cope with it. One or more of them could be terse and barely polite while I know they're whispering about me, saying I have a lot of nerve ingratiating myself with their father—or grandfather—respectively. Or, they could be very assertive and/or obnoxious people and just tell me to my face that they disapprove of my being a part of the family."

"Do you really think that Nolan would put up with either scenario?"

"No, which means it would start an argument that would likely end with something like, "'If *she* doesn't leave, *I'm* leaving!'""

"I really don't think that's going to happen."

"But it could," Chas argued vehemently.

"Okay, it *could,* but it's not very likely. Maybe *you* should give these people what you hope to get from them: the benefit of the doubt."

"I know," she said. "I will. I just . . . I'll just be glad when it's over."

"Or maybe you'll have such a good time that you *won't* be glad when it's over."

Chas tossed him a skeptical glance, then looked out the window, and Jackson allowed her to stay in her own thoughts during the remainder of the drive. She knew from things Nolan had told them—and pictures they'd seen—that he had a daughter who lived in northern California with her husband; they had three children who were all grown, and one of them had recently gotten married. They were attending various colleges. Nolan had another daughter in New York who was divorced and had no children. He also had a married son in Florida; they had a son who had been married a few years and they were expecting a baby. Their daughter would be starting college in the fall.

Chas had difficulty keeping track of names. She wasn't even sure she could keep the daughters straight from the daughters-in-law, and Nolan rarely used names when talking about his grandchildren. He'd just say, "My granddaughter did this," or "My grandson called." Chas was worried about getting names right, remembering who was who, or rather embarrassing herself because she *couldn't* remember. Then it occurred to her to consider *why* she was so concerned about impressing them and so worried that they wouldn't accept her. As the answer came to her mind, tears came with it.

Jackson noticed and took her hand. "What is it?"

Chas explained the course of her thoughts and he asked, "So, what's the answer?"

"They're the only family I've got. Other than Granny, I never had family. I always *wanted* to be part of a family. I have you and Melinda, but that's different."

"Yes, it is."

"If they don't like me . . . don't accept me . . . then my hopes for being a part of a family will be gone."

"The more kids you have and the older they get, the larger your family will become."

"I know, but . . ."

"It's not the same; I know. But you can't control how they will feel or respond. You can only be yourself."

"I know."

"And Nolan will always love you no matter what. So will I."

"I know. Granny gave me a good life; she made up for not having a family. She really did."

"She was amazing," Jackson said. "And I'm sure she would be pleased that you're making an effort to do this today. You didn't *have* to come, you know. You could have called Nolan and made an excuse. But you're doing this because you know he wants you to, and in spite of all your worries, I think you want to meet these people. Because if you don't give this a fair chance, you'll always wonder. And it could be a long time before everyone is together again."

"I know," she said. "You're right. Thank you for being so patient with me."

Jackson chuckled. "I have a long way to go to get even in the patience department." He kissed her hand. "It'll be okay. And even if it's not, we'll make the most of it, and we'll recover. We've certainly survived worse than disgruntled relatives."

"Yes, we have. And like you said, the babies will charm them." She glanced back at them. The baby was asleep, and Charles was looking out the window, unusually calm and quiet. "They could charm just about anyone."

When they arrived at the house, Nolan met them at the door, all smiles and thrilled to see them. He took Charles from Jackson and made the usual fuss over him, and Charles was familiar enough with him that he was fine with being the center of attention in Nolan's arms. When Nolan began making introductions, Chas felt expectedly overwhelmed. Then a marvelous thing happened. In the same moment she realized that these people were actually her aunts and uncles and cousins, she realized that they were hugging her, telling her how nice it was to meet her and her family, and how pleased they were that she'd been found. There was no negativity at all. In fact, both of Nolan's daughters got tears in their eyes as one said to the other, "I do believe she looks a bit like him." And the other responded, saying, "I never imagined making peace with him in such a way."

The rest was easy. Once the initial introductions were done, everyone's attention registered the fact that Chas and Jackson had brought a baby seat in with a little blanket over it. Chas pulled the blanket away, and everyone crowded around to get a peek, with so many oohs and aahs that it was comical. The remainder of the day was amazing! The food was fantastic, and Chas got lots of compliments on her salad and cake. Visiting with these people and getting to know them was one of the best things that Chas had ever done. Jackson had been right: she was having such a good time that she didn't want it to end.

When it came time to leave, she told them all that they were welcome to come to the inn anytime, and if any of them ever wanted to rent a room, she'd give them a really great deal. They all started talking about wanting to at least see the inn before they left town, and they made an impulsive plan to come as a group the following evening. On the way home, Chas felt grateful for the day, and for knowing that she would get to see her family again before they all dispersed and went back to their homes across the country.

"You were right," she said to Jackson, taking his hand. "There was nothing to worry about. It was incredible!"

"Yeah, it was. And you've got a whole notebook full of email addresses, so you can keep in touch."

"That *is* amazing, isn't it."

"Yes, I think it is."

CHAPTER 14

When Polly and Elliott returned from their honeymoon, life quickly settled into a comfortable routine that didn't seem much different than before. It had become completely natural to have Melinda staying in the house. Polly came to work as usual. Elliott hung around and was eager to help Jackson with anything that needed doing. He had applied for more jobs, but as of yet hadn't gotten any positive response.

They'd been home less than a week when Jackson flew to Virginia with Elliott to help him wrap up all of the loose ends of his life there and clean out his apartment. It brought back memories for Jackson of doing the same thing. They were able to fit everything that really mattered into Elliott's car and left the rest to be sold or donated to charity. Elliott's original plan to rent a truck seemed pointless when Polly's home was already furnished and equipped, and he only needed his personal things. Together they drove to Montana, a route that also reawakened memories for Jackson. When he'd last driven this road he was still recovering from the violence he'd endured, and he'd arrived at the inn with a ring and a marriage proposal. Chas had eagerly accepted, and they'd been married that same week. He smiled to recall it, and enjoyed telling Elliott details of the story he'd never heard before.

"Can I ask you a question?" Elliott asked following several miles of silence.

"Sure," Jackson said, keeping his eyes focused on the road ahead, since it was his turn to drive.

"Chas is a religious woman."

"Yes," Jackson drawled, tossing Elliott a skeptical glance. "That was a statement, not a question."

"And you go to church with her."

"That was another statement."

"You do, right?"

"You know that I do."

"So . . . is it out of respect for Chas, or . . ."

"It was, initially."

"But not anymore?"

"Nope. Now I go to church because I want to, because I know it's true. You already knew about that."

"Yeah, I know. I guess I was just wondering about . . . certain points."

Jackson noted Elliott's thoughtful expression and asked, "What's on your mind?"

"Just . . . thinking," he said, then nothing more for a minute or so. "I guess . . . the whole wedding thing was really . . . nice. I'm glad we had your bishop come and do it. He said some really good things. I just . . . never really thought about marriage being a commitment with God *and* your spouse. It's a great concept. My mom was religious, and . . . well, I should clarify that she took me to church on Christmas and Easter, and we had a Bible in the house. I guess that doesn't really qualify as being religious. I guess it would be more accurate to say that my mom believed in God, but she was such an unhappy person that it didn't seem to be doing her much good."

"Maybe if she'd gone to church more often than Christmas and Easter . . ."

"Yeah," Elliott said with a little smile. "Maybe." A long moment later he added, "But you; you're happy."

"Yes, I am."

"And you became a lot happier after you met Chas, and then I think it went up a notch after you married her. But something's different since . . . I don't know when, exactly. Something changed. You're so . . ."

"What?" Jackson asked with mock defensiveness. "What am I?"

Elliott chuckled. "You're . . . well . . . it's like . . . you're at peace with your life, with who you are."

For the sake of provoking Elliott to really think about what he was saying, Jackson asked, "Aren't you?"

"Oh, I love where my life is at," he said. "Don't get me wrong. But . . . I just keep thinking about some of the things that were said at the wedding . . . and the way I felt, and . . . I wonder if there isn't more."

"More what?"

"More . . . happiness, or maybe a . . . deeper happiness."

"I would agree with that," Jackson said. "Marrying Chas made my life so good that I couldn't imagine ever needing anything else. But the PTSD was bad; it was real bad—especially after my mother died. The counseling helped more than I could ever say; it helped a lot. But the really deep healing came through more spiritual means. I was baptized in February."

"Really?" Elliott grinned and turned more toward him.

"I told you about this already."

"Yeah . . . but I didn't know it meant . . . baptized." He chuckled. "You were baptized? Like water sprinkled on your head and stuff?"

"By immersion, actually. The same way Jesus was baptized. You go under the water and come up again to symbolize a new birth. Yeah, I really was."

Elliott chuckled again.

"Is that funny?"

"Not . . . funny *ha ha,* but maybe funny strange. I mean . . . you . . . baptized; a baptized Mormon."

"Yeah," Jackson said in a tone he would have used back in the days when he was Elliott's boss and he wanted him to feel intimidated.

"I'm not questioning it," Elliott said. "I just think . . . wow . . . that's a big change. You were never religious, and you certainly weren't Mr. Righteous either."

"No, I wasn't. There's a lot about my past I'm not proud of, a lot that I regret. But with baptism all those things are wiped clean. It's a new start—literally. I stopped drinking soon after I met Chas."

"And now you don't even drink coffee, right?"

"That's right."

"Why?"

"It's kind of a . . . health code, I guess. We commit to do certain things that will respect our bodies and keep them healthier. Coffee just isn't good for you."

"Okay, I get that," Elliott said and was silent for several miles. Jackson let it rest, figuring Elliott might need space to think, and he certainly wasn't afraid to ask a question if he had one. Then a thought occurred to Jackson and he knew he should voice it. It was the perfect opportunity, and to Jackson, it was one of the most important points of his beliefs. He had a feeling it would mean a great deal to Elliott as well.

"Do you mind if I tell you something that's important to me?"

"I would love it," Elliott said.

"When I fell in love with Chas, it changed my life. I'd never imagined that it was possible to even feel that way about a woman."

"Yeah, I know what you mean."

"I know you do. The thing is, when you love someone that much, when they become the center of your life, I can't even imagine how you could ever face losing them. Ever."

"Yeah," Elliott said with conviction. "I . . . don't even know what I'd do without her."

"Obviously, losing a spouse to death would be one of the most horrible things a person could face, especially if they really love each other. But imagine how it would feel to believe that death was the end. How could you cope with wondering if you'd ever see them again?"

"Are you saying that death *isn't* the end?"

"What point would there be to life if death were the end?"

Elliott thought about it. "I have to admit that's a pretty profound question. I'm going to have to think about that."

"A lot of people believe in life after death, but they also believe that relationships have no significance in the next life, or heaven, or whatever you choose to call it. Can you even imagine that what you feel for Polly would have no relevance once your spirit leaves your body?"

Elliott thought about that too. "No, now that you mention it, I can't imagine these feelings ever ending."

"Well . . . next February, once I've been a member for a year, Chas and I are going to the temple, and the kids are going with us. We're going to be sealed. It's an ordinance that makes marriage and families eternal. When death happens—and inevitably it will—the separation will only be temporary. Facing such a thing would be more difficult than I can imagine, but there is a great deal of peace in knowing that death is not the end. We *will* be together forever."

Elliott watched Jackson closely, as if doing so might help the concept sink in. Jackson glanced back and forth between Elliott and the road. Elliott finally sighed, then cleared his throat, then said, "You really believe that."

"I more than believe it, Elliott. I know it's true. I have had feelings . . . experiences . . . that cannot be explained. I absolutely know that Jesus is the Christ, and I know that the church I belong to is His true Church on the earth. Simple as that. I know it's true."

Again Elliott just stared, and Jackson gave him the opportunity to take it in. After a couple of minutes Elliott turned to look out the window, deep in thought. Jackson finally concluded the conversation by saying, "If there's ever anything else you want to know, feel free to ask."

"There is one more thing."

"Anything."

"Can I go to church with you when we get back?"

"That would be great," Jackson said. "Have you talked to Polly about this?"

"Do I need her permission?"

"No, but I think she needs to know how you feel. When Chas and I got married, obviously I didn't share her religious beliefs, but we had a very clear understanding on where we stood. With religion not being a part of either of your lives when you came together, I don't think you can make big changes without making it a mutual matter. If she doesn't want to go with you, you need to respect that. You need to be open with each other about your feelings, but not pushy. Does that make sense?"

"It does."

"Chas never pushed, never nagged. But she was there with the answers when I needed them."

Elliott nodded. "Okay, I'll talk to her. Thanks, buddy."

"Anytime. Oh, and for the record . . . I'm really glad you're moving to Montana. It's nice to have a friend."

"Ah," Elliott said with dramatic exaggeration. "That is *so* sweet." Jackson slugged Elliott in the shoulder, and they both laughed. "Seriously, though," Elliott said. "I'm glad too. It's gonna be great raising our kids together."

"Yeah, I believe it will."

After more miles of silence, Elliott said, "Do you still think somebody from the Nuccitelli family is going to show up in our lives again?"

"I don't know. The more time that passes, the more I want to believe that it's over."

"But . . . that gut instinct tells you it's not."

"That's right," Jackson said. "And what about your gut instinct?"

"The same."

"But there's not a lot to be done about it. When it happens—*if* anything happens—we'll take it on the best we can."

"I'm with you on that."

"Then we should be fine," Jackson said and silently prayed, *Please Lord, be with us in this.*

* * * * *

Jackson and Elliott were both thrilled to finally arrive home, but no more thrilled than Chas and Polly were to see them. A few days after their return, Jackson extended an official invitation to Elliott for him and Polly to join the family at church on Sunday. Elliott said he would talk to Polly and let Jackson know. Elliott called back the next day and politely declined without giving a reason. He didn't seem upset or unhappy; he simply stated that now might not be a good time. Jackson had no idea what the reasons were, and he couldn't ask without being nosy or impolite. He expressed his disappointment to Chas, but she assured him that with time they would likely come around. But whether they did or not, they would all continue to be good friends, and the example of the lives that Jackson and Chas lived as Latter-day Saints would always be evident.

The last week of September Elliott finally got a job as a security guard for a huge corporation in Butte. They were all pleased that he was now employed, and Polly was especially pleased because this job would be less dangerous than that of a police officer. He would have rotating shifts, including nights, so his schedule would be challenging, but Jackson told him to appreciate at least *having* a schedule, which wasn't the case, more often than not, with the FBI.

A few days after Elliott got the news about his job, Melinda got news that Brian was coming home. She'd spoken to him on the phone a few times, and she'd proposed the idea to him that Jackson and Chas had carefully proposed to her—that Brian come and stay at the inn for a while to help with the transition back into normal life. Melinda had reported that at first he was reluctant, but after she had reminded him that Jackson had once been a Marine and that he'd also survived PTSD, Brian was finally convinced that spending some time with his uncle might be a good thing. Jackson had also talked to Dr. Callahan and had arranged some appointments for Brian. With any luck, Brian would agree to meet those appointments and the family would be more capable of helping him with the doctor's expertise in the mix.

The night before they were scheduled to pick Brian up at the airport, Melinda was so giddy that Jackson felt sure she wouldn't get a wink of sleep. He fell asleep himself within minutes, helped along by a general sense of fatigue these days. It was the simple result of having an infant in the house, as well as a toddler that still woke up in the night occasionally. He came awake to the usual sounds of Isabelle's need to be fed.

"I've got it this time," Chas said. Jackson rolled over and went back to sleep.

His next awareness was coming out of a nightmare. It was similar to other crazy dreams he'd had since the shooting incident at the inn, and nothing like the PTSD nightmares that had plagued him for so long. What struck him differently was a lingering sense of uneasiness. He recognized the feeling well. It was that gut instinct that had served him so well through his years in the military, and even more so as an FBI special agent. That gut instinct had never failed him. It had confused him sometimes, and had often frustrated him. But in the end, when all the facts came forward, he had to acknowledge that it had never been wrong. And right now the feeling was stronger than ever that the issue with the Nuccitelli family wasn't over.

Sleep was an impossibility while he once again asked himself hard questions and logically assessed the situation. He couldn't think of a single reason why anyone from *either* of the crime families involved in the situation would have any reason to come back here, or have any problem with anyone involved—except the logic of knowing how such people thought and worked. As Elliott had put it, they were often out to get revenge for getting what they deserved. And Harry Nuccitelli had gotten what he'd deserved. He'd gone to prison. Jackson knew that the information his wife had given to Elliott with a guarantee of anonymity had strengthened the case against him in regard to other things, and Harry was serving two life sentences. While certain members of his family might have a problem with that, the shooting had been witnessed by multiple people. Bridget had willingly given her statement of what she'd witnessed, and Jackson knew the other information she'd offered could never be traced back to him or Elliott. The last that Jackson had heard from his FBI affiliates who had handled the case, Bridget was still considered a part of the family and was under its protection. But Jackson had no idea how other members of the Nuccitelli family might feel about what had gone down. Jackson hated feeling this way, and he hated having it hang over him. But what could he possibly do about it? After pondering *that* question for over an hour, he came to the same conclusion that he'd come to over and over in regard to the same problem. He could only do the best he could do, and then he had to put it in the Lord's hands and rely on the promptings of the Spirit to protect his home and family. He knew there was nothing he could physically do, so he prayed fervently that they would all be guided and protected, and he still felt good about not saying anything to Chas. If there was nothing anyone could do, there was no point in alarming her or anyone else. Surely, with time the matter would sort itself out.

* * * * *

"It certainly is a blessing that I have family with an inn," Melinda said while she was helping Chas make certain that the room Brian would be using was all in order. Brian would have the room right next door to the one Melinda had always used during her stays. It worked out well, since this room had a large shower instead of a bathtub, which would be better for Brian as he continued to recover from his injuries.

"Even if we didn't have an inn," Chas said, "we would certainly be glad to open our home for family any time. Especially to you. You're the perfect guest. You help more than you ever cause any extra work or fuss. I love having you here. And I'm grateful that Brian agreed to come here. I really think that Jackson can help him."

"We're just assuming that he *needs* that kind of help."

"I suppose we are, but I think it's a pretty safe assumption. I can't imagine how any person could face the horrors of war and not be traumatized. If the trauma gets addressed head-on, maybe it won't affect him too badly."

"I do hope so," Melinda said. "I'm just so grateful he's coming home, and he's not going back."

"We're all grateful for that," Chas said and hugged her sister-in-law tightly. "It will be so good to see him! It's been a long time."

"It will be *so* good to see him," Melinda said and returned to making up the bed.

Jackson appeared in the doorway of the room. "Come on, sis. We've got to go."

"Oh!" She glanced at her watch. "Goodness." She giggled like a little girl. Then she glanced toward Chas in apology.

"Don't you worry about this. It will only take me another five minutes to have the room ready."

"Thank you," Melinda said and hugged Chas again quickly.

Jackson gave his wife a kiss, saying, "Isabelle is still asleep. Polly has the baby monitor and the other baby in the office."

"Thanks," Chas said. "Be careful."

"Always," Jackson said and hurried Melinda out to the car.

* * * * *

Jackson knew that Melinda had caught sight of Brian the same moment he did. It was impossible to miss him, dressed in his uniform and walking with crutches. Caught up in the anticipation of having Brian get close enough to see his mother, Jackson was taken by surprise when someone nearby began to applaud, and several other people joined in. It took a few seconds to realize they were applauding Brian. Jackson watched his nephew closely, wondering how he would respond to the attention. If it had been him, he probably would have had mixed emotions. While neither Jackson nor Brian were the type to seek praise or be the center of attention, it still meant something to know that the sacrifices made on behalf of this country were recognized and appreciated. Brian slowed down a little when he realized this was about him. His expression was difficult to read, but Jackson caught a subtle glimmer of some humble gratification. Jackson joined the applause.

Brian saw his mother, and they moved toward each other. Melinda wrapped her arms around him and Brian dropped the crutches in order to hug her tightly. The applause increased. Jackson picked up the crutches and turned toward the small crowd like some kind of bodyguard, nodding his appreciation and holding up his hand to put a graceful halt to it so that Melinda and Brian could enjoy their reunion.

When the hug was done, they both wiped away tears, and Jackson handed the crutches back to Brian after he had hugged him as well. A couple of people approached Brian, thanked him for serving, and asked to shake his hand. While they were waiting for his baggage, an older gentleman approached Brian, shook his hand, and asked about his service. The older man had served in World War II, and the two men shared a poignant conversation until the baggage arrived and it was time to part.

Jackson's memories of being a Marine were stirred when he hefted Brian's duffle bag onto his shoulder. He picked up the other bag, and they walked together to the parking garage. Brian moved quickly on the crutches and seemed to be doing well except for the uncooperative leg. Once they were at the car, Jackson set down the bags and held Brian's crutches while he got in.

"Sorry for all the trouble," Brian said.

"It's no trouble, kid. We're glad to have you back."

Brian nodded and forced a smile. Jackson put the bags in the back of the SUV. Melinda sat in the backseat with Brian so they could talk more easily. Jackson drove out of the airport parking lot and asked, "Are you hungry? I wouldn't imagine you got enough on the flight to hold you for long."

"No, thank you . . . I'm fine," Brian said.

"Okay," Jackson added, "but when we get to the inn you can eat as much as you want any time of day. There's always food available."

"Thanks."

Melinda was her typical motherly self through the drive home, asking Brian every question imaginable about his time in Iraq, his injuries, his hospital stay, and other things that men usually took no notice of. But Brian was kind and patient with his mother. Melinda had told Jackson that he had always been kind and patient, except for a couple of teen years when he had been typically snotty. They shared a good relationship, which was especially good since Brian wasn't married. If a man didn't have a wife, it was good to have a mother to turn to. Jackson had spent most of his adult life without either, and he couldn't help thinking that he would have been better off to have remained close to his mother.

When they arrived at the inn, Brian commented, "Oh, it's just like I remembered. I love this place!"

"Glad to hear it," Jackson said. "You're welcome to stay as long as you like."

Chas ran out to meet them and hugged Brian tightly while he was still holding on to the side of the car and Jackson was getting his crutches out of the back.

"You don't look too bad off," Chas said, taking his face into her hands.

"I'm much better now," he said, and she kissed his cheek. "I'm glad to be home."

"We're all glad for that," Chas added. "Come on in and make yourself comfortable. Jackson will take your bags to your room. It's on the second floor, but we've got an elevator to make it easier."

"Oh, that's good," Brian said, taking his crutches.

He went carefully up the steps to the porch with Chas and his mother on either side of him. "I've got some soup on the stove," Chas added. "Are you hungry?"

"Some soup sounds great," he said.

They all shared a lunch of hot soup and fresh rolls that Polly had just picked up at the bakery that morning. Brian seemed relaxed but a little dazed. After he'd eaten, he admitted that he hadn't slept well the night before; the flight had been long, and he could feel the jet lag coming on.

"Rest as much as you need to," Jackson said. "If you miss supper, you know where the snack fridge is. There are always sandwiches and stuff in there."

"I know where it is," Brian said, "but I don't want to miss supper." He turned to his mother. "You call my room and wake me."

"I will," she promised and hugged him before he hobbled into the elevator and went up to his room.

That evening at supper, Brian was more quiet than his usual self. He looked tired—or perhaps, more accurately, he looked drained and weary. Jackson knew that look. Or rather, he knew the feeling.

While Jackson was helping Chas clear the table, he whispered to her that he wanted to have some time alone with Brian. A few minutes later she casually asked for Melinda's help with something in the kitchen, and Jackson asked Brian if he'd like to see the addition on the house now that the workers had all gone home for the night.

"Sure," Brian said eagerly and followed Jackson outside and through a doorway that didn't have a door on it yet.

"The exterior will be done soon," Jackson said. "Then it will be all closed in before winter weather and they can work on the inside."

"It's gonna be great," Brian said, looking around. He maneuvered the crutches with little trouble, following Jackson through the rooms, and even up the stairs to look around there as well.

Jackson sat down in what would be a window seat in the master bedroom. At the moment it was only made of plywood, but eventually it would be covered with decorative oak and a cushioned seat. It was nearly as long as a small couch, and Brian sat down as well, turning slightly to look out the hole where a window would be installed in a few days.

"So, how you doing, kid?" Jackson asked.

"It's good to be home. I mean . . . it feels like home. It's nice to be with family."

"You'll always have a place with us," Jackson said. "And I hope you do feel at home here."

"Thanks. That means a lot. I guess when you were my age . . . in the Marines . . . you didn't really have a home to go to."

"No, but . . . that was partly my fault. I managed. But I wasn't wounded. Maybe if I had been, I'd have had more incentive to go home."

Brian didn't comment, and the silence became awkward.

"You know," Jackson said, "you don't have to be brave with me. Other people in your life may have no idea what you've seen, and what you're feeling, but I get it; I really do. And I've learned the hard way that believing you can hold it all inside and deal with it like a man only ends up making you less of a man in the long run."

"What do you mean?" Brian asked, but his tone was interested, not defensive.

"I got some counseling for my PTSD after the incident. I thought I'd dealt with it, but it got worse. I tried to ignore it. Then I was having nightmares that would wake Chas. It's hard to feel like a man when the woman you love finds you screaming in your sleep, then has to calm you down while you cry like a baby. What you've been through may have an effect on you for the rest of your life, and when you find the right woman to settle down with, I think you need to make sure she knows that it *is* a part of who you are. But I think that if you face it head-on and deal with it, instead of just hoping it will go away, you can be a lot better off *before* you try to start over and have a normal life." Brian said nothing, and Jackson asked, "Are you with me?"

"Yeah, I'm with you." Brian's chuckle had a bitter edge. "Dare I say that even considering that life could be normal again just feels . . . absurd?"

"I know what you mean. Let me guess. You can't close your eyes without seeing it. Sometimes you hear it in your head so loudly that you can't hear what people in the room are saying. Sometimes you wake up in the dark and you don't know if you're really safe, or if you're still in a war zone."

"Yeah, that about covers it." He looked straight at Jackson. "How did you do it? How did you cope? You're doing good now, right?"

"I am, yes. After the Marines, I struggled with difficult memories, but as I said, I was never wounded. I saw some horrible things, but I . . . joined the FBI. I guess it got swallowed up in seeing different kinds of horrible things. I started drinking. I never thought I was an alcoholic because I didn't let myself get drunk, and I was very selective about *when* I would drink. Chas was the one who showed me that I *needed* the liquor to cope. So, I gave it up. Then the whole incident in South America happened. It's like every unresolved issue just merged into it and I really thought I was going to lose it."

"But it's better now?"

"Oh, so much better! I checked myself into the psych ward. I was blessed to find a doctor that I wished I had found years earlier. His specialty is PTSD." Jackson took a deep breath and hoped this would be received well. "I took the liberty of getting you an appointment with him. If you don't want to go, I'll cancel it. I don't want you to think that I'm being manipulative or intrusive. I just want to see you get back to normal as quickly and painlessly as possible. Personally, I think that PTSD isn't taken seriously enough with our veterans. Of course, they take it more seriously than they did in previous wars. It was hardly acknowledged in World War II. I think there are probably still old men walking around with that stuff in their head. It's better understood now, but I think you've got to take control of the situation and not wait for somebody to fix it for you. So, what do you say?"

Brian shrugged. "Well, sure. I'll go. What can it hurt? All I could think about while I was in the hospital was just getting back to the States . . . to just be with my mom again. I gotta tell you I was relieved when she suggested I come here. At first I thought I didn't want to be a burden to you and I shouldn't come here, but then I realized that you would get it; that I needed you. I can't tell you how glad I am that you get it." His voice cracked, and he looked away. "I don't wanna feel this way. My leg is never gonna be normal, but at least I got to keep it. Sometimes I think I'd give up my leg if I could not feel so broken inside. But men have given up more than that and they're *still* broken inside; women too. I know war is as old as the world, but it sure doesn't make a whole lot of sense."

"No, it sure doesn't. But we're going to get you through this, Brian. I'll drive you into Butte for the appointments, as many as you need. And we can talk anytime—and as much as you feel like you have to. We're family. You hear me?"

Brian nodded and choked back tears. Jackson gave him a hug and wasn't surprised when Brian started to cry. Jackson just kept an arm around him and let him do so, like a lost child come home, but irrevocably damaged. After a minute Brian eased back and wiped at his tears, chuckling with embarrassment. "Is that the manly stuff you were talking about?"

"Yeah, that's it. But Chas told me on many occasions that it took a lot of strength and courage to be able to face such feelings and deal with them, as opposed to hiding them. At first I didn't agree with her. But I do now."

"I'll take your word for it."

"You do that," he said. "Your spirit just needs time to heal, the same way your body does. So don't be too hard on yourself, or too impatient. Just promise me that you'll be open and honest with me, as opposed to keeping feelings to yourself that could make it worse."

"I promise."

"I really mean it, Brian. Things could hit you . . . memories, feelings . . . and you're going to want to keep them to yourself. You've got to promise me that you're going to talk to me about them; if not me, then the counselor. Do you promise?"

He thought about it longer this time, but he said again, "I promise."

"Good." Jackson stood up. "I know for a fact that there's some really great ice cream hidden in the back of the freezer—because I hid it there."

"Sounds great," Brian said, and they went back to the house to find the women already eating ice cream at the kitchen table. But Jackson dug out the carton he'd hidden, and they all declared it was much more decadent, so they all had some of that as well.

"How are you doing, sweetheart?" Melinda asked her son.

"I'm fine, Mom; really."

She looked dubious, and Jackson took the silent signal of approval from his nephew. "I'm taking Brian into Butte the day after tomorrow to meet with the counselor that helped me with *my* PTSD."

"Oh, that's great!" Melinda said.

"And we also have an agreement that Brian's going to talk to me about anything that's troubling him; either me or the counselor. There are reasons why he *shouldn't* talk to you about some of this stuff. When he feels up to it, I think he can talk about how he feels about things that have happened, but not necessarily the details. Does that make sense?"

Melinda nodded. While Jackson looked directly at Brian, he added, "I know it can feel awkward to be so forthright about it, but we're family, and we're not going to pretend that it isn't real. There will be no ignoring the pink elephant in the room, if you know what I mean."

"Yeah," Brian said. "I know what you mean."

"Listen to you!" Chas said to her husband. "All that counseling made you so smart . . . about pink elephants and stuff."

"Yeah," Jackson said facetiously. "Now we should change the subject. Let's talk about something important, like . . . what color we're going to paint the new bedrooms."

"We always argue when we talk about that," Chas said.

"Then it should be very entertaining." Jackson winked at Chas. "You know when it comes right down to it, I'll let you have your way. But someone once told me that a little stimulating disagreement over matters of principle keeps people on their toes."

"*Who* told you that?" Melinda asked.

"Chas did." He pointed at her with his spoon.

"And you think paint colors are a matter of principle?"

"It is if we want it to be," Jackson said and smiled. To have the freedom and privilege to be concerned over such things was something he felt deeply grateful for. And he had Brian and others like him to thank for it.

CHAPTER 15

The following day, Jackson found some things that Brian could do to help with maintenance projects for the inn. He knew that staying busy was important. Brian seemed to be doing fairly well except for the need to rest frequently. But he'd been through a tremendous ordeal with his injuries and the subsequent surgeries.

When it came time for Brian's appointment, Jackson could tell that he was dreading it, but they had a good talk while they drove into the city. Jackson introduced Brian to Dr. Callahan, then he left to do some errands and arrived back at the office just a few minutes before the session ended. While Brian was in the men's room, Callahan said to Jackson, "He's going to be fine, but he needs to stick with the appointments. The next few weeks could be crucial. Without breaking any confidence, I can tell you that he's struggling a lot more than he's letting on, and he could be in for some serious depression if he doesn't stay on top of it."

"Okay," Jackson said. "I'm glad we've got you. We'll keep an eye on him."

"I want to see him a couple of times a week for a few weeks, then we'll cut back. I assume he's staying with you while he deals with the worst of it."

"Yes, he is," Jackson said, then smiled. "Whether he likes it or not."

"That's the spirit," Callahan said. "And how are *you?*"

"I'm fine," Jackson said.

"Fine with your own PTSD? Or fine after people got shot in your home?"

"I'm fine," Jackson said with a chuckle, certain that with how little the more recent episode was bothering him, he didn't require counseling.

On the way home, Brian was very quiet, but he admitted that the session had been good. He liked the doctor, and he knew that continuing his visits was important. A couple of days later Jackson took him to see a doctor who could follow up on the injuries and make sure everything was healing well. The doctor told Brian that he could give up the crutches now, but only if he was comfortable with his pain level. He'd reached a point where walking on the injured leg wouldn't slow his healing. Brian walked out of the office carrying the crutches as opposed to using them, even though Jackson could tell that it was painful. He used them off and on for the next few days, then gave them up completely.

Over the next couple of weeks, Brian's moods were on a roller coaster. Jackson sometimes felt like watching out for Brian took more effort and vigilance than watching out for Charles, who was toddling around the house and getting into everything. But he was glad to be able to do it. As close as Melinda and Brian were, Jackson could tell that the common bonds he shared with Brian had made him more comfortable in being able to talk through the issues. Jackson did his best to keep Brian talking and to keep him busy, even if it was with tedious, mundane tasks.

On a warm autumn afternoon, Brian borrowed Jackson's SUV to go into town and get some things he needed. He was also doing a couple of errands for Jackson while he was out. He'd been glad to reach a point where he was able to drive, due to a reduced pain level in his leg and to his no longer needing pain medications. Jackson set to work in the office, going over some things that needed his attention. He heard the door and looked up from his desk to see a woman enter the office. He recognized her immediately, and his heart leapt to his throat, then dropped to his gut as he rose to his feet. He wasn't sure if it was memories of the past or fear of the future that caused the reaction; probably both. He wondered if this was the moment his instincts had been preparing him for.

"Hello, Mr. Leeds," she said kindly.

"Hello," Jackson said.

"You must be *Mrs.* Leeds," the woman said, and Jackson recalled that Chas was in the room.

"Yes," Jackson said, "this is Chas, and please call me Jackson." Carefully meeting his wife's eyes, he added with caution, "Chas, this is Bridget Nuccitelli. She was staying here while we were in Salt Lake."

"Oh," Chas said and didn't appear to be anything but glad to meet this woman. Jackson noted fear in Bridget's expression that was quickly replaced by relief when Chas extended a hand, saying, "It's nice to meet you." She added with genuine concern, "How are you doing?"

"I'm . . . adjusting," she said. "Thank you for asking." She motioned to a chair. "Do you mind if I sit down? I really need to talk to both of you, and I'm glad to find you here and together. But if this isn't a good time . . ."

"It's a great time," Jackson said. "The baby's asleep, and my sister took our son out for a walk. Please . . . have a seat."

They were all seated and Jackson reached for Chas's hand, hoping she wouldn't catch on to how nervous he felt. Had Bridget come to tell them there was still some element of danger in regard to what had happened here? Her very appearance seemed to coincide so much with the uneasiness he'd been feeling that he had to consciously slow his breathing and take care to appear unruffled.

"You're very kind," Bridget said, "especially after all the trouble my husband brought into your home."

"That had nothing to do with you," Jackson said.

"Well, indirectly it did. I knew he was up to something unsavory. Why else would he insist that we use false names? Mind you,

I've suspected for many years what was really going on, or I should say what the family business *really* entailed. But it was clear that one of the requirements of being married to Harry was to look the other way and keep my mouth shut. Unfortunately, I wasn't made aware of those rules until we'd been married a few years and we had two kids. By then, it was also evident that I needed to keep those rules in order to keep my children—and myself—safe. I'm the best possible safety net for my kids." Bridget looked down, embarrassed. She chuckled tensely. "Sorry. I don't know why I'm telling you all that. We don't even know each other."

"It's okay," Jackson said. "Maybe you need to tell *someone*. I hope you know that you can trust us."

"I guess that's it," she said. "I believe I *can* trust you." She looked at Jackson. "You handled everything to do with my husband's case so gracefully, without putting anyone in a position to take blame. I guess your experience in the FBI has taught you something about how things work in families like mine."

Bridget sighed loudly. "Anyway . . . I shouldn't ramble on. I know I could have sent a thank-you card or something to tell you all of that, and you're wondering why I would go to the trouble to come all the way to Montana."

"That thought had occurred to me," Jackson said.

"There's something left undone," she said, and Jackson swallowed his urge to shout, *I knew it!* "Apparently," she went on, "when Harry and I came here, Harry brought something with him that he'd secretly taken from his father. Harry and his father haven't gotten along for years; truthfully, his parents are closer to me than to him. Ironically, they're relieved to have him behind bars. He was causing problems for the family *and* the business. But there's something that Harry told his father he'd hidden, something that could be very incriminating." Bridget leaned forward, focusing more intently on Jackson. "I'm certain that my father-in-law has done many things that are illegal and unethical. I don't condone those things, and I have no awareness of anything specific. I do know that he's mellowed a great deal over the years, and he's a good man in many ways. I don't know what he's looking for, but I'm certain that once it's in his hands, the matter can be fully put to rest. The thing is . . . we've looked everywhere, and I suspect from something Harry said to me before . . . that day . . . that it might be hidden somewhere in the room where we were staying. If I could just . . . look, and then I'll be gone, and with any luck no one from my family will ever show up here again."

Jackson opened a drawer and found the key, which he handed to her without expressing an opinion one way or another. As an ex-FBI agent *and* a responsible citizen, he would give a lot to have this incriminating evidence against the elder Mr. Nuccitelli, but he also knew that such things were not black and white, and getting something to stand up in court was way too much of a long shot. He wanted Bridget and her children to be safe and cared for. He knew the typical dynamics of this kind of family, and he felt good about simply giving her what she was asking for.

As Bridget took the key from his hand, she said, "Would you come with me, please? I think it would be better."

"Of course," Jackson said, and both he and Chas followed her up the stairs.

"The inn is beautiful, by the way," she said, hurrying past the parlor in a way that Jackson understood. The memories of what had happened there were difficult. For him, they'd been diluted by being here every day. For her, coming back here must have been traumatic.

"Thank you," Chas said. "It is very dear to us."

"Yes, it is," Jackson added.

Jackson and Chas stayed in the doorway while Bridget went straight to the pictures hanging on the walls. The third one she turned over had an envelope taped to the back. Jackson and Chas exchanged a surprised glance as Bridget took the envelope down and put the picture back in place. Jackson didn't even want to know what was inside. He simply felt glad to know that it was really over.

On their way back down the stairs, Bridget said, "I want to thank you for everything." She paused at the bottom of the stairs and turned fully toward them. Tears rose in her eyes as she said to Jackson, "I don't know what brought you through the door at that moment, but I'm certain you saved my life. There's no way to express sufficient appreciation for such a thing—not only for myself but for my children."

"You can't really believe he would have killed his own wife," Jackson said, hoping to offer some reassurance. He'd asked her that question once before, but somehow he found the possibility difficult to believe—even for a guy like Harry Nuccitelli.

"Oh," she said, getting more emotional, "I think he would have. The strain in our marriage was horrid. He just became more and more difficult, but you don't divorce out of a family like this. He'd threatened to kill me, and I had believed for some time that he was capable of carrying out that threat. I *do* believe he would have done it, and he would have found a way to see that someone else took the blame. His father was *never* like that, Mr. Leeds. I want you to know that."

Jackson just nodded. "I'm glad everything turned out okay for you. We wish you all the best."

"Yes," Chas said, "take care of yourself."

"Knowing that Harry will never see the light of day again makes such a thing possible."

She smiled and moved toward the door. Once she was gone, Chas turned to Jackson and said, "Funny, I've just had a feeling that something was left undone with all of that, but I didn't want to say anything."

"Are you serious?" Jackson asked with a chuckle.

"Yes, why?"

Jackson just hugged her and said, "It would seem you have good instincts."

* * * * *

Jackson was relieved after Bridget left. His feelings about the issue not being wrapped up had been validated. Now he could finally let go and put this behind him, once and for all. But that night, lying in bed, the feeling rushed over him, as strong as ever—perhaps more so. He resisted the urge to curse aloud. Chas was asleep and wouldn't have heard him, but God would have heard him, and he needed God's help more than ever.

Jackson prayed fervently to know *what* remained undone. Was there some truth to Elliott's theory? Was it really possible that someone in the Nuccitelli family would blame him for Harry going to prison? Was he or his family really in some kind of danger? Jackson spent half the night analyzing those questions, pleading with God to guide him so that they would all remain safe. He didn't want to be in a panicked frame of mind if there was no reason to panic. On the other hand, he didn't want to be in some level of denial and overlook the need for taking some kind of precaution that should be taken.

He finally made peace with believing that as long as he did what he'd been doing all along, they would be all right. He just needed to be careful, stay sharp, and listen to the Spirit. Then he had to put the matter in God's hands and go about his life without indulging in fear. Fear would only blow the whole thing out of proportion and make them more vulnerable. Trusting that the Lord would make up the difference had served him miraculously well in the past. It was certainly the best option for the present. He just wondered how many times he was going to have to talk himself through the same formula before he could truly accept it.

* * * * *

Jackson woke up to daylight and the memory of a nightmare. In it his fears for the future mingled into a montage of memories from the past. But more clear than the images he'd seen in his sleep were the feelings they had provoked. Lying there staring at the ceiling, the pounding of his heart gradually slowed into a normal rhythm while he assimilated the reminders all around him that his life had changed; *he* had changed. A soft rustling from the other side of the room drew his attention there and he turned to see the reason for the changes. The only thing that Jackson had done right since the day he'd met Chas was to actually listen to what she had to say. Everything good that had happened to him, every good choice he'd made, every positive change he'd made had been initiated and motivated by her. He recalled again the emptiness he'd felt in his dream, reminiscent of the hollow life he'd lived before coming to the Dickensian Inn and finding the love of his life and the key to every unanswered question. The ache that had entered his heart dissipated with evidence of the present. He watched her rocking gently back and forth, smiling down at the sleeping baby, watching the maternal glow that came so naturally to her. When she stood up to put the baby in her crib, Jackson just had to be close to her. He quietly crossed the room and stood behind her, putting his arms around her waist.

"You're awake," she whispered so as to not wake the baby.

"I've been watching you," he said, kissing the side of her neck. "You're so beautiful."

Chas turned in his arms and looked up at him. "When you say things like that, it . . ."

"What?" he asked when she didn't finish.

"I don't know," she said, her eyes turning moist. "I just . . . I'm so glad I can be with you forever."

Jackson pressed a hand to the side of her face. "Sometimes I feel so . . . unworthy of that; of you."

"No, Jackson. Never. You're a good man. You deserve every possible happiness." He looked down and she added, "What's going on? Is something wrong?"

He shook his head and looked at her. "Sometimes the past just . . . comes back to me. It makes me so grateful for what I have now; for you, our children, and the gospel. And the promise of what the future will bring for us. But . . . it can be hard to appreciate how far I've come without remembering what I came from. Sometimes the regrets feel so . . . heavy."

"Whatever your life may have been before you came here is simply irrelevant, Jackson. It's in the past. There's no need to ever think of it."

"Except that . . . it does make me appreciate all that I have now." He tightened his arms around her. "It helps me realize how very blessed I am."

"In that case," she smiled, "you can think of it for a minute here and there, just to keep you humble."

He smiled in return and kissed her, drawing her more tightly to him.

"You know what I think is wonderful?" he asked, his face close to hers.

"What?" she asked, and he kissed her again.

"I think it's wonderful that God actually created us to feel this way." Again he kissed her. "And being married to someone who makes you feel this way is . . ." He kissed her once more, as opposed to futilely trying to come up with an adequate adjective.

"Amen," she whispered and their kiss became all consuming. At that very moment, Charles made noises from the other room to indicate that he was awake. They both chuckled and Chas said, "Since God created us to feel this way, we have children."

"So we do," he said and took advantage of the opportunity to kiss her once more.

"Don't worry. He'll go back to sleep . . . eventually . . . this evening some time."

"I'll be looking forward to it," he said and reluctantly let her go so she could get Charles out of his crib. He stood there for a moment, marking his gratitude for all he'd been blessed with, determined to be worthy of such blessings. Few men were given such a glorious second chance, and he would strive to never take it for granted.

* * * * *

Jackson hurried to get dressed, knowing he needed to go into town right after breakfast to take care of some business at the bank. He was putting on a casual sports coat that he often wore when he left the house, when the thought occurred to him that he shouldn't leave the house without his weapon. The thought momentarily took his breath away. He'd prayed day and night to be guided by the Spirit to know when there was a need to take any kind of action to protect his home and family. *His weapon?* Was it that crucial? It only took him a moment to know that he shouldn't question the prompting. He just needed to do it. He had a permit to legally carry a concealed weapon, and he had enough experience with doing so that it didn't feel so strange. In fact, it simply boosted his confidence—not only in knowing he could protect himself if need be, but in also knowing that God was with him. Everything was all right before; it would be all right now. At least that's what he told himself in order to push away the fear and trepidation he felt. He knew he could only do his best, and then he had to give the rest to the Lord. He removed his jacket and put on the well-worn shoulder holster that he dug out from the bottom of a drawer. It felt comfortable and at home. He checked the weapon and snapped the clip into it. He made sure the safety was on and holstered it before he put his jacket back on, checking in the mirror to make certain it wasn't visible. He wondered for a moment what the day might bring. Then it occurred to him that perhaps it would bring nothing. Perhaps it was just God's way of letting Jackson know that they were in tune with each other. Or maybe it was simply some kind of test to see if he would be obedient.

After breakfast Chas gave Jackson the usual kiss they exchanged when one of them was leaving the house. Then she hugged him, and he knew he was busted.

"What is this?" she asked, pushing his jacket aside to reveal the gun at his side.

Jackson sighed and gave her the only answer he could; the only honest answer. "I just felt like I needed to wear it."

Chas's brow furrowed, and her eyes showed alarm. "Why?"

"I don't know why, Chas."

Jackson could feel her mind working, and he felt it was best to say nothing while it did so. Once enlightened, she said, "There is only one reason an innkeeper would feel the need to carry a gun. You don't think it's over yet. You think the mob still wants something from us."

"Me," he said. "I'm the one who sent Harry to prison."

"What other option did you have?"

"I know how this works, and you know how this works. People like the Nuccitellis see things differently."

"How long have you been feeling this way . . . that it's not over yet?" He hesitated and she added, "It's that instinct thing of yours, isn't it? And you've been holding out on me because you didn't want me to worry."

Jackson sighed again, looking at the floor. "No, I didn't want you to worry. I *still* don't want you to worry. I *never* felt like it was over."

"Since the day it happened?"

"That's right."

"And once Bridget came?"

"I felt better . . . for a few hours." Jackson took hold of her shoulders. "Listen to me, Chas. If I had believed your knowing how I feel would have helped keep us safer, I would have said something. My level of concern isn't really that high. It's just . . . a nagging feeling that it's not over. That doesn't necessarily mean we're in danger. It just means it's not over. I've prayed for protection and guidance. I felt like I should wear the weapon. We were kept safe before. There's no reason to think it will be otherwise now."

Chas pondered her husband's words and tried to feel reassured. She had to admire his simple faith in these matters. Of course, his faith had been strengthened immensely when such an obvious prompting had saved lives. It would seem he'd learned to mesh his gift of powerful instincts with the gift of the Holy Ghost—and she admired him for it. Panicking or expressing fear when he was handling it so well would not help anyone or anything. Instead she forced a smile and said, "You're my hero, Jackson Leeds." She kissed him. "I'm going to say a prayer and leave it up to you and God to keep us safe. I think the two of you make a good team." She smiled again and added, "Be careful."

"Oh, I will," he said and walked out the door. Chas watched him go, getting a little bit of an idea of how it might feel to have a husband in law enforcement who went out the door *every* day wearing a gun, knowing that danger was always a possibility. She was glad he had a gun and that he knew how to use it. She just prayed he wouldn't have to, and she prayed that this would soon be *really* over. She couldn't imagine what else might happen, but perhaps it was best if she didn't *try* to imagine. It was likely best if she didn't think about it all.

Jackson stepped outside to get into his car and noticed a black sedan with tinted windows sitting in the parking lot. They had no guests, no visitors. At the very same second that his senses were alerted to this being a problem, the driver's door opened, and a man wearing a dark suit and sunglasses got out. Jackson stopped where he was, waiting, alert, and glad to have acted on that prompting. With any luck the gun would remain in the holster, but it wasn't difficult to see that this man *also* had a weapon beneath his jacket. He opened the back door of the car, and an older man got out, also wearing sunglasses. But he was dressed in a pink golf shirt and tan slacks. He looked like the kind of man he'd expect to find sitting at the head of an expensive dining table, gorging himself on food and drink and giving orders. In a word, he was such a stereotypical mob boss that Jackson almost laughed.

He wondered if these people had some kind of unspoken code in the way they dressed and behaved. But what was he doing in the parking lot of the Dickensian Inn? Montana was a long way from the east coast.

"Mr. Leeds," the older man said. It wasn't a question.

"That's right," Jackson said with the same tone of confidence. "What can I do for you?"

"You know who I am." Again, he was *not* asking.

"Should I?" Jackson asked, not wanting to feed his ego.

"I would think that my face would have been on some 'most wanted' poster back at the FBI office where you lived for so many years."

"Not in *my* department," Jackson said.

The man lifted his brows. His driver-slash-bodyguard leaned back against the car and folded his arms, bored but cautious. "You *don't* know who I am?" he man asked, sounding mildly deflated.

"I could probably add things up and make a fair guess. You *do* have a vague resemblance to Harry Nuccitelli. And since I've been wondering when one of his relatives might show up, I'm having to assume that's who you are."

With an arrogant lifting of his chin, the man said, "You sent my son to prison."

"Your son sent himself to prison," Jackson said without missing a beat. "When a person does something illegal, they make a choice that has consequences. You can only get away with not getting caught for so long. What I did, Mr. Nuccitelli, is prevent your son from taking *more* lives. As I see it, I did you all a favor by *not* killing him. I could have done it. And I could have passed it off as self-defense, no problem."

"Maybe it would have been better if you had. Prison's a hard place to live out your life."

"Prison is what he earned, and that's what he gets. It had nothing to do with me."

"I think you misunderstand the purpose of my visit," Mr. Nuccitelli said, taking a step forward. Jackson pushed back his jacket, casually but in a way that made it clear he was armed. Mr. Nuccitelli stopped and held up his hands, and the driver became more alert. "I really do just want to talk to you, Mr. Leeds. I have no intent or desire to harm you or anyone else. You have my word that nobody's gonna get hurt. You did me a favor, Mr. Leeds. I came to thank you, and I'm hoping you'll be willing to do me another one."

Jackson studied this man while he studied his instincts. He prided himself on being able to tell when someone was lying. Either this guy was a really great liar, or he was actually telling the truth. He needed to hear more. "I think you'd better clarify that."

"I'd be happy to. Is there somewhere besides the parking lot where we can talk?"

Jackson thought about that for a minute. "I'd be happy to invite you in . . . if I get the weapons at the door. There's been too much blood spilled in my home to make me anxious to trust you—or anyone—with a gun."

"Totally understandable," Mr. Nuccitelli said and motioned toward the house. Jackson followed him and his driver until they were near the back door, out of sight from prying neighbors or anyone driving by. The driver handed over the pistol from beneath his jacket.

"And the one on your ankle," Jackson said.

"What makes you think I've got a piece on my ankle?" he asked.

"Someone like you *always* has something on his ankle," Jackson said.

The driver sighed and pulled a small pistol from an ankle holster. He handed it to Jackson, who turned to look at Mr. Nuccitelli. With the way he was dressed, it was clear he was not wearing a weapon, but he comically lifted both pant legs enough to prove that he had nothing there as well. Jackson motioned them through the door, and then into the office, but he stayed behind them, keeping an eye on them. He put the driver's weapons in the safe and locked it, but he kept his own gun in its holster. The two men sat down and waited. Jackson also called the inn's phone number from his cell phone, knowing Chas would answer it with the cordless handset she was carrying.

"Hi," he said. "I didn't leave. I'm in the office having a little meeting."

"With whom?" she asked, and as he sat there behind the desk, he wanted to pinch himself. He actually had the head of the Nuccitelli family and his bodyguard sitting in his office. He couldn't even begin to imagine where this was going to go. But as long as Mr. Nuccitelli kept his word that no one was going to get hurt, he wasn't as concerned as he might have been otherwise. His instincts were telling him this meeting was a good thing. As long as he remained alert, he was all for trusting his instincts.

"You wouldn't believe me if I told you," he said to Chas, "I'll let you know when I'm done. Oh, and call Elliott and tell him that since there's sunshine today, we can go ahead and clean out the garage like we planned."

"You were going to clean out the garage?" she asked.

"Just tell him," he said. "I've got to go."

Jackson hung up the phone and leaned back in his chair. "So, you've come a long way to ask for a favor, Mr. Nuccitelli. Maybe you should let me know what this is about."

"Please, call me Gus."

"Okay, Gus. Get to the point."

"My son was out of control. His mother and I have been wondering what to do for years. Of course, it was horrible losing Bruce—*especially* knowing it had to do with the Dinubilo family. I've been trying for years to get all of that to settle, but I've been outnumbered. Truthfully, we've been hoping—by we, I mean me and my good wife—that something would happen to stop Harry. He's angry, and he's got a chip on his shoulder. The thing is, I've been working my way out of the business; have been for years now."

Jackson lifted his brows and nodded toward the formerly armed companion. "If you're not in *the business,* why the armed escort? I've always thought it was the sign of a paranoid man."

"I *am* a paranoid man, Mr. Leeds. I've done a lot of stupid things in my life, and I've made a lot of people angry. But I'm telling you I haven't done anything illegal in years. My good wife, bless her soul, she's been trying to talk me into making changes ever since our kids were little. The kids didn't do it to me, but by the time I started getting grandkids, and I could see how messed up my kids had become, I started looking at things different, you know? The textile business is good. It's more than enough to support the family. My brother I can't vouch for, and I know Harry's been up to some nasty stuff, even if it can't be proven. But I'm telling you I'm clean and I'm gonna stay clean."

"I'm glad to hear it," Jackson said. "But what exactly does this have to do with me?"

"I trust you, Mr. Leeds, and I'm hoping you can trust me."

"We don't know each other nearly well enough for trust."

"But I know *about* you. You're a good man. You saved my little Bridget's life. She's one of the best things that ever happened to this family. Harry never deserved her. We're gonna help her get a divorce so she can get on with her life. I think she actually loves us enough to stay a part of the family in spite of the way that boy treated her." He paused and added, "She told me you helped her find those papers Harry left here."

Jackson hesitated to comment, trying to assess his instincts. "All I did was give her the key to the room."

"You were kind to her, and you trusted *her.* You will never know how important it was for me to get those papers back. Harry could have ruined all of us. If I'm gonna be ruined, I'd like the information that takes me down to at least be true."

Jackson took in Gus's words and believed he was telling the truth. "You're right about one thing," he said. "I'll never know. I don't think I'd want to."

Gus went on. "Now, I know you've got no reason to trust me, and I don't really expect you to. That's why I'm prepared to prove that what I have to offer you is true."

"Offer me? If you're offering me something, then I assume you want something in return. Is this the favor you're wanting from me?"

"It is. But I think it will be more to your benefit than mine . . . or should I say, more to the benefit of enforcing the law in the great state of Virginia."

"And what do you want out of it?"

"I want a clean slate. Like I said, I haven't done anything illegal for years. I'm done with that. But I want to get off the FBI's wanted list. I want to clean up my family's reputation. What my brother does is his business. I don't even speak to him anymore."

"And what does the FBI get in return for this . . . wiping of the slate?"

"The name of the mole . . . and proof . . . and a guarantee that the source—that's you—remains anonymous."

Grueling moments of silence passed while Jackson kept his expression steady and fought to cope with a pounding heart and a seething stomach. He knew this man was hoping for some evidence of either his astonishment or his doubt. He felt both. But even more so he felt instinctively certain this man was being straight with him. Then Gus Nuccitelli leaned closer to Jackson and said, "I'm sure you recall that incident not so many years ago when your team got sold out. One of your friends died that day."

"Oh, I remember," Jackson said, trying to stay cool. He'd been put on administrative leave. He'd been suspected along with everyone else. It was the reason he'd gotten online in search of an out-of-the-way bed-and-breakfast. And he'd come here.

"And not long after that, an agent—who *was* a mole—took himself out and tried to take a couple of your guys with him."

"Oh, I remember that, too," he said. He'd been in the kitchen with Chas when he got the phone call. He remembered throwing up in the kitchen sink. It was Veese and Ekert who had almost died that day. But Jackson—as well as everyone else—had assumed that incident had gotten rid of the mole. He was waiting for the point to this explanation, and the knots in his stomach were growing tighter.

"Don't you find it interesting that certain criminal organizations manage to stay just one step ahead of the FBI?"

"I *do* find that interesting," Jackson said.

"I want you to know I had nothing to do with any of that. I only heard about it later. I can't tell you where or how I heard it. But I can tell you that the man who killed himself wasn't acting alone. There was someone else, someone higher up." He paused and tightened his gaze on Jackson. "Someone who wanted that girl who saw my Bruce get shot to come *here.*"

Jackson wanted to throw up again. But he swallowed his nausea, kept a straight face, and simply asked, "You have proof?"

Gus Nuccitelli held out his hand toward his sidekick, who reached into his inside jacket pocket and pulled out an envelope. He handed it to Gus, who handed it to Jackson. He hesitated a moment, then opened it. A quick glance showed photos, and a photocopy of a document that had been shredded then taped back together. And there was also a flash drive.

"It's a recording," Nuccitelli said. "I'm not gonna tell you who I stole that from. Let's just say they'll never know it's missing, because I duplicated it. My trail is clean. The evidence is clear. Do we have a deal?"

Jackson swallowed carefully. "I'm *ex*-FBI, you know."

"Still respected there; still have friends."

"Yes, I do. And yes, we have a deal . . . so far as it's in my power. I will use my influence as far as it's possible."

Nuccitelli breathed a deep sigh. His relief was genuine. "With any luck, it'll save some lives up the road."

"Most likely," Jackson said, still seething inside.

Gus Nuccitelli and his driver—with his weapons returned— were soon on their way, promising never to return. Jackson noticed as they left that the car had Virginia plates. They'd actually driven the distance, which meant that their coming here would be virtually untraceable. No flights or rental vehicles. Jackson stood on the porch and watched them leave, still sick to his stomach. He was, however, overcome with the miracle that had just occurred.

CHAPTER 16

Nuccitelli had barely left when Elliott drove in. He got out of his car and came up the steps. "What's with the sunshine message? You need help?"

"I do," Jackson said. "Although if I'd needed it when I thought I might, you'd be too late."

"I was at a dental appointment."

"It's okay," Jackson said and sat down on a step. Elliott sat beside him. "Gus Nuccitelli was here . . . with an armed escort."

"Are you *serious?*"

"Oh, yeah."

"What did he want?"

"He wanted to thank me for getting his son off the streets. And he wanted to make a deal."

"What kind of deal?" Elliott sounded understandably suspicious.

"He wants a clean slate. He's cleaned up his act; says he hasn't done anything illegal for years. He wants off the wanted list. Of course, we couldn't prove anything when he *was* doing illegal stuff. Obviously, we also can't prove whether he's actually keeping his nose clean. He just wants a clean slate."

"And you believe he's telling the truth?"

"I do. Nobody's that good a liar."

"You always could sniff 'em out," Elliott said. "What's he going to give us for this clean slate?"

"This," Jackson said, handing him the envelope.

"What is it?" Elliott asked as if he feared it would blow up in his face.

"Something I think you should deliver personally. I'll pay for the flight, but I don't want to do it. You'll know who to talk to. You'll know what to do."

"What *is* it?" he repeated.

"A mole."

Elliott opened the envelope and gasped. "Tom Myers? A mole?"

"That's how it appears. It's not for you and me to assess the evidence. We just have to put it in the right hands. But . . ."

"But?"

"I feel it in my gut." Jackson wiped a hand over his face and blew out a harsh breath. "He was with me in South America, Elliott. He wasn't behind the operation, but he was there. Now I wonder if he had something to do with giving me up. He was always one of those guys that just seemed to . . . make everything a competition. And I never felt like he liked me. But you work with who you're assigned to work with. And . . ."

"And?" Elliott pressed.

"He's the one who arranged for Cortney to come here. Now I wonder if it was intentional. Did he know she was connected to the Dinubilo family? Did he know it was likely that trouble would follow her? And catch up with me?"

"Why would he do that? Even if he *is* a mole, what could he have been hoping to gain?"

"There were two or three different times . . . before you came on board . . . when things happened that made him look like a fool. In my opinion, it was because he *was* a fool. I was only doing my job, but when I got praised and advanced, he took it personally for reasons I never understood. The position he's got now, they offered it to *me*, but I didn't want it. I preferred the field work. But more than once he made a snide comment to me about his having a job I thought I was too good for." Jackson looked directly at Elliott. "Is it possible that he's got some . . . ridiculous grudge against me? Could he have really hoped that sending Cortney into my protection would end badly for me?"

"We may never know."

"Yeah, well . . . once that information gets into the right hands, we'll know he isn't going to do any more damage."

"And you really want me to take it?"

"Yes."

"Why? I mean . . . I'm glad to, but . . . why?"

"Because if I get within a hundred miles of him, I might be tempted to kill him, and it wouldn't go over well with my new religious convictions."

Elliott's chuckle had a bitter edge, and he slapped Jackson on the shoulder. "Consider it done . . . um, delivering the information . . . not killing him."

They exchanged a wan smile before Elliott left and Jackson went into the house. He found his wife folding laundry in the bedroom, with the baby lying in the center of the bed and Charles playing nearby.

"What's wrong?" she asked once she got a good look at his expression.

"Sit down," he said. "We need to talk."

"What is it?" she said as they sat on the little couch, close together.

"The good news is that . . . it's over, Chas. It really is over. I can feel it right here." He pressed a fist to his chest. "The bad news is that . . . well, I've got some tough things to deal with."

Chas took his hand. "I'm listening," she said. "I'm here for you . . . always."

"I know," he said and smiled at her. "That's the *really* good news. That's how I know I'll get through this. I can get through anything as long as I have you."

* * * * *

Even though Brian could now drive himself into Butte for his appointment with Dr. Callahan, Jackson went with him, glad that Callahan had been able to fit him in for his *own* appointment. He'd talked all of this through with Chas. He'd pondered it; he'd prayed about it. Remarkably enough, he knew where he stood and how he felt. He just wanted a professional opinion to be certain he wasn't setting himself up for any future panic attacks, nightmares, or other unexpected adventures that he'd rather avoid.

At the moment, he was still horrified by the breach of trust, especially when he recalled so many instances of working with this man, putting his life and the lives of others on the line. But Jackson also felt strangely comforted in knowing that there was some explanation behind some of the strangeness of past events—especially in regard to this incident with Cortney coming to their home. It had never felt completely right. Now he felt certain it had been somewhat of a setup. But he felt increasingly certain that it was truly over.

He felt as if he'd found a trusted ally in Gus Nuccitelli. Perhaps they had something in common in having witnessed far too much grief and suffering from the effects of organized crime. But more than anything, Jackson felt gratitude. In spite of the fact that evil people were rampant in this world, doing all kinds of damage through deceit and greed, Jackson had seen and felt the guiding hand of God in these matters. He was safe. His home was safe. His family and friends were safe. And it was over.

After telling all of that to Dr. Callahan, Jackson was given an A-plus. "You are officially cured," he said. "What you've been through is hard, but you've been able to weigh it sensibly and not let it overtake your life. You could still have moments when it comes up, when you feel angry, or . . . Have you felt angry? Because you didn't say anything about that."

"Yes, I've felt angry. But it hasn't been so long since I finally got over being angry with every person who had ever hurt me. I had to work hard to reach the point where I could take anger out of the equation and forgive. I've got too much life to live to waste any time being angry with this guy. He'll get what he deserves. The minute I felt angry, I asked God to take it. He already paid the price for all of that. It would be senseless for me to try to carry it around. I know you're not a religious man, but I know you understand what I'm saying."

"I do understand it, and I'm very impressed. I think the fact that *you* have become a religious man is one of the best things that could have happened to you. You almost make me want to consider it."

"Well, if you ever get serious about considering it, you know where to find me."

"Yes, I do," Callahan said with a broad smile.

On the drive back to Anaconda, Jackson and Brian talked about how far they had come, and how glad they were to be family.

* * * * *

Elliott and Polly took an impromptu trip to Virginia so that Elliott could wrap up a few little things that were still undone and show off his wife to all his friends and coworkers there. They had a marvelous time, and Elliott returned to tell Jackson that the information had been delivered to someone they absolutely knew they could trust. And it had been handled so discreetly that no one would even mildly suspect that when this information came forth, it had come from Montana. The deal had been made on behalf of Gus Nuccitelli. The matter was closed.

The only residue that Jackson felt from the whole thing was an ongoing regret for the way such horrific violence had occurred here at the inn. Polly was doing well; she and Elliott were deliriously happy by all accounts. Jackson could see his family happy and thriving. He'd even come to terms with believing that it had been right for Cortney to come here and stay; if she'd gone elsewhere, it was likely that innocent lives would have become collateral damage. And Tom Myers's perfidy might never have been exposed. But he still had a problem with what had actually occurred at the inn. He felt like their home would never be quite the same, and he hated that feeling. Certain there was nothing he could do about that, he just tried not to think about it.

Distraction came in a way that Jackson would have preferred to avoid, but he couldn't deny that he wasn't terribly surprised. He'd suspected that something would hit Brian hard, because he knew the problems were far from solved, and he knew the war was still going on in Iraq. When news came that one of Brian's closest buddies had been killed, it seemed that all of the grief and fear and horror that Brian had been working hard to keep in check just exploded. Jackson spent almost two straight days holed up with him in his room, trying to talk him through it, and trying to talk him into seeing Dr. Callahan. But Brian refused to leave the room, and Jackson didn't dare leave him alone, since he was continually expressing a desire to end his own life. When Brian flew into a rage one too many times, Jackson belted him in the jaw just hard enough to knock him unconscious, then he called 911 to have him taken to a hospital where he could get the help he needed. Jackson loved him like a son, but he couldn't fix this. And with Brian in the hospital, Jackson could focus on trying to keep his sister together.

The paramedics arrived and found Brian just coming out of it, but still groggy enough that it wasn't hard to get him restrained on a gurney. One of them said, "How did you manage that?"

"Oh, you learn all kinds of great tricks in the Marines," Jackson said.

As Brian was being put into the ambulance, he came around enough to be terrified and angry. Jackson looked at him hard, told him his family loved him, and that everything was going to be okay. Then he tried not to cry as the ambulance drove away. His sister was already doing plenty of that.

Word came the following day that Dr. Callahan had made Brian his high-priority patient, and he felt confident that with a couple of weeks of inpatient treatment, he would be well on his way to healing from all of this and having a manageable life. Since family wasn't allowed to visit at first, Jackson was glad that the new section of the house was almost completed. The timing couldn't have been more perfect. Chas kept Melinda distracted with what seemed like ten thousand decorating choices that needed to be made while the painters were finishing up with the colors that Chas had chosen—with no input from Jackson. But he trusted her good taste and knew it would be beautiful. It would be home, no matter what color the walls were painted.

Autumn merged into wintery weather as the construction crew finished the last of their work. Jackson met one last time with the contractor to go over the final report of expenses, and Jackson was glad to tell him how pleased he was with the work. They discussed some remodeling work that he and Chas wanted to have done in the inn as well, with the possibility of getting that started after the holidays.

With the house officially finished, some new pieces of furniture were delivered, and the women kept busy with adding some décor and purchasing things that were needed for the new kitchen and bathrooms. They began moving their things slowly into the new addition, but they couldn't upset the business of the inn too much on days when there were guests. They'd decided to do the biggest part of the move over the Thanksgiving holiday when the inn would be closed for a couple of days. Since Polly and Elliott would be having Thanksgiving dinner with them, they were all for pitching in to help with moving some furniture.

The Friday prior to Thanksgiving, Jackson took Melinda to Butte to visit her son. Brian looked great and seemed in good spirits. While Brian and Melinda were visiting, Callahan told Jackson that the work he'd been doing with Brian had been pretty intense, but it had also been very productive. He told Jackson that

Brian's suicidal desires had been very real and deeply wired, and if Jackson hadn't been there for him, it likely would have happened. The thought was chilling, but it strengthened Jackson's gratitude for the prompting he'd felt to bring Brian to their home. Callahan was glad to report that Brian's suicidal feelings were mostly under control. He had gotten past his pain enough to have a strong will to live. He'd been able to take hold of his strong sense of patriotism and set goals for making his community and country better by being one less victim of war. Rather, he wanted to be a survivor who could raise a good family and be a strong voice for all that was good about this country, all that was worth fighting for. Callahan was planning to release him the following week, certain the timing of having Thanksgiving dinner with his family would be good for him.

"Dinner?" Jackson said. "Heck, I need him to help move furniture."

They laughed together and Jackson thanked him, yet once again, for being the means to miracles in their lives.

"He's so much better," Melinda said to Jackson in the car on the way home. "I think he's going to be okay."

"Yeah, I think he is."

"I don't think he would have been without you . . . and Dr. Callahan."

"Don't give me the credit. I was just doing what I felt prompted to do."

"You mean . . . what God told you to do."

"That makes me sound like a prophet or something," Jackson said and chuckled. "I just listened to the promptings of the Spirit, Melinda. We've talked about it before. We've talked about it a lot. You know all this stuff."

"I know but . . . now I guess . . . well, it keeps getting more and more personal. I think God's trying to tell *me* something."

"Really?" Jackson gave her a hard stare for as long as he dared while still keeping his eyes on the road. "And what is that?"

"I want to be baptized, Jackson. I'm ready."

Jackson laughed with delight and took her hand. "Yes," he said, "I believe you are. I've been wondering when you'd be smart enough to come around."

"Will you go with me to talk to the bishop about it on Sunday?"

"I'd be happy to, but I think at least part of that conversation needs to be private."

"Okay," she said, then let out a contented sigh. "When Brian got called up to go to Iraq, I was afraid my life would go downhill and never recover. Now I feel like it's better than ever. I miss Sasha and the kids. I've never gone this long without seeing them, but . . . the time I've spent with your family has been such a blessing in so many ways. We've had numerous miracles."

"Yes, we have," Jackson said, and he spent the remainder of the drive listening to his sister recount all of those miracles, going all the way back to how they had been reunited after more than twenty years. Now neither of them could imagine life without having each other in it. They'd both definitely gained a deeper appreciation for having family in their lives, and even more so for making God a part of their lives as well. This combination gave them much for which to be grateful.

* * * * *

The Sunday before Thanksgiving

Chas came awake and wished she hadn't. She felt tired. Both Charles and Isabelle had been restless during the night, and she hadn't gotten nearly enough sleep. She turned over carefully, recalling that one or more of the children was probably still in the same bed with her, unless Jackson had moved them. Her sense of smell picked up on something unusual, and she opened her eyes. What she saw changed her mood immediately. In a moment that almost never happened, both Charles and Isabelle were sound asleep in the bed between her and Jackson. Jackson was wide awake, watching her with a sparkle in his eyes and a subtle smile hovering on his lips. A huge bouquet of multicolored roses was lying about halfway down the bed, below where the babies were sleeping.

"You see this, Mrs. Leeds?" he said in a whisper. "I couldn't have planned it better myself if I'd tried. What I see right now is everything that makes life worth living. What I see is a life I never dreamed I would have, and I thank God every day that I do. What I see is what I'm going to spend my life trying to deserve. What I see is what I'm going to have with me forever." He smiled and touched the tears trickling out of her eyes. "Happy Sunday before Thanksgiving, my love." He laughed softly. "Could you have imagined *this* four years ago today when we first met?"

Chas laughed softly as well. "No, I don't think I could have *ever* imagined this. But you're right. It's everything worth living for." She reached across the babies to kiss him. "I never dreamed I could be so happy." She kissed him again. "And the flowers are beautiful. Will we have those in heaven?"

"I would think so," he said. "But as long as I have you and our babies, I'll be good."

"Yeah, me too," she said, and Charles began to stir. His stirring provoked Isabelle into stirring. And the day began.

At church, Jackson was able to arrange an impromptu meeting with the bishop on behalf of his sister, although they had to miss part of their usual meetings. Melinda insisted that Jackson go in with her initially. Her announcement that she wanted to be baptized clearly pleased the bishop. He asked her a few questions that made it evident that she was indeed ready, although he said that he wanted to talk to her privately as well. Before Jackson left the room, the bishop asked Melinda who she would like to perform the baptism.

"I don't know. I hadn't thought about it," she said. "Does it matter?"

"The authority is the same no matter which priesthood holder you choose," the bishop said. "How about your brother?"

"Me?" Jackson said, startled. "But I don't have the priesthood. I haven't been a member for a year yet."

"You have the Aaronic Priesthood," the bishop said. "And that's all you need to perform a baptism. Someone with the Melchizedek Priesthood will need to do the confirmation."

Jackson was stunned. "I can do that? Really?"

"You really can . . . but, of course, that's up to Melinda."

"Well, of course! That would be perfect."

"I'd be honored," Jackson managed to say without choking on his own words. Then he was glad to be dismissed so the bishop could speak privately with Melinda. He hurried into the men's room and into a private stall before the tears let loose. His own baptism was one of the greatest moments of his life. He *never* would have imagined four years ago when he'd walked into Chas's life that such a string of miracles would take place. Now he was being given a tremendous opportunity, a privilege he hadn't anticipated. Considering everything else in his life that was good, he couldn't imagine anything he would rather do now than be the one to help his sister cross this bridge into a better life.

Once he had control over his emotions, Jackson went to the Relief Society room where Chas was in the usual meeting with the other sisters. He peeked in discreetly and caught sight of her, with Isabelle asleep on her shoulder. A sister near the door saw him and nudged Chas to get her attention. She saw Jackson, and he motioned with his finger for her to step outside. Once alone in the hall, Jackson said, "Melinda's talking to the bishop, but I couldn't wait to tell you. He said that *I* can be the one to baptize her."

"You *can?*" she asked and got tears in her eyes. She would have hugged him, but the baby was asleep against her. She put one arm around him, and he hugged them both. "That's so amazing!" she said. "For all of my years in the Church, there is apparently a lot I still don't understand about such things."

"You're still ahead of me," he said and kissed her quickly before she went back into her class and Jackson went to wait for Melinda.

When she came out of the bishop's office, they set a tentative date for the baptism. Then Jackson sat on the couch in the foyer with his sister to talk about this marvelous turn of events.

* * * * *

That evening the home teachers came for a visit. One of these men had been Chas's home teacher long before she'd met Jackson. The other was a more recently assigned partner. Jackson and Chas both knew Ron very well; he'd been around to help them through many challenges. Lloyd was someone they didn't know as well, but he was kind and genuine, and it was easy to feel comfortable with these men. Jackson shared the news of his sister's forthcoming baptism with the home teachers, and they were thrilled. Melinda beamed and answered some questions about how she'd come to this. Charles began to get restless, and Melinda offered to take him out so that Jackson and Chas could continue their visit. Isabelle was asleep on the couch beside Chas.

"She spoils us," Jackson said to Ron and Lloyd. "We don't know what we'll do when she leaves."

"How is her son?" Ron asked, aware of the situation.

Jackson gave a brief report, glad that it was a good one. They chatted about the new addition to the house and how they would be moving into it soon, then Ron asked, "Forgive me if I'm being nosy, but this thing that happened here in the summer has been on my mind a lot for some reason. I just can't help wondering how you're doing with that. I'm sure it must take time to come to terms with something so . . ." He couldn't think of a word.

"It's been rough," Jackson admitted, but Lloyd looked confused. Jackson explained to him, "There was a shooting here. It was in the papers."

"Oh," Lloyd said with more compassion than curiosity, "that was *here?*"

"I'm afraid so," Jackson said. "Thankfully, my family was in Salt Lake at the time, but it was still tough." Without even thinking about it, Jackson found himself spilling his every feeling about how the inn didn't feel the same to him; it felt violated and desecrated, and he wished he could shake the feeling.

"Perhaps the house simply needs to be dedicated," Ron said. Jackson looked at Chas to be assured that she was as ignorant as he. "It's like . . . well . . . simply put, a priesthood blessing for the house, to protect it from evil and invoke the Lord's blessings to be here."

Jackson reached for his wife's hand, feeling as if his prayers had been answered. And he hadn't even known for certain all these months what to pray for. He'd believed he would just have to deal with these feelings and hope they went away. Now he had an answer.

"That would be wonderful," Jackson said. "I didn't know any such thing was possible."

"Then I'm glad we're here. Should we do it now?"

"Can we?" Chas asked eagerly.

"Absolutely!" Ron said. "And since your new addition is finished, I'm certain it will be included in the blessing as well."

Jackson found Melinda and Charles and invited them back into the room. Now that Charles had a cookie in each hand, he was being more cooperative. Since there were no guests at the inn that night and the phone was turned off, they were guaranteed privacy. They all knelt together, and Jackson held Chas's hand while Ron used his priesthood authority to ask for God's greatest blessings to be upon this house. He commanded any evil presence or influence to leave, and for any negative residue of past episodes within these walls to be swept away. He asked for angels to stand round about this structure as sentinels. He asked that it stand strong against evil and calamity. He spoke of the light of the gospel filling every crevice of the house, both the old and the new. He said that children would be raised here in an atmosphere of love and thanksgiving. He was silent for a long moment, as if he might be listening for inspiration. Then he said with a subtle crack in his voice and deep conviction, "For many years to come, this will be a place of refuge for the troubled in spirit who seek healing and peace. Strangers and loved ones alike will be drawn here to find new beginnings and rest to their souls. Unlike the innkeeper who turned Joseph and Mary away in ancient times, this inn will be as the stable that offered rest for the Savior of the world, and all who come here will feel the light of Christ and be given the opportunity to take it into their lives if they choose."

Ron ended the blessing, and the others all spoke a heartfelt amen. Jackson didn't feel embarrassed by his own tears, even before he realized everyone else had tears in their eyes as well. That awful feeling he'd had hovering with him for months now was gone. He couldn't think of any better way to celebrate the anniversary of his meeting Chas. Together, they had everything they could ever want or hope for.

* * * * *

The following day, Melinda's daughter Sasha called to give her a big surprise. She'd spoken to Jackson on the phone about it a couple of weeks earlier, but they'd decided to surprise Melinda. Sasha and her husband and kids were coming to Montana for Thanksgiving. They would be flying in Wednesday morning and staying until the following Monday. Melinda was so excited she couldn't stop laughing. Sasha's visit combined with Brian getting out of the hospital and doing so well made her giddy with happiness. She had to admit that having her baptism on the calendar only added to her long list of all for which she had to be grateful.

Thanksgiving dinner was probably the best that had ever taken place under that roof—at least as far as Chas or Jackson had ever experienced. Every member of Jackson's family was there, and Chas's grandfather came as well. Elliott and Polly were also there, and they all agreed that some friends were every bit as good as family. "Sometimes better," Polly said, since her own family connections were something from which she was glad to be free.

The previous evening they had moved the bedroom and nursery furniture from the inn into the new house. There were still some odds and ends that needed to be put away, but everything was where it needed to be. Thanksgiving dinner would always take place in the formal dining room of the inn. It had been that way for generations in Chas's family, and it would continue to be so. As they all went around the table and shared their personal reasons for feelings of thanksgiving, many tears were shed. It had been a year full of fear and drama. But lives had been spared and many blessings had come.

On Saturday morning Melinda was baptized with all of her family present. Her children and grandchildren couldn't begin to understand her reasons for doing this, but she hoped that with time they would. But they were respectful of her decision, and she told Jackson more than once that having her family there was an added blessing she hadn't expected. As Jackson lifted his sister up out of the water, then embraced her, he felt certain that his parents—both of them—were very pleased. How could they not be?

On Sunday morning Jackson awoke in his new bedroom, still trying to adjust to the change, but loving every minute of the adjustment. They could hear a little chime anywhere in the house if one of the doors to the inn opened or closed, and from their kitchen they could see the office and hallway on a little monitor connected to security cameras. Their new house had a separate front door with a decorative sign that said *Private Entrance,* and by next summer the fenced-in patch of dirt behind the addition would be transformed into the perfect yard for barbecues and playing children. But Jackson realized he had overlooked something. He got out of bed and dug into one of Chas's drawers in the dresser that had been moved from the old bedroom. As soon as she was awake, he dangled a shiny key in front of her face.

"Remember when I gave you this?" he asked.

She snatched it from his hand. "I *do* remember!" she said.

They both immediately went downstairs and out their new front door—in their bathrobes—wanting to do this while the children were still asleep. "Okay, do it," he said. "Make it official."

Chas smiled at him, recalling the day he'd given her the key. It had been the Sunday before Thanksgiving, a year ago. He'd just purchased the doorknobs and locks for the new part of the house, and he'd given her the key with the anticipation that when the house was done, they'd have a formal unlocking the front door ceremony.

"I think I imagined a little more pomp and circumstance."

"Or more formal attire," he said with a chuckle. "Nah, this is better. This is between you and me."

Chas had to lock the door with the key, in order to *un*lock it. She did so with a great flourish and a dramatic, "Ta dah!"

Jackson scooped her into his arms, carried her over the threshold, and kicked the door closed. He set her down and hugged her tightly. "Welcome home, Mrs. Leeds."

"And the same to you," she said and kissed him.

"It's been quite a year," he said. "A lot's happened since I gave you that key."

"Yeah. With any luck, things will calm down a little."

"What about all the people who will come to our inn, seeking refuge and help?"

"As long as it's one adventure at a time, I think we can handle it."

"As long as it doesn't entail organized crime, it shouldn't be too bad."

"Look at it this way, when you add up everything we've survived so far, we can get through anything, right?"

"Anything," he said and kissed her again. Then they realized that both of the children were awake. And the day began.

About the Author

Anita Stansfield began writing at the age of sixteen, and her first novel was published sixteen years later. Her novels range from historical to contemporary and cover a wide gamut of social and emotional issues that explore the human experience through memorable characters and unpredictable plots. She has received many awards, including a special award for pioneering new ground in LDS fiction, and the Lifetime Achievement Award from the Whitney Academy for LDS Literature. Anita is the mother of five, and has one adorable grandson. Her husband, Vince, is her greatest hero.

To receive regular updates from Anita, go to anitastansfield.com and subscribe.